At the City Limits of Fate

Michael Bishop

Edgewood Press

At the City Limits of Fate
Copyright © 1996 Michael Bishop

"Beginnings" copyright © 1993 by Michael Bishop for *Christmas Forever* (Tor,1993).

"000-00-0000" copyright © 1985 by Michael Bishop for *Last Wave #5* (Winter, 1986).

"Snapshots from the Butterfly Plague" copyright © 1990 by Omni International, Ltd., for *OMNI* (December, 1990).

"Among the Handlers" fcopyright © 1995 by Michael Bishop for *Dante's Disciples* (White Wolf, 1995).

"At the City Limits of Fate" copyright © 1982 by Flight Unlimited, Inc., for *Shayol #5* (Winter, 1982).

"Epistrophy" copyright © 1994 by Michael Bishop for *Tombs* (White Wolf, 1994).

"For Thus Do I Remember Carthage" copyright © 1987 by Byron Preiss Visual Publications, Inc., for *The Universe* (Bantam Spectra, 1987).

"Allegra's Hand" copyright © 1996 by Dell Magazines, Inc., for *Asimov's Science Fiction Magazine* (June, 1996).

"God's Hour" copyright © 1987 by Omni International Ltd., for *Omni* (June, 1987).

"In the Memory Room" copyright © 1987 by Michael Bishop for *The Architecture of Fear* (Arbor House, 1987).

"Life Regarded as a Jigsaw Puzzle of Highly Lustrous Cats" copyright © 1991 by Omni International, Ltd., for *Omni* (September, 1991), with an immediate *Omni*-authorized appearance in *You Haven't to Deserve* (Atlanta Task Force for the Homeless, 1991).

"Reading the Silks" copyright © 1989 by Omni International, Ltd., for *Omni* (August, 1989).

"Icicle Music" copyright © 1989 by Mercury Press, Inc., for *The Magazine of Fantasy and Science Fiction* (November, 1989); and by Michael Bishop for *Spirits of Christmas* (WYNWOOD™ Press), whose editors originally commissioned the story.

"The Ommatidium Minatures" copyright © 1989 by Byron Preiss Visual Publications, Inc., for *The Microverse* (Bantam Spectra, 1989).

"I, Iscariot" copyright © 1995 by Michael Bishop for *CRANK! #5* (Summer, 1995).

Front cover art and design copyright © 1996 Rick Berry

ISBN: 0-9629066-6-2

To these editors with respect and gratitude:

Pat Cadigan and Arnie Fenner
Bryan Cholfin
Kathryn Cramer and Peter Pautz
Peter Crowther and Edward E. Kramer
Ellen Datlow
Gardner Dozois and Sheila Williams
Scott Edelman
Edward L. Ferman
David Hartwell
Jane Hill
Byron Preiss and David Harris
Jeanne Schinto
and
Steve Pasechnick
for helping to assemble
At the City Limits of Fate

"Religion is the first thing and the last thing, and until a man has found God and has been found by God, he begins at no beginning, he works to no end."

H. G. Wells

Contents

Beginnings

"In my end is my beginning."
— T. S. Eliot, "East Coker"

Across the sky, carrion birds that rarely landed in the Temple grounds flew cagy loops. Over the head of the skinny captive next to me, legionaries had nailed a board calling him our king. They'd set my tree at an angle to his. I could read not only his *titulus* but also the sign above the maggoty-white face of the kid to his right.

REUEL BEN ADLAI, the sign said in Aramaic: THIEF.

And my placard? I couldn't tilt my head far enough back against the upright to see it, but I knew what the Romans' paid sign-painter had daubed there:

MISHAEL OF HEBRON, THIEF.

Two robbers, with a king in the middle. The king even had a caption in the occupiers' tongue:

IESUS NAZARATHAEUS REX IOUDAEORUM.

"Listen," I said, "if you're really our deliverer, tell these foreign pigs to take us down." Smoke from the camps of pilgrims in town for the Passover, and from the cooking fires of the hawkers along the Golgotha road, swept up the hillside past us. Yeshua and Reuel both turned their faces into it to meet my burning eyes.

Reuel said, "Hush. If you can't fear dying, at least fear God."

I spat—barely enough to dampen a midge.

"Where you and I deserve this," Reuel said, "the Nazarene has done nothing."

"Deliverer! He can't even deliver himself. He's earned my scorn, and the people's, through his blasphemy." I said this as loudly as I could—even though I didn't credit his blasphemy for the unsayable reason that I didn't credit a Father to blaspheme against.

Reuel looked not to me but to Yeshua. "Adonai, remember me when you go up to your throne."

"This very day, you will have a place beside me in our Father's kingdom," Yeshua told him.

"And dogs will adorn themselves with rubies," I said.

Thunderheads massed beyond the Kidron and thrashed toward the city like a kelp-laced sea. Dust whirled. My tree shook like a mast. So did the uprights from which Yeshua and Reuel hung. Most of the hawkers below us kicked dirt on their fires and hurried for shelter. One of the legionaries guarding us, earlier a victor at dice, twisted Yeshua's robe around his neck like a shawl, then catcalled the people—vendors, pilgrims, a few timid followers of the Nazarene—scurrying to escape the rain.

Fire ran from the nail holes in my wrists to my armpits and down my flail-bitten sides. I yelped against both it and the wind-rocked swaying of my tree.

—I would also give *you* water, Mishael. Behold my pain.

These words, spoken to my inward hearing, drew my gaze to Yeshua's uncomely face. Sweat and grime lined its creases. His eyes (the whites like discolored bone, the irises as dark as falling olives) met mine with something not quite reproach and not quite pity; even so, the mingling of condemnation and ruth in them mysteriously doused the hot ache in my arms and flanks. I shuddered, or else the wind again sped through our little copse of execution posts.

"Who spoke?" I shouted, even though I knew—for Yeshua's message had come to me like a dream pronouncement, clear word by word but upon awakening a riddle.

"Hold your tongue, lout!" cried Priscus, the legionary who had won Yeshua's robe.

"I want to know who spoke!"

Priscus jabbed me in my shame with the square end of his spear, and I ran a splinter into my hip reacting to this poke. The only officer on the hillside, a centurion whom the sentries had not yet called by name, turned aside.

—Steady yourself, Mishael. Go steady. It is I.

"But you make no—"

"Shut up, lout!" said Priscus. "Do you want another?"

—Commune as I do, inwardly. What you write in your heart, Mishael, I will receive under its seal.

Yeshua, the fraud addressing me, hung from his tree like one nearly dead. Some women down the hill, crook-fingering among themselves, ignored the pitch-and-churn of the oncoming pall to grapple upslope toward us. Their garments popped like flags, their voices flew away in the windy babel. From another part of the road, a man—one of Yeshua's unreliable cronies— made his own slow trek upward.

—How trust you? I asked Yeshua in the inward speech he'd just advised. Even an ignorant village sorcerer could pick the mind of one nailed to a post.

—Split a log and I am there, Yeshua said nonsensically. Pick up a stone and I sparkle in its seams.

3

—But nothing in you sparkles of the Messiah. How trust you, Nazarene, when I know even the Father for a lie?

A shrieking gust rattled our posts in their sockets and tore Yeshua's robe from Priscus' neck. It flapped down the back of Golgotha like a market thief fleeing a pack of angry vendors. The man climbing toward us caught the robe on his outstretched arm and clutched it to him.

—Whoever curses the Father may find forgiveness, Yeshua said, as may that person who curses me. But whoever blasphemes the Holy Spirit will discover forgiveness neither in this city nor in the lasting one to come.

"A dog returns to its vomit," I said. "And the fool to his folly."

Priscus considered poking me again, but refrained when the women struggling uphill on one path and the robe-clutching man doing so on another had drawn close enough to hail Yeshua even over the wind's keening. In fact, Priscus retrieved the robe he'd diced for. With his centurion's approval, he even let the interlopers linger amidst our posts. They regarded me, when they looked up at me at all, as if I'd fallen among them from a shadow kingdom of demons and blights.

—What happens at the end? I asked Yeshua. What becomes of us, when the world has dwindled into a carcass?

—Do you know the beginning, Mishael, that you can ask so beseechingly after the end?

—Yeshua, I can't help but ask.

—In our end is our beginning.

—I beg you, riddle me not.

—Whoever stands at the beginning stands blessed.

—My blood flows out. And my strength.

—For whoever stands at the beginning will fully comprehend the end. Even dying, that one will live.

Out of aching rage, I cried, *"Demons take you!"*

—Mishael, you knew me at the first. Here, you hang with me

in the extremity of my sacrifice. Give over your taunts and die into the beginning.

Riddles! How had I known Yeshua "at the first"? I rolled my balding pate against the upright and shut my burning eyes. The Mount of Olives, the Temple, the Antonia Fortress—all now lay under a bruised-lavender fleece of clouds. This buckling, sky-borne fleece was visible to me even with my eyes closed. I could feel the oddly freshening winds and hear above Golgotha the expectant cries of carrion birds.

Yeshua spoke aloud, "Woman, look upon your son." I opened my eyes. Yeshua didn't mean for the woman to look at *him*, but at the male lackey who had just arrived. To this bearded man, Yeshua said, "And, you, embrace your mother."

Obediently, the lackey pulled the woman to him (her pinched face briefly seemed a window on a younger self, but only for an instant) and helped her back down the hillside to the road we doomed captives had earlier stumbled out on.

Weeping, the other three women tripped along behind them, but stopped at some distance and refused to move even another cubit toward Jerusalem.

"I thirst," Yeshua said.

"Wait for the rain," Priscus said.

But his superior, the centurion, put a sponge on his spear tip, thrust it into an amphora of spoiled wine, and lifted it to Yeshua's lips. Yeshua leaned his head to mouth the sponge, sipped from it feebly, then turned his head aside. The purple on his lips trickled down his chin into the raw gulley of his breastbone.

"It's over." Almost at once, Yeshua slumped from the nails driven between his wrist bones, and his body hung like a plucked fowl tied to a stake.

"Has his spirit left him?" called one of the women.

"The bastard's dead!" Priscus shouted down to her, and the women, after briefly conferring, trotted toward the city gate through the first cold knives of rain.

A thunderclap sundered the air, a ram's horn trumpet blew from an eastern wall, and Golgotha shrugged like a leviathan rolling under a Roman freighter. Our execution posts shunted upward, dropped, tilted out of true.

Reuel screamed. The centurion, Priscus, and a legionary named Macer fell with a single cry on the laced leather strips of their body armor. Then the centurion glanced up in awe at Yeshua and said something lilting and unintelligible. Priscus, on the other hand, jumped up and pricked Yeshua under the ribs with his spear. As if he'd just split a wine skin, blood and water gushed out.

It was about the ninth hour of the day. Passover torrents rattled the olive groves, beat upon the city's pavements, and pocked the grassless hillsides. I lifted my eyes bemusedly to this downpour.

—Taste the rain and I am on your tongue, a voice told me. Sanctify the end and a beginning comes to birth.

Three muddy legionaries stood at an awkward remove, eyeing Reuel and me with glum dutifulness. The rain had stopped. The thunderhead had pulled itself threadbare, revealing in the east several fringy blue armlets. Yeshua had died, but Reuel and I still clung in our pain and contumely to the afternoon's last daylight. Such fires crackled in my bones and along my sinews, however, that I would have gladly let go of my life.

A fresh squad of soldiers from the Antonia Fortress slogged out of the city and up the hillside.

The squad's leader said, "Rufilius, we've come to break their legs. The Jews don't want them to die out here on their plaguey Sabbath."

"Go ahead," Priscus said. "The sooner I get off this muddy hill the better."

The centurion Rufilius said, "Omit the one in the middle. His spirit's left him."

"Already?" said the leg-breakers' leader. "Didn't last long for a king, did he?"

The soldiers wondered about Yeshua's short time aloft. He must have had some hidden illness. He must have had more woman to him than man. Or maybe fear had cleft his heart.

Rufilius stepped away from the others. "Get on with it!" he barked.

The men drew lots for the honor of using the hammer. A big kid named Capito won. He teased Priscus about the mud-flecked robe he'd won dicing. A true Roman would rather win a hammer swing than any piece of a Hebrew's womanish garb. A legionary named Strabo produced a wine skin, and all of them but Rufilius drank from it.

Reuel groaned weakly. This drew the soldiers' attention, and Capito, hefting the mallet, stumbled over to Reuel's post and smashed his legs below the knee with two or three wayward blows. Reuel cried out.

But only once. His feet slipped clear of the *stipes*, and the weight of his body dragged down his lungs, to keep him from groaning more.

"Capito, you don't know what you're doing," said Priscus, laughing.

"Then what better way for me to learn?"

The road to the city gate had begun to fill once more with hawkers, pilgrims, onlookers. The Passover camps teemed again with life. The curious stood huddled on the road's margin, gaping up at our little forest and the haphazard doings of the legionaries. More of Yeshua's followers had gathered in the storm's wake than had visited Golgotha during the brunt of his agony. As before, women outnumbered men.

"So, Mishael, what thievery brought you to this shameful pass?" Capito asked me in clumsy Aramaic.

"A l-l-lamb," I said.

"A lamb?"

Priscus laughed scornfully. "Sacrificial animals. Lambs, goats, rams, doves, pigeons."

"Oh, so he stole offerings meant for the stiff-necked God of the Jews?" Capito looked up at me again. "Good for you. Such treachery deserves a boon."

A boon? I thought.

Capito broke only my right leg—with a crisp, well-placed strike of the mallet head. I yelped and cursed, then slumped whimpering through gritted teeth.

At length, though, as the legionaries busied themselves drinking and pointing out pretty female pilgrims to slander, I got my good leg under me and lifted myself against my tree's upright, easing the tax on my lungs. In fact, in this way, I could go on breathing. In, out; in, out; each gasping breath a stab and a hiss.

—I am the vine, the vinedresser, the vintager, the wine.

No one but me, I think, heard this new riddle. The guards, except for Rufilius, were bickering like street urchins; Reuel, meanwhile, had strangled to death a scant half hour after the breaking of his legs.

Flies tiptoed through my sweat. Cooking smoke curled into my eyes and nostrils.

—I am the wheat, the gleaner, the baker, the bread.

This riddle pricked me. In the hour before sunset, a party of Jews came toiling up Golgotha. Two thickset, well-dressed elderly men led it. Two younger men followed with a cart, behind which marched four or five women. The cart held an assortment of stoppered earthenware vessels and a pile of clean linen strips.

"I have permission from Pilate to take away the Nazarene's body," said the richer-looking of the two old Jews. He showed his authorization to Rufilius.

"And who are you?" said Rufilius, squinting at it.

"Joseph of Arimathea."

Yeshua's other disciples—if they warranted that title—refused to name themselves. The women wept audibly, while the old

Pharisee standing next to the Arimathean gazed up at Yeshua with a look of heavy strickenness.

"I don't care if you take them all," Rufilius said. "Just be quick about it."

The young men who'd pulled the cart, with the bumbling help of Joseph and his portly friend, uprooted the central tree and lowered it hand over hand to the ground. They used a metal claw to draw the spikes from Yeshua's wrists, then carried his body to the cart bed. The women treated the most visible signs of his scourging with aloes and myrrh, rubbed him from crown to foot with spices, and bound him as they would a baby in linen ribbons very like swaddling clothes.

Indeed, this last sight recalled to me the face of Yeshua's mother, and not only from that peculiar moment just before the thunderstorm.

"Bread," I said to myself. "House of bread."

"This man lives," the old Pharisee said. "Less than an hour till sunset and he lives."

Out of respect for the coming Sabbath, Priscus offered to kill me with his spear. The Pharisee snorted and appealed directly to Rufilius.

"Once you've broken their legs," he said, "the law says you forfeit any further right to help them die."

"*Whose* law?—Capito, break that thief's other leg."

"It's too late for that," the Pharisee said. "Because the Sabbath nears, you must yield him to whoever comes to take him down."

"He'll die within hours anyway," Rufilius said.

"Then why not allow us to spare you the bother of disposing of him?"

"Let them have their *king*," Priscus said. "Let them have all three. Who's to question your report, sir?"

Yeshua's death had awed and then dispirited Rufilius. "All right. Take them." He formed up his men (both his own guards and the late-arriving squad of leg-breakers) and marched them downhill in a tipsy gaggle. They chanted smutty cadences all the way to the city gate.

"Call me Nicodemus, Mishael of Hebron," the Pharisee said. "I think perhaps you've paid for your thievery."

As they'd brought down Yeshua, they brought me down. (They also soon reclaimed the body of Reuel.) They washed me as best they could and placed me gently in the cart. A asecluded garden of tombs bordered the execution site, and Joseph of Arimathea told Yeshua's cronies to cart us there, there to lay Yeshua and Reuel in a pair of tombs of Joseph's ownership.

I rode to the tombs beside the two dead men, and at every lurch I gasped. The work of the soldiers' whips had left my back a map of welts and ridges.

"A scourging, nearly ten hours on the tree, a broken leg, and the man still lives," Nicodemus said. "Is this the rabbi's last sign?"

"He would've done better to work it on his own behalf," the woman said.

Nicodemus and his wife, with the help of an awkward boy of twelve or so, lowered me into the lustral bath in the cloister of their comfortable house in Jerusalem. Rainwater helped feed this mikveh. Because of the recent storm, then, it shimmered and brimmed as I went down into it. Nicodemus's wife scooped a pair of leaves and the husk of a dead wasp from the surface and departed with the boy. I sat unsteadily on the lowest of the mikveh's three stone steps as the cool water nibbled at me like schools of tender fish.

"We should have that leg tended to," Nicodemus said.

"Not now. Just this. Thank you."

"I'm astonished you're able to support yourself at all, Mishael, even with the water to buoy you. Yeshua and that other man died out there—yet you look old enough to have sired even the unjustly condemned Nazarene."

The Sabbath had arrived. A torch in the cloister rippled in

smoky reds and oranges in the surface of my bath. Nicodemus was of two minds about my presence in his mikveh. That I had entered it to soothe my body rather than to cleanse my spirit troubled him. Seated on a stone bench nearby (ready to rescue me if I fainted and slipped all the way under), he talked to cover my silences and to distract himself from the grief rising in him. Mostly, he talked of Yeshua. His voice laved me as the water did, as if lapping me from the coast of an unexplored country.

". . . of water and the spirit," he said at length.

Those words, quietly uttered, slapped like a wave. "You've built an idol in your heart to Yeshua," I said.

Nicodemus took a moment to reply. "At the moment he died, the curtain in the Temple tore from top to bottom."

"Who told you that?"

"A person I trust." The torchlight reflected in Nicodemus' eyes made him seem both younger and weaker. "Touched by the rabbi's words and deeds, I visited him one night to ask him about one of his teachings. Answering, he implied that he was God's incarnate son, sent to die for us."

"I almost died for myself," I said. "And Reuel surely died for Reuel. In his case, Yeshua's dying made no difference. Am I to believe that everyone else will live forever?"

Nicodemus shrugged.

"Another question: How may that which does not exist call into existence a 'son'?"

It took a moment for Nicodemus to absorb this strange— indeed, unheard of—notion. "Your words pollute my mikveh, Mishael." He didn't try to to evict me from it, however, but perched there like an ugly plaster statue of himself.

"Yeshua's mother looked . . . very human," I said.

"And why not? She is."

"Her face and the Arimathean's burial clothes reminded me that I once saw her cradling Yeshua as an infant." My head felt light as a sea medusa's bladder.

11

Nicodemus rose to his feet. "Don't mock me, thief. I already doubt the wisdom, if not the good-neighborliness, of bringing you to my home."

"No mockery," I said. "I once saw your incarnate Son of God as a baby, his butt cheeks rash-mottled and his swaddling clothes wringing and smeared."

"Explain this," Nicodemus said.

While I explained, Nicodemus paced his cloister.

In Hebron, I was orphaned at twelve. I fed myself by doing hundreds of petty errands and sometimes even cutting purses. In the countryside, I pruned vines, tended sheep, and harvested wheat. A lustful vintner from Herodium used me for two years as his catamite. At fifteen, I broke free, turning to thievery for my livelihood.

One spring, in open pastureland, I chanced upon a shepherd who told me of a couple from Galilee who, for some bothersome Roman administrative reason, had gone afoot and donkeyback to a nearby village. There the woman had given birth. My informant and several other shepherds had befriended the couple, carrying them water, figs, dates, and portions of hot-spiced lamb. They kept this up for two or three days, embarrassed and angered by the lack of hospitality that most of their fellow Bethlehemites had shown the travelers.

If I hungered, the shepherd said, I should call upon these people. They had leftover food aplenty and errands I could run to repay them for sharing it with me.

I found the woman (in truth, a girl only a bit older than me) and her grizzled husband sunning themselves on a ledge in front of the limestone hole where they had taken shelter after villager after villager had rebuffed them. Their ribby donkey colt grazed downslope in a stand of thistles. They gave me bread, cheese, raisins, some savory lamb. I clearly recall the donkey amidst the thistles, the food, and the couple's candid, undemonstrative friendliness—but I can't, today, recall their names. This was over thirty years ago, and in my wanderings to that point, landmarks and raw luck had always meant more to me than people and their uncertain alms.

I stayed two days with the Galileans, gathering firewood, grooming the colt, washing their infant son's wrappings and laying them out on the rocks to dry. Once, I even went into the village with the halt-footed husband so he could fulfill some undone part of the registration procedure.

That night, back from this tiresome chore, I lay down in a corner and slept. Twice, at least, the baby woke me crying, obviously indifferent to the notion that God might prefer his human heir to behave with rabbinical dignity, even in a cave. The mother quieted her very babylike infant by slipping it an inflamed-looking nipple.

The next day, the couple had me watch their child in the cave while, outside, they put balm on a running sore on the donkey's withers and loaded the animal with their belongings. I've never liked babies much. They make too much noise, a lot of it mysterious or silly. This one, lying in a stone trough lined with straw, followed me with eyes as lively as a pair of dungball-pushing beetles. It prated an abracadabra babble and puffed out its cheeks. When it began to fuss, focusing on me with an acuity I had never seen in a newborn, I went to it and undid the linen straps in which its mother had so tightly wound it.

Outside, to protest its loading, the donkey reared, brayed, and sliced the husband's robe with one quicksilver forehoof. Then, ducking its head, it trotted downslope, heedless of the man and woman's shouts. When they chased it, I looked about the cave for some unpacked item to take. All that presented itself was a delicate cedar box that held, I discovered, a single gold ingot small enough to rest on my palm. I carried the box outside and hid it in a thorny shrub.

The baby, free of its swaddling, began to thrash and wail. I hurried back inside to calm it. It shut up as soon as it saw me

13

hovering over it. Its eyes—how to say this?—had the cunning glitter of a very old man's; they also had a kind of pity-filled gaiety, a gentleness that struck to my very heart—like an adz head, or an insult.

I pinched the baby's nose with two fingers and pulled its head out of the straw, then let go of its nose so that its head dropped back with a jolting bounce. The baby made a dovelike murmur. I grabbed one of its big toes and twisted it. This time the baby voiced a yelp, which grew into an insucking cry that brought its parents running.

"Shhhhh," I went. "Shhhhh, shhhhh, shhhhh."

The naked baby continued to wail. I grabbed it up from its feed-trough manger. Afraid that it would either pee on or spit up all over me, I quickly turned it around, suspending it over the cave floor with its pudgy arms outstretched and its bony feet adangle. This pose so surprised the baby that it shut up, hiccoughing rather than screaming. At that moment, though, its mother ducked inside.

"He dirtied himself again, mistress," I said. "But I've taken care of it. See. He needed air."

(The look on that child-woman's face appeared again today on the face of Yeshua's mother.)

She said, "Mishael, give him to me," and took the baby out of my hands. She cradled it against her shoulder, examined it, cooed to it. "Now, leave."

So I did, surprising, as I darted out, both the woman's husband and their well-laden donkey colt.

Later, after the couple had left for Jerusalem for their son's circumcision, I returned to the hills for the hidden cedar box and the gold ingot inside it.

"An incredible story," Nicodemus said. "But for your sake, I hope you lie."

"No."

"Then I fear you pollute not only my mikveh but also the rabbi's sojourn on Golgotha."

"Neither of us knows the end of that story."

"You know nothing at all, Mishael."

"Whoever stands at the beginning will fully comprehend the end." For the first time, this saying made sense to me.

"You comprehend nothing."

"Perhaps your Nazarene is who he said he was."

"He's dead, isn't he?"

"In our end is our beginning."

"He *died* up there!" Nicodemus said in heartfelt anguish.

"Hallow the end and a beginning comes to birth."

"Dead, dead, dead, dead, dead!" Nicodemus had removed the belt of his tunic. With each word, he flicked the belt into his mikveh, right under my face: pock, pock, pock, pock, pock. "And you, man, deserve no boon at all!"

"Of water and the spirit," I said.

With one well-placed blow of his hammer, Capito broke my other leg. Not long after that, I hobbled across.

000-00-0000

000-00-0000

ABSOLUTE ZERO: You have entered a small auditorium or theater to see an animated documentary of the history of place holders in the affairs of the human species. I am your narrator. I have no name, but my voice identifies me as female. At present, of course, you find yourself staring at a blank or blackened screen and listening to the unemotional cadences of my voice-over. Experimental films, whether live-action or animated, have never particularly interested you (the third game of this year's World Series is being broadcast tonight on commercial television), but someone with affectedly modish tastes and an irresistibly bullying manner prevailed upon you to come, and so here you are, your sole consolation the absence of a line at the ticket counter and hence the lack of any need to function as a place holder in an annoying queue. Still, the house is three-quarters empty, and the loud garrulity of your companion has made you shrink into yourself like a sick man's penis. You slump down so far in your seat that no one but those in immediately adjacent rows can see you. The strain of this posture induces you to remember that yesterday you obtained a replacement for a lost Social Security card and that a computer error gave you the disquieting number 000-00-0000. Moreover, it frightens you that the film you are about to watch (if ever a visual image breaks in upon the screen's blindness) has no title.

> "*zero, absolute*: lowest temperature point that is
> theoretically possible: 0° Kelvin, -273.2° Centigrade
> or -459.8° Fahrenheit; the point has been very closely
> approached, but cannot be attained in experiments."
> Siegfried Mandel, *Dictionary of Science* (New York: Dell,
> 3rd printing, 1972), p. 365.

000-00-0000

"ZERO AT THE BONE": This caption dawns at the bottom of the screen, beneath a flash-frozen flood of spectacularly cold light. A glacier of empearled lambency. You begin to believe that either on the Centigrade or the Fahrenheit scale, absolute zero has been attained. Two weeks into October and the operators of this theater are cavalierly running the air conditioning at topmost tilt. This frightens you, too. You begin to shiver, but have no strength to stand and stalk out. Zero at the bone. Where have you heard *that* before? A literary allusion, isn't it? But who first said it? Nobody. Nobody that you can remember, and with your vitiated will and your brand-new, identity-mocking Social Security card, you're nobody, too. Take heart, Mr. 000-00-0000. Even yet, you are more than I, for I am as fearfully close to a nonentity as anyone could ever be. You hold your place in the clammy flesh, but I mine only at the sufferance of the anonymous animators who sponsored this

18

project and only as a voice. I have no Social Security number at all. I am probably of a completely different nationality. French, maybe, or Japanese. *Hiroshima, Mon Amour.* (Does my accent identify me?) I have attained 0° Kelvin on the scale of my own self-esteem and hence have reached absolute zero in an absolute personal sense. Only my task as narrator preserves me from total nullity. Aught that I am, I ought not to exist in any guise, even a scratchy vocal one. It scares me, 000-00-0000.

> "*zero:/* an insignificant person; a dull nobody. For synonyms see OAF [U.S. slang, mid 1900s-pres.]" Richard Spears, *Slang and Euphemism: A Dictionary of Oaths, Curses, Insults, Racial Slurs, Sexual Slang and Metaphor, Drug Talk, Homosexual Lingo, and Related Matters*, Abridged Edition (New York: Signet, 1982), p. 448.

000-00-0000

"A LONG TIME AGO, THE HUMAN SPECIES DIDN'T KNOW NOTHING": Everything that you have heard me say to this point, *only* you have heard. It all represents a kind of inadmissible prologue that I have laid down solely to establish a connection between us. "A long time ago, the human species didn't know nothing." There. That voice-over narrative hook, as coyly inelegant as it may be, begins the sound track proper just an instant or two after your eyes have registered the two-dimensional snowfield captioned "zero at the bone." Bones are often fossils, and fossils take us back to the beginning. Or near it.

> NARRATOR: A long time ago, the human species didn't know nothing. By which we mean to report that although early human civilizations were far from mathematically illiterate (else how could they have practiced astronomy or built the pyramids?), the concept of zero, today such a commonplace

that even kindergarteners comprehend it, eluded discovery
for centuries. Addition, subtraction, multiplication,
and division all went forward without benefit of the
empty-headed symbol that Einstein himself once referred
to as a "goose egg." So did score-keeping in such popular
diversions as gladitorial combat and roc-potting. Indeed,
until the advent of the symbol itself, mathematicians (and,
yes, royal scorekeepers) were forced to acknowledge this
troublesome nonesuch by leaving strategic gaps in their
rows of figures. Blathermore and blahforth, blah blah blah
blah blah

On the screen, my dear 000-00-0000, a montage of Leonardo
da Vinci-ish sketches (animated, of course) depicting all the histori-
cal tidbits I continue to rehearse verbally for you and your seatmates.
But I've gone under like this (again) to address you (once more) on
a subliminal level because *they* are NOTHING to me. What I say for
your ears only, Mister Nowhere Man, must therefore lift you from
the status of theatergoing cipher to (at least) that of marginal entity,
even if I myself remain only a place holder in the emptiness of your
soul.

"Although there are only nine counters in each row of
the abacus, there are actually ten possible arrangements.
Besides using any number of counters from one to nine in
a row, it is also possible to use *no* counter—that is,
to leave the place at the counting position empty. This
escaped all the great Greek mathematicians and was not
recognized until the ninth century, when some unnamed
Hindu thought of representing the tenth alternative by a
special symbol, which the Arabs called 'sifr' ('empty')
and which has come down to us, in consequence, as 'cipher'
or, in more corrupt form, 'zero.'" *Asimov's Guide to
Science* (New York: Basic Books, 1972), p. 876.

000-00-0000

A FUNNY THING HAPPENED TO ME ON THE WAY TO THE VACUUM:
Your companion has fallen asleep in his seat. An animated documentary on the topic of mathematical place holders has turned out
to be not at all to his taste. Buffoonishly, in outright competition
with my voice-over, he snores as loudly as earlier he talked. (*You*
wish that in the torn upholstered theater chair next to you reposed
only a gap.) Even though the actor Zero Mostel is dead, your
companion resembles a poignantly weary Zero Mostel, his jowls
wagging, his projector-illuminated lips puffing with each crass
expulsion of breath. Too bad for him. At this point, the film is
almost amusing. The animators have conjured a colorful promenade of cartoonish figures who have borne the unfortunate fore-
name Zero, including the actor whom your companion resembles,
a Greek philosopher whose writings on various metaphysical
matters were lost forever in the fire at Alexandria, a buck-toothed
character in the comic strip *Beetle Bailey*, and a certain JS ("The
Unknown Citizen"), whose first name might as well have been
Zero, because although there was no official complaint against him,
the government has recently issued him a Social Security card
bearing upon it the cipher-laden series 000-00-0000. The animators have rendered this last archetypal figure without a face.
Helplessly, you put your hands to your not ill-sculpted features to
see if they are still there.

> "It's a joy to see Messrs. Mostel, Silvers and Gilford
> romping through this farce, and it reminds us again of
> the unfortunate way in which the movies have neglected
> and wasted the enormous talents of these three comics.
> Mostel is much more than a comic—he is, simply, one
> of the very greatest actors alive." Steven H. Scheur,
> ed., *Movies on TV: 1978-79 Edition* (New York: Bantam
> Books, Eighth [revised] edition, 6th printing), p. 261.

But, of course, he isn't alive anymore. Neither are most of the unsung human beings who survived well into this century, many with considerably more auspicious forenames than Zero.

000-00-0000

ZERO DRIFT: More snow, more instructive cartoons. You note the absence of a comforting lump under the outer edge of your left buttock and realize that your billfold is gone. A battered wallet with plastic inserts for credit cards and family photographs. You actually employ only a few of these transparent envelopes. (A K-Mart photo-booth mugshot of your father, fifteen years old, is precious to you, but the only paternal feature that you can recall with any degree of certainty has its proper home in the 1950s, i.e., the man's graying, military-style crewcut.) One such plastic insert *does* contain your Social Security card, and the loss of that piece of official identification truly frets you, deflecting your attention from both the film and your companion's snoring. Did your wallet slip from your back pocket and fall to the floor? A clumsy search in the dark finds nothing to support this hypothesis—unless the person behind you has already picked it up and hidden it in his or her clothes. Or maybe your pocket was picked by one of the unwashed attendees milling about in the lobby before the houselights went down. If so, the thief has acquired 1) only a dollar or two, 2) an homogenized likeness of your father, who either died in the recent past or else joined the brainwashed minions of a charismatic religious sectarian, and 3) tentative control of the nine zeros on your Social Security card. You imagine the thief doing everything in his power to divest himself of this fearful numerological curse, planting the card on some unsuspecting stooge, who, upon discovering it, either drops it in a tempting spot in a public place or else surreptitiously passes it on to yet another anonymous victim. You imagine this cycle continuing until every person in the world has briefly experienced the private celebrity of administrative extinction.

22

"*zero drift* n : a gradual change in the scale zero of a
measuring instrument (as a thermometer or a galvanometer)"
Webster's Third New International Dictionary (G. & C.
Merriam Co., 1976), vol. III, p. 2658.

WEIGHTLESSNESS: The narrator of this untitled film weighs even
less than I do. She has only her voice to project into the void. And
weightlessness, of course, occurs automatically in environments
possessing, either naturally or artificially, the "negative" attribute
of ZERO GRAVITY. Like absolute zero, zero gravity is difficult to
attain in the everyday operation of the world. The narrator of this
"animated documentary," for instance, sounds inordinately serious
about my coerced attendance tonight, the loss of my wallet, and the
(falsely) ominous misassignment to me of a nine-digit Social
Security number whose digits are in fact ciphers or place holders.
Objectively speaking, clinically speaking, we are all place holders,
but the subjective dimension has the power to redeem us from the
anonymity of vast perspectives and the omni-potent longview. I am
chuckling sardonically to myself as I scrunch here, and I would urge
the faceless woman upon whose heavy subvocalizations I have been
involuntarily eavesdropping ever since the projector began to purr,
"Lighten up." My friend Zero Mostel (not his real name) has already
pronounced judgment on the filmmakers' ponderous approach to
their subject matter, and I would wake him up and suggest going
home except that I would rather endure his snoring than his
inevitable angry response to any tactless hint that he may have been
sleeping.

"*zero-sum game* n : a game in which the cumulative winnings
equal the cumulative losses." *Ibid.*

"NOTHING CAN BE CREATED OUT OF NOTHING."—LUCRETIUS: And you of course compound the denial of my reality by speaking around me to an unidentified second-person auditor as if I were not even here. Look at the caption on the screen, 000-00-0000, the one from Lucretius, and let me inform you that I have not misread your unspoken anxiety and that your flippant response to my compassionate intrusions (for I have addressed you by *name* each time I've undercut my own narration to talk to you) qualifies as a self-defense mechanism. I have not manufactured my analysis in the absence of facts, I have NOT made something from nothing.

> "Recent discoveries in particle physics have suggested mechanisms whereby matter can be created in empty space by the cosmic gravitational field, which only leaves the origin of spacetime itself as a mystery....
> "We have seen how the quantum factor permits events to occur without causes in the subatomic world. Particles, for example, can appear out of nowhere without specific causation.... Thus, spacetime could pop out of nothingness as the result of a causeless quantum transition." Paul Davies, *God and the New Physics* (New York: Simon and Schuster, 1983), pp. 214-215.

000-00-0000

I THINK I'M TURNING JAPANESE: Handbooks on proper English usage tell us that the plural of the word *zero* may be either *zeros* or *zeroes*. Both before and during the years of World War II, the Japanese built 10,937 "Zeroes" (or "Zeros"). This was an aircraft properly called the Mitsubishi A6M, a single-seat fighter famous for its use by the Japanese Navy in *kamikaze* assaults on U.S. vessels in the Pacific. The pilots of the notorious Zeros (or Zeroes) divebombed their explosives-filled airplanes into American carriers, destroyers, and troopships, sacrificing their own lives for the sake of the embattled homeland. Perhaps the Mitsubishi A6M

24

became known as the Zero because its kamikaze pilots were expendable ciphers in the Japanese war effort, persons of no individual consequence, nobodies. This is certainly what they became, physically, at the moment of sacrificial impact, but as a transplanted countrywoman of these fallen heroes (rarely, if ever, heros), I must point out that they also attained the absolute zero of apotheosis in their own native religiometaphysical faith. Nobodies became somebodies, if only briefly, through violent self-negation, subtracting their Zeros (or Zeroes) from the sum total of the Divine Wind. A zero-sum game of existential profundity, played for keeps. Everyone is temporarily a celebrity in death, and the victim of violent self-sacrifice even more so. This is an amusing paradox that I tell you, 000-00-0000, to offset the gravity of my public narration.

> "I remember not so long ago being in the Imperial War
> Museum where they have the front section of a *Zero*
> fighter cut through the cockpit. One can actually stand
> looking into the cockpit. And one can see what's actually
> underneath the plane; looking up into the interior, one can
> see every rivet. An enormous sort of tragic poetry
> surrounds that plane in the Imperial War Museum. One can
> see all those Japanese men at work; women in their
> factories in some Tokyo suburb stamping the rivets into
> this particular plane. One can imagine the plane later on
> a carrier in the Pacific...." J.G. Ballard, "Interview with
> JGB by Graeme Revell," *Re/Search*, No. 8-9, 1984, p. 47.

Uncertain of my age, maybe *I* am one of those women. Maybe I am the *daughter* of one of those women.

ZERO VISIBILITY: But individuating myself in this way, in an aesthetic experience predicated on the abstract universality of its components, has terrified you, hasn't it? You have no desire to know the crass autobiographical details of my background, such gross distinguishing factors as my parents' nationality, the fortuitously erotic placement of a birthmark I can only dimly remember, the psychic scars of past rejections. You don't want to see me stamping rivets into an airplane. And you don't want to hear me plaintively confess the ways in which I abased myself for a man who knocked me up and then vanished from my life as thoroughly as if someone had dismembered his body and cleverly deep-sixed the pieces. (I had an abortion.) You prefer knowing me as a script-bound voice. You don't want to see me at all. You *can't* see me. Of course, the limits on your ability to visualize me derive from the homeopathic nature of your own self-defining anxieties.

See *Webster's Third New International Dictionary*, vol. III, p. 2657, for details.

000-00-0000

DISINTEGRATION <ZERO HOUR> EVOLUTION: Has my analysis annihilated you? The projector continues to purr, but the preternatural fixity of your eyeballs suggests a kind of defensive catatonia. Maybe I can knock down your irrational defenses with tenderness.

NARRATOR: Lorenz Oken, a German philosopher and biologist, had the bent of a Pythogarean mystic. He believed that reality couches itself in a variety of mathematical symbols. According to Oken, zero is simultaneously nothingness and infinity. Positive and negative numbers issue from zero in opposite directions, and this process parallels the descending and ascending order of animate and inanimate objects in our natural world. Oken also held that, metaphysically speaking, zero is God and that the decay of matter to "mucus" and the ascent of living creatures toward higher and higher

26

levels of self-awareness reveal God's wish to embody himself in nature. This philosophy, so attractive to American Transcendentalists, has a tacit counterpart in that of the kamikaze pilots who killed themselves for the state. It is not so bad to be Nothing. Sometimes, in fact, it is everything. If zero is God, and if our entire cosmos arose spontaneously from nothing, think for a moment on the vast potential of a single person's self-conscious anonymity.

The number 000-00-0000, you see, permits interpretation as nine place holders awaiting the substitution of weightier counters. Hiroshima, mon amour, need not haunt us *forever*.

"*love* n . . . 7: a score of zero in tennis and some other games: NOTHING" *Webster's*, vol. II, p. 1340. [Probably from the French *l'oeuf*, the egg, because of the zero's resemblance to a goose egg when the score is recorded on a chalk board or a slate visible to the contestants or the spectators at a tennis match.]

"*zero hour* n : compare H HOUR, COUNTDOWN, CRISIS, and DAY OF RECKONING" *Webster's*, vol. III, p. 2658 [semifaulty citation].

"*zero population growth*: a short-term consequence of the atomic bombing of Hiroshima, a long-term consequence of the death of love. (Game, match, set)" Richard Bowers, Paul Erlich, and Charles Remington. *A Latter-Day Devil's Dictionary* (Garden City, New York: Doubleday, 1969), p. 191 [altogether faulty citation].

GROUND ZERO: And so of course we come down to this. We zeroize (or, rather, *you* zeroize) the seeming impossibility of a relationship between us by projecting my whispered appeals into the intangible narration of an artsy-fartsy film or by dismissing them as the grating rhonchus of a male companion who forced your attendance at this cornily hip event. But I am *not* invisible, I am *not* merely a voice emanating in matter-of-fact nuances from the speakers in this converted chemistry auditorium, and I am most definitely *not* a buffoonish double for someone resembling the late Zero Mostel. That that unfeeling person (the place holder separating us) knocked me up I can't deny, and that I am the nisei offspring of immigrant parents I have never done anything to hide from you. Look at me. How could I? And so we sit here side by side an ocean apart (the Pacific, presumably) suffering the chill of the air conditioning and the absolute zero at the bone of our fears of and for the other. The emphatic details of my identity obliterate you. They wipe you out. It is not your wallet that you have lost but your way through the labyrinth of my intimidating personal history. You have forgotten, if you ever knew, that "except for zero itself, every number raised to the zero power is defined as equal to 1." (That is what we could have been.) Or maybe the comic misassignment to you of Social Security card 000-00-0000 is no misassignment at all. Maybe, in this single mordant instance, the state has not erred. It has atomized you as you have atomized me, but by impersonal chance rather than by deliberate choice. Which is why it is astonishing that either of us should continue to hurt.

Look, 000-00-0000, the lights are coming up.

000-00-0000

Snapshots from the Butterfly Plague

Two cruel Aprils ago, a swarm of monarchs—see-through amber and hosiery black—wheeled down on a baby carriage parked next to a boathouse on Mockingbird Lake. The butterflies landed on the baby's face, then clung there like a swaying tower of miniature flags. (Twenty Thousand Flags Over Georgia.)

From my bicycle on an trail above the boathouse, I saw it all. It never occurred to me to think those monarchs were murdering the kid, suffocating him the way Edward the Second's assassins crushed the poor king under a table. But the returning mother's scream, along with a whispery stampede of retreating infanticides, made me think again.

As everyone knows, incidents of lepidopteran hostility increased after that bewildering first incident. From Montreal to San Diego, kaleidoscopic kamikaze strikes on ballparks left dozens of players, and countless fans, battered almost to insensibility by siroccos of pitiless silk.

The culprits weren't monarchs only, but azures, swallowtails, metalmarks, hairstreaks: squadrons of flamboyant loveliness that dropped out of the sky or exploded from peach trees, wheat fields, cattle pastures.

And when butterfly silkstorms fanned into our cities, smearing windshields, appliquéing engine grilles, Osterizing themselves in revolving doors, cycloning through subway stations like opalescent confetti, randomly canonizing winos, bag ladies, and whores (even as, tenderly, they snuffed them), Uncle Sam mobilized the National Guard.

Frightened boys in combat gear gassed every butterfly-flooded urban canyon, or else they *shot to kill* with evil-looking automatic weapons. In fact, on the Fourth of July, in the parking lot of Atlanta/Fulton County Stadium, a platoon of burr-headed guardies machine-gunned a flight of anglewings, pearl crescents, and red admirals. The carnage—if that's the word—was spectacular. So was the noise.

Jodi-Marie and I watched from a wall above the parking lot. To us, the deafening *tat-tat-tat!* was like a firefight with the wash line of a shah: brocades disintegrating, Shantungs tattering in air, the entire blazing wardrobe of a royal household parachuting into orange and purple scrap.

"It's for the birds," Jodi-Marie said as we illegally pedaled the shoulder of Oklahoma's I-40 between Yukon and Hydro.

"What's for the birds?" I said. (Probably, it was fancying myself a Tour de France competitor on a day so hot it could have been radioactive.)

"Damn it, Dennis, I said it's *like* that old flick, *The Birds.*" Jodi-Marie reached out to halt me, bestriding the mountain bike I'd bought her like some leggy, Lycra-clad gal in a *Bicycle Guide* ad. "Except it's butterflies instead of birds."

Jodi-Marie hadn't been born when *The Birds* came out. Me, I'd been at Duke, digging the Beatles and pot-smoking my way to a hippy peacenik vision of Shangri-La.

Still, Jodi-Marie wanted points for the allusion—which, by then, was so old-hat I had to tell myself that she *did* deserve some credit; after all, it's hard to stay abreast of things when you're self-propellering your tassels in the Cheetah Lounge five to seven hours a night.

That's why she liked me: my inherited cash and my savvy about the world. I wasn't just some crusty old bum—I was a mature, and well-heeled, bicycle vagabond.

"*This time*," I began to say, "*the birds are on our side*"—but a highway patrol car swam out of the heat shimmer.

Smoky was debonair in his widebrim and shades. "Hey," he said, "you shouldn't be up here." (On the high, holy "Motorized Vehicles Only" macadam, he meant.) To illustrate his point, he told a story about some hitchhikers, over by Guthrie, set upon by a wheeling conflagration of scarlet swallowtails. They were driven screaming to their knees, not to mention their deaths, by yards and yards of belligerent red chiffon.

"They looked like men on fire—like they'd been whooshed by flamethrowers or something."

"Scarlet swallowtails are from the Philippines," I said. "You don't get them in temperate zones."

Smoky waved. The air did dizzying hulas over the concrete, out on the prairie. "This look 'temperate' to you, bubba?"

"It's just so hard to believe a bunch of silky butterflies can really kill people," Jodi-Marie said.

Smoky—his real name was Clayton McKenna—said, "A ton of nylon may be softer than a ton of bricks, but a ton's still a ton, missy." He told us that truckers, people in cars, bus passengers, and speeding Hell's Angels were probably safe, but that hikers and cyclists were "playing butterfly roulette."

Then, Good Samaritan-like, McKenna paced us four miles past El Reno to U.S. 270, which we followed northwest to Watonga, Woodward, Fort Supply, Forgan, and, eventually, the oxymoronically monickered Liberty, Kansas.

Actually, birds *weren't* our allies—not any longer. In only their past nine to twelve generations, an army of workaholic U.N. entomologists bemusedly reported, nearly every lepidopteran species worldwide had chemically mutated to secrete into its blood a sickening toxin—hydrogen cyanide—that no self-respecting bird or bat would ever want to taste again.

Besides, the bug men said, butterflies from every continent but Antarctica were now ecumenically flocking, as if joined in common cause to chasten humanity with their spectacular oneness. And, of course, if sheer beauty had no power to shame or reform, the little organza beasties weren't averse to pummeling the bejesus out of us with a myriad hallelujahing wings.

Seven miles up the nauseating zebra haze of Highway 83, due north of hayseed Liberal, our incandescent mountain bikes coasted into the lot of a dusty complex of cinderblock buildings called—I kid you not—LAAMAAR DE LONG'S HOLISTIC ECOLOGICAL GREAT PLAINS CHURCH & ROADSIDE MOTH-O-RAMA.

"Some damnfools say it's Nature biting back," Laamaar De Long told Jodi-Marie and me in the welcome cool of the moth-o-rama's parlor, "but that's a earthshoe liberal's two-bit notion of cosmic justice. I don't buy it."

Laamaar was a wide man, as wide as his given name, as wide as the GREAT PLAINS. Fifty or so, he put me in mind of a lumpy-faced critter from my daddy's favorite comic strip, *Pogo*—but whether hound, skunk, gator, or bear, I couldn't say, only that the gruff old coot was at once endearing and sinister.

"It isn't Nature biting back," he said. "It's God or something like Him souping up the ordinary with a whizz-bang glory."

Later, our admission money in hand, De Long walked Jodi-Marie and me through his bare-walled moth-o-rama. "These are the night fighters of God's holistic ecological invasion force. I've always been an after-hours guy, so it had to be moths I beelined for when going into, first, a business and, later, a religion."

We walked by glassed-in dioramas sheltering peacocks, lunas, regals, sphinx moths, owlets: an aviary of tender plumes hammering in the aqueous half-light of the viewing chambers.

"Nowadays, butterfly houses are 'in'—a dime a dozen," said De Long, "but my moth-o-rama's a one-of-a-kind affair. I'm damned proud of it."

The male lunas—pale green and glowing, like bioluminescent fungus—seemed especially restive. I wondered if their furred antennae were picking up the pheromone broadcasts of the females winging solo over the ticking evening wheat.

Jodi-Marie placed her hands on the glass, whispered consolingly to the moths, muttered that they deserved to be free, then said it was time to catch some muscle-restoring shuteye. Come morning, our itinerary long since decided, we'd strike out for Wolf Creek Pass, the Grand Canyon, Las Vegas, and, Jodi-Marie's own hubris-tic grail, Hollywood. (Hooray.)

"Make camp here on my grounds," De Long said. "You're my first real customers in days. I'd like the company."

Having taken a judgmental dislike to the old fellow, Jodi-Marie didn't want to accept. I convinced her it was okay.

A full moon floated over the wheat. It glimmered like a beach ball as we bucked on the canvas ground cloth in our thermoplastic tent.

Despite the Butterfly Plague now in process, we were biking to the coast so that Jodi-Marie could "become a star." She wasn't an unintelligent young woman, but she couldn't sing. Her voice was a metallic whine. She couldn't act, not even enough to disguise her distaste of Laamaar De Long from De Long himself. And once past her perfunctory B-girl bump & grind, she couldn't dance any better than a hamstrung sow tripping down a meat-packing line on its way to become Spam.

Nevertheless, in the plastic-defracted glow of the August moon, Jodi-Marie said, "I *am* going to make it. It's my destiny, Dennis. Remember that stripper who did it with fans?"

"Pardon me, Jodi girl, but I'm not *that* old."

"What was her name? Sally Something. Sally . . . Rand."

"Yeah, but she *didn't* use fans."

"Sure she did."

"It was feathers. Big ones. Ostrich plumes."

"Okay, okay. What difference does it make?"—but the kink in her voice said that the distance between fans and ostrich plumes was vast. Then, as if to dispel a gathering funk, she told me the dream she'd been having nightly for over a week:

She is sashaying down the runway of the biggest crystal palace since the world got into the business of World Fairing. Big-time exhibitionism. She herself is the fairest of the Fair, feathered in exotic lepidoptera from Africa, Asia, South and Central America, the palmy Caribbean: tailed batwings, languid owls with disturbing eyespots, yellow birdwings, Paris peacocks, tigers, emerald-banded swallowtails, G I A N T purple emperors, modest zebras, blood-red flambeaux. They hide what she wants to hide. They show what she wants to show. They flutter when she struts. They crackle, sigh, and hover exactly when she wants them to.

Jodi-Marie's eyes had begun to glass in reverie. Butterflies swam in her pupils. I almost fell in love with her dream-stitched image of herself—her pied, and striated, and moiré-patterned self-infatuation.

"*Come back inside!*" boomed De Long from much too near us in the moonburned night. "I'll break all my moth cases. You can let the fuzzy fellas shingle your pretty self for as long as it t-t-tickles your fancy, gal."

"Cripes!" said Jodi-Marie, pushing me off.

I fought to catch myself, to recover my shorts.

De Long blathered on: "My wife ran off with a weather-radio man six years ago. All I want's a look-see, gal. Isn't that what you want to give me? Isn't that what you've been dreaming of?" He peered down into our tent like a boozy sodbuster colossus.

"I was dreaming of *show business*," Jodi-Marie said. "What you snuck up on was private."

I got angry: "If it's a peep show you want, buy a VCR."

"Eskimos share their wives," De Long said reproachfully, then staggered back to his tinhorn moth-o-rama.

Jodi-Marie figured De Long for a would-be rapist; I argued that he was only a lonely, wifeless fool.

So we stayed, and tried to sleep, and the moon tumbled by like the ball in an exhausted roll-on deodorant.

Later: BOOM! BOOM! BOOM!

Our after-the-fact deductions told us that De Long had fired a 12-gauge shotgun at the panels in the moth-o-rama's roof, blasting holes in them, widening these holes, then blasting again— until every tin panel was a window and the moths in his dioramas (earlier freed by hammer slams) went helixing up through the holes like a tornado whirling black-and-white oragami toys, scissored scraps of celluloid, and weightless kernels of popcorn excelsior whooshingly upward: a tornado run in reverse on the drive-in-theater screen of the Seward County sky.

"They're heading toward the moon," Jodi-Marie said, "like moths toward a—"

"A flame," I concluded for her.

And, in fact, a superorganism of moths was climbing together to blot out the moon. Lepidoptera in the fields beyond the structure joined the escapees in windmilling aloft.

Jodi-Marie and I watched draft-borne argosies of the creatures bank, interthread, flap higher and wider, eclipse the stars, and greedily devour the slow-to-set moon. Then we packed up our gear and scrammed. For miles, though, we couldn't outpace the signs in the sky of an imaginative business gone horribly awry.

Killing the plants on which the larval caterpillars fed, said the hotshot U.N. entomologists, would knock out the berserk adults far more efficiently than machine-gunning them as they whirled over parking lots; better, even, than spraying them with chemicals while they basked in hardwood groves or wildflower meadows.

The entomologists were wrong: Every species worldwide had modified its feeding habits to such a degree that it could live on carrion as well as plants. We saw flocks of British Camberwell beauties, or mourning cloaks, perched like Ritz-dyed lichen on the carcasses of road kills: dead dogs, steamrollered cats, raw red opossums.

Almost overnight, in evolutionary terms, adult lepidoptera had become opportunistic scavengers. They also engaged in predation, slaying in wily bands whatever they wanted to eat.

But there was more: These new lepidoptera had abandoned the four-part life cycle of egg, caterpillar, chrysalis, imago—in favor of 1) sex between contending adults, 2) a three- or four-month pregnancy, and 3) the dropping of fully formed winged infants (as few as one, as many as a thousand) that scavenged, preyed, and grew, no matter the species, as large as a grown man's hand. Then they would fly off with the reconnoitering squadrons to which their parents still belonged.

Said one worried bug man, "I'm afraid that, today, the damned things are like souls: immortal."

For, although it was easy to kill free-lancing adults, it did appear that, left alone, these mutant lepidoptera *did not die*. Their biomass burgeoned like April kudzu. Meanwhile, silkworms, inchworms, bagworms, woolly bears—all the different makes of caterpillar—were conspicuous by their extinction.

Jodi-Marie and I had stopped to rest in a turnout at the top of Wolf Creek Pass. Near water birch, Englemann spruce, and aspens, I only half listened to her harangue about the necessity of choosing a stage name to replace her real surname, Woznicki.

Among a stand of wind-nudged aspens on the Pagosa Springs side of the mountain, one tree burned like a lamp sipping natural gas; the blaze of its foliage was a startling bluish white.

"*I'd like something sweet and happy-sounding,*" Jodi-Marie was saying, from far away. "*Something gay. Well, not gay. Joyful. Upbeat. Fun-like.*"

My bonfire tree was an aspen, but an albino, a breathtaking freak.

"*Like Jolley. Jodi-Marie Jolley. Or Goforth. Or Harmon—short for 'Harmony.' Whaddaya think?*"

A crash in the undergrowth near the burning tree. A rattling of leaves. A murmur. Faint snappings of branches. The leaves on my albino aspen burst into the San Juan Mountain sky and spread out overhead in bands of gaudy, living cirrocumulus.

The butterflies shooting from the aspen—huge mustard whites, slightly smaller azures—had scared me, but even more scary was the party of bare-chested savages trudging up the mountain toward our turnout. Eight or nine in all, they were young men and women (whites or chicanos, so far as I could tell) who had glued to their faces the scales of monarchs, sulphurs, blue tigers, British orange tips—even the prismatic scales of various unpigmented species—so that their faces sparkled like those of rain-forest Indians made up for ritual war.

"My God," Jodi-Marie said. (I heard her.) "Those women down there—they aren't even wearing halter tops."

I didn't say she was only barely wearing one herself. Besides, the savages did have capes, hand-painted linen wings that snagged the underbrush and glinted menacingly.

"Those are Mariposa People," I said. "Come on!"

But an arrow, colorfully fletched, lodged between the spokes of Jodi-Marie's front tire.

"*Now!*" I shouted, pulling it out and snapping it in two.

Together, plummeting, we rode the dropside of Wolf Creek Pass, coasting headlong to save our lives, falling handlebar by handlebar toward Pagosa Springs. Suddenly, a dreamy cloud of butterflies—lemon, ivory, sapphirine, emerald, scarlet, orange—loomed below us, smack in the middle of Highway 160.

"Duck your head," I cried. "Go through them! Stay inside the edging line!"

We were wearing helmets, our chin straps flying free, and when we hit that eddying, airborne palette, sky, mountain, and roadway disappeared. The world consisted solely of buoyant fabric scraps, nostril-tickling quilting squares. Waves of bitter insects filled my mouth. Sleeves of wind-plastered scales rippled from my arms. The highway was an unraveling gallery of Roualts, Chagalls, Klees, Pollocks, Mondrians.

Jodi-Marie and I broke from the silk squall. Wobbling crazily, we still might have wrecked, but an unpaved escape lane for runaway semis ski-sloped abruptly up to our right.

I shouted, "*Go up it! Go up!*"

She did. I did. We both did.

This uphill cut was bumpy and gravelly, but it rescued us from screaming ever faster downward, and when its gravity finally caught us, and we toppled, neither the Mariposa People nor the butterflies themselves were anywhere to be spied in the spruce-lined defile of Wolf Creek Pass.

"A bunch of crackpot millennarians," I said. "They think the end has come and the only way to save the world, and themselves, is to smear their faces with butterfly scales and sacrifice 'mundanes' like us to their Great Butterfly Manitou."

"Not really," Jodi-Marie said.

"That's the first lot I've ever seen, but it's plain what they wanted—namely, to kill us."

"You mean, they'd've left our bodies out as meat for a bunch of hungry butterflies?"

"You got it."

Later, walking our bikes, holding them back from the mountain's relentless tug, Jodi-Marie asked, "Why *mariposa*?"

"It means butterfly," I said. "In Spanish."

Later yet, in a motel in Pagosa Springs, Jodi-Marie, clad only in the wings of a big crimson towel, pirouetted for me.

"I've found my new name. 'Mariposa.' 'Jodi-Marie Mariposa.'"

"It's a syllable longer than your own name."

"Yeah, but it's prettier. And it goes with Marie."

I just looked at her. On the TV, I watched an entire program about mutating lepidoptera and their terrible impact—ecological, economic, emotional—on lands and peoples from the Philippines to the Seychelles.

We saw butterflies everywhere we rode: through Ute country, on Arizona's Navajo reservations, tree-clinging festively in Kaibab National Forest, swooping in gala formations past the layer-cake strata of the Grand Canyon, eating dead animals on all the desert ranches between Cortez and Kingman.

It was scary to pass them. You had no idea if they were only scavenging or cagily biding their time. I'd have felt much less anxious sighting a tornado at twelve o'clock high.

Las Vegas was all neon glitz, but the painted ladies, Mormons, clippers, striped blue crows, and crimson tips darting among the swimming pools and casinos made even Las Vegas's crisscrossing searchlights and jitterbugging electronic signs seem as prosaic as flashlight beams.

We stayed at Caesar's Palace, saw a stage show featuring thirty sequin-dusted girls, and fed more than five hundred quarters into the slots. At last, three citrus swallowtails in a row gave us a jackpot, and a welcome excuse to stop.

"You could probably get on here," I said. I meant as a chorus girl, but Jodi-Marie smiled wanly and shook her head.

"It's Hollywood or bust," she said.

I avoided the obvious joke, and, early that evening, we pedaled out of Vegas down Interstate 15, our handlebars laden with water bags: Neither of us was too keen on dying of thirst in the Devils Playground or some funky desert salina. But with the man-eating butterflies of the dying twentieth century, we were willing to take our chances.

It took us three days to bike the dry lakes of southeastern California. The only lepidoptera we chanced upon were single-tons, because butterflies care for the yucca-spiked desert about as much as most people do.

In any case, we did a lot of riding at night. When we finally reached "civilization," the insane freeway grid that is Greater Los Angeles, we felt like two lost sand grains ourselves. We spent our first night in a motel not too far from Dodger Stadium. You could hear the traffic on the Hollywood Freeway, and the conch-shell roar of sun-tanned people in Hawaiian shirts, and the faint, recurring, businesslike cracks of either baseball bats or dreams.

"Maybe you'll be discovered," I told Jodi-Marie.

The pity was, standing with her on a balcony ledge somewhere on the bleak edge of Shangri-La-La Land, I understood, belatedly, that I wanted to discover her myself.

The plague grew worse. Galaxy arms of butterflies—hordes of skippers, moths, and swallowtails—reduced atmospheric visibility to a level prefigured only by the worst of L.A. smogs. You could not go outside without stepping on a carpet of wings, or breathing in a mist of scales, or overhearing the provocative whine of pastel membranes razoring the wind.

There was also the continuous noise of insect husks colliding. Air-conditioning systems clogged. Swimming pools began to resemble outdoor Oriental carpets. Unprotected infants died. Street people emigrated inland. The Hollywood sign took on a filigree of moving orchids.

The President declared Greater L.A. a federal disaster area—redundantly, in my opinion. The Environmental Protection Agency, with the California Department of Transportation, proposed spraying lepidoptera-specific poisons from water cannons mounted on trucks, boats, and helicopters. "Much too risky," said the mayor, and the plan was discreetly scrapped.

Meanwhile, Jodi-Marie "Mariposa" was getting nowhere but mauled in all her casting interviews—when, that is, she could hack her way down the butterfly-choked boulevards to her appointments, using a portfolio of publicity photographs as a machete.

Away from southern California, the Mariposa People slaughtered every member of a wealthy Texas oil family, the head of a prominent logging clan in Seattle, and a rich arms manufacturer and his wife in Ohio. At each site, they left messages accusing the government of "criminal inattention to the REAL NEEDS of the people."

All this was going on even as the funds I'd assumed bottomless were, according to a registered letter from my lawyer in Raleigh, steadily ebbing. Global crop failures and triple-digit inflation had a great deal to do with the depletion of my trust, but so did my lifestyle.

"Jodi-Marie," I said, "you'll never get a job until you find another stage name."

September, October, November—all gone. Our first Christmas

in L.A. No tree in our bleak Koreatown walkup, but the starstruck wannabes on Sunset Boulevard had plenty of baubles, nose-rings, and tinsel-town pretensions to make up for the lack. When the daily Butterfly Alert was favorable, I would ride over to see them.

Jodi-Marie's new surname was O'Connor (in honor of a favorite teacher in Savannah). But in five weeks, it had landed her exactly as many parts—i.e., none—as had Mariposa. Then, three days before Christmas, she bicycled home from a longshot interview not far from the Rancho La Brea tar pits, to announce that she had been . . . *"discovered!"*

"Tonight," she said, showing me an address, "I've got to go for a screen test with a . . . a Mr. Marvyn Sabbatai."

"Okay," I said, smelling a rat. "I'm going with."

We took a cab. Mr. Oliver Lux, Sabbatai's aide, had given her the fare. We ended up at a house of cedar shakes and rustic stone off the Topanga Canyon Road. The oleagenous Lux appeared angry to see me, but he ushered us into a leather-padded room full of books and videocassettes. Then he left.

"Sabbatai's big-time," Jodi-Marie whispered. "Just look."

"Name a film he's directed."

"He's not exactly a director, Dennis."

"Great. Why are we here?"

"He's a producer, a special-effects man with cash. He's worked with Spielberg, Kubrick, Ridley Scott."

"Of course he has," I said.

Sabbatai's library was dimly lit. If you're legit, I thought, why isn't there a film-school diploma on your wall? The place felt like the sanctum of a latter-day opium-eater. Across from the door that Lux had exited by, another door quietly opened.

Sabbatai came through it. At first, all we could tell about him was that he was tall and slender and seemed to be wearing a rumpled dressing gown and a pair of silk pyjama bottoms as badly in need of pressing as his gown.

Marvyn Sabbatai was less a man than a papier-maché golem

42

made up of, and animated by, the thousands of Asian black swallowtails comprising his gown and pyjamas. His hands and face also consisted of butterflies, but bronze, golden, or fuschia ones, with feathery earthtone moths all over his scalp for hair.

What sort of creature was this man? A human being? A robot of butterflies? A holographic special effect?

His entire body ceaselessly acrawl with beautiful insects, he turned about to face us as if my unspoken question were banal, its answer either irrelevant or unresolvably moot. He paced. He would not sit down. Finally, though, he halted.

"*You'll do,*" he whispered to Jodi-Marie. "*My faithful Oliver wasn't lying.*"

"Do for what?" I said.

It took a moment to realize that his whisper was actually a rubbing of wings at the anatomical focus of his "lips." He had "whispered" because what else can butterflies do to create sound? Thus, his "voice" was a chilling approximation of speech, something you might hear from a man with a cancer-gnawed larnyx.

"*Do for the film I'm going to produce.*"

"And what's that?" I asked.

"*My multimillion docudrama:* Hostile Butterflies. *Our lovely Miss O'Connor will play—humanity.*"

Sabbatai, gesturing, strode back and forth. Individual moths and butterflies detached themselves, briefly undulated away, then floated back to alight again among their fellows.

"*Are you afraid of insects, Jodi-Marie? Afraid of challenges? Afraid of stardom? Afraid of me?*"

"No, sir. I don't think so."

"*Then you won't mind butterflies landing on you. Or me, for that matter, touching you—here.*"

He approached to touch her, and I . . . well, to stop him, I tried to grab the lapels of his dressing gown. He flew apart. I fell through him. Jodi-Marie screamed. My hands sifted sparkling scales.

Sabbatai—if he existed—had panicked into fragments, a minor riot of everywhere-skittering wings.

A door opened, Oliver Lux within it.

I scrambled to my feet. Parts of Sabbatai were shredded under my fingernails, parts were ground like mica or tinted Mylar into the burgundy carpet, other collops blossomed gaudily on his walls and bookshelves.

"Come on!" I said to Jodi-Marie.

I grabbed her hand. Our cab was still waiting, paid for in advance by Lux. We hightailed it out of Topanga.

"*You'll do*," the night whispered. "*All of you will do.*"

January, February, March. And, all too cruelly, April again. Things had fallen apart. The center had not held. My money was gone. I'd hocked our bikes. Nowadays, we walked between Koreatown and Sunset Boulevard, or, depending on the status of the Butterfly Alert, scooted along the streets like bent-over soldiers.

Sabbatai, who had reputedly pulled himself together again, was orchestrating everything; or else the butterflies—maybe the more likely scenario—were orchestrating him: The filming of *Hostile Butterflies* was the only major project in the works in Hollywood. Clearly, the inhuman Mr. Sabbatai had put out a pheromonic casting call; greater L.A. had become, as I told the bewildered Jodi-Marie, a "mind-tripping Peter Max-ville."

A few freak thunderstorms gave us several days' relief, pelting butterflies out of the sky, plastering them like scrolls of flocked wallpaper to freeways, sidewalks, awnings, cars. But when the sun came out again, Sabbatai—who, according to Variety, had signed a fifteen-year-old hooker with AIDS for the symbolic role he'd almost given Jodi-Marie—reinvoked his potent legerdemain, and the city brimmed again with psychedelic silk.

In fact, a coalition of U.N. entomologists and meteorologists reported that 72% of the planet's lepidopterans had migrated, or were now satellite-trackably "in the act of migrating," to sunny southern California.

•

Jodi-Marie fell ill. Disappointment, existential ennui, and simple hunger drove her to the day-bed in our flat. Through our Venetian blinds, the ceaseless blur and hum of wings served only to amplify her little-girl delirium. I asked her if she wanted me to get her out of L.A. in a has-been-hippy friend's microbus.

"No, Dennis. This is where I belong."

Why, I had no earthly idea. I was surviving on peanut butter and stale bread. Jodi-Marie was getting by on lukewarm lemon tea and Skippy-flavored kisses.

One day in May, hacked off at God, I left her to the odors of sickness drenching our walkup.

Under the blizzard of insects rustling like palm fronds above Olympic Boulevard, I stumbled toward the studios. Along the way, I saw dozens of camerapeople busily filming Marvyn Sabbatai's latest, probably last, magnum opus.

They were everywhere. Squinting, aiming, shooting. Producing enough full-color footage to preserve the end of this world in complex celluloid montage for . . . not for our posterity, I guess, but for whoever or whatever succeeded us.

Sabbatai himself, magnificently reconstituted, stood swaying on a sixty-foot scaffold, visible from half a block away on Olympic. Gripping a huge megaphone of butterflies, he "whispered" through it as loudly as the Malibu surf: *"Full sun! Cameras! Action!"*

A third again as tall as his tower, he spoke to the sky over Los Angeles County and Santa Monica Bay. His exhortations had the unbrookable force of Yahwistic command. Monarchs, malachites, coppers—a thousand, thousand species—converged on the city, homed on Sabbatai's scaffold, geysered above it in an iridescent stalk as wide as teeming West Hollywood.

I fell to my knees. Stoplights blinked. Traffic halted. A blast-furnace wind hurricaned around me, stealing my breath and parching my lungs. But still I saw that the lepidoptera billowing aloft were not only rising, transfiguring sunlight, but spreading out atop their streaming pillar like the cap of an hallucinatory thermonuclear mushroom.

My air was gone. The ground was gone. The sun was gone. This was Armageddon. Sabbatai was its impresario. Then he mutated on the scaffold, coming to resemble—briefly, at least—Laamaar De Long, his body a carnation-and-chrysanthemum-covered effigy on a float in an upwardly mobile Rose Bowl Parade.

Sabbatai—De Long—Shiva the Destroyer. Therefore, the head of the Holistic Ecological Church of Liberty, Kansas, was also an usher into everlasting mystic liberty.

Butterflies were nibbling on my eyelids. Somebody indignantly shooed them away and helped me up.

Beneath the roiling mushroom cap sitting on our city, I hitched a ride on the back of a fume-stained van defeatedly sputtering east on Olympic.

Jodi-Marie was out of bed. Venetian blinds lay jumbled on the floor like spilled swords. The window overlooking Koreatown stood open. Butterflies wobbled around the room in a Mack Sennet frenzy. Jodi-Marie sat by the radiator under the window listlessly grabbing the insects, cramming them into her mouth.

"Good," she said, holding out a handful. "Try some, Dennis."

I seized her hand, brushed the crushed insects away. "They're foul," I told her. "*Foul!* You can't do this."

"Dennis, I'm hungry. You, too. Eat."

I guided her back to the day-bed. I laid a damp washcloth over her eyes. I knelt beside her. I waited.

Later, dumbfounded, I watched her arch her back and die. "NO!" I cried.

(Outside, butterflies kept erupting heavenward.)

"Jodi-Marie Woznicki," I said, "I love you." Did I mean it? Or was saying so a sop to my own conscience? Then I remembered the dream she'd told me under the August moon at Laamaar De Long's, and I knew:

```
         I AM                      I AM
       sashaying                 sashaying
    down the runway   \     /  down the runway
    of the biggest crystal \  /  of the biggest crystal
    palace in the history of  \/  palace in the history of
such palaces since the world  {}  such palaces since the world
       got into the business {{}}   got into the business
of bigtime World Fairing,  {{}}  of bigtime World Fairing,
    I myself the fairest  {{}}   I myself the fairest
of the Fair in the bigtime {{{}}}  of the Fair in the bigtime
exhibitionism by which I  {{}}  exhibitionism by which I
show the world my stuff,   {}  show the world my stuff,
      strutting it with pride     strutting it with pride
          and yes, oh yes,          and yes, oh yes,
         the utmost utmost          the utmost utmost
           life-affirming,            life-affirming,
           self-affirming,            self-affirming,
             validating                 validating
               LOVE                       LOVE
```

Was this a shallow vision? An empty faunching for celebrity?

Well, it wasn't the "vision" I loved: It was Jodi-Marie. No matter how childish or crass, her goal was higher than mine.

For mine was to drift, take my pleasure, and die.

Now I can heal myself, not quite at leisure, of the spiritual rot that once numbed me to everything about her I couldn't take in at a glance.

Beauty—the visible sort—has always slain me. Now it does so again: a lovely, silken megadeath.

Thanks to God and Marvyn Sabbatai, it slays us all: the quick and the dense, the naked and the overdressed, etc., etc., *for this is*

47

the way the world ends, this is the way the world ends—not with a bang but a flutter.

But to hell with all that T. S. Eliot crap. Here's my epitaph for Jodi-Marie: HER TALENT WAS HER LOVINGKINDNESS. . . / SHE STAYED TRUE THROUGH THE BEAUTIFUL WORST.

Meanwhile, so many goddamned butterflies! Batwings, birdwings, peacocks, the whole iridescent, suffocating schmear.

To die beneath them is an exasperating loveliness, and I would do anything if, as a final boon, they would shape for me aloft the clear, forgiving face of Jodi-Marie Woznicki.

Among the Handlers

or

The Mark Sixteen Hands-On Assembly of Jesus Risen, Formerly Snake-O-Rama

And He said to them, "Go into all the world and preach the gospel to every creature. . . . And these signs will follow those who believe: In My name they will cast out demons; they will speak with new tongues; they will take up serpents; and if they drink anything deadly, it will by no means hurt them; they will lay hands on the sick, and they will recover."

Mark 16: 15, 17-18

Men in soiled workclothes occupied the cracked red leather booths. Some pointed at their cronies with wrist-twisted forks. Two or three ate alone, a folded newspaper at hand or a scowl of wary dragged-out blankness protecting or maybe legitimating their aloneness. None of them any longer took heed of the smells saturating Deaton's Bar-B-Q: scalded grease, boiled collards, sauce-drowned pork. And the sinuous anglings of the sandyhaired kid waiting their tables drew the notice of only one or two.

Becknell, a hulking 32-year-old in a filthy ballcap, said: So how you like a peckerwood that lifts up snakes handlin yore vittles?

His boothmate, Greg Maharry, said: You mean Pilcher?

Course I mean him. Anyways, it aint my idea of telligent ressraunt policy.

Criminy, Maharry said, who're you to bellyache bout young Pilcher's cleanliness?

Who am I? Becknell squinted at Maharry.

You spend most days up to yore butt in axle grease.

So?

I reckon Hoke knows as well as you to wersh his hands.

Mebbe. But grease's clean gainst them slitherin canebrakes thet Sixteener bunch of his favors.

You ever lifted a snake? I bet you never.

Think I aint got the sand? Greg, thet's——

Hoke Pilcher eased around the honeycombed divider from the kitchen with his tray aloft. Becknell, bigger than Maharry by a head, released a long sibilant breath while Maharry gave Hoke a queasy smile. Hoke lowered the tray to waistheight so that he could remove to the table the loaded barbecue platters, two sweaty amber longnecks, and two heavyweight mugs bearing icy white fur from Mr. Deaton's walk-in freezer. Holding the tray against the table edge, Hoke began to rearrange the items on it for easier transfer.

Mr. Becknell, he said, I aint been to an assembly out to Frye's Mill Road in moren a month.

Becknell said: You blong to thet bunch, don't you?

Yessir. But I've never lifted a snake there. He wanted to add, Either, but swallowed the impulse.

How come you not to've?

No anointin's ever come on me. So far I've mostly just shouted and raised my hands. Waitin and prayin, I guess. Hoke reached the longnecks onto the table, then the mugs with their dire chiseled coldness.

Becknell said: My golly. Yo're a Mark Sixteener thout the balls to do what you say you blieve.

Leave him go, Albert, Maharry said.

Why?

Minit ago you was blastin him for bein a Jesus Only. Now yo're chewin on him for the contrary.

Thet's where yo're flat wrong, Greg.

O.K. Tell me how.

I'm chewin on him for claimin one thing then actin somethin allover yellowbelly else.

Hoke set Maharry's hubcapsized pork platter in front of him and shifted the tray to unload Becknell's wheel of shrimp and chicken, with onion rings and hot slaw around them for pungent garnish.

Becknell said: And if you really blong to thet bunch, whyn hell don't you go to their services?

It's sorter complicated, Mr. Becknell.

You aint turned heathen?

Nosir. I'm tryin—

A heathen's shore as Judas lost, but a Mark Sixteener thet acts like what he sez mebbe has a chanst. Mebbe.

Hoke felt his grip loosen and the tray tilt. Becknell's chicken, scarletbrown in its breathtaking sauce, slid down his mattress-striped overall bib along with an avalanche of slaw and shrimp pellets. The onion rings flipped ceilingward and dropped about Becknell and Maharry like mudcaked nematodes. A longneck toppled. A razorthin tide of beer sluiced across the table and off it into Becknell's lap. He roared and jumped, catching a falling onion ring on one ear and nearly upsetting Maharry's bottle. Maharry grabbed it in a trembling fist and held it down. Hoke's tray, which had hit the floor, rattled from edge to edge.

My cryin cripes! Becknell said. You summabitch!

It was an accydent, Maharry said. Go easy now.

Using the towel on his belt, Hoke picked chicken and slaw off Becknell. He righted the fallen longneck, daubed at the beer, and turned this way and that between the unbroken platter under the table and the reverberating plastic tray. His boss, Mr. Deaton, burst into the diningroom with so many wrinkles on his forehead's pale dome that Hoke could not help thinking of a wadded pile of linen outside a unit of the Beulah Fork Motel. Deaton, stooped from working under the greaseguard that hooded his stove, unfolded to full height.

Hoke, what you done now?

Ruint my clothes, Becknell said. Ruint my meal. Stole my peace of mind.

It wasn't apurpose, Maharry said.

Thet's the second spill you've had today, Deaton said. The second.

See, Maharry said. He didn't mean it personal.

Albert, Deaton said, I'll bring you replacement eats in ten minutes. He thought about that. No, seven.

Free?

Awright. Spruce up in the ressroom. I'll pay for either yore drycleanin or a new pair of overalls. He turned to Hoke. Criminy, boy. My Lord.

My mind's gone off, Mr. Deaton. I cain't focus.

S thet right? Well. I cain't afford to keep you till you git it right. Ast Matilda Jack to pay you off.

I'm fired?

Yore word, not mine. Just git yore money and beat it on out of here.

Sir, I need this job.

Mebbe you can git you somethin out to the sawmill.

I done ast.

Ast again. Now git. Have mercy.

Hoke tossed the filthy sodden towel onto the table, amazed that the disaster had scarcely dirtied his hands, much less his clothes. He strode through Deaton's Bar-B-Q under the mirthful or slipeyed gazes of maybe a dozen other customers and wrenched back the frontdoor.

From airconditioning to pitiless summer swelter. Hoke hiked straight across Deaton's parking lot, filched a cigarette from his shirtpocket. The sky pulsed so starwebbed that the neon sign winking Bar-B-Q, Bar-B-Q, could neither sponge those stars away nor make Beulah Fork's maindrag look like anything other than a gawdy podunk road.

Hoke lit up. Smoke curled past his eyes, settled in lazy helices into his lungs.

Thirty minutes later, still afoot, Hoke stopped on the edge of Twyla Glanton's place, a clearing off Frye's Mill Road. He registered the insult of the jacked-up candyapple-red pickup with chromium rollbars parked alongside the deck of Twyla's doublewide. The truck belonged to Johnny Mark Carnes, a deacon in the Mark 16 Hands On Assembly of Jesus Risen, a congregation whose tumbledown stone meeting center lay farther along this black-topped strip. Like Albert Becknell, Carnes had ten years and maybe forty pounds on Hoke.

Almost aloud, Hoke said: Pox on yore hide, Carnes. Then waded through fragrant red clover and sticky Queen Anne's lace toward the deck. He felt gut-knotted in a way reminiscent of the cramps after a dose of paregoric. What did he plan to do? No clear notion. None.

His tennis shoes carried him up the treated plank steps of Twyla's deck, anyway, and before he could compute the likely outcome of this showdown, his fist began to pound the flimsy aluminum stormdoor over the cheap wooden one that was supposed to keep Twyla Glanton safe from burglars, conartists, and escaped murderers out here in the honeysuckle-drenched boonies of Hothlepoya County. Yeah.

Carnes himself opened the door, then stood in it like the sentry that Hoke would have hoped for, except that Hoke wanted someone else in the role and took no pleasure in any detail of Carnes's manifestation there but the fact that he still had his britches on. Unless of course . . .

Pilcher, Carnes said. Kinda late to come callin on a lady, aint it?

You've just said so.

I been here a while. Somethin we can do you for?

Even with the light behind him, Carnes presented a handsome silhouette: narrowheaded, wideshouldered, almost oaken in the stolidity of his planting. Actually, the light's fanning from behind improved his looks, dropping a darkness over his sunken piggy eyes and also the waffleironlike acne scars below and off to one side of his bottom lip.

Could I just talk to Twyla a minit, Johnny Mark?

From somewhere in the doublewide's livingroom, Tywla said: Let him in.

Some folks you let em in, it's nigh-on the War tween the States to git em out again. Carnes stood stockstill, unmoving as a capsized tractor.

Twyla appeared behind him. Her look surprised Hoke. She wore a swallowing purple sweatshirt, luminous green and purple windsuit pants with a band of Navajo brocade down each leg, and pennyloafers. Her sorrel hair had a mahogany nimbus, from the backglow, and strands floated about her teased-out helmet like charged spidersilk. Hoke, looking past Carnes at Twyla, felt the pilotlight in his gut igniting, warming him from that point outward.

A pearl onion of sweat pipped out on his forehead.

Never before had he seen a Mark Sixteener woman in any garb but anklelength skirts or dresses. Certainly not Twyla, whose daddy had lifted serpents, and who called out his name at every assembly, and who, at Li'l People Day Care in Beulah Fork, had a steady job, where she so staunchly refused to wear jeans that she often got the other workers' goat. Hoke, though, had given her a private pledge of fidelity.

He said: Colby Deaton fired me tonight.

The jerk, Twyla said. Babes, I'm so sorry.

Tough way for a guy to git him some sympathy, Carnes said.

We've missed you out to church, Twyla said. You orter not stopped comin cuz of me. I'm still yore friend.

Thet aint it, Carnes said. He's afraid to come.

Not of snakes, though. I wunst saw him grab a pygmyrattler with a stick and a gloved hand.

No, not of snakes, Carnes said. Thisere wiseboy's scairt of me. Cause I'm even more pyzon than they are.

Wadn't afraid to come up here with yore showoffy truck out front. Or to knock on Twyla's door.

Yall stop yore headbuttin! Twyla pushed Carnes aside and the stormdoor out. She laid a cool hand on Hoke's shoulder, bridging him into the doublewide, beckoning him out of the dark to either self-extinguishment or redemption—if these options did not, in fact, mesh or cancel. Go on home, babes. Sleep on it. Tomorry's got to have a perter face.

I'm footsore, Twyla. Bout wore out.

I'll wear you out, Carnes said.

What you'll do, Johnny Mark, is none of the sort.

Then praytell what?

Yo're gonna carry him home. In yore truck.

Play chauffeur for puley Mr. Pilcher here? Dream on.

No dream to it. And do it now. S bout time for me to turn in anyways.

So Hoke sat hugging the passengerside door of the jacked-up candyapple-red truck as Carnes accelerated the woods and flung back under his tires long humming stretches of asphalt. Possum eyes caught fire in the headlamps. An owl stooped in cascades through a picketing of trees, and a fieldmouse, or a rabbit, or some other fourlegged hider in the leafmulch was rolled to its back and taloned insensate.

Past this kill, through some roadside cane that loblollies deeper in overtowered, a quartet of ghostly deer—two does, two fawns—made Carnes brake. The deer negotiated a quicksilver singlefile crossing. The truck fishtailed heartstoppingly and squealed to juddering rest on the shoulder in time for Hoke to watch the flags on the deers' rumps bounce into the pines' mazy sanctuary.

Carnes muttered, strangled the steeringwheel, exhaled hard.

Nice job, Hoke said.

Don't talk to me. Carnes took an audible breath.

We could've died if we'd hit just one of em. Hoke spoke the truth. In this part of Hothlepoya County deer on the road comprised an often deadly, yearround hazard. Hoke knew—had known—a highschool girl cut to ribbons by a buck attempting to leap the hood of her boyfriend's car. The buck had landed on the hood and, asprawl there, struggled to free itself from the windshield glass, one bloody leg kicking repeatedly through the glittery hole.

Don't compliment me, Pilcher. Ever.

Awright. I won't.

You aint got the right to tell me nothin. Cept mebbe yo're a sorry excuse for a Sixteener.

Hold it a minit.

And mebbe not even thet. Speak when spoken to. Otherwise, hush it the hell up.

Who made you God?

Carnes pointed a finger, holding its tip less than a wasp's body from Hoke's nose and staring down it like a man sighting a rifle.

I did speak to you, pissant, but I didn't ast you a blessed thing. He dropped the point.

Hoke wanted to say, Up yores, but leaned back against his door instead, shrinking from the despisal in Carnes's face. Who would know or care if Carnes killed him out here on this road, then rolled his body into the cane? Twyla. Thank God for Twyla Glanton.

And thank God Carnes didn't have a row of snake boxes in the bed of his truck or, even worse, a solitary crate here in the passengerside footwell. Hoke could imagine sitting over an irritated pit viper—copperhead, rattler, whatever—with one foot to either side of the box, the rotting vegetable smell of its scales rising alien and humid to gag him, its heartshaped head searching for a way out. Meantime, though, he had Johnny Mark Carnes less than a yard away, still wired from their close call with the deer, still palpably resentful of Hoke's presence in his truckcab.

Whym I drivin you home, pissant?

Hoke set his teeth and stared.

I ast you a question. You can answer. You better.

Twyla told you to.

Ast me to. Nobody tells me to do anythin, Pilcher, least of all a outtake from the flank of Adam.

Hoke thought a moment. Then he said: You got no bidnus movin in on her. I had my eye on her first. From all the way back in school, even.

I beg yore pardon.

You heard me.

Losers weepers, huh?

I love her, Johnny Mark.

God loves her. You just got yore hormones in high gear.

I spose you got yores set on idle?

You wisht. Look, pissant, what can you give the lady but puppydog looks and a fat double handful of air?

Somethin thet counts.

Deaton canned you tonight from yore waitressin. You live in a verbital cave.

It's not a cave. Don't say waitressing. Men do it too.

Yore mama died of a lack o faith drinkin strychnine.

No, Hoke said. The Spirit went off her cause strife had fallen mongst the people. She had faith aplenty.

And yore daddy hightailed it to who knows where, Minnesota mebbe. No wonder Twyla took her a second look at you.

Like yo're a prize.

Got me balls enough to uplift serpents to the Lord and make us babies in the marriage bed.

Hoke shut his eyes. Yo're already married.

Not for long. Carnes smiled. Comparisons're hateful, aint they, pissant? Least you've got yore faith, though.

Yes, said Hoke quietly.

Which gives you a family in Jesus. Protection from slings and arrows, snakebites and pyzon. Right?

Right.

So come on to meetin this Friday. Forgit Twyla's migrated affections. Us Mark Sixteeners want you mongst us. Where else you got to go, Pilcher?

Nowhere.

Aint thet the truth. So come on Friday. I got someone you need to meet there.

Like who?

S name's Judas, Pilcher. He's a longboy. Called for the betrayer cause they aint no trustin when or who he next might bite.

Hoke put his hands on his knees and squeezed. Carnes had him a new diamondback, name of Judas. Well, of course he did. Subtlety had never much appealed to Carnes, else he would have linked with Methodists and driven a white twodoor coupe off a Detroit assemblyline.

Now git out, he said.

Yo're sposed to take me home.

Carried you far as I aim to. You aint but a mile from thet crayfish den of yores anyways. Out.

Hoke got out. Carnes put the boxy truck in gear, flung sod and

58

gravel backing off the shoulder, and shouted out the window after a screechy turnaround: Don't I deserve a nice thanks for totin you this far?

Thank you. Hoke eyed Carnes blankly, then stared away down the blacktop at dwindling taillights and the broken ramparts of pines bracketing it. Shithead, Hoke said, turning to foot it the rest of the way home, morosely aware that he had no idea which of them, Carnes or himself, he had just cursed. Nor did the incessant burring of the cicadas among the cane afford him any clue or solace.

He had never lived in a cave. He lived with Ferlin Rodale, a former schoolmate now doing construction work, in a dugout of bulldozed earth, old automobile tires hardpacked with clay, and plastered-over walls strengthened with empty aluminum softdrink cans. Ferlin had seen such houses on a hitchhiking trip to New Mexico, then brought back to Hothlepoya County—whose director of Department of Community Development had never even heard of such structures—an obsession to build one locally, despite the higher watertable and wetter climate. Anyway, to Hoke's mind, Ferlin's dugout qualified as a house. Even the head of Community Development had allowed as much by issuing Ferlin a building permit even though his tirehouse lay outside every local engineering code. It wasn't finished, though, and wouldn't be for another six to eight months, if that soon, and so Ferlin and Hoke lived in the shell of the place, sleeping in a U-shaped room that faced south under a roof of plywood, black felt, and grimy plastic sheeting.

Mebbe it is a kinda cave, Hoke said, limping home through the woods. Carnes is sorta right, the bastid.

Well, so what? Ferlin had wired it for lights, sunk a well, and laid PVC piping so that both sinks and the cracked and resealed commode had water. Hoke paid fifty dollars a month for a pallet in the lone bedroom and split the electric bill with Ferlin. His own folks had never had so nice a place, only a rented fourroom shack, aboveground, with pebbled green shingles on the walls and a tarpaper roof. If Ferlin's house struck some ornery people as cavelike, well, better a cave than a windbuffeted shanty on lopsided fieldstone pillars. Mama and Daddy Pilcher should've enjoyed such luck—even with the beer cans, bottlecaps, cigarette packages, candywrappers, clamlike fastfood cartons, and other junk littering Ferlin's clayey grounds.

In a footsore trance Hoke shuffled over the murderously potholed drive leading in, a drive lined about its full length with blackberry brambles, dogwoods, and pines. He had only starlight and lichenglow to guide him, just those undependable helps and the somewhat less fickle guyings of nightly habit. At length he approached a sycamore, a striated ghost among the scaly conifers, on which Ferlin had hammered up a handlettered placard:

TRESPAsERS !!!—
WE AIM to PLEZE But SHOT to KILL!

Hoke stopped, perplexed. Did that mean him? Ferlin had prepared the sign to secure them solitude, even down to the premeditated detail of its misspellings, working on the already frequently borne-out surmise that the image of a surly cracker with a shotgun would scare off uninvited visitors better than a storebought KEEP OUT notice. Hoke, shambling by, gave the sign a fresh twist out of true and chuckled bitterly.

Half the people in Beulah Fork probably thought that Ferlin and he, not to mention every Mark Sixteener in the county, were ignorant sisterswyving mooncalves. Well, damn them too, along with Carnes.

I know a thing or two the President don't, Hoke said. Or a perfessor up to Athens, even.

Like what? he wondered.

Aloud he said: Like I love Twyla and don't want to die in front of her with a snakefang in my flesh.

This saying stirred Ferlin's dogs, a redbone hound named

Sackett and a mongrel terrier named Rag that began barking in echoey relay. They came hurtling through the dark to meet the intruder and possibly to turn him.

Hush, Hoke said. S only me.

Sackett took Hoke's hand, in the webbing between thumb and forefinger, and led him up the trail, his whole ribby fuselage atremble. Rag pelted along behind, kinking and unkinking like an earthworm on a hot paving stone.

From the dugout—doors wide open, plastic scrolled back to the clocking stars—Hoke heard a breathy female voice singing mournfully from Ferlin's totable CD player. It sang about a blockbusted blonde with a disconnected plug at the Last Chance Texaco. Ferlin sang along, overriding the soft female voice, his screechy updown falsetto an insult to his dogs, to Hoke, to the very notion of singing.

Thank God the Last Chance Texaco cut was fading, drifting like a car whose driver has nodded asleep. But as Hoke crossed the dugout's threshold, into earthen coolness and the glare of one electric bulb swinging on a tarnished chain, the next song began and Ferlin ignored Hoke's arrival to play airguitar and hoot along with Rickie Lee Jones, albeit out of sync and out of tune, the words in his throat (*Cmon, Cecil, take some money! Cmon, Ceece, take you a ten!*) like cogs mangled and flung from the strident clockwork coming-apart of his lungs and throat. Ferlin wore a jockstrap and flipflops, nothing else, and when he finally looked at Hoke, he checked his wrist, which bore no watch, raised his eyebrows, and kept on screeching, his stance hipcocked, showbizzy and questioning at once. At the end of Rickie Lee's cut, he mouthed, *But, baby, don' dish it ovah if he don' preciate it.* . . . .

Then Ferlin turned off the player and came over to Hoke with a look of almost daddyish concern on his freckled hatchet face. Squinting and grinning, he said, Home a mite early, aint you?

Deaton canned me. Hoke told Ferlin the whole story, even the parts about stopping at Twyla's and catching a spooky ride in Johnny Mark Carnes's pickup.

But you don't like Carnes, said Ferlin.

I don't like walkin neither.

You walkt in. I didn't hear nothin stop out on 18.

Hoke crumpled into a lawnchair Ferlin had salvaged from the county landfill. Carnes got him a new snake he's callin Judas, he said. Wants me to make the next service out to the assembly so's I can charm it.

Ferlin whistled, a sound like a mortar shell rainbowing in. You aint handled with em yet, and he wants you to lift a serpent name of Judas right out the gate?

Looks thet way.

S why my religion don't include handlin, less a course it's women. Them I'll handle. Devotedly. Ferlin never attended services anywhere, but to willing females he tithed regularly the selfalleged five inflated to ten percent of himself that at this moment he had pouched in his jockstrap.

Such talk. Eddie Moomaw told me to git a new roommate if I planned to stay on a Sixteener.

Ferlin played airguitar. *O mean Mark Sixteener,* he sang: *Climb outta yore rut!*

Hush thet, Hoke said.

But Ferlin kept singing: *You don't like my weiner, So you show me yore butt!*

Didn't I ast you polite to stop it?

Ferlin threw his airguitar at the wall and paced away from Hoke. You got to watch yore fanny. Some of them Sixteeners'll drag you down for pure selfrighteous spite.

Meanin Johnny Mark Carnes?

Him, ol Moomaw, and anyone else over there thet cain't pray a blessing thout first tearin the world a new a-hole.

The world hates us Mark Sixteeners.

It don't unnerstand yall, Ferlin said. Neither do I.

So I shouldn't go this Friday?

You hear me say thet? I just said to watch yore fanny.

So mebbe I orter go?

Ferlin said: I wouldn't visit thet stonecold snakeranch of yall's thout a direct order from God Hisself.

Groaning, Hoke pulled off his tennis shoes and claystained sweatsocks. His feet sang their relief, his anxiety over his lost job, the more judgmental Mark Sixteeners, and Carnes's new diamondback a smidgen allayed by the night air and his roomy's profane straightforward banter.

Then he said: Ferlin, I have to go.

Nigh-on to hatchling naked, Ferlin squatted over his svelt black CD player. Balancing on the spongy toes of his flipflops he punched up a song about Weasel and the White Boys Cool, his wide chocolate irises reflecting a crimson 9 backwards from the control console. Ditchfrogs, a cicada chorus, and Ferlin all crooned along with the disc (*Likes it rare but gits it well, A weasel on a shoadohdah flo*), but this time so low and softly that Hoke did not feet slighted. Ferlin had heard him, and as soon as cut number 9 ended, and before number 10 began, Ferlin said:

What would happen if you didn't?

I'm not rightly shore. The Holy Ghost'd probably go off me for good.

Meanin what?

I'd send my soul to perdition for aye and awways.

Better go then, Ferlin said, knobbing down the volume on cut 10. Hell's a damned serious bidnus and forever's a smart jot longern Monday.

Hoke gave him back a forlorn chuckle.

Answer me one thing: Why would a fella with half a brain and a workin pecker take up a pyzonous snake?

To git Spiritjumped and throughblest totally. You won't never know, Ferlin, till you've gone puppetdancin in Jesus's grace yoreself.

Sounds like really rollickin sex.

S a billion times better.

The expert speaks, Ferlin said. Hothlepoya County's Only Still Cherry Stud.

They's moren one kinda virgin, Hoke said. Not bein married I've never slept with a woman. But not bein sanctified you've never come under the Spirit's caress.

Ooooooo, Ferlin said. Got me. Got me good. He fell over next to his CD player, writhing as if gutshot. When Rickie Lee finished singing about her gang's all going home, leaving her abandoned on a streetcorner, Ferlin stopped thrashing and lay motionless: a rangy unclad departmentstore dummy, flung supine into a junkroom.

Hoke struggled out of the lawnchair. He hobbled over to Ferlin and around the CD player on whose console a red 0 had brilliantly digitized. He nudged Ferlin in the armpit with his toe. When Ferlin persisted in his willful unflinchingness Hoke said, Thanks for the words of wisdom, dead man, and retreated to their U-shaped bedroom to dream of Twyla and climbing knots of sullen upraised snakes.

Ferlin drove Hoke in his customized 54 Ford, a bequeathment from Ferlin's daddy, to the Friday-night meeting of the Mark 16 Hands On Assembly of Jesus Risen farther down Frye's Mill Road, on an island between that road and a twolane branch going who knows where. Ferlin dropped Hoke off near a private cemetery about fifty yards from the church itself, with a nod and a last cry of advice:

Be careful, Pilcher, who you take a rattlesnake from!

Hoke recognized the saying as one of the shibboleths of a wellknown Alabama handler selfbilled the EndTime Evangelist, a big amiable man who preached a foursquare Jesus Only doctrine heavier on redemption than judgment. A year ago he had visited their hall, blessing it with both his message and his serpent handling; and when a longtime Mark Sixteener upbraided an older teenager near the front for wearing a teeshirt printed with the profane logo of a rocknroll band, the evangelist helped avert a nasty dustup, saying:

Leave him go, Brother Eddie. You've got to catch the fish before you can clean em.

Hoke remembered that saying and also the preacher's caution against accepting a pit viper from just anybody. Anyway, even should an anointing drop on him like a garment of spiritwoven armor, Hoke would steer clear of Johnny Mark Carnes. A spirit of deceitfulness and envy in a house of worship could undo even an honest-to-Christ mantling of the Holy Ghost, as his own mama had learned too late to prevent her from dying of a pintjar of strychnine so polluted.

Polluted pyzon? Ferlin had said once, reacting to Hoke's story. Aint thet redundant?

A child of the world would think so, but a Sixteener would knew from experience that it wasn't. It wasn't that such petty feelings could defeat God, but rather that the Spirit generally chose not to consort with folks nastily prey to them. If It withdrew when you had fifteen pounds of diamondback looped in your hands, of course, you would probably find beside the point the distinction between a defeated Spirit and just a particular One. . . .

Dented pickups and rattletrap jalopies surrounded the stone church. Years ago—a couple of decades, in fact—it had housed a country grocery and a fillingstation. Then it had closed. It had reopened for three or four summer seasons as a roadside produce market, setting out wicker baskets of peaches, grapes, and tomatoes, along with two hulking smokeblackened cauldrons for boiling peanuts. Then the place had closed again. An oil company removed the gaspumps. The owner died, and the owner's family sold out.

A Mark Sixteener from Cottonton, Alabama, purchased the building and turned it into a touristtrap herpatology museum called Snake-O-Rama. This entrepreneur equipped the interior with several long trestletables, furnished the trestletables with three or four glasswalled aquariums apiece, and stocked the aquariums with

serpents. For two bucks (for grownups) or fifty cents (for kids),
you could go in and ogle diamondbacks, copperheads, cottonmouths, watermoccasins, pygmyrattlers, timberrattlers,
kingsnakes, greensnakes, racers, coralsnakes, gartersnakes, one
sleepy boaconstrictor, and, for variety's sake, geckos, chameleons,
newts, an aquatic salamander called a hellbender that resembled a
knobby strip of bark with legs, and an ugly stuffed gilamonster.

Hoke had visited Snake-O-Rama on an eighthgrade fieldtrip
with Mr. Nyeland's science class, the year before he laid out of
school for good. But tourist traffic on Frye's Mill Road was light to
nonexistent, and the number of subsidized trips from the Hothlepoya
County schools fell so dramatically during Snake-O-Rama's second year that the welloff Mark Sixteener who ran the place—most
members of the Assembly were collardpoor— arranged to sell the
building and land, not including the old family graveyard nextdoor,
to a dispossessed offshoot of his church from west of Beulah Fork.

The Pilchers began attending the new Assembly as a family.
Hoke's mama died only months later—a death the coroner ruled
an accidental poisoning—and his daddy soon thereafter fled such
crazy piety. Hoke, though, had hung on, convinced that these
handlers, poisondrinkers, and ecstatic babblers were now kin and
that one day Jesus would bless him if he lifted up and chanted over
a handful of coiling snakes. For the most part, Hoke had found that
belief fulfilled in his association with the Sixteeners, especially in
his friendships with Twyla, an elderly couple called the Loomises,
and the family of the black preacher C.K. Sermons, whose surname
jibed so exactly with his calling that even a few in their Assembly
wrongly figured it a pulpit alias.

In fact, of all the twentyodd folks who met regularly in the
former Snake-O-Rama, only Johnny Mark Carnes and two other
men in their 30s, Ron Strock and Eddie Moomaw, had ever shown
him anything other than acceptance and aid. Their help had
included shoemoney, a Bible, and Sam Loomis's appeal to Colby
Deaton to give Hoke a job at Deaton's Bar-B-Q.

The trio of Carnes, Strock, and Moomaw, though, saw him as a pretender, a pain in the buttocks, and, in Carnes's case, a misbegotten rival for Twyla Glanton, even though Carnes already had a wife from whom he had separated over her disenchantment with hazardous church practices and his evergrowing inventory of scaly pets. Eddie Moomaw called Hoke the orphan and, in a service not long after Hoke moved into the tirehouse, rebuked Hoke for living with an unredeemed heathen, taking as his text the prophetic recriminations of Ezekiel 16:

Then I wershed you in water; yes, I thoroughly wershed off yore blood, and I anointed you with oil! Moomaw had said, his eyes not on Hoke but instead on a wildeyed portrait of Jesus on the Snake-O-Rama's rear wall.

Amen! said many of the unwary Sixteeners, Hoke included. *Tell it, Brother Eddie!*

Brother Eddie told it, at last bringing his eyes down on the target of his rant: You offered yourself to everyone who passed by, and multiplied yore acts of harlotry!

Amen! Woe to all sinners!

Hoke stayed silent, but his napehair rose.

Yet you were not like a harlot, Moomaw said, because you scorned payment!

Sicm, Brother Eddie! Hie on!

Men make payment to awl harlots, but you made yore payment to awl yore lovers, and hired em to come to you from awl aroun for yore harlotry!

Amen! Go, Brother Eddie! At this point, only Carnes and Ron Strock were seconding Moomaw's quoted accusations. No one else understood the reasons for such condemnation. No one else could follow the argument.

I will bring blood upon you in fury and jealousy! Moomaw said, pointing the whole top half of his body at Hoke, snakily twisting shoulders, neck, and head.

At that point C.K. Sermons rose from his altarchair. His skin the purple of a decaying eggplant, he clapped his enormous hands as if slamming shut a thousandpage book.

I will be quiet n be angry no more, he said. The boy you scold does not deserve such upbraision, Brother Eddie. He goes where he muss to put shelter over his head.

Amen! Twyla said. *Amen!* said the Loomises. *Amen!* said a dozen other Sixteeners.

A course he's a orphan. He's done long since lost his mama n daddy. But didn't Jesus say, I will not leave you orphans, I will come to you?

He said it! Deed He did!

So what if the Pilchers come to us stead of vice versa? So what? They's moren one way fo the body of Jesus to surroun this worl's orphans! Moren one way to stretch comfort to the comfortless!

Amen! Praise God!

Thus rebuked, Eddie Moomaw retreated to his own altarchair grimfaced and blanched, his tongue so thick on the inside of his cheek that its bulge looked like a tumor. And only C.K. Sermons raised snakes heavenward that night. Of course, he had also—alone among the evening's worshipers—tossed back a small mayonnaise jar of strychnine (making a comical pucker at its bitterness), foretold in tongues, and restored Brother Eddie to concord with their fold by exorcising from his body a demon of resentment named Rathcor.

Rathcor! Sermons shouted, one hand hard on Moomaw's chest, the other shoving downward on his head. Rathcor, come ye forth in shame n wretchedness! *Now!*

And Rathcor had departed Moomaw, half its vileness in a sulfurous breeze from Moomaw's mouth and half in a startling report from his backside. These smells had lingered in the stone building, a stench that Hoke recalled as burnt cinnamon, bad eggs, and decomposed pintobeans.

S awright, Sermons told everyone. Just means the demon's done hightailed it. Means Brother Eddie's free.

Brother Eddie had smiled, lifting his hands into cobwebby shadow and praising the Lord. But his hostility toward Hoke, not to say that of Carnes and Strock, never fully evaporated, and Hoke could only wonder if a portion of Rathcor had lodged in the most secret passages of Moomaw's anatomy—his nose, his ears, his anus, his dick—because Hoke could not imagine, from Moomaw's present behavior, that Sermons had cast Rathcor out of him entire.

Greet one another with a holy kiss.
Romans 16:16

The closer Hoke drew to the kudzu-filagreed building the louder grew the buzzing syncopated music leaking through its mortarted joins. He heard tambourines, trap drums, an electric guitar, a trumpet. This music, pulsing like strobes in the grimy windows, told him he had arrived late, the service had already begun. The stolid rockwalls and the roof of steeply pitched shakes seemed almost to expand and contract with the singing and its jangly backup, like a jukejoint roadhouse in an old Krazy Kat cartoon.

The people crooned: *Oh, weary soul, the gate is neah. In sin why still abide? Both peace n rest are waiting heah, And you are just outside.*

And a fervent chorus: *Just outside the door, just outside the door, Behold it stands ajar! Just outside the door, just outside the door—So neah n yet so far!*

Hoke halted, clammy with the cold suspicion that through this old gospel hymn the Sixteeners were addressing and jeering his tardiness:

Just outside the door, just outside the door—So neah n yet so far!

Then go on in, he told himself. Walk through the gate and face em like one of their forever own.

He did, pushing in more like a gunslinger entering a saloon than a believer in search of his sweet Jesus Only. The ruckus from the toothache-imparting guitar and trumpet, not to mention the rattle of drums and tambourines, smacked him like a falling wall. The handclapping, pogojumping Mark Sixteeners—men to the left of the pewless sanctuary, women to the right—ladled a soupy nausea into Hoke's gut. Usually, such motionful devotion wired him for most of the fiercest God frequencies, but tonight a fretfulness lay on the people, a catching mood of upset, even derangement.

At the end of Just Outside the Door, Sermons leapt to the altardeck from between his wife, Betty, and their 13-year-old daughter, Regina, already a jivy trumpeter. The only black male in the building, Sermons wore a sweated-out Sunday shirt and a bolo tie with a turquoise cross on its ceramic slide. He harangued the sweltering room:

I grew up wi the cutaway eyes n the sad caloomniation o folks who figgered me n my kin just a lucky step up from the monkeys.

We hear you, Brother C.K.!

Caw it bigotry, peoples. Caw it hate or ignorance. Caw it puft-up delusion.

Amen!

Whatever anybody caws it, peoples, it hurt—like stones n flails. Sometimes, Lawd Lawd, it still lays me out, even me, faithful servant to our Risen Jesus thet I long since become in my rebornin.

Glory!

Now the chilrens of this worl done started comin after our own. Mockin, namecawin, greedy to troublemake.

Satan has em, C.K.! Satan!

Lissen what they done to Sister Twyla—to make her move off our Risen Jesus to the dead Christ they socawed churches strive to burry eyebrow deep in works n talk!

Preach it!

They bite like unprayed-over snakes! They want to pyzon the chilrens of the light!

God'll repay!

Sister Twyla, cmon up here! Testify to what the heathen n them lukewarm Christians of Beulah Fork's sitdown churches done to knock back yore faith!

C.K. Sermons reached out a hand, and Twyla, modest in a lightyellow anklelength poplin dress, emerged redeyed from the women. She floated across the floor to the platform. She did not mount it, but pivoted to face everyone with a sweet timid smile. People upfront parted to make her visible to worshipers farther back.

Hoke stood admiring. Three nights ago she'd worn her hair in an unrighteous teased-up globe. Now it hung long, reddish streaks flashing in the sorrel every time she moved her head, a small ivory barrette for ornament. Hoke could tell, though, that she'd had a monster bout with tears: her eyesockets looked scoured, shiny with knuckling.

Bless yall, she said. Praise God.

Praise God!

Yall notice, please, thet Hoke Pilcher's come in. It'd be good if you men greeted him with a holy kiss, like Paul sez to do, and you womenfolk guv him a sisterly nod.

Hoke felt an abrupt heat climb from his chest and settle in his cheeks. The women to his right nodded or curtsied while in their half of the sanctuary the men milled into ranks to bestow on him the holy kiss spelled out in Romans 16. Sermons, Eddie Moomaw, and Hugh Bexton leapt down from the altardeck to greet him—mechanically in Moomaw's case, it seemed to Hoke—and Ron Strock and Johnny Mark Carnes used their go-bys to pinch one of Hoke's reddened earlobes or to razz him about the irregularity of Twyla's appeal.

I need to remember this tactic, Carnes said, nudging Hoke's cheek: Big entrance, ten minits late.

Ferlin couldn't git his Ford cranked. I wadn't—

Stifle it, Pilcher, Carnes said. Lady's gonna talk.

Twyla absentmindedly rubbed her palms together. Early Wednesday mornin, she said, I had my car tires slashed and my deck strewn with toy rubber snakes. My trees got toiletpapered and my trailer aigged.

Cry out to God, said Camille Loomis, the Sixteener nearly everyone called Prophetess Camille.

Thet's not all. On Wednesday I went to Li'l People, where I've done worked three years now, and Miss Victoria let me go. Said some of her parents don't want their babies tended to by a known snake handler.

C.K. Sermons said: Christian parents, no doubt.

Sposedly. Anyways, I'm a known handler. Like a known car thief or a known ax murderer.

Yo're a known blessed friend, said Sam Loomis.

I cain't work a minit longer cause I might feed somebody's darlin a bowl of baby rattlers. I might wrap a watermoccasin up in the poor kid's didy.

We'll hep you, said Angela Bexton.

I know yall will. Like Brother C.K. sez, it hurts—this persecution by the world.

Somebody suggested a love offering.

Wait, Twyla said. The world thinks we've gone crazy cause we abide in and by the Word. Thet's what the silly children of this world've come to.

Amen!

But much as I love them little ones I seen to awmost ever day for three years, I love the Word—I love the Lord—more. I won't walk outta the light to satisfy any false Christian I may offend by abidin true.

Praise God!

And as Moses lifted up the serpent in the wilderness, even so must the Son of Man be lifted up.

Amen! Praise God!

Jesus sez thet in the Book. Which is to affirm thet I will lift serpents myself at ever pure anointin.

In His name! Amen!

I will do it to lift up the Word thet is also Jesus Risen, else this brief life will fall out in ashes and I myself blow away like so much outworn dust.

Twyla's speech, carrying news of her persecution and the witness of her resolve, stunned Hoke. He could not move. His embarrassment had drained away, though, and in its place welled pride. His love streamed over and then from Twyla like a flood of rich silt. Others among the Sixteeners did move in response to her testimony, reclaiming their instruments, cranking up a gospel shout, swaying to the acid caterwauling of Ron Strock's guitar and the ripple blasts of young Regina's trumpet, leaping about like stifflegged colts, footstomping and handclapping not in unison but in a great cheerful boil that somehow melded them in faith and triumph. Finally, Hoke absorbed through his pores their backasswards confederating spirit. And then he too began to move.

The bite of the serpent is nothing compared to the bite of your fellow man.
—Charles McGlocklin, the EndTime Evangelist

Later C.K. Sermons leapt again to the altardeck. His wife, Sister Betty, a lightskinned AfricanAmerican with the figure and selfpossession of a teenaged gymnast, broke out a video camera. She shouldered it like an infantryman shouldering a bazooka. Hoke had noticed such cameras at other Jesus Risen services, usually in the hands of local TV crews looking for two or three filler minutes for an 11:00 P.M. news broadcast. The red light on Sister Betty's camera glowed like a coal, or a serpent's eye.

Sister Twyla did no preachin tonight, said Sermons. She testified. You see, I just heard some wayward mumblin bout how womens don't blong up here preachin.

They don't, said Leonard Callender.

Nobody disputes it, said Sermons. I know they got no caw to make mens subject to they preachments n foretellins. And Sister

Twyla knows it. Futhamore, nothin like thet's happened here tonight. Yall unnerstand?

Praise God we do!

Good. We got new bidnus to tend to, new praises to lift. And none of it'll go Jesus Risen smooth if they's wrong thinkin or foolish resentments mongst us.

A fiftyish man named Darren DeVore bumped Hoke's shoulder. S mazin to me, he whispered, how we got us a nigger preacherman and female testifiers.

Thet so? said Hoke, stepping away.

My daddy woulda cut the fig off thetere fella and led the uppity women outside to catch some rocks.

Whynt you tell it so everbody can hear you?

I aint my daddy, Brother Hoke. I've changed wi the times. Grinning, he angled off through the other men toward the altar platform.

We need some prayin music, Sermons told the band. We got to pray over these pernicious snakes.

The band struck up a hardrock hymn, Regina Sermons cocking her elbows and blowing out her cheeks like a swampfrog. Twyla, Hoke noticed, had a tambourine. She hipbanged it in proximate time to the hymn's rhythm. Only the women sang:

> *When Judah played the harlot,*
> *When proud Judah mocked her God,*
> *God stripped her of her garments,*
> *Nor did He spare the rod.*
>
> *Yet His love was such, O mighty such,*
> *Judah He toiled to save:*
> *He proffered her His Jesus touch,*
> *And with sweet rue forgave.*

As the women sang, C.K. Sermons, Eddie Moomaw, and

Hugh Bexton prayed over the snakeboxes against the church's rear wall. The boxes showed bright handpainted portraits of Jesus, Mary, and the disciples. The men prayed with their eyes shut, hands palm upward at shoulderheight or squeezed into juddering fists at their bellies, their voices either high monotone pleas or low gruff summonses.

Shan-pwei-koloh-toshi-monha-plezia-klek! shouted Prophetess Camille, her head thrown back as if inviting a knife to unhinge it at her wattled throat. *Fehzhka-skraiiii!*

Camille sez they's a demon in here, Sam Loomis told Hoke over the tubthumping music.

A demon? Rathcor?

A betrayer. A worker of hoodoo what'll drag hypocrites and baby blievers straight to hellfire.

Camille turned in a slow circle, her arms hanging down like rusty windowsash weights. *Auvlih-daks-bel-woh-oh-vehm-ah-pih!* she cried. *Neh-hyat-skraiiii!*

Camille sez we got moren one in here! said Loomis. But the betrayer he's done fell to pitdiggin!

Sermons did a solitary congadance from the snakeboxes to the edge of the altardeck with three or four serpents in each hand. He dipped from side to side in an ecstatic crouch as the Jesus Risen band veered into a rave-up of Higher Ground. Eddie Moomaw and Hugh Bexton slid forward to bookend Sermons, the way the thieves on Golgotha had flanked the crucified Jesus, Bexton with canebrakes and pygmyrattlers squirming about his wrists like overboiled spaghetti, Moomaw with only a single snake but that one a silky diamondback of such length that it looped his forearms in countergliding coils.

Hoke knew this snake for Judas even before Carnes took it from Moomaw. Carnes began to handle it in an orgasmic frenzy. He may have even moaned glory in his upright congress with Judas, but the rattle and blare of the Sixteener combo, along with the worshipers' continuing babel, drowned even the loudest utterances of the chief three handlers.

In spite of Prophetess Camille's warning, Hoke could feel a benevolent essence—the Holy Ghost—seeping from overhead and even sideways through the stones into the former Snake-O-Rama. He halfexpected everyone to sprout plumelike flames from the crowns of their heads, like so many outsized cigarette lighters snapping to radiant point.

It entered Hoke, this Spirit, and, amid the crazy din, he too began to dance, jitterbugging in place, barking praise, reconnecting with his dead mama and his absconded daddy as well as with the raptured majority of the Sixteeners. This was what it was like to open to and be tenanted by the Comforter, Jesus Risen at His ghostliest and most tender.

Yes. It was like a blesséd fit.

Hoke began to stutterstep diagonally through the other happy epileptics, a chess piece on a mission. He could smell the Holy Ghost, Who had now so totally saturated the room that C.K. Sermons and the other handlers pranced about veiled in a haze thick as woodsmoke. The smell was not woodsmoke, though, but cinnamon sourdough and overripe juiceapples, offerings to eat and drink, not to laud. Hoke elbowed through this fragrant haze, seeking its source. He suspected that it had its focus somewhere near C.K. Sermons.

Sermons gave Regina—the band now lacked a trumpetplayer—two snakes; and Regina, more child than woman, lifted them through the layered gauze of the Spirit, to the Spirit, one snake climbing as the other twisted back to flick her pugnose with its quick split tongue. Sister Betty videotaped Regina's performance.

Other Sixteeners began to handle, one man thrusting a snake into his shirt, another tiptoeing over a diamondback as if it were a tightrope, enacting Jesus's promise, Behold, I give you authority to trample on serpents. . . .

Sister Camille fell down ranting. Twyla, Polly DeVore, and

Angela Bexton knelt beside her with prayercloths and stoppered bottles of oliveoil, dimestore items with which to minister to her as holy paramedics.

Hoke, still dancing, had reached the front, hungry for the boon of a serpent from C.K. Sermons. For the first time since joining the Sixteeners, he knew the Holy Ghost had anointed him to handle, as it had anointed nearly every other person in the church tonight. But Sermons had already distributed his entire allotment of snakes. He stood on the platform with a Masonjar of strychnine, praying over it, preparing to drink.

Hoke floated past Sermons and many others . . . to Eddie Moomaw, who still had three or four living bracelets to hand out. He looked peeved that no one had yet come to relieve him of them. Sister Betty, Hoke noted sidelong, recorded the chaos with her video camera, paying as much heed to him and the other congregants as to her own husband and child.

Then Hoke went flatfooted and reached out to Moomaw, his face helplessly grimacing. He mewled aloud. Moomaw handed him a canebrake, a pinkishbeige timberrattler not quite a yard long, a satinback that winched itself up to his chin, shaking its rattles like maracas.

Hoke was anointed, fearless. Gripping the canebrake with both hands, he inscribed 8s with it in the air before him. He slipped into a floating whiteness where the rattler focused his whole attention and no other material body in the Snake-O-Rama impinged on him at all.

Furiously, the snake continued to rattle warning, but Hoke had surrounded and entered it just as the Spirit had done him, and it would not strike. Hoke knew this with the same kind of bodyborne knowledge that made real to him his possession of ears, elbows, knees, even if he made no effort to touch them. He and the snake shared one spellbound mind. In fact, he felt so loose, so brainfree, that he imagined the serpent an extract from his own person: his spinalcord and brainstem in a sleeve of patterned velvet.

77

Then something in the immaterial sanctuary of Hoke's trance bumped him. *Bumped* him. Someone in the Hands On Assembly was shouting louder than anyone else, louder even than the scouring racket of the Jesus Only band.

Hoke sensed the soft white pocket of his trance blurring at the edges, breaking down. Forms and voices began to intrude upon him. The timberrattler in his hands separated out of the albino plasma that had sheltered them, taking on the outline and bulk of a realworld menace. Hoke finally understood that the loudest screaming in the room was his own. He clamped his mouth shut, thinning out the sound, and turned to Moomaw to rid himself of the agitated canebrake.

Regina Sermons, still powerfully anointed, stood handling beside him, but even without looking at Hoke, she edged away to allow him to make the transfer.

Eddie Moomaw took the snake from Hoke, smiling mysteriously sidelong. Why the smile? Was he disappointed that Hoke had escaped unbit? sorry that a snake had already come back to him? peeved that no one else had returned one? Hoke shook his head and retreated a step.

C.K. Sermons, holding his Masonjar, wiped the back of his hand across his mouth. Good to the last drop! he said. Praise God! He beamed at Sister Betty's camera, spread his arms wide, revolved on the deck like a musicbox figurine.

Hoke decided he had to get some air. He turned to thread his way doorward.

Carnes blocked his path. Welcome back, Pilcher, he said. Here. Have you another. . . .

Judas folded into Hoke's arms like eight feet of burdensome firehose. Hoke had no time to sidestep the handoff. To keep from dropping it he shifted the diamondback and, as he did, saw on Carnes's face a look of combined glee and despisal. More from surprise than fear, Hoke lost his grip. Judas, suddenly alert and coiling, dropped. Hoke went to one knee to catch the snake, managed a partial grab, and found himself eye to yellow eye with Judas. Fear washed through him, a quickacting venom, and he shielded his face with the edge of his hand. The snake struck, spiking him just below the knuckles of his pinkie and his ringfinger, a puncture that toppled him.

Somebody screamed piercingly, and this time the rising sirenlike wail belonged not to him but to Twyla Glanton. Judas crawled over Hoke's fallen body. It bit him again, this time in the upperarm, then rippled over the concrete in a beautiful coiling glide.

Help him! shouted Twyla, arrowing in. Hush thet racket and help him, else he's bound to die!

Not if he's got faith! said Carnes.

The band stopped playing, the prophets stopped babbling, and Sermons, Bexton, and Moomaw hopped down from the altardeck to see about Hoke. He could hear the cicadas outside, whirring dryly, the sad bellyaching of ditchfrogs, and the faraway hum and buzz of pickup tires rolling on asphalt and ratcheting over a cattleguard.

Git him a doctor, somebody!

Now, Twyla, if we do thet, Carnes said, aint we sayin the Word's not the Word? Before Twyla could answer, Carnes looked down at Hoke. Boy, you want a doctor?

Nosir. Just some kinda ease. Hoke sprawled, burning where Judas had fanged him.

He'd say thet, Twyla said. Just to fit in better here at th Assembly.

He won't ever fit in better if he truckles to this world's medicine, said Carnes.

Sermons knelt beside Hoke. He don't want a doctor, Sister Twyla, cause he knows from whence comes his hep.

Praise God!

Look here, said Twyla. Thet's a big Judas of a snake. It spiked

79

him twyst. Thet much venom'd drop a buffalo, much less a peakèd skinny boy.

Faith can toss mountains into the sea, Carnes said.

Twyla grimaced. When was the last time yore faith tossed a mountain into the sea?

Kept me safe handlin thatere serpent, Carnes said. S moren anybody can say for Brother Hoke.

Hoke'd done handled, Sermons said. You caught m when the Spirit'd gone off him.

Hugh Bexton returned with Judas around one shoulder like a great drooping epaulet braid. He stood directly over Hoke, and Hoke could see Bexton and the snake looming like paradefloats against the cracked ceiling. Judas seemed to probe about for a baseboard chink or a skylight, a way to escape. Occasionally, though, it coiled the upper portion of its length floorward and flicked its tongue, swimming over Hoke with the airy loveliness of a saltwater eel.

If Brother Hoke dies faithless, said Camille Loomis, he'll go straight to—

—hellfire, Sam Loomis finished for her.

It was told me from on high, said Camille.

What happens to the hoodoo workers here amongst us? Twyla said. Do those betrayers go to hellfire too?

Not till they die, Camille said.

But they laid the hoodoo on Judas and got poor Hoke bit.

Camille sounded sad or embarrassed: No, missy, them hoodoo workers just showed up his weakness.

What garbage, Twyla said. What backassward crap.

The Loomises looked at each other and backed away. Hoke watched Judas swimming, climbing, loopsliding in dimensionless emptiness. The Loomises' curse—*straight to hellfire*—rang in his head. The faces of those still hovering over him revealed a peculiar range of passions, Twyla's running from cajolery to outrage, Carnes's from amusement to satisfaction. Sermons made a series of increasingly sluggish peacemaking gestures. Judas bobbed down in a slowmotion arc and once again laid its yellow gaze on Hoke.

Somewhere beyond the diamondback's scrutiny glowed a single pulsing red dot.

Hoke thought: I'm going straight to hellfire.

Like Jesus, Hoke rises from himself and strides out of the cooling tomb of his own bones.

He leaves Twyla, Carnes, Moomaw, Sermons, and all the other Sixteeners and ambles into the quiet darkness—no cicadas, no frogs, no trucks—outside the Hands On Assembly of Jesus Risen, formerly Snake-O-Rama. He walks and walks. In less time than it takes to leap a ditch he comes to a steeppitched road lined with blackberry brambles, dogwoods, pines.

A sycamore almost concealed by this other foliage bears a handlettered sign:

TRESPAsERS !!!—
WE AIM to PLEZE But SHOT to KILL!

He has come home to his roommate Ferlin's tirehouse in a hard-to-reach pocket of Hothlepoya County. Neither Sackett nor Rag rushes out to greet him. The house itself blazes like a firebombed tiredump, turbulent coalblack smoke billowing away, climbing into the sky's midnight fade.

The conflagration does not devour the house, but surrounds, dances on, and leaps from it. Pungent smoke skirls ceaselessly from the twoply radials and the halfburied whitewalls. Hoke calmly observes the fire, then cuts painlessly through its pall, and enters the dugout's U-shaped livingroom.

Ferlin! he shouts. You to home?

The interior startles him. It looks like an immense tiled lavatory. The walls glitter like scrubbed kitchen appliances, even if their white enamel faintly reflects the movement of fire and rippling smoke. Although he has no trouble breathing here, he must hike forever—longer than it takes to leap a ditch—to reach the glass cage, a bulletshaped capsule, across from Ferlin's frontdoor.

Hoke rides the capsule down. Flames twist in the glass or clear hard plastic shaping it, flickering from side to side as well as up and down. Beyond these flames the countryside (yes, countryside) looks infinitely hilly. Figures—faceless sticks dwarfed by the buttes and spires in the brickbrown landscape—cower in half-hidden rock niches or flee over plains like fiery icefloes.

Occasionally a longnosed fish, or a mutant parrot, or a para-chuting man-of-war drifts past the capsule, each with some raw disfigurement: a gash, an extraneous growth, an unhealthy pur-pling of its visible membranes. Hoke wants to pull these wounded critters inside the capsule and heal their wounds with hands-on prayer.

Can God dwell in any of these freaks? In any part of this infernal canyon? Hoke thinks so. How could he have trespassed here without help?

In the subbasement the capsule halts. Hoke emerges, and an ordinarylooking man in a chambray shirt and a pair of designer jeans meets him. The man does not speak. His sunglass lenses betray neither friendliness nor hostility. Hoke discovers his name only because it is stitched in flowing script—JUDAS—over his heartside shirtpocket (if he has a heart). He greets Hoke with a crooked thrifty bow.

This man, this Judas, leads Hoke through a tunnel lit at distant intervals with baseboard lights fashioned to resemble lifesized Old and New World serpents: cobras, mambas, pythons, shieldtails, eggeaters, rattlesnakes, vipers, and so on, each of these sinuous devices plugged in at ankleheight and aglow with an icy radiance that both animates and eerily Xrays the shaped light. Hoke can see the skull, vertebrae, and tubelike organs of each makebelieve serpent.

Leading the way, Judas lists to one side or the other of the tunnel, but Hoke walks straight down its middle, trying to ignore the threat implicit in the baseboard lamps. The tunnel—itself a hollow, kinking serpent—goes on and on. Sometimes its twisty floor and curved walls seem to tremble, as if bombs have fallen close to hand.

At length the tunnel opens into a chamber—Hoke regards it as a satanic chapel—with a crooked wingless caduceus where the cross would hang in most decent Protestant churches. Ringing the chamber's squat dome are bleak stainedglass windows whose cames outline serpents in a stew of motifs, all colored in deep brown, indigo, or slumbering purple, with intermittent shards of crimson or yellow to accents the snakes' hooded or bulgingly naked eyes.

In these cames Hoke sees the same kinds of snakes in two dimensions that he saw rendered in the tunnel in three, except that here the serpents are all venomous cobras or pitvipers. The conflagration outside the chamber inflicts a sullen glitter on the dome's glass, but Hoke draws some comfort from it, as he would from a fire on a stone hearth.

Unlike the church on Frye's Mill Road, Judas's antichapel has pews. Three rows of benches face the pulpit, each one covered in snakeskin. Behind the pulpit, a choir loft made of long white bones and ornate ivory knobs faces outward beneath a stainedglass triptych.

With a gesture, Judas urges Hoke to find a place among the pews. Hoke chooses the curved middle pew and sits halfway along its scaly length. Judas mounts to the pulpit, growing two feet in height as he uncoils from a deceptive stoop. For the first time since arriving down here, Hoke can study Judas's face.

It is the machinemolded face of a departmentstore dummy, with just enough play in the blockfoam to permit the creature to smile faintly or to twitch a lip corner. When he removes his sunglasses, he reveals yellow eyes like a diamondback's and his face deforms into the soft triangle of a pitviper's head, with severe dents in the cheeks and a smile that has widened alarmingly. The rest of Judas's body maintains a human cast, and, hands gripping the pulpit's sides, he leans forward to regale Hoke, his lone congregant, with a stemwinding sermon. Outside, bombs or depth charges continue to explode, and Judas responds to the tremblors by rubbernecking his head around and whiteknuckling the lectern that seems to hold him erect. Hoke pays close heed.

Judas's sermon has no words. It issues from the creature's smile as hisses and sighs. Flickers of a doubletipped tongue break the sibilance, and at each pause Judas seems to rethink the next segment of his message. Then, as the crux of his text demands, a quiet or a vigorous hissing resumes, along with more tongueflickers and sighs. Sometimes Judas pounds the lectern or ambles briefly and shakily away from it. Hoke can make no sense of any of it, but Judas's voiceless sermonizing continues without relent. Hoke would like to make a getaway back through the tunnel, but his dead mama taught him never to walk out on a preacher and so he sits longsufferingly in place. Maybe Judas wants to torment him the way Carnes and the handlers tormented their spiritdrugged snakes.

Long into his sermon, a blue film creeps over Judas's eyes, turning them a sickly green. This milky film thickens. As it does, Judas's eyes go from green to seagreen to turquoise to a dreamy cobalt. These cobalt veils blind Judas, but he goes on hissing his wordless rant.

When Hoke thinks he can take no more, Judas stops hissing and rubs his snout with his human hands. The skin over his snout loosens all the way back to his capped eyes. Judas grabs this scaly layer and peels it back. Then the skin on his hands splits, and the new hands beneath these glovelike husks break through to peel away the old skin, including his chambray shirt and designer jeans.

With one reborn hand on the pulpit for support, Judas steps out of this old covering and sets it aside. The husk rocks on its feet like a display mannikin fit only for junking. The new Judas, meanwhile, clings to the pulpit in the guise of a human female:

another mannikin, but an animated one for the women's department. With chestnut hair that cascades down and trembles over her shoulders, this female version of Judas picks up her discarded skin by the shoulders, carries it to the choir loft, and places it in one of the five chairs there. The integument of this molt rattles dryly, its snaky head deforming again into something recognizably human, as if its serpentshape had never really taken.

Hoke sits mesmerized. He no longer wants to run, simply to understand. At the lectern again, the female snakeperson goes on changing, her face shrinking and triangulating, her tresses pulling back into her skull and weaving into satiny snakeskin. Looking past her, Hoke sees that the molt in the choir has come to resemble his daddy, who ran out on his mama and him shortly after she had yoked them with the Sixteeners.

You bastid! Hoke shouts at the thing.

Outside, very near, a bomb falls. The explosion rocks the domed chamber, audibly warping the stainedglass in its cames, swaying the pulpit, and rattling the hollow imago of his daddy, which totters in its chair. The imago has no eyes, only gaping vents, but it stares at Hoke without love, remorse, or any plea for understanding. It sits, just sits, teetering slightly when ordnance explodes.

The snakeperson at the pulpit ignores Hoke's daddy and launches into another harangue—a hissyfit, Hoke thinks—that expands and expands. Usually Hoke's bladder, given the length of these speeches, would expand too, threatening rupture and flood, but here in Ferlin's subbasement his bladder has lots of stretch and he too much endurance.

At last, though, the second Judas's eyes grow a milky film and a second shedding occurs, revealing a new snakeperson and leaving behind a female husk that the third version of Hoke's guide places in the choir loft next to his daddy. The face of this shell takes on the features of his mama, while the third snaky preacher begins a brandnew tirade.

Hoke nods. At length, a third molt puts a fresh male husk in the loft with his folks. This tedious process occurs twice more. By the end of the diamondback's fifth hissyfit, every seat in the choir is occupied. The choir now comprises five false human beings whom Hoke sees as wicked likenesses of his daddy, his mama, Johnny Mark Carnes, Twyla Glanton, and Ferlin Rodale. They rustle to their feet, and the sixth Judas sheds its preacherly garments to join them in the loft as an immense coiled rattler.

How can they sing an anthem when they have no voices? Why does the sixth Judas lace her long anatomy among the other five betrayers, then raise her triangular head above the zombie face of Johnny Mark Carnes?

Ulo-shan-pwei-koloh-ehlo-scraiiii! says the sixth Judas in a female voice familiar to Hoke. *Neh-hyat-kolotosh-mona-ho!* Her split tongue flits among these syllables like a hummingbird sampling morningglory blossoms. Then, on her warning rattle, the choir, once mute, joins her in pealing out a hymn that Hoke well knows:

O for a thousand tongues to sing. . . .

Hands pressed against him, their warm palms on his chest, upperarms, forehead. One pair had a viselike grip on his temples, flattening his ears and struggling to touch fingertips behind his head.

Here he comes, a voice said. Glory.

Bring m out, Jesus. Bring m on out.

Hoke let the faces surrounding him clarify in the glare of a ceilinglamp. As his pupils narrowed, even the darker faces among the four took on definition. He recognized Twyla Glanton and then every member of the Sermons family.

Praise God.

Twyla's face came toward him, and she placed one ear less than an inch from his lips. Say again, she said. Her sorrel hair touched his face.

Lift him from the pit n set him upright midst us, said C.K.
Sermons. Bless his ever goin forth n comin home.

Say again, Twyla said again.

Hoke tried—no sound, but his lips quirked.

Looky there, said Regina Sermons. He be smilin.

Hoke stayed with the Sermonses the next three days. They prayed
with and over him, often laying on hands. They fed him unsalted
rice, applesauce, bananas, and tea made of chamomile flowers,
passionflower leaves, and crushed rosebuds. With no other medical attention but this food and prayer (Antivenin is the antichrist
and doctors are its antifaith disciples, Carnes had liked to say),
Hoke recovered quickly.

On Sunday morning, the Sermonses held an outdoor service
on the decks of the splitlevel gazebo in their backyard. No one
brought snakes into it, although Hoke knew that the Sermonses
kept a dozen or more in crates along the rear of their double garage.
Twyla, Ferlin Rodale, and Sam and Camille Loomis (who had
forgiven Twyla her words at the Friday-night snakehandling service) attended this informal gathering. Oddly, though, no other
member of the congregation showed up, and Hoke began to
suspect that something more dire than his own rattlerbites had
disrupted Friday's worship.

The Sermonses refused to talk about such matters while his
body went about healing itself. When not praying or reading the
Bible with him, they gave him his space, including free run of their
house and grounds.

Their brick house sat on an acre off White Cow Creek Road,
ten miles west of Beulah Fork. It appeared to have been lifted from
a hightone suburban subdivision and set down again in the share-
cropper boonies. It had three bedrooms, a study, and a den with a
hightech entertainment center: largescreen TV and VCR combo,
multideck stereophonic CD soundsystem, and, because none of the
Mark Sixteeners were teetotalers, a wellsupplied wetbar. The

Sermonses could afford such a place because C.K. sold insurance as well as preached, and Betty worked a deskjob in the Hothlepoya County Health Department, even if her job struck Hoke as peculiarly at odds with the noninterventionist doctrines of their Hands On Assembly.

On Monday evening, Twyla, Ferlin, and the Loomises came for another call. This time, though, C.K. herded everyone into the den to watch the videotape that Betty had shot three evenings earlier. Hoke understood that C.K. had organized the gathering as a small party in honor of his recovery. If it had any other purpose, beyond showing off Betty's skills as a camerawoman, he could not have named it.

This past Friday a true anointin came on Brother Hoke, C.K. said. Yall watch n see.

Somebody had wound the tape exactly to the point at which Eddie Moomaw passed Hoke a timberrattler. The tape showed Hoke handling, there among the other Sixteeners. The hopping and stutterstepping of the worshipers, the clangy music, the scary inscrutability of the snakes—everything on the tape united to make Hoke see himself and his friends as part of an outlandish spectacle, separate somehow from their everyday selves. He recognized himself, and he didn't. He recognized Twyla and the Sermonses, and he didn't. Betty's tape tweaked the familiar old church and the ordinary folks inside it into a gaudy circus tent, with jugglers, acrobats, and clowns.

My Lord, Ferlin said.

You know you'da loved to been there, Twyla said.

F yall think this's gonna work on me like a recruitin film, yall just don't know Ferlin Rodale.

Where is it? Hoke said. I don't see it.

Betty Sermons leaned over and patted his forearm. Where's what, baby?

The Spirit, Hoke said. Thet night it was so thick in there you coulda bottled it.

It don't tape, Betty said. Never has.

Hush, Prophetess Camille said. This's where Brother Hoke passes his serpent on back to Eddie Moomaw.

Hoke watched himself hand off the timberrattler. Then he watched C.K. take a hearty swig of poison and Carnes explode into view to unload an even bigger snake on the video image of himself. On the Sermonses' largescreen, Hoke accepted and then almost dropped the diamondback.

Yall're flakier than a deadman's dandruff, Ferlin said.

From a threestage recliner, Sam Loomis leveled a hard gaze on Ferlin. Who taught you yore manners, young man?

Beg yore pardon, sir. I've just never liked snakes.

They've awways spoken well of you, Twyla said.

The videotape continued to unspool, flickering and jumping in testimony to Betty's active camera technique.

Here comes the bites! Regina said.

Hoke flinched. So did Ferlin, who looked off at the framed underwriter certificates on the wall. Hoke kept watching and soon saw himself sprawled on the concrete floor, surrounded by Twyla, the Loomises, Sermons, Moomaw, Bexton, and two bigeyed little boys—the Strock twins—who had wriggled free of their mama's restraining arms to hunker next to Hoke and gawk at him in cheerful expectation of his demise.

Brats, thought Hoke.

Aloud he said: This's where I died. Then walked home to Ferlin's. And rode a elevator straight to hell.

Except, of course, the largescreen showed no sequence of events like that at all. Instead they saw Judas writhing above Hoke in Hugh Bexton's arms, and Twyla saying, *What backasswards crap*, and the Loomises moving stiffly out of view. Then the screen showed a dozen worshipers milling, smoke rolling over the floor from beneath the altardeck, a painted churchwindow shattering, and a fractured brick tumbling end over end on the concrete.

Sermons and the others raised their heads to register the

broken-out window. Smoke began to rise through the church from baseboards, closets, windowsills, and the junkrooms behind the altar. The pictures of the outbreaking fire careened even more madly than Betty's earlier shots. Folks scrambled to flee the building. A sound like the amplified crumpling of Styrofoam dominated the audio; shouts, children crying, and the slamming of car and pickup doors echoed in the background.

C.K., Darren DeVore, Leonard Callender, and Ron Strock—there to shoo away his twins as much as to assist Hoke—picked Hoke up and hustled him in a hammockcarry to the door. Other men crated up and rescued their snakes, sometimes appearing to put their decorated boxes and the creatures inside them before their own wives and kids. The tape's last poorly exposed shots included a pan from the church's burning facade to the gleaming asphalt road going past it.

What was thet all about? Hoke said.

A fire got goin in the dry kudzu behind the church, Twyla said. It burnt us out, comin through the back.

How? Why?

Somebody done set it, C.K. Sermons said. A enemy like unto them cropburners in the gospels.

Only part standin today is walls, Betty said.

Twyla allowed that the fire could have started from a flungaway cigarette, but that C.K.'s investigation on Saturday morning did make it look that somebody had piled dry brush and maybe even two or three wheelbarrows of waste lumber, ends and pieces, against the church's rear wall. Then the sleazes had soaked the piles with kerosene, covered them with kudzu leaves and evergreen branches, and sneaked up during the snakehandling to drag the brush away and light the kindling.

Why'd anybody try to kill yall? Ferlin said. Yall're in a damnfool hurry to do it yoreselves.

Rathcor had his claws in it, said Camille. And whilst them

snakes were out, I bet you cash money thet Carnes, Moomaw, and DeVore awl played divil's innkeeper.

You don't know thet, Twyla said.

She sez it she's nigh-on certain, Sam Loomis said.

Plus it looks like Carnes's done skedaddled outta thisere county, C.K. said.

Hoke cavecrawled into himself. The Mark Sixteeners had lost their meetinghall, Johnny Mark Carnes had vamoosed without a faretheewell, and a disagreement of fierce consequence had split the Assembly—Eddie Moomaw and his cronies arguing that the fire bespoke a judgment for allowing a descendant of Ham to preach and handle snakes amongst them; the Loomises, Twyla, and their friends adamant that Moomaw had laid a vile scapegoatment on the Sermonses for reasons having less to do with theology than with low blood, covetousness, and whitetrash pride. There had been no full Mark Sixteener fellowship on Sunday morning not merely because their church had burnt, but because a schism along skewed racial and maybe even economic lines had cleft the Assembly.

Why'd Johnny Mark run? Hoke said.

I tracked him, Betty Sermons said. Taped his ever step wi thet big Judas snake of his. He figgered if you died, we'd put it out to Sheriff Ott thet he murdered you.

Then the bigger fool he, C.K. said. Law aint gonna squash no Sixteener for killin a Sixteener.

Why not? Regina said.

Same reason it aint like to vestigate our church fire as a arson, said C.K. dyspeptically, as if the strychnine he'd drunk had soured his stomach.

Or look too hard at the mischief out my way, said Twyla.

Rewind, said Regina.

Mam? said C.K. Sermons.

Rewind. Show me playin wi them ol snakes again.

Betty Sermons rewound the tape, and everyone watched Regina handle her rattlers again. Then the TV rescreened Hoke's work with the canebrake. Was that Hoke Pilcher? he wondered. Yes, but Hoke Pilcher under a throughblest anointing. In spite of everything else—snakebite, hellfire, schism—the sight of this miracle poured a tart joy into him, and Hoke perched before it, utterly rapt, oblivious to his surroundings.

That autumn Twyla Glanton moved from Hothlepoya County to Cottonton, Alabama. There she found a job as assistant city clerk and joined a small offshoot of the Hands On Assembly of Jesus Risen. In early October Hoke got Ferlin to drive him to Cottonton to see her, but Twyla had begun to date a surveyor in the Alabama highway department, and Hoke's visit brought down embarrassment on everyone but Ferlin.

Johnny Mark Carnes, according to Eddie Moomaw, had opened an upholstery shop near Waycross. In this shop, he recovered easychairs, divans, carseats, footstools, threestage recliners, and a variety of other items, from pewcushions to the padded lids of jewelryboxes. Occasionally, according to Moomaw, he used snakeskin, for which reason he made frequent unauthorized jaunts into the Okefenokee Swamp.

The Mark Sixteeners in Hothlepoya County remained divided. The Moomaw faction held brush arbor services on New Loyd Hill until the first frost in October. The Sermons family met with the Loomises, the Callenders, and the Bextons in either their garage or the splitdeck gazebo in their backyard, depending on the weather. Both groups suffered snakebites over these weeks, but no one died. Neither faction attracted anyone new to its meetings except the occasional media reporter and GBI agents in scruffy but futile disguise.

Hoke attended the services of neither group. He had gone to hell in a disorienting feverdream, but the conflicts among the local Sixteeners, especially in the absence of Twyla, had tormented him a thousand times worse than either his snakebite or his resultant delirious trip to the sheol tucked away under Ferlin Rodale's tirehouse. Why attend services if a spirit of feud and persnicketiness held the real Spirit at bay? Hell had nothing on a holeful of serpents or an assembly of quarrelsome believers. Hoke would gladly risk eternal judgment if he could avoid the latter two kinds of snakes.

Aside from spiritual issues and Twyla's leavetaking, Hoke's biggest worry was putting money in his pockets. Ferlin forgave him rent shortfalls and overdue payments for the electric bill, but Hoke cringed to impose and even in his exile from Deaton's Bar-B-Q often ventured into Beulah Fork to prune shrubbery, cut grass, sweep parking lots, or carry out groceries. Sometimes he went with Ferlin on roofing or carpentry jobs, earning his hire by toting shingles, bracing ladders, and sorting nails into the pockets of canvas aprons.

In December, Colby Deaton rehired him to bus tables, wash dishes, and run errands, and Hoke stayed with this job—despite the ragging of halfwit good ol boys like Albert Becknell—until early March, when he quit to begin a new line of work, catching and selling poisonous snakes.

A Japanese tuliptree had flowered in the wilderness among dog-woods and redbuds still under winter's spell. Hoke stopped with his crokersack to marvel at it. The tuliptree had set out its pink blossoms on whitespotted grey limbs altogether bare of leaves. These flowers danced like ballerinas against the naked boughs. Another coldsnap, no matter how brief, would kill the flowers; a violent rainstorm would knock them to the leafmulch, and no one would ever guess that they had bloomed.

At the base of an uglier tree nearby—Hoke took it for a blighted elm—a timberrattler slithered languidly up into the day from a hole down among the tree's roots. Hoke had come for just this event, the emergence of a congregation of snakes from their hibernating place. Because it was still early, he could expect more snakes to follow this one to the surface. Dens in which to safely pass an entire winter commanded allegiance, and snakes that had successfully hibernated returned to them fall after fall. Many serpents slept coiled together in the same den, moccasins with cottonmouths, diamondbacks with canebrakes, an immobile scrum of pitvipers in coldblooded wintersleep. And this first rattler, Hoke knew, signaled like a robin the coming of even more of its kind.

In his lowcut tennis shoes he crept up to the elm, seized the canebrake behind its head, and quickly bagged it. Then he crouched and waited. This strategy brought results. In an hour, with the latewinter sun steadily climbing to the south, he caught four more snakes, bagging them as efficiently as he had the first.

Even this small early haul promised a decent payoff. He could get ten dollars a snake from some of the Sixteeners and possibly as much as fifty if he captured a rattler longer than six feet. Snakes died over the winter, or escaped, or emerged from their crates bent like fishhooks from clumsy handling. Conscientious handlers would replace and retire their injured snakes. That turnover meant a career of sorts, if Ferlin would allow him to breed members of like species inside or near the tirehouse. And Sam Loomis had told Hoke of a research center in Atlanta that bought pitvipers for their venom, yet another likely customer and income source.

Hoke caught three more emerging snakes, and then there was a lull. Well, fine. All work and no lolligagging made Hoke a dull dude. His gaze wandered to the tuliptree again and to the pink chalicelike blossoms fluttering in it—pretty, so pretty. Then Hoke started. A human figure sat in an upper crook of the tuliptree, balanced there as shakily as an egg on an upended coffeecup. The figure shifted, and Hoke recognized her as his dead mama, Jillrae Evans Pilcher. He stood up.

Good to see you again, Hoke.

You too, Hoke told his mama. He meant it.

What day is it, honey?

Sunday, he said.

Well. You orter have yore tail over to the Sermonses then, shouldn't you?

Hoke explained about Rathcor and Carnes and Judas and the schism that had come to the Mark Sixteeners in the aftermath of the fire at the former Snake-O-Rama. He explained why he would never encounter the Holy Spirit among either of the church's contending factions and how attending the services of one or the other turned him into an angry uptight nitpicker, a heathen nearlybout. God, he said, would more likely happen to him here in the woods.

My me, said Jillrae Pilcher. The classic copout.

Mama, I cain't do everthin the same blest way you would.

Look quick, she said. They's more comin.

Hoke looked. A halfdozen pitvipers had boiled up through the tunnel from their den. They burst forth into the dappled noon in a slithery tangle. Hoke chuckled to see them, but made no sudden grab to catch one. He glanced back at the tuliptree, his awkwardly perched mama, and the pink blossoms stark against the reawakening woods. His mama faded a little, but because he held his glance, the pink grew lovelier, the sunlight crisper, and the separate trees beyond the tuliptree both more distinct and more mysterious, a pleasant contradiction. Then a snake raced over Hoke's instep. He had no need to look away from the tuliptree at the escaping serpents because their touch told him nearly everything and the woods into which he continued to peer told him the rest.

What is it? said his mama, clinging to the forking branches over her head.

Hoke smiled and blew her a kiss.

The woods behind the tuliptree filled with a haze like a cottony pollen, and this haze drifted through the dogwoods, redbuds, and conifer pillars until it hung from every limb of every tree within a hundredfoot radius of Hoke's dying elm. The awakening snakes boiled out into the haze. Hoke knelt and picked up pitviper after pitviper, two or three to each hand. Standing again, he handled them in the enabling white currents of the drifting pollen grains. His mama, looking on, faded toward invisibility. Hoke lifted a

95

handful of serpents to her in heartfelt farewell. The woods rang with a shout, his own, and the haze pivoting around Hoke's blighted elm either drifted or burned away.

Ferlin burst into the clearing.

My God, he said. Way you uz yellin, I figgered somebody'd done kilt you.

No, said Hoke, bagging the snakes in his hands. I'm just out here laudin God.

Alone? said Ferlin, closing the distance between them.

Only takes two or three, said Hoke.

Not countin them divilish snakes there, who's yore second, Pilcher?

Hoke gestured at the tuliptree, realizing as he did that Ferlin was unlikely to have seen his mama stranded amid its blazing pink flowers. He set his crokersack down and dropped a friendly arm over Ferlin's shoulder.

How bout you? he said.

[Author's note: I owe a significant debt to Dennis Covington's *Salvation on Sand Mountain: Snake Handling and Redemption in Southern Appalachia* for much of the background of this story. Charles McGlockin, the EndTime Evangelist, whom I quote three times from Covington's book, is a real person, but all the other characters and situations are imaginary; resemblances to real human beings, living or dead, or to actual situations in the histories of real snakehandling congregations are entirely coincidental.]

At the City Limits of Fate

Highways have mirages as dizzying as any desert's. It was late April, and I was bound southwest out of Atlanta on I-85. That's why I did a double take when my little Toyota sped past the apparition on the shoulder: it did not melt into either air or just another fatigue-jacketed hitchhiker, but reasserted its peculiarity in my rearview mirror. You see some strange types trying to bum rides, but seldom does the heat haze over the concrete reveal a samurai with a fisherman's net and a begging bowl.

Almost against my will, my foot eased off the accelerator.

Hitchhikers usually frighten me. Whether carefree college kids, Woody Guthrie lookalikes, skinheads in GI green, Brooks Brother businessmen trudging along with gasoline cans, or maidens in distress (no matter how nubile), I do *not* stop for them. In 1973 my uncle Richard picked up a young woman dressed like Lawrence Welk's champagne lady. She blew his brains out, lost a slipper nudging his body into a drainage ditch, and drove his automobile to Valdosta, where the GBI eventually arrested her. Although Cinderella may soon qualify for parole, Uncle Richard's in to stay.

Ah, but this hitchhiker, this black-clad refugee from the Tokugawa shōgunate. I thought I knew where he was going, I was going there myself. I also thought that no one dressed in such conspicuous garb would risk slaying the Good Samaritan who succored him. But backing toward him down the shoulder, I could hear a paranoid part of me whispering, *"This is crazy, Perry— this is suicidally out of character."* I was scared to death to be doing what I was doing, but I was doing it anyway.

Think what an ugly year it had already been: John Lennon shot dead in New York, the President bushwhacked in D.C., the Pope gunned down in Rome. Crazies abounded, and you never knew where they might lurk. Nowadays you scanned the front page the way you had once turned to the sports section for the box scores. And, as a further reminder of the irrationality of the age, at the behest of Brock Fowler, my editor at *Atlanta Fortnightly,* I was on my way to a backwater little burg called Kudzu Valley. Persistent rumors had given the place an unsavory reputation.

"Lift?" I shouted out the passenger window at the make-believe samurai. Without so much as a don't-mind-if-I-do, this bearded young fellow (early twenties, I judged him) picked up his duffle bag, tossed it into the back seat, and got in beside me, deftly disposing the skirts of his robe and the remainder of his gear. My heart was racing like sixty, and a moment later that's where my speedometer needle stuck, too. Truculently, my passenger stared straight ahead.

"Going to Kudzu Valley for the anniversary?" I asked him.

"That's so," he acknowledged grudgingly.

"It's lucky I saw you then. I'm Perry Shipp. I do feature work for *Atlanta Fortnightly* magazine." This elicited no response. "What's *your* name?"

"Shirokazi Jirō."

"Unusual name for a Caucasian, isn't it?"

At last he looked at me. A mere kid costumed like a Kabuki actor impersonating a samurai, he had even painted a few red character lines around his eyes and on his unblemished forehead. "It's an acceptable name for a human being, though. I'm not responsible for the genetics of the matter."

"Your parents from Kudzu Valley?"

The young man threw me a quizzical look. This was a loaded question. On April 31, 1976, a full two and a half years before the gory debacle at Jonestown, Guyana, it was rumored that a dozen of Kudzu Valley's inhabitants had staged a mass suicide to protest the threat posed to their community by the construction of the Cusseta Dam, a project that was quietly shelved later that summer. Circumspection, intrigue, blackmail, and roadblocks had kept word of the alleged suicide from the nation at large. Meanwhile, as a matter of "responsible policy," local news-gathering concerns had squelched this story as another invidious rumor along the lines of "John Kennedy is still alive in a Dallas hospital" and "McDonald's grinds red wigglers into its hamburger meat." Nevertheless, a number of my colleagues believed that Kudzu Valley was Georgia's secret Jonestown.

As a response to my question the hitchhiker said, "I am Shirokazi Jirō, descendant in the second generation of Wilton Emberley of Kudzu Valley, who, at the age of thirteen, engaged in an air-rifle battle with the infamous bullies of White Cow Creek. Receiving a BB in the left eye, my father plucked forth the ruined orb, dug out the BB shot, and fired this dented pellet back at the warrior who sent it. I am endowed with a courage like unto that of my father's."

"You've got that down pat," I said. "Was Wilton Emberley one of those who took part in the—well, uh, the protest?"

"No. No, he wasn't." Jirō relaxed perceptibly. From actorish formality his speech shifted into a more conversational mode. "Mrs. Brumblelo, the admirable old woman who thought up and staged the protest, she was a great-aunt of mine. My dad, her nephew, he was killed in a car crash on his way to a rock festival in the late sixties. Mom remarried a broker with a big house in Peachtree City. For four years I attended a prep school in Atlanta. Right now I'm studying language arts at Emory."

"Under the name Shirowazi Whosis?"

The young man did not respond, either to answer my question or to correct my impertinent rendering of his pseudonym.

"Why are you going back to Kudzu Valley now? The fifth anniversary of an event that supposedly never took place is a pretty ridiculous occasion."

"Do you see my headcloth?"

I could not help seeing it. Red and white, it was knotted behind his left ear. The excess hung over his shoulder, flapping against his chest in the wind from the open window.

"A headcloth like mine signifies one of two things, Mr. Shipp— either that I'm a laborer or I'm mentally unbalanced."

"You want me to assume the latter, I take it."

He smiled. "Everyone knows that students don't work."

"You're going to Kudzu Valley because you're mentally unbalanced? Listen that's—"

"Crazy," said Shirokazi Jirō. His smile mutated into the ghost of a mocking grin. "I know."

Unsettled by our brief talk—memories of Uncle Richard had sprung to mind—I tried to restore my equanimity through chatter: "A nice act you've got yourself." I glanced in my rearview mirror at his duffle bag. "Looks like you intend to stay for a while, amuse the home folk, play out your gig. That it?"

"I want to meet the mayor."

"Mr. M.?" Who else but Mr. M.? Scuttlebutt held that Mrs. Bernard Bligh Brumblelo had appointed Mr. M., a former instructor at the state university, to the chair of the Yukio Mishima Cultural Association of Kudzu Valley. This unlikely organization had eventually arranged the rumored suicide on the Post Office lawn, a ceremony that Mr. M. had neither reported in advance to the proper authorities nor fulfilled his tacit obligation to attend. To some extent, then he was mayor by default, the most prominent and well-connected citizen among the population's survivors.

"If that's his name," Jirō replied.

I had a sudden frightening insight, one predicated on the madness of all the wouldbe hit men who had shaken the political and/or cultural foundations of western civilization during the past half-year. "You want to kill Mr. M., don't you?" I blurted.

The youth favored me with another cryptic smile. "I don't really want to talk anymore. Could we listen to the radio?"

"Push the right-hand knob."

He did so. The radio came on. He adjusted the dial until he had found a station to his liking. To counteract the interference of the wind he turned up the volume. His samurai trappings aside, he was apparently an aficionado of good old Anglo-American rock.

To my dismay and bewilderment, the recurring lyric of the song on the radio was *"I think I'm turning Japanese, I think I'm turning Japanese...."*

At one o'clock on that brilliant April afternoon, having meanwhile forsaken I-85 for a shimmering state blacktop, we were approaching Kudzu Valley. Our journey, I felt, had transported us into a half-mythological era long before the Meiji Restoration. Kudzu, of course, is a Japanese import, and its clambering vines had turned the valley into a vast green edificiary of pagodas, topiary shapes, temples, and castle keeps. By contrast, the town itself is a dusty tract in the midst of this profligate vegetable architecture. Oddly, at the northeastern city limits a huge Shinto gateway, or *torii,* brackets the blacktop: you cannot enter the town without driving beneath this structure, which, at clear midday, shines a blinding lacquered red.

I stopped my Corona Mark 11 a good distance from the gateway. The city limits sign beside the right-hand pillar said

KUDZU VALLEY—POPULATION 704, but to me these characters reduced to a single word:

FATE.

It had been four years since my last abortive trip to Shirokazi Jirō's hometown when I had been working for the *Columbus Ledger,* and on that occasion no splendid red torii had straddled the two-lane. Even my rider seemed surprised to see the gateway. Did I wish to pass beneath it and commit my undistinguished life into the hands of psychological foreigners? I seriously considered dropping Jirō off and returning to Atlanta minus both my story and what little remained of my journalistic reputation—but I feared what he might do. Fate had arranged our meeting solely to inflict upon me the unwanted duty of my samurai's keeper; to deny Fate's commission would be to admit an existential cowardice.

"What's the matter?"

"Got to get some pictures," I ad-libbed. I grabbed my camera equipment and took several shots of the torii before returning to the driver's seat. "Where do you want to go?"

"City hall, Mr. Shipp."

It was easy to find. Most of the buildings in Kudzu Valley— Builders Supply, Unfug's Electric, Variety Five & Dime—occupy the same elongated, tin-ceilinged shell on East Broadway. The weathered bricks in this shell, of regional red clay, were cut with piano wire and an old-fashioned wheel assembly; many of them have a distinct bluish cast. (Nobody makes bricks that way anymore.) However, the city hall on the denuded lot opposite the Farmers and Merchants Bank radiates a cool modernity at odds with the dustiness of nearly every other building. It has blond bricks, plateglass doors, polarized windowglass, and a sterile-looking stainless-steel plaque inscribed with the mayor's full name and the date of its official opening: April 31, 1979. The Economic Development Administration, according to the plaque, supplied a grant of $162,000 to finance the construction of this space-age facility.

"You suppose Mr. M. knew Jimmy?" I asked my companion as we entered the dim air-conditioned hall.

"Sir?"

"Jimmy. Miss Lillian's boy."

"Oh. I don't know. But my great-aunt did."

We found Mr. M. in a big, tiled office. He was sitting at a desk whose facing featured several carven *tengu:* goblinlike creatures that are half bird, half human. The mayor seemed to be the only person in the entire city hall. He was reading a book. Although still a young man, a pink spot in the middle of his pate was threatening to become a tonsure. On the wall behind him, framed in oak, fluoresced a black-light poster of the Japanese novelist Mishima in his famous pose as Saint Sebastian, his near-naked body bristling with arrows the way a porcupine bristles with quills. Jirō stared over Mr. M.'s head at this arresting piece of decor.

"I prefer Kawabata, the Nobel laureate."

"Do you?" replied Mr. M., looking up from his book. He was altogether unabashed to see visitors in his doorway.

"He never posed for such tripe."

"I daresay he didn't have the body."

Jirō swaggered into the room in his robes and face paint. "You don't contend that Mishima's overwrought literary style is on a par with the classicism of Kawabata?"

Mr. M. glanced over his shoulder at the poster. "I don't *read* him, young man. I *look* at him."

Stricken mute by this riposte, Jirō sashayed to the desk and fingered the leaves of a dwarf willow in a blue ceramic pot. Unless something were said, I felt sure that the next order of business would be a tea ceremony and the composition of apposite haiku.

"We've come for the anniversary," I announced.

Even in the office's inexplicable dimness (surely the mayor could afford to turn on the lights) a cagy gleam came into Mr. M.'s eyes. He stood up to scrutinize my features. "Ah, Mr. Shipp, another newspaper reporter. Of course. The day after tomorrow—no, no, *tomorrow*—marks the second anniversary of the dedication of this city hall."

"That's not—"

"You'd like a tour, I presume. You and the bearded geisha busily defoliating my bonsai."

Jirō drew back his fingers. "I am Shirokazi Jirō, descendant in the second generation of...." Haughtily, he went on to the end of his spiel.

"And another native son," commented Mr. M. "Welcome home." Irony rather than welcome informed these words.

I hoisted my camera into view. "May I get a photograph of you at your desk, Mr. M.? For my story."

"Absolutely not. The city hall is the story, not its current occupant. Let me show you around."

This suggestion, ipso facto, led to its fulfillment. Jirō and I saw the city clerk's office (uninhabited), the maintenance engineer's cubicle (likewise), the soundproofed council chamber (ditto), and the spacious meeting room where the voting machines were stored. The furnishings in these rooms bespoke an interior-design debt to Copenhagen rather than to Kyōto, a fact that somewhat allayed my uneasiness. However, in this last chamber, directly across from the voting machines, was a wall of elegant Georgia marble upon which hung a large still-life of poppies. Bright, evil-red poppies.

As I stared at this painting, Mr. M. said, "The ulteriority of this visit does not escape me. In the first place, this solitary *ronin*"—nodding at Jirō—"desires revenge and, having recently come into his majority, believes he can effect it. Secondly, you, Mr. Shipp, want what journalists drolly term a *scoop*." He made the word sound like something to be scraped off a shoe. "I, however, wish only to preserve the status quo, for the common door to your two disparate purposes hinges on my undoing, and I really don't want to be undone."

"Now," I said, still regarding the poppies, "you're no longer talking about the anniversary of the city hall."

Mr. M. ignored this comment. "If you want a photograph, Perry Shipp, Your Reportership, why not take one of young Mr. Emberley in front of this still-life? The red of his face paint perfectly matches that of the poppies. You do have color film, don't you?"

Eagerly, Jirō, the costume buff, approved this plan. He even suggested that he pose with his fisherman's net, his begging bowl, and his *katana,* or samurai fighting sword. I was reluctant to see this last instrument, but Jirō hurried into the heat to the car to fetch back these items. Not a drop of perspiration beaded his handsome young face when he reappeared in the meeting room, the scabbard-bound katana canted across his chest on a ribbonlike sling. So attired, he posed before the poppies.

"Mishima in reverse," said Mr. M. By way of clarification he added, "An Easterner in the guise of a Western saint versus a Caucasian in the guise of a Japanese warrior-monk." He neither smirked nor smiled. His own ironies did not amuse him. "I suppose it's my duty to be hospitable to the zealous. My duty and my burden."

Ducking his head to take off the scabbard (I had finished snapping his picture), Jirō shot the mayor an unreadable glance. We then wandered back down to Mr. M.'s offfice, where he asked us if we had found lodgings for our stay. Our noes prompted him, rather surprisingly, to invite us to spend the night in his own home, once the residence of his late cousin and Mrs. Bernard Bligh Brumblelo's friend, Clarabelle Musgrove Sims. I wanted to decline this offer, but before I could do so, Jirō enthusiastically accepted for both of us.

Mr. M., it struck me, had opened his gates to a Trojan Horse inside which his enemies were brazenly proclaiming their readiness to torch his topless towers. Had the man abandoned his senses? I would have to go with Jirō to keep him from beheading our host as he slept.

"You'll have to share Cousin Clarabelle's old room," the mayor said. "It's the only one upstairs that's even remotely livable."

My handsome young companion merely smiled.

As we left the city hall, an elderly black man in bib overalls and a perforated cap hailed us. "Affernoon, Mr. Muraosa," he cried. "Sho' hot, ain' hit?"

Despite the initial "m," *muraosa* wasn't the mayor's name. Bewildered, I looked at Jirō.

"It means 'headman' in Japanese," he whispered. "It's like saying, 'Afternoon, Mr. Mayor.'"

"Oh," I astutely responded.

Following Mr. M.'s directions, I drove the three of us to the Sims House, an ornate Victorian affair about three shady blocks from the business district. This house completely dominated a secluded neighborhood bereft of kudzu but abounding in magnolia trees, elms, and hydrangea bushes. Its many lofty cupolas and gables gave it a vague resemblance to Ōsaka Castle (to which the Shōgun Ieyasu once laid stubborn seige, and which the besieged ultimately destroyed by fire), and at the foot of the steppingstone walkway to the front door was a torii exactly like that at the northeastern city limits, only smaller. Jirō and I followed Mr. M. beneath the torii and up the charming steppingstones to the house.

"This is a holy place," the young man discreetly informed me.

How could he tell? The Shintō gateway? The fragrant serenity of the neighborhood? My feeling about the house contradicted Jirō's—unless by "holy" he meant something disturbingly akin to "haunted."

After showing us around downstairs, Mr. M. led us into the solarium for iced tea and sugar cookies. A squat little person wearing a pleated linen cap and white culottes served us. I could not tell whether this person was male or female, white or black. Strictly speaking, Mr. M.'s employee did not qualify as "black," for his or her skin suggested a kind of splotchy albinism, as if exposure to sun or maybe even to acid had peeled away the blistered epidermis, revealing the unpigmented layers beneath. The servant had a broad nose and conspicuously everted lips, but these physical character- istics did not strike me an undeniably Negroid. As for Mr. M., he did not call his stocky employee by any name, and the employee's only response to his commands and our polite expressions of gratitude was a genderless giggle. Jirō, I thought, observed the servant's comings and goings with both hostility and suspicion— despite his civil tongue.

At first our conversation proceeded by stops and starts. I tried to ask Mr. M. about the events that had allegedly led to the scuttling of the Cusseta Dam project and eventually to his elevation as mayor—but, adroitly, he turned these questions back on me. How did I justify abusing the hospitality of a dedicated public servant by my many impertinent references to an event that had never taken place? Had he been a less tolerant person, he implied, he would have showed me to the door and pointed the way back to Atlanta. From the corner of my eye I saw young Jirō was regarding the mayor with beetled brows and compressed lips, but he did not interrupt to take my side or to accuse our host of lying.

At this point I played what I thought to be my trump card. From my inside jacket pocket I removed a photocopy of a document entitled "The Yukio Mishima Cultural Association of Kudzu Val- ley, Georgia," a confession of sorts from our host's own hand. Shortly after the alleged events of April 31, 1976, a GBI agent had sneaked into the Sims House and photographed the most bizarre and incriminating of Mr. M.'s files and records. Later, of course, powerful state functionaries with either blood or business ties to Kudzu Valley had suppressed these illegally acquired documents— but, through clandestine methods of his own, Brock Fowler at *Atlanta Fortnightly* had obtained copies and had entrusted one such set to me. I held up the folded pages of my photocopy so that Mr. M. could see them.

"You don't deny authoring this account, do you?"

"What is it?" he replied laconically.

"Entries from your personal diary from the period between June 1, 1975, and June 1, 1976. Here's an excerpt from the last entry: 'Yesterday afternoon everybody in Kudzu Valley, Georgia, with the exception only of children under the age of six and a single responsible adult, committed *seppuku*'—that's ritual suicide—'on the lawn of the U.S. Post Office building.' Later you write, 'I have become Kudzu Valley, Georgia. Dear, dear God, what am I supposed to *do?*'"

Mr. M. was not given to laughter; he favored me with a wan smile. "Oh," he said. *"That."*

"Well?" I prompted him.

"A short story based on the rumors that were so rife in this area a few years ago. I sent it to *The Georgia Review*. I daresay that's where your snoopsome colleagues gained access to the manuscript. I submitted it under an uninspired pseudonym. It was rejected, and I wasted no time putting it back on the market."

"A short story?"

"Which was finally published last year in a paperback consisting of *several* fictive narratives. As you must have already noticed, Mr. Shipp, I am *not* the only surviving adult inhabitant of our town. Surely, as a responsible journalist, you understand the treacherous chasm separating make-believe from fact—unlike that misguided young woman at *The Washington Post* who forfeited her Pulitzer and her professional credibility for fabricating the story that garnered her the award. At least, Mr. Shipp, I *hope* you have such an understanding."

I gaped at the pages in my hand. No, they did not much resemble a diary. Typed, double-spaced, on only one side of the paper, they looked like a prepared manuscript. Fowler, my editor, had apparently fallen prey to the uncritical enthusiasm of one of his novice newshounds, and I, too, had permitted my desire for a scoop to blind me to the many anomalies of our "evidence." The recent Pulitzer fiasco notwithstanding, this lapse was one more reason I was working for *Atlanta Fortnightly,* a shoestring operation on the verge of bankruptcy, rather than the estimable and solvent *Washington Post.* My eyes clouded over. My mind retreated into masochistic review of a career that had stumbled from one two-bit assignment to the next. I had screwed up again.

Mr. M. did not let me continue this demoralizing contemplation of the past— at least not in silence. He asked me questions that forced me to dredge the successive low spots of my career into the tea-colored light of his solarium.

I told both him and Jirō that I was approaching my fortieth birthday, that I had spent my entire adult life as a correspondent for such respectable but obscure newspapers as *The Harris County Journal, The LaGrange Daily News,* and *The Columbus Ledger-Enquirer* (my last assault on the Big Time). Nearly a third of my working hours had been spent in fanny-numbing attendance at meetings of local school boards, city councils, county commissioners, or parent-teacher groups. At the *Ledger* one of my most exciting stories had centered on the efforts of a junior-high class to send President Carter the Biggest Registered Letter in the History of the Universe. Usually, however, I waxed lyrical over more prosaic matters: burst sewer lines, penny-ante holdups, pot raids, washed-out roads, tax digests, library openings, and rigged highway bids. Nothing had come of my first investigation of the Kudzu Valley rumors, perhaps because no one had wanted anything to come of them. None of the residents would talk to me (or to anyone else, thank God), and I had despaired of ever making my mark as Dixie's answer to Woodward and Bernstein.

Two years ago, however, I had written a fanciful feature story for the *Ledger* about a West Georgia family's sighting of a gnome *(Hominibus parvissimis)* in the Roosevelt State Park, near Warm Springs; and this little article—in which my gnome deplored the litter strewn about by park visitors—had caught the attention of Brock Fowler, who was just then launching *Atlanta Fortnightly.* (A few readers, cranks and literalists, had taken my article at face value, despite an editorial disclaimer about my "vivid imagination"—but I don't want to go into that here.) Anyway, Fowler hired me to do a monthly column and occasional investigative work for his groundbreaking magazine, and I left Columbus for Atlanta. Predictably, this enterprise was not prospering, and today I was the only remaining member of the magazine's original staff, primarily because I had reluctantly agreed to three separate pay cuts over a sixteen-month period. Moreover, although Fowler had not yet changed the title, for the last five issues *Atlanta Fortnightly* had been appearing monthly. My career was similarly out of synch. And had been for almost two decades.

Euphorically self-pitying, talking nonstop for an hour and a half or more, I spun out my woeful monologue. Indeed, when I finally clamped my lips shut, the tea-colored light had acquired the hue of creek water and my body felt seined of every darting minnow of energy. Jirō and Mr. M. were observing me with a kind of noncommittal compassion. Before I could prevent it, a surge of salty gratitude welled in my eyes. I swiped at it with the back of my hand and averted my gaze.

"It's all right," Mr. M. assured me. "I'm quite cognizant of the twin traumas of unrewarded merit and derailed ambition." A beat later he added, "Things have improved considerably of late, however."

His servant then waddled in to remove our tea glasses, the cookie platter, and our embroidered place mats. After he or she was gone, Jirō turned to our host and spoke a long-deferred accusation:

"No matter what you say about your short story, or your diary, or whatever it is, I *know* that my great-aunt took her life on the Post Office lawn."

Replied Mr. M., unperturbedly, "Please remember that she was unwell and that infirmity excuses many rash acts. Try to forgive her."

Because we had received no dinner invitation and were wary of eating a full-fledged meal in the Sims House, Jirō and I bought a couple of greasy scrambled dogs at a little café on East Broadway. The young man drew many perplexed and perplexing stares, for which reason he did not talk at all during our outing. Or maybe he was simply preoccupied with what he had seen and heard at the house.

When we returned, Mr. M.'s servant carried my overnight case and camera equipment up the stairs to Clarabelle Musgrove Sims's old room. Another servant—a virtual twin to the first, but for summer livery and a motoring cap—appeared from the vestibule and tried to take Jirō's duffle bag. He objected strenuously and carried it himself. Inside our spacious old room I asked him why he had been so vehement in his refusal.

"Mr M.'s servants are not people," he told me, bolting the door. "They're *oni*."

"Only what?"

"Not 'only'—oni," the young man patiently explained. "Oni are Japanese demons. These two are in thrall to Mr. M., and they're not to be trusted. I don't like their looks."

I grimaced my disbelief.

"They're fairly small as oni go, but they're strong. One of them could have carried *all* our belongings upstairs. You noticed their caps? They're wearing them to hide—"

"Jirō, your imagination's running away with you. What's Mr. M. doing with a pair of Japanese demons for servants?"

"Covering up the truth of what happened here five years ago. Preserving the status quo."

"And how did he get them?"

"By betraying my grandfather's sister and all the other members of the Mishima Cultural Association who sacrificed their lives for this community. Evil always rewards its own. These oni are Mr. M.'s reward."

"I thought you said this was a holy place."

"It is. The torii proclaims it as holy. But even the holiest of places is subject to pollution, Mr. Shipp."

I shook my head.

Jirō flung his duffle bag across the room. "And *you're* the one who wrote about a gnome complaining of litter in Roosevelt State Park!" Disgustedly, he retired to a corner and began reading a set of World War II combat comics that had fallen from his bag. An odd cultural taste, I reflected, for someone studying language arts at Emory.

I, meanwhile, fetched out a notebook and began recording my impressions of the day's events. Tomorrow was the fifth anniversary of S Day, and I wanted to be ready for whatever it might bring.

Our room—once the sanctorum of Clarabelle Sims—was furnished in austere samurai fashion. Movable paper screens gave us the option of partitioning the room (though we chose not to do so), and our beds were mere pallets atop the reed mats that lay like islands on the ancient heart-of-pine floor. A closet, a portable television set on an unfinished end table, and a tiny bathroom were among the few concessions to Western notions of comfort. Indeed, the walls lacked windows, and our light came from a pair of pole lamps designed to resemble the glaives carried by feudal Japanese monks. At ten o'clock we turned out these lamps and said our good nights—the first word from Jirō since our argument. Knowing that my young friend was plotting revenge, for a long time I lay in the dark with my eyes open. Then I feigned the regular breathing of one deep in sleep and hoped that this sound would narcotize my roommate.

It did no such thing. At midnight (the luminous numbers of my digital watch gave me the hour), the would-be *ninja,* or assassin, raised himself from his pallet, removed his sword from its scabbard, and crept to the door. Hearing the bolt snick back, I prepared to spring across the room to prevent Jirō from carrying out his plan. But when he tugged at the knob, the door did not come open and a throaty growl of warning answered from the corridor.

"What's that?" I exclaimed under my breath.

Jirō, a shadow in the darkness, whirled about to face me. "The oni," he whispered bitterly. "We've been locked in, Mr. Shipp. They're guarding the door to make sure we stay here."

The growls outside grew more ferocious.

"Maybe they're for *our* protection," I hazarded.

"Fat chance. Mr. M.'s maybe, but not ours."

"It looks to me as if our host is justified in setting a guard before our door. You wanted to kill him."

"I still do."

"Exactly."

"But he wants to do the same to us. He's locked us in not just for the night, Mr. Shipp, but for as long as he can keep us here."

"That's foolish, Jirō. He can't get away with it. Fowler has a pretty good idea where I am. If I'm gone too long without reporting back, he'll call the authorities, send somebody else to investigate."

"Okay, then. He wants to keep me here for as long as he can. He wants to control *my* actions."

The oni in the hall—I had actually begun to think of them as demons rather than as dwarfish albinos—continued to make menacing noises. I was glad the door was locked. Not my roommate, though. His katana glinting coldly in the warm dark, he turned back to the door to insert its blade into the crack beside the lock plate. Although I begged him to stop, he kept working at the mechanism until a metallic *pop!* told us he had succeeded. Taking one step back, he again pulled on the knob, and the door burst inward like a hatch on a space vehicle exploding into vacuum. This explosion swept the oni in behind it, and the naked electric lights in the corridor half blinded me. I lunged to my feet empty of every intent but my own survival.

Through blurred eyes I watched Jirō expertly decapitate the first of the two demons. This was the one that had served us sugar cookies in the solarium. Its growling head rolled across the floor to

113

the foot of my pallet. Looking down, I saw that a pair of stubby
horns grew out of its leprous forehead. From the matted hair just
above its brow a beady third eye returned my astonished gaze.
There was no blood, only a nauseating stench. I then looked up to
see the second demon butting Jirō in the stomach, endeavoring to
inflict a mortal wound with one of its cap-covered horns. Despite
his cumbersome robes, my roommate fell back nimbly from this
attack—but the oni still managed to stay in close where he could
not wield his sword effectively. Cold and continuous, the creature's
howls of bloodhunger seemed to make the entire house reverber-
ate.

I snatched my camera from the floor, shouted "Cheese!" at the
top of my voice, and took the oni's picture when it spun to face my
sparkling lens. Jirō struck the demon in the back of the neck. Its
head hurtled from its body, and I had to dance aside to keep from
tripping over this phosphorescent, three-eyed bowling ball. My
momentum carried me to the door, which I reflexively slammed
shut. Jirō leapt to my side and slotted the interior bolt—despite his
earlier having tried so singlemindedly to free us from our illicit
house arrest.

"I thought you wanted out!"

"Look, Mr. Shipp, look!" He pointed across the room at the
portable TV set on the end table next to the bathroom. Its screen
was glowing, filling the room with an uncanny silver light. "It's
Amaterasu's mirror, Mr. Shipp. Come on, we've got to kneel
before it."

Only during football season did I do prolonged obeisance before
my TV set. Moreover, unattached noggins and headless bodies
seldom create an ambience conducive to my full viewing enjoy-
ment. Jirō's promptings struck me as absurd, if not downright
crazy.

But, as if showing us a close-up of a sunrise or the apocalyptic
flash of a nuclear explosion, the face of the set grew brighter and

brighter. I turned my head. In the continuing outflow of light, however, I saw that the bodies of the two demons had oxidized, leaving behind only their grotesque heads as testimony that they had ever existed. Awed, I submitted to Jirō's command to kneel.

"She won't appear until we've made her an offering," he told me from the corner of his mouth.

"Who won't appear?" I demanded, shading my eyes.

"Amaterasu, Goddess of the Sun. She wishes to speak to us from her mirror." He wiped the blade of his sword and laid the weapon on the floor below the television set. "Do you have any jewels, Mr. Shipp?"

"Jewels?" (My incredulous whisper was a falsetto.)

"It would be good if our offering approximated the items in the imperial regalia of Japan. The TV set is her mirror, of course, and my katana's a good surrogate for the imperial sword—but we need some jewels. That's the final item in the regalia."

Muttering to myself in terror and perplexity, I fumbled among my camera gear for several lens attachments. To these I added my watch, a zircon tie tack, and my senior class ring, an assortment of "jewels" that Jirō took from me and placed with his sword in front of the set. If these failed to summon the goddess, I thought somewhat numbly that maybe my plastic credit cards would do. I had no other valuables.

The glow on the screen, a silver-gold nimbus, contracted to a cyclopean rectangle in which the features of a ghostly woman began to take shape. Her skin was silver-white, her hair like crimped strips of aluminum foil, her godly mien so overwhelming that at first I did not recognize her for what she was—an apotheosized avatar of Mrs. Bernard Bligh Brumblelo, Jirō's deceased great-aunt. Over the long centuries since her petulant sulk in a Japanese cave and her tentative reemergence, Amaterasu had aged.

"Curtis?" she said. "Curtis Wemberley?" (The liquid consonant in this last word she pronounced without falter.)

"Ma'am?" said Jirō reverentially.

"You've taken your vengeance. You've fulfilled your task."

"No, ma'am, I haven't. The traitor's still alive. I've got to take care of him, too, Sunny One."

As if to emphasize his aliveness, Mr. M. knocked on the door and asked if we were all right. Having heard a commotion, he felt obliged to inquire. He hoped he wasn't needlessly disturbing us.

"Ha!" said Jirō, but not very loudly.

"Curtis," said Amaterasu in the ghostly guise of Mrs. Brumblelo, "you're not to harm a hair on that man's head."

"But—"

"Dear me, don't argue. If he betrayed our Cultural Association, he's atoned for that 'sin' a thousand times over."

"How?" exclaimed Jirō.

"By shepherding Kudzu Valley through a crisis. By living in his dotty cousin Clarabelle's house for six years. By preserving my shrine in her old bedroom. He's an insufferable snob in some ways, I freely confess, but he's performed an important caretaker function."

"He tried to kill us!"

"Not him, Curtis—the oni. They're headstrong creatures at best, and I sent you here to dispatch them before they ventured into town to perpetrate their mischief. And so you could slake your thirst for vengeance, of course. Now hold your tongue while I talk to Mr. Shipp."

Our host knocked harder on the door. He wondered aloud if we had heard the noises he had just heard.

"Now, Mr. Shipp," said Amaterasu, the Sunny One. "I want you to know that you have not come here on a wild-goose chase. The alleged mass suicide about which you have heard so much piquant speculation—well, it *actually occurred!*"

The goddess's haggard, actinically bright face faded away—to be replaced by an overexposed videotape of the seppuku ceremony in which, five years ago, she had taken her mortal life.

"Here, Mr. Shipp, you see how Spurgeon Creed, Ruby and

Clarence Unfug, Lisbeth and Q.B. Meacham, Fontessa Boddie, Tom and Lonnie Pederson, and I performed our first ritual cuts and how Augustus Houseriser stood behind us with a sword to abbreviate our agony. Only eleven folks were involved, not the entire adult population, and our sacrifice, willingly undertaken, saved this place from a latter-day flood. Go back to Atlanta and tell our story, Mr. Shipp. Five years is enough time for this community to sit on what happened here. Even our clever Mr. M. can't expect to stonewall forever."

The face of the goddess displaced the horrifying scene on the Post Office lawn. The glow surrounding her features intensified. Soon the screen was nothing but a small rectangular window on a brilliant Hiroshima radiance. Neither my roommate nor I could look at it anymore.

"Secure your trophies, Curtis," said Mrs. Brumblelo's disembodied voice. "Secure them and come visit me. It's been ever so long since we've had a spirit-to-spirit chat."

Whereupon the screen went grey and Mr. M. contrived to burst into the room despite our interior bolt. (Undoubtedly he had given us a defective lock so that he could arrange access whenever he desired.) Jirō did not wait to see what he wanted. He lifted the heavy sleeves of his robe, flapped one wing across his face in Bela Lugosi fashion, and shrank to the size of a tengu, becoming, in the process, a living representative of the carven goblins on Mr. M.'s desk in city hall.

A wind attended this shrinkage, and although it was still rather dark in the room, I saw young Shirokazi—whose surname means Blackwind—fly to the heads of the oni, pick them up in predatory claws, and go careering past our host, into the corridor, and down the stairs like a dustdevil of avenging darkness.

The youth's departure sucked the stench of the fallen oni after him, and when I turned on the nearest pole lamp, Mr. M. and I were met on a battlefield cleansed of almost every token of prior conflict. Not since the honeymoon evening of my third failed marriage had I experienced such a strange sequence of events.

117

"I've got to go," I told my adversary.

"Tomorrow's the anniversary, Mr. Shipp "

"I know. I've observed it already. My roommate's deserted me, and I've got copy to write."

"Do you intend to write about everything you saw here?"

"Absolutely. I've got a commission from the Sun Goddess."

"As you wish." Mr. M. turned on his heel, apparently satisfied that he could not triumph over such resolve. Deprived of his oni, he was powerless to do me any violence.

I hurried to gather up my belongings. While doing so, I brushed past the TV set on which Amaterasu—Mrs. Brumblelo's deified ghost—had spoken to young Shirokazi and me from a typhoon of incandescent ions. It did not surprise me to find that the set was a Sony.

The following April, my "scoop" dismissed as a clumsy fraud akin to last year's debacle at the *Post,* Fowler's magazine long since defunct, I stood on the shoulder of I-85 trying to hitch a ride back to Kudzu Valley. None of my pictures had turned out. Either I had had my cameras on the wrong settings or I had used them without providing them with film. I had yet to fulfill my destiny, and only by passing beneath the lacquered red torii at the city limits of that little town could I hope to take my fate into my own hands again.

If only I could lay my hands on Mr. M.'s television set . . .

I was dressed as a *rōnin*, a masterless samurai, and my unusual garb soon led a young woman in a Datsun to stop for me. She may have thought I was a mirage. A reporter's notebook lay on her dashboard; a variety of photographic equipment cluttered her back seat. She leaned over to the passenger side and unlocked the door.

"*Arigato*," I told her.

That means "thank you" in Japanese.

Epistrophy

Julian Wrysodick slumped in harness as I rolled his three-wheeled chair down the beach in a storm of spray and buffeting gusts. His hands posed like crabs on the woolen-clad bones of his thighs. His ungainly grey head lolled in the buffeting gusts. He smelled simultaneously of witch hazel, camphor, and urine, even as his weird fetor carried inland on the buffeting gusts. I wished that my cousin Ferrel, Wrysodick's regular attendant, hadn't taken the flu and called me away from the Seacourt library; that Wrysodick himself had acknowledged his senescence and infirmity and remained indoors, out of the spray and buffeting gusts.

The cold winter twilight flapped around us like unbattened sailcloth.

"Rudy!" Wrysodick barked over one shoulder. "Rudy, why in breezes have you stopped?" His voice? A ratcheting of unoiled gears.

"This is crazy, Mr. J."

"It pains me you think so."

"*Look* at it. We could get caught out, sir. Squall blowing up. Darkness. These buffeting gusts."

"Ferrel wouldn't balk at accompanying me."

What's this accompanying business? I thought: I'm pushing you. Aloud: "No balking to it. I'm simply pointing out the inadvisability."

"You fear a reprimand, or worse, if I croak out here."

"Well, of course."

"Fine. You probably should. Buffeting gusts." He showed me the custard-grey white of one eye and the whiskery corner of a grin.

"So it's all right if I take you back?"

"Ferrel wouldn't. Not old Ferrel. He'd push on." (Yeah. Into the buffeting gusts.)

"Yessir," I said.

"There's something I'd like you to see, Rudy. In fact, there's something *I* want to see. And that . . . well, that's what counts, isn't it?" He lifted a bony index finger off his leg and wobbled it at a dune-populated cape jutting into the slate-grey chop fifty yards ahead. "Go. Go go go."

I shoved. Wrysodick's chair, designed for a variety of outdoor terrains, including heavy sand, shot forward so quickly that I seemed almost to dogtrot after, rather than to impel, it. Quite a buggy. Why fret the birdshot spray, the menace of falling night, the endlessly buffeting gusts?

After all, the chair had headlamps on each of its otherwise useless armrests, not to mention glowing red running strips on its tires and sides. To a sand crab, we must have looked like a runaway Ferris wheel.

With less hassle than I would have imagined, we negotiated the cape and several shell-studded flats that eventually opened out on a small peninsula of snow-white sand, as if a crew of engineers had poured a concrete base beneath the peninsula's square tip and anchored that platform to the underlying shelf by a method that educated morons like me would never grasp. My chairbound charge gaped into the buffeting gusts.

I rolled Wrysodick toward the spit. From the bottom up, it went like this: concrete subfloor, overfloor of pristine white sand, and, atop this sugary layer, tucked away in an open-faced shelter of cut, intricately fitted, and well-waxed driftwood, the very thing that Wrysodick had wanted to show me and to see again himself. Namely, a jukebox.

By now, the sky had given up all its light, the wind had acquired the droning keen of a dynamo, and Wrysodick had taken on an extra pound or two in the paralyzing soddenness of his woolen clothes. He no longer stank of astringent, camphor, and pee, but of something fleecelike and doggy. When I leaned down to speak directly into his ear, I saw that his ashen bat-fetus face had begun to glow from memory or present-day content. Or possibly both.

In the pink, I thought. Suddenly, the old geezer is in the pink, a sheen of self-satisfied reminiscence.

"Here?" I yelled.

"No closer. Roll me up. *Roll me up!*"

I would have gladly rolled him up into a bony pellet, like the casts that owls commonly regurgitate, and hurled him into the Atlantic, but reality stayed me. Instead, I rolled the chair. The headlamps on its armrests played like spots on the shimmering formed-plastic tubes and chromium trim of the box, somehow animating all its curves and sponging the night around us with an intangible swirl of emeralds, rubies, sapphires, and flashing lemon drops. The box's console stood five and a half feet tall. Towering over Wrysodick, it throbbed before us like a Titan's heart.

"The Wrysodick 1440, the first model I put into production after the war," Wrysodick said.

Which war? I wondered. And then, cogitating, knew he meant the one that we had ended with atomic bombs, two prodigiously buffeting gusts.

"When material controls ended, I jumped," Wrysodick said. "Back into the game. This beautiful baby was the result."

"You designed jukeboxes?"

"Dreamed. Designed. Crafted. Produced."

"Ferrel said you were a manufacturer of phonographs, stereo equipment, that sort of stuff."

"A jukebox *is* that sort of stuff, Rudy."

A nod at the Wrysodick 1440. "Does it play?"

Even shivering in near-terminal decrepitude, he scoffed at the implied notion that it would not. This unit had its own built-in power source. Wrysodick told me how to activate that power source; how to adjust the volume against the booming of the sea and the wind's shrill vocalizations; how to prime the disc player with a slug that automatically returned itself; and, finally, how to punch out a selection from the twenty-four catalogued in side-by-side rows above the elaborate *Wrysodick* nameplate and the undulant U-shaped tube framing the stained-glass drum of this model's sexy abdomen. I did everything he said, right up to the point of button punching.

"Punch seventeen, Rudy."

"Seventeen?"

"It's been seventeen years since she died."

I punched seventeen: "Misterioso," by Theolonious Monk. With the jukebox's volume on its highest setting, the notes of this oddly syncopated, almost discordant cut banged out at us like the jamming of a quartet of deeply peeved skeletons. The xylophone in it hinted so strongly at smart-aleck bone rattling that I began to shiver even more vehemently than Wrysodick, who grinned like a cadaver. The paired vertical tubes on the front outer edges of the box pulsed in juking rhythm with the music and our chattering teeth.

"Who?" I managed. "Seventeen years?"

"Irene. My wife. My one and only beloved."

"Did she like *that*?" Another nod at the glowing machine.

Wrysodick couldn't see this nod, but had no trouble reading my question. "She liked everything on that baby. It's all jazz, all twenty-four selections." Something flew by overhead: seagull, sandpiper, or scrap of newsprint. Wrysodick flinched, a self-protective jerk of his massive grey head, as this flimsy UFO fluttered beyond us toward a waste of sea oats and eroded dunes. Then, like a turtle coming back out of its carapace, he recovered:

"Monk on piano. Milt Jackson on vibes. John Simmons on bass. Shadow Wilson on drums."

"Never heard of any of them but what's-his-name," I said. "The lead player, Thelonious."

"They recorded that and a cut called 'Epistrophy'—it's on the box too—in the summer of 1948."

"Nearly twenty years before I was born."

"Really? Well, I was at the height of my powers." A quick involuntary head twist. Another recovery. "The *height*, Rudy."

"Yessir."

"Misterioso" plinked mysteriously to a conclusion. Three minutes plus of cool sardonic playing that Irene Wyrsodick had contrived to soar on and that had clearly lifted Julian off the ground too. Even after the mechanical arm inside the console had returned the vinyl disc to its stack, the Wrysodick 1440's sculpted tubes went on geysering. Inside them, in the liquid chemical still roiling there, I could see—or thought I could—tiny floating grains clumping and separating again, dissolving and briefly remanifesting. I left Wrysodick and knelt beside one set of paired tubes.

"What makes them do that?"

"The chemical in there—irenex, I call it—has a really low boiling point." Head loll. Finger twitch. "Small heaters at the bottoms of the tubes." He chortled. He smirked. "*Voila!* Instant Technicolor ebullience."

"It's pretty." I had to admit. It was. A lot prettier, to my way of measuring, than the ivory and bone collisions of "Misterioso." I fingered the console's ever-present slug out of its return slot.

123

"One more time," Wrysodick said.

"Seventeen?"

"What else? Seventeen."

I stood and pored over the other selections. I would have liked to hit a Sinatra, a Dick Haymes, a Jo Stafford. I would have liked to punch Charlie Parker doing "I Didn't Know What Time It Was" (because I didn't), or Ella Fitzgerald on "I Ain't Got Nothin' But the Blues," or Dizzy Gillespie's "Lorraine," or almost anything other than seventeen. Still, I did my duty by Wrysodick, there in the buffeting gusts, and, as they buffeted, dutifully punched seventeen. Thelonious plunked, bubble tubes boiled, waves crashed, and the wind flung shrapnel against the polished backside of the jukebox's driftwood lean-to and flung them in buffeting gusts.

"Irene loved this spot," Wrysodick said. "We put her to rest here."

Behind his chair again, I peered around. "Where?"

"There. Inside my machine. We cremated her. Her bones went into a box, the box into a compartment of the 1440."

"I thought with cremation you got ashes."

"You get *cremains*, Rudy. Lots of ash. Some charred bone fragments. Those we boxed up and stashed in the Wrysodick."

"So what did you do with her ashes?"

"Most we put into the cedar box with the bone fragments. A sprinkle, though, went into each of the bubble tubes."

"The bubble tubes?"

"Sure. Why not? She dances in those things. She inhabits this place."

"Ferrel never told me."

"Good. I'd've fired him if he had. No one has a right to reveal my eccentricities but me."

After a beat or two I said, "Is it legal? Burying someone in a jukebox?"

"My wife. Our property. Our choice. Sure it's legal. If it isn't, nobody's going to tell me so."

Once again, "Misterioso" plinked to an off-key conclusion in the deafening salt air. Meanwhile, Irene Wrysodick, or some gritty part of her, danced in the bebop tubes of her husband's flamboyantly beautiful music box.

On our way back to his big stucco house, Wrysodick lurched heavily against the straps in his chair.

A heart attack, the coroner said. No autopsy confirmed this assessment. Rather, as stipulated in Wrysodick's will, a cremation was followed by a beach-front memorial service at the site of the enshrined jukebox.

Ferrel got me an invitation by arguing that the person in whose presence the patriarch had died—no one, by the way, ever accused me of either negligence or treachery—had an inviolable right to attend. Who, after all, had last spoken with Julian Wrysodick? Who had beheld his definitive death throe? Who had wiped his mouth of sputum in the buffeting gusts?

At first, I hadn't wanted to go. But Ferrel told me that Emily Singleton, the eldest daughter, had mixed the cremains of her dad with those of her mom and put them all in the cedar box inside the 1440. And some of Wrysodick's ashes had gone into the bubble tubes, there to commingle with those of the beloved mother of his children.

As a result, the ceremony itself, consisting of a text from First Corinthians and seven or eight becoming jukebox numbers, moved me a lot. I began to love Julian Wrysodick and the woman who had predeceased him by seventeen years. I even began to find a happy, if well-hidden, lilt in the Thelonious Monk piece "Misterioso."

After the funeral, Ferrel Kidd, my uncle Garrick's son, and I stopped by the Seacourt Public Library so that I could pick up some work I needed to do at home. We sat down at a table in the community meeting room to talk.

Ferrel is two years younger than I, a card-carrying member of Generation X. At events less solemn than funerals, he wears outsized dungarees, granny glasses, and a Fishbone baseball cap backwards. I still hadn't quite adjusted to seeing him in a charcoal chalk-striped suit, even if he had long since shed the jacket and dropped his suspender straps.

"When my time comes," I said, "please find some way to put my mortal remains in a jukebox."

Ferrel raised his grown-together eyebrows. "You realize, cuz, they don't make Wrysodick 1440s anymore? Hell, they don't manufacture Wrysodick boxes at all."

"A comparable competitive model, then."

"What would do? A Seeburg? A Rock-Ola? A Wurlitzer? I don't think any of em quite suits."

"I'm snowed, Ferrel. Think of something."

"Tell me what's snowed you."

"The beauty of it. The late Mr. and Mrs. Wrysodick, they jazz each other continually in the rainbow-colored tubes of his name-sake machine."

"Yeah."

"Beats going into the cold clayey ground or being randomly scattered at sea."

"I guess," said Ferrel without enthusiasm.

A few months later, Tropical Storm Eliot struck the coast and wreaked havoc. Buffeting and collapsing every building on the Wrysodick estate, this storm built in gusts, soared inland on gusts, and slammed down the jukebox shrine and tomb of the Wrysodicks in a rageful succession of gusts.

Not long after, Ferrel and I threw in together and bought burial plots in a modest Seacourt cemetery. A blue note to end on, but the discordant truth.

For Thus Do I Remember Carthage

Augustine wants no company, and perhaps the last person that he
expects to intrude on him this evening is an importunate astronomer from far Cathay.

A fever has besieged the old man. In the bishop's house next to
the basilica of Hippo Regius, Augustine mulls the imminence of his
own death. Not yet officially a saint, he broods, too, on the
portentous events of this past year.

An army of 80,000 Vandals has besieged Hippo. Under their
wily king Genseric, they seem inevitable occupiers. Boniface,
Count of Africa, has held them at bay throughout the summer with
a force of Gothic mercenaries and a few ragtag volunteers from
among the male population of upper Numidia—but Genseric's
fleet has blockaded the harbor and Vandal soldiers have disabled the
power plant providing Hippo with electricity. Augustine must read

the psalms copied out and affixed to his bedchamber walls by the flicker of an olive-oil lamp rather than by the steady incandescence of one of Seneca the Illuminator's clever glass globes.

"This earthly city cannot last," the bishop tells himself, "but the City of God . . . the City of God endures."

Possidius appears inside the door of his bedchamber with a tray of pears, bread, and marinated chick peas.

Bishop of Calama, a town twenty leagues to the south, Possidius fled to Hippo last October to escape the oncoming barbarians. (Two Numidian bishops less wise than he were tortured to death outside the walls of their cities.) He has lived in Augustine's episcopal quarters ten months now, but has been fussily nursing the brilliant old man for only these past two weeks.

"Go away, Possidius," murmurs Augustine.

"A modest *convivium*," the other replies. "Excellency, you must eat."

"I know I must, but sometimes, Possidius, it's hard to remember why. Christ forgive me my fatalism."

"To keep up your strength, sir. And, this evening, because you have a visitor."

"No, Possidius, I don't. I've forbidden visitors. Physicians are especially unwelcome."

"This isn't a physician. Vindicianus, your doctor, has almost lost patience with you, Excellency."

Gently again, the old man in the voluminous black birrus says, "Whoever it is, is sadly unwelcome. Not for his shortcomings, but for mine."

Tears streak Augustine's face, conspicuously splotching it. He has been reading the Davidic psalm beginning, *"Blessed is he whose transgression is forgiven, whose sin is covered,"* and the balm of its verse *"Thou shalt preserve me from trouble"* has surely induced these tears. Frequently, of late, he succumbs to tears, and Possidius cannot tell if he does so from pity for the plight of Roman Africa, or from an unspeakable gratitude to God, or from some ancient shame for

which only he of all men would scruple to indict himself. Undoubtedly, he weeps for a panoply of reasons, but the bishop of Calama
is unable to sort them out.

"He's a stargazer, Excellency, who hails—he declares—from
the capital of Africa." Possidius places the tray of fruit, bread, and
leguminous porridge on Augustine's writing desk.

"Carthage?"

"So he says. But he's spent the past thirty years—his entire life
since the century turned—looking at the stars from various cold
escarpments in Northern Wei."

"Ah, yes. Flying machines and dragons aren't the only miracles
from that mythic land, are they?"

"Telescopes, Excellency. Horseless chariots. Boxes that talk,
and others in which tiny images of people dance about one another
like butterflies. Seneca the Illuminator says they've perfected
machines in Cathay at least a *century* in advance of any made by the
Daedaluses of Rome or Constantinople.

"But the greatest miracle, Excellency, may be that your visitor
has returned to Numidia at exactly the time that Genseric's Vandals
were bearing down on us through Mauretania. This astronomer
sneaked through their siege lines to enter the city and to find our
basilica. He wants an interview. Morally, sir, I think you should
grant it."

"Morally," the old man mutters. On his feet for the first time
since Possidius interrupted his reading, he totters to his writing
desk and picks up a pear. He burnishes it on his robe and lifts it to
his chin, not to bite it with his bad teeth but to sniff it for submerged
memories. He has lived three quarters of a century, and a year
besides, and that Possidius should be defining morality for him—
fabled Defender of the Faith against the errors of Manichees,
Donatists, and Pelagians—strikes him as droll. But God knows that
he has often needed chastening, and perhaps tonight the Deity has
applied Possidius as a scourge.

"Does my would-be visitor have a name?"

129

"Iatanbaal, sir."

"Christ save us. A pagan name. Does this man have any Latin, Possidius, or am I to talk to him in my execrable Neo-Punic?"

The refugee from Calama smiles. "Iatanbaal speaks Latin well enough. It's his first language. For three decades, however, he has been talking in the tongues of Babel, some so queer that I am uncertain what to call them."

" 'Given of God,' " Augustine muses.

"Excellency?"

"in Neo-Punic, *Iatanbaal* means 'given of God.' " He places the pear back on his desk, squints at it as if it has just scolded him, and lapses into reverie.

"Father Augustine," Possidius prompts.

The white-bearded apostle turns his ravaged face to the bishop from Calama. "Oh, yes. Our visitor. Iatanbaal. 'Given of God.' In that case, let him come in."

ii.

It startles Augustine to find that Iatanbaal—why did he expect a younger man?—is hard on sixty. The astronomer, who drops to his knees to kiss the bishop's hand, owns just as many gray hairs as he but a less lined, a less troubled countenance.

The stargazer wears a tight tunic in decadent late Roman style, but a pair of leggings—*trousers*—favored by Hsiung-nu horsemen in the service of the Wei Cathayans among whom he has lived and worked since the turn of the fifth Christian century. Over one shoulder, he carries an ornate bag of some length and bulk. The bishop also notices that on his left wrist Iatanbaal wears a thin strap bearing on it an oblong jewel, very like obsidian.

This jewel is featureless, but when the astronomer stands, it strikes the edge of Augustine's writing desk. Suddenly, a row of crimson characters gleams on the black stone's surface. The gleam fades as quickly as it flared, however, and Augustine crosses his hands on his breast to stare at the enigmatic bracelet.

"Pardon me, Excellency," the astronomer says, and their eyes lock. "This device is a miniature time-gem."

The bishop realizes that he and his guest are the same height, with irises the same slatey Berber gray. In other circumstances—the besieging Vandals elsewhere, his own death a decade rather than days away—they might have been good friends. Augustine lets his gaze fall again to the "time-gem."

Each time that Iatanbaal depresses a metal stem on the edge of its jewel, tiny crimson characters appear. At one moment they say, *VII:XXXVIII*. At the next, *VII:XXXIX*. The astronomer explains that these numerals signify the hour and the minute, and that in Northern Wei he had the horological artisans of Lo-yang make him an instrument with Roman digits—a feeble thrust at his homesickness. He shows his host that the time-gem takes its power from a coinlike disc, or energon, within the jewel. Augustine finds the Cathayan word for this disc unpronounceable.

"Seven-forty," he declares when new numerals—*VII:XL*—wink into view. "By what criteria do you establish the hour?"

"In Northern Wei, Father Augustine, scientifically. But while traveling, by sun and simple intuition."

Augustine waves his hand, dismissing the entire matter. "Why have you come to me, Master Iatanbaal?" He can see that his guest wants to tender the time-gem as a gift, and he has no desire to accept it, either as token of esteem or as bribe. Death's specter has transported him beyond flattery, beyond manipulation.

"Because in your *Confessions*—a copy of which the former bishop of Alexandria let me see—I found you have an unusual philosophy of time, rivaling in sophistication the theories of our most learned Cathayan astronomers." Iatanbaal refastens his time-gem's strap. "It leads me to suspect that you alone of all Romanized westerners may be able to comprehend the startling cosmogony formulated by our Wei genius Sung Hsi-chien. Comprehend, Father Augustine, and thus appreciate."

"I wrote my *Confessions* a long time ago." Augustine eyes the

131

astronomer warily. What he penned about time in that book was that before God made heaven and earth, neither they nor time itself had any existence. Time did not begin until God spoke the word that inaugurated creation. Before time, there was no time, and what God did then (the conjecture that He was readying Hell for pryers into mysteries being a facetious canard), no mortal human mind may plumb or reckon. Is that so astonishing a theory of time? Is it really profound enough to bring an African astronomer home from the Orient to congratulate him for anticipating the speculations of a Cathayan genius? Augustine can scarcely credit such a motive.

"But, Excellency, you repeat and extend your discussion of time in the eleventh and twelfth books of *The City of God*. I read your latest masterpiece in Alexandria, too, but this time during a brief stop there on my way back from Cathay. In the eleventh book, you write—I've memorized the words—'*the world was made, not in time, but simultaneously with time,*' while in the twelfth you eloquently inveigh against those who hold that history is cyclic and that this world is born but to die and rise again. Sung Hsi-chien has found empirical proof of your positions in his astronomical observations and in certain clever tests of his cosmogonic theories, and this, I think, is a brave coincidence of minds."

"Empirical proof?" Augustine's fever has made him woozy. He sits down at his desk. "Master Iatanbaal, what need of empirical proof has faith predicated on reason?"

"Why, none, I suppose, but Sung Hsi-chien and five generations of Cathayan lens-grinders, astronomers, cosmogonists, and sky-ray readers have nonetheless provided it. I was fortunate enough to help Sung with his researches, Father Augustine, and so possess the understanding to outline these proofs for you."

"I don't require them."

"No, of course you don't. But you of all philosophers should wish to learn them. And so I've come to Hippo Regius to instruct you in Sung Hsi-chien's 'New Cosmogony.'"

"*Febris acuta* grips me. I'm dying, Master Iatanbaal."

"Here, eat." The astronomer pushes Possidius's tray toward the bishop, then hefts his long, leathern bag onto the other end of the desk. From it, he pulls a tube of ivory and silver; an ebony box with a small glass port on its upper face; and two enameled packets that Augustine decides are accesories to the odd little box. How he knows this, he cannot guess. But, sipping thoughtfully at his chickpea marinade, he waits for Master Iatanbaal to unriddle the mysteries of his peculiar equipment.

"A telescope," the astronomer says, lifting the tube and then turning it so that the bishop can see it. "Outside Lung-hsi, in a tower on the Great Wall, the Wei Cathayans have a telescope so much larger than this one, Father Augustine, that it dwarfs the pillars of the Parthenon. An instrument even larger dominates a hill near Lo-yang, and the biggest telescope of all stares heavenward from a dome outside Ching-chao. These far-seers, along with the work of imperial astronomers and scientists, have altered in amazing ways our old notions of the heavens."

Augustine dunks his bread in the piquant marinade. Telescopes larger than temple pillars? he thinks, working his bad teeth. This importunate scoundrel is lying.

"The Wei have also invented a type of colossal telescope that gathers and focuses invisible sky-rays from distant stars. The best is beyond Ku-shih, in the Takla Makan Desert, and Sung and his helpers visit it several times a year in a pterodrac—a mechanical flying dragon—commissioned by the Emperor. I myself have flown in this pterodrac, Father Augustine, but the Wei—a secretive folk—do not generally allow foreigners to do so."

A madman, the bishop thinks. Colossal telescopes and draconoid flying machines. But the most insidious thing about him is that he presents these fantasies as if they were Holy Writ.

Iatanbaal lays the telescope aside and seizes on his ebony box, shifting it so that its tiny eye points directly at Augustine. "A luminotype chamber," he says, fingering a lever on its side. "With this, Father Augustine, one can preserve the image of any object or person as it exists at the very instant that the operator depresses this lever. The Cathayans call such images——" he uses a word even less familiar to Augustine than Greek—"but I say *luminopicts*, or 'light pictures,' and in Northern Wei no aristocratic household is without a gallery of such images in its family shrine."

"Nonsense."

"Excellency?"

"Why do you show me these vanities? Why so cynically regale me with lies?"

Iatanbaal, heretofore the mildest of guests, bristles at this, but lets go a sigh and takes back his composure. "Lies? No lies, Excellency. The opposite. Your entire life has been a quest for truth, and your whole career as an ecclesiastic a battle for truth against pagans and heretics. My prime motive in coming to you—in traveling thousands of leagues; in risking life and limb to defy the Vandal blockade—was to bring you the elegant cosmogonic truths that I have learned in Cathay. To instruct you in them so that you may add them—before you die—to *The City of God*, the most glorious religious philosophy of history ever conceived."

"*Magnum opus et arduum*," Augustine murmurs. Praise has always softened him, and although he may finally be immune to flattery, he cannot always think ill of flatterers. Aloud he says, "That book is finished. I can add nothing to it."

"I speak of *The City of God* in your mind, Father Augustine, not of dry words on paper. This grander *City of God*, the Platonic one that you seek to revise with each new breath and each new discovery. . . Excellency, unless I misjudge you terribly, that magnum opus will never be finished until your soul departs your body."

This approach nearly disarms Augustine. He concludes, however, that Iatanbaal is ingenuously patronizing him and hardens his heart against the man.

"I fear my soul is soon to do that. Please, sir, precede it in departing. I tire."

"By Christ, old man, I've not come all these years and all this distance to have you spurn my message!"

"Away, astronomer."

"God does not will it!"

"Possidius!" Augustine cries. "Possidius, this man is—"

"You don't believe me, do you? Here, then, look!" Iatanbaal opens one of the packets beside his luminotype chamber; he thrusts into the bishop's hands a smooth square of parchment bearing on one side an image of five robed Cathayans.

The Cathayans are rendered monochromatically, in palpable light and shadow, their faces both alien and distinct, their garments as brilliantly limned as silk at noonday. Augustine slides his thumb across the surface of this provocative square.

"A luminopict," Iatanbaal says. "The older man, at center, is Sung Hsi-chien. The rest are students—gifted disciples."

"A clever painting under an equally clever glaze."

"This is no hand-drawn artifact!" Iatanbaal barks. "This is a luminopictic image from life, caught on a light-sensitive substance by the rapid opening and closing of this mechanical eye!"

"Do you destroy the box to remove the image? And must you make a second box to catch a second image?"

"You mock me, Father Augustine, and I—"

Possidius enters the bedchamber, his eyes widening at the sight of Iatanbaal's equipment. Augustine signals his weariness to his fellow bishop by nodding. Possidius, a wraith in black, approaches the astronomer and drops a hand on his shoulder.

"It's time for you to go."

The violence with which Iatanbaal shrugs aside Possidius's hand alarms Augustine. "Even the prodigal son received a warmer welcome than the one you hypocrites have tendered me!" Tears of resentment and frustration squeeze glistening from his lower lids.

"The basilica of Hippo Regius has a hostel for visitors," says

Possidius. "Many now dwelling in it are refugees from other parts of Numidia, but you, too, may find a bed there. This defamation of our hospitality is unwarranted."

"Your flea-ridden hostel be damned!"

"Sir," says Possidius. "Sir, you try our—"

"I have no intention of deserting Father Augustine—not until death itself abstracts him from history!"

The old bishop, stunned by the presumption of the astronomer's promise, pounds his fist on the writing desk. "And what gives you the right to impose yourself on a dying man in this unconscionable way?"

"One thing only: I'm your son, old man, I'm your son."

The fever in Augustine makes his head feel like the inflating hood of a cobra. He can think of nothing to say.

"Once, Father, you wrote of me, praising my virtues but taking no credit for them, 'I had no part in that boy, but the sin.' More recently, supposing me dead and quoting Cicero, you declared, 'You are the only man of all men whom I would wish to surpass me in all things.' A most poignant declaration."

"But you *are* dead," the bishop manages, woozier than ever with both brain heat and the fever of incomprehension.

"Iatanbaal means 'given of God,' Father. Adeodatus does, too, and my name—my true name—is Adeodatus."

iii.

Augustine remembers Carthage. There he acquired a concubine, a lovely woman not of his class; and the happiest issue of that union was the boy whom they named Adeodatus, 'given of God.' In those days—Christ be merciful—he was a Manichee, a dualist proclaiming his belief in two contending gods, one benevolent and caring, one so malign and cruel that you could fix on it every sort of calamity plaguing the world. That was nearly sixty years ago, and recently a letter from Paulinus, bishop of Nola, has accused

Augustine (but facetiously, of course) of championing dualism again:

"What, after all, is *The City of God* but a manifesto dividing Creation into two camps? It seems, Aurelius Augustinius, that you will never completely elude the ghosts of your wayward past."

One such ghost has just popped up. Adeodatus, the boy whom he thought had died with the noble Nebridius in the undertow off the beach at Ostia, has entered his life again. He has done so only days before an enfeebling fever will—how did "Iatanbaal" phrase it?—oh, yes, *abstract him from history*. Forever, presumably. A father-and-son reunion that renders mundane even the parable of the prodigal son in the Gospels.

How did Adeodatus survive those currents? And did Nebridius, Augustine's dearest companion after Alypius, also manage to thrash clear of them?

A single oil-burning lamp hisses in the bedchamber. Possidius has retreated to his own room. Genseric's soldiers shout obscene challenges along the walls on the inland side of the city. Their shouts clash, echo, fade, resurge.

Augustine's son—a "boy" of sixty—sits cross-legged on the floor, recounting in a monotone the story of his and Nebridius's adventure off the Italian coast. Adeodatus had been sixteen and his father's friend thirty-five.

"Nebridius, Father, had no adventure. Promptly dragged under, he must have drowned. I, on the other hand, was whipped out to sea and sent bobbing into open water. Prayer kept me afloat. Libyan pirates picked me up somewhere west of Naples. For the next nine years, I was a helpless witness to their raids around Sicily and the coastal towns of Mauretania and Egypt. Finally, I escaped into the arms of some Greek mariners when my captors trusted me to carry out a certain theft unsupervised, and it was these kind Greeks who transported me to Alexandria. . . ."

Heavy-lidded and hot, Augustine listens to Adeodatus with half his attention. The details of this tale are not important; vitally important, however, is the fact that after venturing to Cathay from Alexandria and living there for thirty years, his son has returned to Numidia. He has come back to keep filial vigil at his deathbed and to bring him . . . well, the Truth.

Adeodatus's voice ceases. The old man feels his son's dry lips kissing his forehead; his own papery eyelids flutter open.

"Go ahead and sleep, Father. In the morning, your fever will have eased, and you'll have no trouble following all the miraculous things I intend to tell you."

"Adeodatus—"

"Sleep, Father. I'll stay with you as long as it takes. As long as you yet have life."

Augustine remembers Carthage. He dreams of that city. There he met his son's low-born mother, and there he deceived the blessed Monica, his own mother, by secretly boarding a ship to Italy while she supposed he was waiting for a fairer wind to depart. City of pagan shrines, rowdy "scholars," vain theatrics, and vulgar circus entertainments. In his dream—his fevered memory—Carthage rises full-blown again, raucous with trade and pageantry. He sees it as it was sixty years ago, four decades before the electric globes of Seneca the Illuminator set its streets and windows ablaze even at profoundest midnight. His memory, translated into dream, quickens for the old man every emotion—the four great perturbations of the mind—that he experienced as a questing youth in Carthage.

Desire, joy, fear, and sorrow.

I knew them all there, reflects the slumbering Augustine. And I know them all again every time I reenvision that city.

God, too, the bishop discovers and rediscovers in either memory or dream, searching inwardly for the One Thing that will fill the empty places created by his own temporary forgetfulness. That One Thing is God. If he sometimes forgets God, he can find Him again in memory, a fact that seems to Augustine a rational proof of His existence. For you cannot remember what you have wholly forgotten, but God—happiness—always resides within;

and when you trip over That Which refurnishes the emptiness, you say to yourself, "This is it," and you know that the processes of your own mind have led you ineluctably back to God.

As memory can resurrect Carthage as it was half a century ago, reasons Augustine in his fitful sleep, so can it reacquaint me with the Deity as He has ever and always been. . . .

Adeodatus has made a pallet for himself in the bedchamber. He is using his doubled-up telescope bag for a pillow.

The cries of the barbarian heretics beyond Hippo's walls—Arian Christians who deny that Father and Son share the same substance—buzz in Augustine's head like evil flies, troubling his hot slumber nearly as much as his memory has. He moans; and his son, somewhere in the dizzy darkness, touches a wet cloth to his brow.

And another thing, Augustine thinks: As my memory holds every unforgotten moment of my life, God contains every possible reality, but without possessing either a past or a future. Everything that has ever happened, is happening now, or will happen tomorrow abides in His all-seeing eye. He foreknew—knows, I mean—that Adeodatus would return to me as I lay on death's threshold, and He has always known exactly what he will say to me tomorrow when he indoctrinates me into the riddle of Sung Hsi-chien's "New Cosmogony."

Dear God, my God, what an unpredictable dramaturge.

iv.

Morning. Augustine's fever has broken. He offers a prayer of thanksgiving for himself and several prayers of deliverance for the people of Hippo Regius. Then he and Adeodatus eat the pears that Possidius brought to him last night.

"The universe is far vaster than any Greek or Roman astronomer has ever told us," Adeodatus says.

The old bishop stays silent. It would not surprise him if the universe were *infinite* in size. Tautologically, the omnipotence of the Creator has no limits.

"And far older. And far more strange than even Ptolemy himself supposed."

Augustine has read—albeit some time ago—Claudius Ptolemaeus's great book on astronomy. Once, in Milan, he even sat down over a Latin translation of a star catalogue compiled by Hipparchus, much of whose original work in Greek Ptolemy summarized and supplemented in his own book.

But Adeodatus has already begun to lesson him:

"First, the Earth circles the Sun, just as Aristarchus of Samos posited. Second, beyond Saturn are three planets that no Western observer has ever beheld. Third, there is a force that I can best call 'attractiveness' that governs the movements of both planetary bodies and stars. Fourth, the Sun is but an unprepossessing minnow of a star in an enormous school of stars that the Cathayans call the Silver Whirlpool. Fifth, as many of these 'schools' of stars swim through the universe as do solitary stars in our local Silver Whirlpool. The Cathayans have their own picturesque word for these enormous stellar families, but let me simply call them *lactastrons*, for they resemble whirlpools of curdled milk. Sixth, light travels at a speed—accurately determined a century ago by an Eastern Chin astronomer named Wang Mi—that is a universal constant. Seventh, this speed, altogether peculiarly, does not increase if you add any other velocity to it. Eighth—"

Just as I first supposed, Augustine thinks. My visitor—my *son*—is a madman. Flesh of my flesh, a lunatic.

Aloud he protests, "How can you add something to something else without making it larger?"

Adeodatus looks perplexed. "I don't know. However, Wang Mi conclusively determined that nothing exceeds the speed of light, and from this discovery there later sprang Sung Hsi-chien's . . . well, I can only translate these astonishing mental constructs as his 'Postulatum of Temporal Comparativity' and his 'Postulatum of Attractive Comparativity.' From them, Father, Sung and his most creative students were able to go on to the formulation of a 'New Cosmogony,' and it is *that* awesome truth—with its implications for faith and eschatology—into which I want to initiate you."

"Add one to ten," Augustine growls. "It sums to eleven. You cannot add something to something else without making it greater than before."

Adeodatus puts a hand on his father's forearm. "Add Christ to God, Father. Have you made the Almighty greater than He was before your 'addition'?"

This argument stymies the old man. "No" is clearly the only orthodox answer. To say "Yes" would be to fall into a heresy akin to Arianism, the chief spiritual error of the barbarian besiegers outside Hippo's walls.

Adeodatus proceeds with his lecture. He talks of lactastrons—milky clans of stars—thousands of *annilumes* away. He points out that the Cathayans have so finely honed the technologies of lens- and mirror-making that they are now able to see the microworlds at their fingertips as profitably as they can the universe annilumes beyond our own whirl of planets. Furthermore, they have discovered the fundamental units of matter—*atoms*, to follow Democritus—and arranged the various earthly elements on a graph now employed as an important pedagogic tool in their science academies. Yet another device—Adeodatus, with a Greek twist, translates it *chromoscope*—enables Cathayan astronomers to deduce the physical composition of celestial bodies and so to classify them. What they know about the creation of the Heavens and the Earth beggars the imagination; not even the poetry of Genesis is grand enough to hymn the boldness of their discoveries.

"You're insane," Augustine declares. "Only a madman would try to turn me to such ridiculous views. These outlandish lies reveal your contempt for me; they blaspheme the Creator."

"Father Augustine, I'm not asking you to deny God or to betray

Christ. Once, the tenets of Catholicism struck you as ridiculous. Don't you remember? You were a Manichee who dismissed the faith of my grandmother Monica as beneath the consideration of an educated man. Yet today, enmired in a self-spun orthodoxy, do you spurn the body of knowledge I bring to you from Cathay because it seems—at first—contrary to your current philosophies and prejudices? When, Father, did your mind petrify? And don't you understand that not one item in my catalogue of wonders sabotages your beliefs at any *essential* level?"

Where does this graybeard boy get the audacity to prate of the petrification of my mind? Augustine asks himself. Why, from me, of course. He inherited it.

Later that day, three men try to pay Augustine their respects— among them Possidius, who brings the prandium, his midday meal of cheese, fruit, and wine; Eraclius, the priest who succeeded the old man in the pulpit of the basilica; and Vindicianus, a physician who wants to apply a preparation of grape hulls and olive oil to Augustine's forehead.

Following his father's wishes, Adeodatus allows the prandium to enter, but not the man who brought it. He likewise turns away the priest ("The cricket chirps," says Eraclius, "the swan is silent") and Vindicianus ("This porridge will draw the harmful caloric from his brain"), who announces on leaving that Augustine probably won't live to regret declining his poultice.

The bishop eats another pear—forbidden fruit, it seems to him, and therefore gloriously sweet—while his son takes the cheese and most of the watered wine. As they eat, Adeodatus continues his recitation:

In addition to planets, stars, nebular bodies, and lactastrons of all shapes, sizes, and degrees of energy production, the cosmos contains such perplexing phenomena as *invisible abysses* (dying stars whose own terrible *attractiveness* has led them to collapse into colossal stellar deadfalls) and *quasistrons* ("almost-stars" that a Northern Wei observer, Hong-yi Chiu, detected twenty-five years ago with the sky-ray-gathering telescopes in the Takla Makan Desert). These latter phenomena, Adeodatus tells Augustine, appear to be the most distant objects in all the created universe. That they should even be detectable suggests that they are pouring into the void more candle power and invisible ray emissions than all the suns in the entire Silver Whirlpool. Perhaps each quasistron is a battlefield in the war between the fallen angels in Lucifer's camp and the seraphic host still loyal to God.

"Those battles occurred near time's nativity," says Augustine. "Even if they continue today in every human breast, they commenced long before God made Adam."

"Exactly. The light from quasistrons has been en route to us from five to ten billion years; we are peering not only to the far periphery of the universe but also to its temporal infancy. We are retro-observing the pangs of Creation."

Augustine's temples throb. He cannot say if he is exhilarated or demoralized by this news. Or even whether he believes it.

"Undoubtedly, most of the quasistrons Hong-yi Chiu has found and indexed don't even exist anymore." Adeodatus shows his father the luminopict again. "Look. This is Hong-yi. This stout, youthful fellow standing next to Sung. It was in his household that I lived for the last six years of my sojourn in Cathay. He believes that quasistrons—the term *almost-stars* was his coinage, and even Sung came to approve it—are the hearts of forming lactastrons and that quasistrons derive their power from invisible abysses—*attraction pits*—devouring all the down-whirling interstellar matter around them. If angelic war preceded the birth of lactastrons, Father, it was a war of unholy violence. But, at least on the macrocosmic level, it has been over for billions of years."

"More mendaciousness," Augustine counters. "Reckoning by our sacred scriptures, we know that not six thousand years have passed since Creation." But the authority with which Adeodatus states his case—an authority akin to Jesus's whenever he chose to speak—has sabotaged the old man's certitude.

"The scriptures are often metaphorical, Father, and Sung's New Cosmogony has invalidated their chronology."

Augustine refrains from citing the prodigal for blasphemy; he's done that once already. "You've been tiptoeing around this Sung's cosmogony all day, Adeodatus. Out with it."

The graybeard boy seems relieved. He begins talking of sky-ray transmission, the ongoing sibilance of the void, and a scientific law whose discovery he attributes to Hong-yi Chiu's father, Hong-yi Pang, who phrased it like this: "All lactastrons but the nearest are fleeing from our Silver Whirlpool at velocities in harmony with their distances."

The "Formula of Hong-yi Pang" as Adeodatus terms it, implies that every lactastron in the cosmos had its beginning in a compact central locale. Time and matter alike were frozen together in a lump in this primeval place. Presumably, upon God's command, they exploded like a many-vented volcano, flinging the ingredients of Creation out into the virgin dark.

But it was old Sung Hsi-chien who formed this idea from his own theories of comparativity, the observations of four genera-tions of Cathayan stargazers, the hypotheses of a forward-looking school of microtheoreticians, and the lactastron law of the elder Hong-yi. Sung called his simple but startling explanation of the origin of the cosmos the "Earliest Eruption Postulatum."

Adeodatus, Augustine senses, places more faith in Sung's theory than in the opening verses of Genesis. Oddly, however, his son's enthusiasm for the Cathayan's cosmogony excites him, too. Excites and frightens.

He gropes for a response: "Billions of leagues, billions of years. Adeodatus, you play among these enormous figures like a boy stirring a stick in an anthill. How did Hong-yi Chiu, this friend of yours, arrive at the absurd conclusion that his 'almost-stars'— his *quasistrons*—are so preposterously far away?" The bishop has real-ized that the vast streches of time in Sung's cosmogony depend for their validity—granting the accuracy of Wang Mi's calculation of the speed of light—on the accuracy of Cathayan assessments of interstellar distances; and so he seeks, half-heartedly perhaps, to attack the postulatum at this point.

A strategy that fails to disconcert his son. Adeodatus speaks of measuring the distance to stars by noting their differences in observed direction when viewed at different times in the Earth's orbit about the Sun. Again translating from the Cathayan, he calls this difference the *transprox* of the star. He goes on to talk of the *chromolume patterns* of heavenly bodies and of how those of his friend Chiu's quasistrons disclose a *sanguineous conversion* typical of celestial bodies receding at high speeds. The evidence for the existence of great distances and of vast stretches of time in the constitution of the universe, he implies, is overwhelming; only an illiterate reversionary would question it.

"Now when I set out for home from Ku-shih, Father," Adeodatus concedes, "a dispute was raging between my friend Chiu and another of Sung's disciples, An Hopeh, about the *meaning* of the sanguineous conversions shown by Chiu's quasistrons. Did the lengthening—the reddening—of the light rays from these almost-stars result from their rapid recession from us or from curious attractional effects that would permit us to think them much nearer our own lactastron, possibily even within it?

"This was an important dispute. If the reddening derived from recession, it would confirm Sung's Earliest Eruption Postulatum. The universe is ever inflating. If, on the other hand, it results from a discordant attractiveness in Chiu's quasistrons, the enemies of Sung's postulatum—those who believe that something other than a primeval eruption began the universe—could rightfully take heart. Further, they wouldn't have to explain from where the quasistrons gather all the 'fuel' to burn so brightly for so long. Because the almost-stars would be *nearer* than Chiu believes, they wouldn't be as perplexingly bright as he has always claimed.

"In any event, Father, An Hopeh had many allies, astronomers jealous of old Sung or simply unhappy with the notion of a universe

145

forever expanding. Not long before I left, however, the dispute seemed to be resolving itself in Hong-yi Chiu's favor. Two of his pupils at the Lo-yang Academy of Sky Studies found some quasistrons surrounded by a faint, glowing pilosity. A luminous hairiness. It had the precise look of very distant lactastrons, and chromoscopic surveys of the light from this pilosity show it to exhibit the same sanguineous conversion—reddening—as the almost-stars embedded in it. This seems to prove that Chiu's quasistrons are truly billions of annilumes away and that Sung is right in crediting the origin of the universe to its Earliest Eruption."

"Enough of this," Augustine murmurs, clutching his head in his gnarled hands. "Please, Adeodatus, no more today."

"Forgive me, Father. I've spoken in such detail only because I wanted you to see that your theory of time coincides with Sung's. So does your belief in the linearity of history. You reject the Greek notion of cycles; so do Sung and his disciples, who believe the universe will die of cold, a plethora of icy, black lactastrons wobbling out into the darkness forever."

"That *isn't* what I believe!" Augustine rages. "We'll have our end not in ice, but in judgment and transformation!"

"You speak of the soul, Father, but I of the palpable world all around us. And, I tell you, Sung Hsi-chien has found insufficient attractive force among the lactastrons to halt the expansion of the universe and draw all matter back into a lump that may eventually explode, to begin this cosmic vanity anew. *His* position coincides with *yours*—a rejection of the periodic rebirth of our world. In that, you're kindred thinkers."

"We're brothers only in our shared humanity!" Augustine says. "What religion does he have?"

Adeodatus is clearly stumped for an answer. After a moment, he replies, "I'm not sure. His work, perhaps."

"I've listened to you for as long as I can, Master Iatanbaal. Harangue me no more. Have mercy upon me and go."

The astronomer—his son—reluctantly obeys, and Augustine

notes with wary surprise that darkness has fallen and that he himself is chill-ridden as well as feverish. Genseric's soldiers rattle their weaponry outside the city gates, and both the Roman Empire and the bishop's care-worn body seem destined for the charnel heap
. . . .

v.

An uproar in the corridor. Possidius is arguing with somebody who speaks Latin with a peculiar accent. Augustine, his intellect a scatter of crimson coals, sits up to see a tall black man pushing into his bedchamber past the flustered Possidius. The black man wears only a soiled tunic and sandals. Over his shoulder, a large, woven bag as filthy as his tunic.

"You can't do this! The bishop is gravely ill!"

"I had a dream," the black man keeps saying, sidestepping the frantic Possidius easily. "My dream told me to come see Bishop Augustine."

Augustine gathers the coals of his mind into a single glowing pile and looks at the Ethiop. This business of the dream touches him: he has never been able to dismiss the requests of those who have dreamed that he could help them. Indeed, Monica, his mother, envisioned his own salvation in a dream, and only a few days ago he laid hands on a sick old man who dreamed that Augustine's doing so would unquestionably heal him.

"Let him stay, Possidius."

The black man bows his head respectfully and says, "My name, Excellency, is Khoinata. Thank you."

"Where's my son?" Augustine asks Possidius.

"In the hostel, Excellency. He has assured me that he won't intrude on you again without your direct summons."

"A policy that I urge you, too, to adopt, Possidius. Leave me alone with this man."

As soon as Possidius, visibly wounded, has left, Augustine asks the Ethiop what distance he has traveled and why he thinks that the bishop of Hippo can help him. Like Adeodatus, Khoinata has

147

sneaked through Vandal lines to enter the city, and he has come all the way from farthest Kush, a great African kingdom, for the privilege of this interview. He believes that what he has brought with him will prove to the imperious Romans that the Kushites are a people with an admirable history and a civilization deserving of the prose of a Tacitus or a Suetonius.

"What do you have?" Augustine asks him.

Instantly, Khoinata gets down on all fours, opens his bag, and begins assembling with impressive dexterity and speed the skeleton of a creature that seems—to Augustine's untutored eye—a troubling conflation of human being and ape.

"My brothers and I found these bones far south of Meroe. They belong to an early kind of man, a kind almost certainly ancestral to you and me. Notice: the curve of these foot bones—the way they fit with these other bones from the lower legs—*that* shows that the creature walked erect. And the skull—look here, Excellency—its skull is larger than those of apes and yet not quite so large as an adult Roman's. One of our wisest chieftains, Khoboshama, shaped a theory to explain such strangeness. He calls it the 'Unfolding of Animal Types,' and I believe it should greatly interest teachers of natural history from Carthage to Milan."

Augustine merely stares at Khoinata.

Khoinata says, "We know these bones are old—very, very old—because Khoboshama counted the rock layers in the declivity where we found them. In addition, he . . . "

Augustine spreads out the coals of his mind. He cannot keep them burning under Khoinata's discourse. He both sees and does not see the skeleton that his guest has arranged like elongate coals on the floor of his bedchamber. The creature has been dead for almost two million years—yes, that's the unlikely figure that his visitor cites—but it lives in Khoinata's imagination, and Augustine has no idea how to drive it from thence.

"Excellency, are you listening?"

"No," the bishop replies.

"But, Excellency, only you of all Romanized westerners are wise enough to grasp the far-ranging implications of . . . "

The old man feels a foreign excrescence on his arm. He glances down and finds that Adeodatus has strapped his Cathayan time-gem to his wrist.

Ignoring the Kushite, he depresses the stem on the side of its obsidian jewel. Suddenly, these characters manifest on the black face of the tiny engine: *XII:I.*

The hour is one minute past midnight.

Something old is ending. Something new is beginning.

Allegra's Hand

Allegra Jamison came to Vista Grove Elementary in early November of my second year as a counselor. At once, she drew bemused or outraged notice for flaunting on her left hand an elbow-length glove of soft, well-worn, cream-colored linen. In no other way did she initially seem remarkable. She struck Beth Peaden, her teacher, as one more pale carp in our mostly Anglo, quasi-rural fishpond.

Except for that glove.

Me, I met Allegra on a hectic Tuesday. Each class has two "ambassadors," heads-up kids who accompany new arrivals around and introduce them to key staff: the principal, Mr. Buchanan; the librarian, Ms. Faris; the music teacher, Ms. Springer; the lunchroom manager, Mrs. Judah; the custodian, Mr. Vicic. As school counselor, I qualify as key. In fact, I brought the ambassador program to Vista Grove three years ago as a gung-ho middle-aged intern. Anyway, Ambassadors Kip Hunt and Hannah Treece es-

corted Allegra to my office before lunch and stood in the hall as I
signed the counselor coupon in her get-acquainted book and gave
her a cartoon sticker for her three-ring binder. Allegra murmured,
"Thanks," and turned to go, hugely affectless for a newcomer.

"Where did you move here from?" I said hurriedly.

"Nother state." Piping soprano; rising inflection.

"Of course. Which one?"

"Sorrow n transience. Dad sez."

That floored me. Fifth graders don't talk like that, even if they
have self-protective instincts keen enough to attribute such off-the-
wall poetry to a parent.

"Ah," I said, hoping to recover with a joke: "Alabama?"

"Yessum. Tescumbia."

What could I say? I knew zilch about Tescumbia. "That's a
handsome . . . a pretty glove."

"Yessum."

"And quite a fashion statement, wearing only one." .

Hannah Treece stuck her head in the door. "One glove, Mrs.
Hewitt. We think she thinks she's a rock star."

"I am, without even singing, my dad sez. If I really was, though,
I'd sew sequins on it."

"Did you lose the other one?" I shooed Hannah back out.

"Nome. It's on purpose, the one alone. Necessary too."

Necessary. Why? Did she have a skin disorder, fungus on her
fingernails, a second-degree burn, a tattoo that a family cultist had
needled into her as a baby? O the questions I wanted to ask. But
why-what-who-where-and-when constructions breed defensive-
ness, suspicion, guilt. A counselor, as much as possible, should
couch all grubby, buttinsky inquiries in the form of friendly
imperatives. For example: *Tell me about your family, kid.*

With my professional scruples on alert and Hannah and Kip
fidgeting outside, I couldn't ask what I wanted to ask, namely, *Why?
Why is your glove necessary?*

Allegra, meanwhile, slipped into the hall.

Gone and soon forgotten. As that comic-strip kid Calvin says, The Days Are Just Packed. I had no time to eat in the lunchroom. Some peanut-butter crackers, peach yogurt, and a stale Caramello would fuel me. After that, an afternoon jammed to the rafters with guidance lessons, small groups, and teacher referrals, several of EXTREME urgency. A new fifth-grade filly with one silly glove just didn't weigh that heavily. I had to teach peacemaking skills to the toughs in a schoolbus shoving match, counsel the niece of a shotgun-murder victim, deal with a Munchausen-by-proxy mother who'd fabricated a case of bang-up asthma for her seven-year-old daughter (as a way to manipulate both her kid and the school system), and write up three cases of abuse and/or neglect for the Department of Family & Children Services, known to everybody hereabouts as DFACS.

"All I want is DFACS, ma'am," agency social worker Epifanio Sudar likes to joke. "Jes gimme DFACS."

So when Allegra Jamison ambled off with Kip and Hannah, she ambled off into the sanity-saving realm of Out of Sight, Out of Mind.

Maybe I saw Allegra in the halls later that week. Maybe I didn't. She returned stage-center shortly after, though, when Beth Peaden referred her with this message:

"Allegra Jamison has a big vocabulary, but few social skills or friends. The glove she wears—she won't talk about it—has prompted mild teasing. Allegra responds with hot looks which only prompt more verbal abuse. Despite daily wear, her glove always looks clean. Either she has extras or she washes it every night. Please talk with her about making friends so she can avoid teasing."

I went down to Mr. Buchanan's office and caught him making a face over a cup of microwaved coffee. "Don't we have a dress code?" I asked.

"Is that a rhetorical question?" Mr. Buchanan resembles a

tubercular Sumo wrestler. When he makes a face, his bottom lip unrolls like a mugging chimpanzee's.

"Not exactly."

"Then don't worry. You look fine."

I said that our dress code (the only rules we usually have to enforce center on cleanliness and proper fit) *might* help us solve our problem with Allegra Jamison. It prohibited gloves, didn't it? Mr. Buchanan picked up and paged through the manual that we send home with every kid at the start of every school year.

"No mention of gloves," he said. "Guess they're okay."

"How can a child write or draw or use a pair of scissors if she's wearing gloves?"

"Allegra just wears one, a left one, and because she's a righty, well . . ." He plopped the manual down. "What's the issue here?"

"Beth—Mrs. Peaden—says it gets her teased."

"Teasing, as objectionable it sometimes seems, can correct beaucoups of odd behavior or dress."

"I don't think it will in Allegra's case."

"Why? Have you talked to the girl?"

"Not yet. But Mrs. Peaden's referral and my own first-day impression—I don't know, it's just that she wears that glove kind of defiantly."

"So she's got balls." Mr. Buchanan ducked his head, peeked up mock-apologetically. *"Mea culpa. Mea maxima culpa."*

"Couldn't you say the dress code prohibits it as a safety measure? A glove like hers—I'd only wear one that long with an evening gown—could catch in a file drawer or under a window sash. It could—"

"So could a sleeve. Should we all go sleeveless? Or, to please the super-safety-conscious among us, nude?" No grin this time; an amused twinkle, only.

"Okay, okay."

"Do your job. You're looking for a mechanical solution. Do your job."

Mr. Buchanan had nailed it: I wanted a decree from on high to sweep Allegra from my IN tray. Why? Because my IN tray was already brim-full. Because Allegra and her kooky glove nagged from a distance at my already dubious peace of mind.

So I cleared the decks—sort of—and summoned the little fashion rebel in. Twò, maybe three, days after Beth Peaden's referral, she entered wearing a threadbare rusty-black smock over a rumpled inky-black dress, thin-soled Kmart tennis shoes, and her ever-present glove. She sat, and I left my desk to undercut the authority-figure intimidation factor. Drumming the fingers of her right hand on her desk's writing palette, Allegra looked sidelong into the *How Do You Feel?* mirror on my rear wall.

"Tell me about your week."

She shrugged.

"I hear it hasn't been all that good. Your classmates give you grief."

"They're geeks. Troublemaking geeks."

"Maybe they don't mean to be."

"Yeah. Like they're remote-controlled or somethin." Such rapid-fire sarcasm!

"I don't think they're remote-controlled, Allegra. They're reacting to *something* outside themselves. Any idea what?"

"Me. I drive em Bonkersville."

"Tell me how you drive them Bonkersville."

Allegra raised her gloved hand, her forearm parallel to the floor at shoulder height. (Progress.) I sat down in a plastic chair that immediately equalized our gazes.

"The day we met you said your glove was necessary. I don't understand. Would you please explain?"

A sneery shrug. "What's to explain? It covers."

"Of course. Your hand. Your forearm."

"Yessum."

"Tell me about the need to cover those parts of yourself."

155

"Adam n Eve wore figs."

"Fig leaves, actually."

" 'Actually'? It's none of it actual. It's all just book stuff. Lies, even."

"Whether fact or lies, Adam and Eve were concealing very private parts of themselves. Your hand, your forearm—they're different, Allegra. More . . . public."

"Mine aren't. They're private. They're mine."

"Of course. I don't mean to imply otherwise. It's just that hands seldom provoke us to shame. Many people take pride in their hands."

"N some do in their privates. Me, *I'm* not ashamed of no part, specially not this hand."

Whoa. I felt like a member of the affirmative team debating the proposition *Resolved: Counselors Make Helpful Friends.* And losing spectacularly. I groped for balance:

"So you wear a glove to insure the privacy of your hand."

Sullenly: "Yessum."

"And that's the only reason."

"No. If I took it off, Mrs. Peaden's army of geeks'd leap on me hardern a jay on a junebug."

" 'Army of geeks'? Allegra, do you think name-calling helps or hinders the friend-making process?"

"Who wants geeks for friends?"

"Geek is a label, Allegra."

"So?"

"A label says nothing meaningful about who your classmates really are." Uh-oh. I'd shifted against my will and training into blah-blah lecture mode.

"Cep how I feel about em."

My jaw began to descend; I stopped it. Touché, I thought. Leaning back, I regarded Allegra as her classmates sometimes must, as a being dropped among them from the planet Monstra.

"Cun I go?" she asked. "Mrs. Peaden's startin math."

Some children have no verbal skills. To draw them out, you have them draw: stick-figure portraits of their families, boxy diagrams of their homes. Allegra had terrific verbal skills, which she used to hedge herself about or to bludgeon would-be intruders. But our first formal interview had come to an end. I didn't know where else to take it, or how to redeem any part from the morass into which I'd let it sink, or what to make of her piecemeal revelations so far.

"Skedaddle then," I told her. "Nobody in this office is a prisoner." (Not even me.)

After school, I drove to a "local" bar—forty miles away— and had two ice-cold bottles of Mexican beer. Hubie, who died during my practicum at St. Elmo's, would have glowed (I think) with flabbergasted approval.

A week later, at lunch, Beth Peaden came by and found me abstractedly downing spoonfuls of blueberry yogurt and poring over a fresh stack of referrals.

"Oh, hi," I said. "Caught me." I wiped my mouth.

"Hoped I would." Beth has trim good looks, a mind like a top-notch tax accountant's, and more empathy for her kids than is strictly healthy.

"Sorry I couldn't help with the Jamison girl."

"Juanita, you helped a lot. As soon as she got back from your office, the difference was . . . huge. She didn't throw eye-daggers at the worst teases, or cut them up verbally, or even try to tattle. Hallelujah."

"You're kidding."

"No. I came to thank you. Thanks."

"Wow."

"Some teasing persists, from Rob Pino and Eddie Staley, but she handles it better. She's even got a girlfriend or two. If anything, I'd like you to talk with Rob and Eddie."

"Sure. That's what I'm here for." As Beth turned to go, I said, "She still wearing that glove?"

"Does Tarzan wear a loin cloth?"

But keeping a secret and flaunting that resolve tend to eat away at beehive institutions like schools. Everyone wanted to know what Allegra's glove concealed. Disease? Injury? Poison ivy pustules? Demagogic Magic Marker slogans? Body art of an erotic or a primitive stamp? And I was as curious as the next obnoxious Vista Grovite.

Unless, maybe, that person's name was Eddie Staley.

Right before our Thanksgiving break, with two teachers and nearly twenty students out with the flu, Mr. Buchanan assigned me to recess playground duty. I checked out soccer balls and bolo paddles, pushed swings, refereed impromptu races, soothed hurt feelings, and ruminated bitterly on the time I could have spent in my office, doing my real job.

I emerged from one such reverie to see Eddie Staley, over by the teeter-totters, his face in Allegra Jamison's, jawing like a pint-sized TV pitchman and side-stepping repeatedly to keep her from escaping. She almost broke free anyway, but Eddie grabbed her collar, yanked her back, and twisted as hard as he could at her gauntlet's linen cuff. Allegra kneed Eddie in the groin—a Jamie Lee Curtis movie maneuver—then clubbed him in the gut with her gloved forearm.

"*Ooof!*" went Eddie. "*Ooooooooow!*" He sank to his knees, one hand on his breadbasket, one at the crotch of his so-fly stonewashed button-flies.

I interceded, catching Allegra by the arm—the right one—and laying a hand on the gasp-racked Eddie's shoulder. "Hands to yourself, Eddie. I saw it all. I don't condone Allegra's retaliation, but you . . . you pretty much got what you asked for."

"Lidl snivel bastid," Allegra said.

I hushed her. Sent her to a more or less neutral corner. Pulled

Eddie to his feet and made him face me. He struggled to stop gasping, to compose himself.

Red-eyed, he said, "I uz jes tryin to make her . . . you know, take off . . . thet dorky glove."

"Suppose I tried to make you take off your dorky jeans?"

Wide-eyed outrage. Or terror. "Unh-unh. No way."

"Exactly. And you've no business trying to disrobe Allegra or anybody else. Got it?"

"Yessum."

"Walk over there and tell her you're sorry."

"She *hit* me."

"I saw."

"Lookit my stummick." He pulled out his shirt, exposed his rounded belly. A diagonally slashing welt had already begun to show crimson above his navel. "Felt like she had a bar in thet glove. A tire iron."

Only he said *tar arn*, and his mouth did a sniveling orbital wobble.

"I doubt that. You'll be okay. Just tuck your shirt back in. The bell's about to ring."

He obeyed me. He didn't apologize to Allegra, though, and I didn't force him to.

Once recess had ended and I sat at my familiar, work-laden desk again, I thought about the welt on Eddie's stomach. Had a kid come to school with such an injury, and had questioning revealed its origins in a domestic dispute, regulations would have compelled me to notify DFACS.

Nicole Staley, Eddie's mother, strode in and stood rigidly at my desk—with no invitation, greeting, smile, or hint of self-consciousness. I stood, said my name, and tried to shake her hand.

"I awready know you. We met at Open House."

"Please sit down." I lowered my hand.

"No thanks. I'll speak to the point and ast you to do the same."

"The point being?"

"Thet glove girl in Mrs. Peaden's class. She hit Eddie."

"An unhappy response to some deplorable goading."

"He says you said you'd take off his pants for it."

The evening before, despite my workload and weariness, I'd made notes on the incident. I read them to Nicole Staley, who listened with persimmon-sucking distaste.

"It's still thet Jamison biddy's fawt."

"How so?"

"Thet glove. It's got to come off. It's a distraction, like fanny holes in kids' jeans or mini-dresses on our priddy baby girls." (*Gulls,* she said.)

"It's just Allegra, Mrs. Staley. It's . . . I don't know, it's just who she is."

"Anybody ever seen her thout it?"

"Not that I'm aware of."

"I think it's a health hazard. A disguise. I think it's hiding"—imaginary trumpet fanfare—"*leprosy*. You know, thet ol Bible disease."

"I disagree. It's even possible that she wears the glove as a religious statement, Mrs. Staley. I don't have the power, or the right, to make her remove it just because it overexcites other people's imaginations."

Mrs. Staley took a photograph from her purse. A Polaroid. She handed it to me. In it, Eddie stood stripped to the waist before a paneled wall, the welt on his stomach throbbingly red, an uncertain half-smirk on his lips.

"After Thanksgiving, we've got a school-board meetin. I might show em this pichur. I might say you thettened to pull down Eddie's jeans."

I returned the Polaroid. "You're within your rights to do just that." An admission that stymied further bluster.

Mrs. Staley put Eddie back into her purse and retreated—

excuse my un-P.C. hyperbole—to whatever cockroachy dustbin had hatched her.

That night I telephoned the number that Allegra had given the school as an emergency contact. I asked for Creel Jamison, her father. "Hold on," an elderly male voice said. "He's my neighbor. Lemme see if he's to-home."

The receiver clunked down hard. I was on countertop hold, listening to tinny sitcom dialogue, a house dog's intermittent yapping, and, about five minutes into my wait, the dinging of a stove timer. Five minutes stretched to ten. The dinging went on and on.

"Hello," I said. *"Hello?"*

The receiver suddenly clunked again, more painfully than before. "Creel here. Talk to me."

(In the background, the elderly male voice: *"Dammitawl, I nearlybout burnt em."* The stove timer stopped dinging.)

I introduced myself to Mr. Jamison. I reviewed for him my meetings with Allegra, noting my concern about her interactions with her classmates and detailing the Eddie Staley playground episode. I informed him that Mrs. Staley had made noises about going to the school board with it.

"Allegra knows better than to hit, ma'am." Mr. Jamison had a youthful voice and a soft Southern accent more businesslike—in a feedstore or lumberyard context—than hillbillyish.

"Believe me," I said, "she was provoked."

"Don't excuse her, ma'am. She still knows better. I hope you gave her serious what-for."

"Primarily, I scolded the boy. He'd been bullying her ever since her arrival."

"Sounds like lopsided discipline to me. Prejudiced, even. You got the Staleys' number? I think Allegra should call em to apologize."

Prejudiced? Out of Creel Jamison's sight, I bristled. But held my tongue and gave him the Staleys' telephone number. An apology might in fact defuse the situation and slide me off the scapegoat's altar.

"Mr. Jamison, I have a sensitive question to ask."

"Ask away." I hesitated. During my hesitation, he said, "Yessum, it's true. In hot weather, I sleep buck nekkid."

A declaration that literally dumbfounded me.

"That's a joke, Mrs. Hewitt. You know, a funny? To break the tension, like?"

"Oh."

"Go ahead. Ask yore sensitive question." Disappointment in my obvious lack of humor tinged his voice, but didn't negate his openness.

"Does Allegra have to wear that long ugly glove to school every day?"

"No, ma'am."

"Then why does she?"

"I guess she likes it. Blonged to her mama."

Ten feet into the meadow and I'd stepped into a cow pie the size of Troup County. I took a swig of my Corona, then banged the bottle—gently—against my forehead.

"What happened to Mrs. Jamison?"

"Vamoosed with a canoeing buddy of mine when Allegra was two. Today they live in west Texas, where the canoeing ain't thet much to brag on."

"I'm sorry." For what? Mrs. Jamison's absconding? Or her diminished (outdoor) recreational opportunities?

"Don't sweat it, ma'am. I don't."

"What about Allegra? Without that glove, things would go a lot easier for her."

"We don't *want* things easy. Else I'd quit Nathan Crowder's truck brokerage and suck tit off Uncle Sugar."

"It's admirable you don't."

"It's taking responsibility. The year thet started bein 'admirable' is the year this country slid into the slops."

If Nashville needed another back-to-basics lyricist, Creel Jamison certainly qualified. I pointed our conversation back to Allegra, though, observing that she believed she had to wear the glove as a cover, the way Adam and Eve had concealed their nakedness from God.

"That's a strange take for a little girl, Mr. Jamison. And she insists it isn't shame that motivates her, but . . . well, necessity. What does she mean?"

"Moren likely, jes what she says."

"Then what, besides the obvious, does her glove conceal?"

"Difference," Creel Jamison said. "Specialness. Which can get you applauded or crucified, dependin."

"But the glove itself signals a provocative difference."

"Not like her uncovered hand would."

"Is she sick? Is her hand a prosthetic device?"

Creel Jamison laughed. "It's real. Too real. And this gabfest's over. Talk to Allegra. She rides her own mounts and curries em when she's done."

"Very folksy. But I—"

"Talk to her. My blessing. But if she ungloves for you, don't Judas-kiss her. Hear?"

Before I could reply, Creel Jamison hung up. Progress, I thought: It's okay he hung up because I know a lot more about Allegra, and I have permission to dig deeper.

After Thanksgiving, a peculiar sort of homage to Allegra manifested itself in Mrs. Peaden's class. Hannah Treece and Lindsay Des Rochers showed up boasting elbow-length ballroom gloves on their left arms. Hannah's, of silky acetate, shone ruby-red. Lindsay's, of deep-brown velvet, scintillated with glitter and raised petal-shaped patterns. Allegra, the fashion rebel, had become a fashion plate.

Sort of.

By Wednesday, Hannah and Lindsay had abandoned their gloves for the ever-popular bare look, and no one else at Vista Grove appeared ready to renew the experiment. Evening-wear gloves wear a body out. They reduce dexterity, raise the temperature from elbow to fingernail, and snag on local excrescences. Only Allegra had the requisite grit, commitment, and stamina to keep flaunting that demanding style.

On the other hand (metaphorically speaking), incidents of ridicule, grab-cuff, and eye-rolling fell off dramatically. I now lacked a solid professional reason to dig deeper into the mystery behind Allegra's glove. I might as well've asked Jody Schuett why he always wore argyle socks.

The last day before Christmas break, I got another referral from Beth:

"Allegra Jamison isn't staying focused. Her grades have dropped. She's missed turning in four homework assignments since Thanksgiving. She seems depressed and frequently visits Never-Never Land. Please talk to her."

Degree of urgency?

Beth had circled MODERATE.

Having my excuse, I hurried to call Allegra in before Vista Grove shut down for the holidays.

She came in clad in her favorite black outfit, with floppy leg warmers over sagging tights, shuffle-along bag-lady shoes, and a cream-colored scarf with a crow printed in the center of its main shoulder-lapping flap. And, of course, her glove; her mother's glove, cream-colored like the scarf.

"Hello, Allegra. You look striking."

She went to my *How Do You Feel?* mirror and pulled from it the taped-up construction-paper portrait of a freckle-faced girl with a diamondlike tear on her cheek. She handed this to me, then sidled with a careless hip bang into my interviewee's desk. "Crap," she said.

"No: you *do* look striking."

Allegra hit me with an I-don't-believe-you-said-that moue. "Thet was like an all-purpose crap, Mrs. Hewitt. Everything's crappy."

"Tell me about it."

She laid her cheek on her gloved forearm, her face toward the cinderblock rear wall. I knelt beside her and massaged the knot of tension in her neck.

"If you had to rank the crappiness, where would you start? At home? At school?"

"It all glops together."

"Your dad?"

"He's . . . he's okay. I love him."

"Mrs. Peaden? Your classmates?"

"What do they have to do with anything? They're jes, you know, around, like rocks or strangers' tombstones."

"Okay. Tell me who *does* have something to do with what's crappy in your life."

"My mama. My brother. Me."

This catalogue brought me up short. Allegra's mama had run out on her and Creel eight years ago.

And her brother? What brother?

I left Allegra to check my file. Surprise: It listed a brother, Desmond, 17. "Dez," however, wasn't supposed to be a current member of the Jamison household, having left Dad and Sis two years ago to take a job in Amarillo, Texas, installing state-of-the-art sound equipment in automobiles, trucks, and all-terrain vehicles. Who needed a high-school diploma when you could patch a CD-player into a Jeep Cherokee?

"Allegra, do you recall the last time you saw your mother?"

"No."

"What about . . . Dez?"

"This morning. Last night. Yesterday morning. The night before. The dawn before that." A sing-song litany.

"This"—I tapped my file folder—"sez Dez is in Texas."

Allegra looked up. "Files lie." She softened. "Or mebbe git outdated."

"Tell me about Dez."

"Would you like to see my arm?" She put her right thumb and forefinger around the cuff of her glove, then held the arm up to me for inspection. I accepted her offer, and indulged my curiosity, by walking over to study the skin between her elbow and the glove's tourniqueted cuff.

A band of tender purple marbled with spoiled-looking green encircled her arm. I wanted to see more. "Is it like that all the way down to your hand?"

"Nome."

"Did Dez do that?"

She pulled her arm away and set it carefully in her lap. "I had this dream bout Dez. It scared me. It woke me up. I slept again, but it came back."

"All right. Tell me your dream."

"Dez was swimming, deep underwater like. He didn't have a suit. Red slits opened n shut on both sides of his neck, and this clear lacy fin ran down his back. He sort of wormed along through the water. His ding-dong—" Allegra pursed her lips, eyed me skeptically.

"His penis?"

"Yessum."

"It's all right. Go ahead."

"His penis floated under him—shyly—till he got to this clump of shells or like jammed-up fish bones on the sea floor. Then it . . . " She grimaced.

"It erected?"

"Yeah. It *pointed*. Like a big thick finger. At a hole in the seashell mound under his face. He hovered over it with his fin ripplin and his you-know pointing."

"Is that when you woke up?"

"Nome. Not yet."

"Tell me what else happened."

"Dez was doing fish stuff with his mouth." Allegra blew a series of invisible smoke rings. "Like thet. Then his cheeks puffed up big n he . . . vomited. Green Jell-O came out n fell in sticky little crystals into the hole in the seashell mound. They got harder, dropping. They looked like stones—jewels—by the time they'd all got down."

"And?"

"I woke up. Scared. Sick, even. After a while, I went back to sleep n dreamt it again."

"Just the same?"

"Jes the same. Cep I knew I was dreamin."

"Allegra, how can I help you?"

"Lemme stay in here. Lemme do some work for you."

I gave her a stack of construction paper to cut in two for seasonal messages home. The discoloration on her arm and the lurid specifics of her nightmare cried abuse to me—emotional, physical, and possibly sexual. The perpetrator? Dez Jamison, who Allegra said had come all the way from Texas to vist them over Thanksgiving and Christmas. I had more questions to ask. Had Dez ever inappropriately touched her? Had she told Creel her dream or showed him her bruise?

Then, writing in my file, I heard several sharp cracking noises in a row. When I looked up, I saw Allegra repeatedly slamming the paper-cutter's blade down on her gloved forearm. I shouted her name, stumbled over, knocked the paper cutter out of her grasp, and tried to seize her left arm so that I could see how badly she had injured herself. It shames me to say that I also envisioned my firing, a police investigation, and a ruinous lawsuit against both me and the schoolboard.

Allegra twisted her arm away and stepped back. "I'm okay!" she said. "It don't hurt! It cain't hurt! Jes don't worry bout it!"

"Child, you have to let me see it. We may need to get you to an emergency room."

"Here, then! Look!" She thrust the arm out at me, but all I could reliably tell was that my paper cutter had slashed a half-dozen transverse tatters into her mother's glove. In its gill-like gaps, I may or may not have seen the emerald sheen of a clandestine stoniness
. . . .

Epifanio Sudar is a 27-year-old social worker with DFACS. On Saturday I called him at home and asked if he would go with me out to Allegra Jamison's place—an unannounced visit—to do a thorough check on her home life.

"It's vacation, Juanita. Don't you ever rest? I've got a Christmas-shopping date in forty minutes."

We talked a while, and he agreed to go with me on Monday, meanwhile cautioning me not to visit the Jamisons alone. "Two fools," he told me, "are always braver than one."

Not that I expected hostility from Creel Jamison, who had sounded both cooperative and bright on the phone, or an ambush at the hands of Dez, whom I knew only from a few file-folder notes and a surrealistic dream recitation from the lips of his depressed younger sister.

Epifanio knows the county, including every confusing back road and byway around Vista Grove. We drove to the Jamisons' in his white VW bug and found their trailer off a dirt lane behind an azalea-ringed clapboard house with a rusty tin roof. The house, I understood, belonged to Creel's elderly neighbor, the man with the telephone.

The trailer—*mobile home* would be a euphemism—rested cattywampus among some scrawny pines, some overturned oil drums, two broken swing sets, two portable storage units, a mound of beer cans, and a mix of lawnmower parts, discarded toys, and ribby-looking bicycle frames. As we pulled in, a feral housecat glanced our way and bolted.

"I'm disappointed," Epifanio said.

"Of course. No one should have to live like this."

"Hey, bleeding-heart lady, I'm only disappointed there's no engineless jalopy up on blocks. With a clunker up on blocks, it'd be perfect."

"Up yours, Epifanio."

We went to the door. Early afternoon. Because no car, clunker or otherwise, sat out front, I feared we might have to come back later. But if Allegra admitted us in the middle of a work day—Creel's work day—we had a better hope of inspecting and evaluating the place than if he greeted us.

Allegra cracked the hollow-core front door and peered out warily. "Mrs. Hewitt!" she said.

"And Mr. Sudar," I said. "May we come in?"

"*He* cain't. I don't know him."

"He's a colleague, Allegra. A county social worker."

"He's a stranger. And a man. Dad sez—"

"That's fine," Epifanio said. "Your dad tells you right." To me he said, "I'll wait in the car."

I entered. Allegra wore a magenta-and-brown horsehair robe whose sleeves swallowed her arms and hands. She put her hands in her arm pits.

"I was sewing. Back there." Nodding over one shoulder.

"Your dad's at work, right?"

"Yessum."

"Where's your brother?"

"Dez? The nekkid fish? He left Sattidy. Swum on back to Texas. Dad sorta kicked his butt out."

"Did Dez put that bruise on your left arm? You never did tell me, Allegra, and I need to know."

"Nome, he didn't. He jes upset me by bein hissef, which he cain't help any moren I can."

I looked around. A living room. A breakfast counter and a galleylike kitchen. A beat-up recliner dominated the living room.

Next to the recliner sat a small bookcase, the shelves of which held a library of maybe fifty paperbacks.

I ambled over and saw Plato's *Republic*; a poetry anthology called *The Voice That Is Great Within Us*; Frances Fitzgerald's *Fire in the Lake*; novels by Somerset Maugham, Herman Wouk, John Steinbeck, Anais Nin; biographies of Gandhi, Babe Ruth, Adolf Hitler, Albert Einstein, John Lennon; five or six back issues of the *National Geographic*; well-paged fairy-tale compilations by Hans Christian Andersen, the Brothers Grimm, Oscar Wilde; and plenty more. Seeing these books, I had a powerful urge to select one at random, plop down in Creel Jamison's chair, and read, and read, and read, as if I had no other duty or concern in the world.

Allegra brushed past me to the bookcase, knelt, and, with her right hand, pulled out a dilapidated paperback, which she thrust upon me.

"What's this?"

"My favorite, *The Arabian Nights*. My favorite story in it is 'The Young King of the Black Isles.'"

"Why, Allegra?"

Still kneeling, and with her eyes lowered, she raised her left arm, letting her robe's sleeve fall back to her shoulder. Her hand, wrist, and forearm—all the way up to the bruise that she'd showed me at school—consisted of a shiny green crystal, or a sculpted assemblage of crystals, that I at first took for a costume glove, a Halloween gauntlet, that she'd put on to get a gasp out of me. But because it ended in a shapely hand, the mirror image of her right one, and graded imperceptibly into the discolored skin below her elbow, I quickly understood that instead of a flesh-and-blood human hand Allegra had this eerily gorgeous member of organic stone.

If she ungloves for you, Creel Jamison had told me over the telephone, *don't Judas-kiss her. Hear?*

"I'm not ashamed of it," Allegra said, still not looking at me. "Nor of any other part, neither."

170

I knelt in front of her. "You shouldn't be."

"It's beautiful. Dad sez. He's awways told me thet."

"I agree with him, Allegra."

"I only cover it to keep from gettin marked out a freak, a real freak. Dad sez they'd come for me."

"Who?"

"Medical doctors. TV folk. The Ringling Brothers Circus. Greasy lidl carnies. Everbody."

"Your daddy's right again." Except, I silently thought, for his medical-doctor phobia.

"He sez we could prolly make money from it, lots of money, but I'd never have no peace again. So it wouldn't be worth the nonstop harassment n fret."

"Your daddy cares for you. Your daddy's wise."

"It's jes thet now it's goin stony-green *right on up my arm*. It'd stopped for a while, but now it's moving again, and I'm . . . I'm *skeered*, Mrs. Hewitt."

I murmured consolation—who knows what?—but also started wondering what it would mean to "Judas-kiss" her in the eyes of her unfashionably principled father. Had I traduced the ethics of my calling by coming to see Allegra during Creel's absence and without his permission? No, not strictly speaking, for I'd suspected abuse and hadn't yet identified a culprit. But now, with Allegra's viridescent hand before me as a faceted rebuke, I felt that I'd pushed the situation's protocols into a swampy moral hinterland. Besides, Allegra—unless I'd totally lost my grip on reality—needed medical attention. The emerald glacier inching up her left arm had more in common with a metastasizing cancer than with a cheery crystallization experiment, and for Creel to make her forego treatment to keep the larger world from ravaging her innocence struck me as unconscionable, and bleakly ironic.

With some effort, I persuaded Allegra to go to Mr. Emmons' house next door, call her dad, and ask him to come home. It was "very important"—she should tell him—that he talk to her school counselor, Mrs. Hewitt, face to face.

Allegra dressed casually (jeans, a flannel shirt, and her mother's glove, the cuts in which she'd mended with some beige thread), then sauntered across the junky yard to Mr. Emmons' place. I returned to the car and explained to Epifanio all I could without divulging the secret of Allegra's hand. I also apologized for the sit-and-wait role to which circumstances had relegated him.

"No problem," he said. "What's the book?"

I showed him.

"Ah, Sherherazade. I hope we get reprieved too. That this hillbilly hothead doesn't shoot us."

"He's not a hillbilly. Or a hothead."

Allegra trudged back from Emmons' place. "Got him!" she cried. "He's comin!" Banged her way inside; peeked back out. "But he don't like it much!"

"Great," murmured Epifanio.

I thumbed through *The Arabian Nights* to the final paragraphs of its lead-in story, "The Further Adventures of the Fisherman." Silently, I read:

Instead of answering these questions the young
man began to weep bitterly. "How inconstant is
fortune!" cried he; "she takes pleasure to pull down
those she has raised." At these words, lifting up
his robe, he showed the sultan that he was a man only
from the head to the girdle, and that the other half
of his body was black marble.

The sultan witnessing this sight admits that it fills him with horror, adding, "I am impatient to hear your history." In that same state—expectant impatience—I awaited the coming of Allegra's father, Creel Jamison.

About forty minutes later, he arrived, swinging into the trailer's yard in a rattletrap truck on whose flatbed a tool chest, a water heater, and possibly the interior components of a heat pump jumped like bugs on a hotplate. The way he slammed to a standstill, hopped down, and flung his truck door shut betrayed his seething anger.

"Uh-oh," said Epifanio.

Creel came on bullishly. He shone stocky, muscular, and handsome, a serrated forelock hanging down across his brow like a grackle's wing. At thirty-six, he looked roughneck young: a nervy, two-fisted teenager.

"What're you doin out here, Mrs. Hewitt?" he demanded.

"We came to see—"

"It chaps my butt to leave Nate mannin all six phone lines for a parley that prolly coulda waited till after-hours, doncha think?"

He stopped, tucking his thumbs into his belt and cocking a solid Levi'd hip. He apparently didn't plan to drag us out of Epifanio's car and pistol-whip us. (Thank God.)

"It chaps my butt!" he repeated.

I got out. Introduced Epifanio. Said that Creel and I needed to confer in private, along with Allegra, and that the matter's urgency had led me to ask her to summon him home, an inconvenience that paled beside the physical and mental health issues requiring our attention.

"Well," said Creel. "The kitten ungloved, eh?" He sounded resigned, not jealously put out.

We talked some more at the car. Creel's easier-going tone, along with my assurance that I'd suffer no harm here, persuaded Epifanio that he could responsibly leave. At first, I'd wanted him to stay, not to protect me, but as an ally in my counseling effort. Creel said no, Allegra's privacy counted more than our convenience. Besides, once we'd conferred, Creel would gladly drive me back to Vista Grove. So Epifanio, looking only mildly doubtful of this ad-lib arrangement, said *adio'* and putt-putted out of the parts-littered yard.

Inside, Allegra sat in Creel's recliner, her gleaming green arm propped on its armrest, her mama's glove in a helical sort of heap on the floor. When we entered, she lifted an emerald forefinger to acknowledge us. And I saw that her ostensibly petrified append-age—down to its separate digits—could move, that it *lived*. As, of course, cancer cells conquer healthy tissue through an insidiously lively process of subdivision and displacement.

Creel and I sat down on bar stools at the breakfast counter and revolved toward Allegra.

"I guess you kinda like this lady," he said.

"She's okay."

"She's duty-bound and friendly-acting. Whether she's okay or not, darlin, remains to be seen."

"Allegra's frightened," I said. "And you haven't taken her to a doctor."

"A minerologist'd be more like it, doncha think? Sides, I have taken her to a doctor. A big-time specialist in Memphis—a do-right Christian—who swore he'd keep her dilemmer strickly confiden-tial. Which he has. So far. For nigh-on ten years. Can we trust you to do the same, Mrs. Hewitt?"

"What did your man in Memphis say? And if this 'do-right Christian' hasn't found a solution, maybe another doctor could help you more."

"Listen. He's presented Allegra's case to all his big-wig col-leagues nationwide. *World*wide. As a game. A hypothetical, for-fun-like problem. Sending along all his test results and whatnot over modems and fax machines and e-mail and so on. For feed-back."

"I'm famous," Allegra said. "Sort of. 'The Girl with the Crystal Arm.'"

I said, "Diagnosis? Prognosis? Treatment? Speculations? Surely, these networking geniuses have told your doctor friend in Memphis *something*, Mr. Jamison."

"Well, some refused to play. No time. No interest. But others said stuff like 'impossible' or 'too weird for rational discourse,' then tried to work on it, anyway. None of em can figure what it was jump-started the microscopic block-laying or crystallization process, though. There's no decent treatments either. I'd sooner chant over chicken blood under a full moon than try again the chemo and radiation routes that made Allegra sicker than her slow stonifying ever did."

"When did it start?"

"I was a toddler," Allegra said, bumping the recliner's footrest down and reciting a family story she knew by heart: "Mama took me to a GP in Holly Springs, Mississippi, where we was living. A nurse there accused her of abusing me, pinchin the tips of my fingers. Cuz my trouble—"

"Yore specialness," Creel said. "Yore uniqueness."

"—my *trouble* started at my fingertips n worked down my hand to my wrist n from there on up tord my elbow, jes like you see it here." She showed me.

"But what caused the 'trouble' to begin with?" I looked from Allegra to her father.

Creel shrugged. "What starts any cancer?"

"You must have a theory."

"The doctors don't, but I should?"

"Do you?"

"Sort of," Creel admitted.

"What is it?"

"Me, I think the trouble came from Angela, her mama. About a year before Allegra was born, Angela became one of them loopy crystal worshippers. Mebbe still is. Thought crystals focused spiritual power n boosted sexual energy. She'd sleep with a piece of glauconite—really, just some greensand breccia—under her pillow. She even raked me down the back with it once while we were—" Creel stopped, embarrassed.

"Did you tell your doctor friend this theory?"

"Uh course."

"And he said—?"

"Thet it was nuttier than Angela's crystal fetish. Mebbe so, but it was moren he or his fella geniuses come up with."

To Allegra, I said, "What about the bruise? At school, you made me think your brother Dez did that to you."

"Her skin bruises that way before the crystallizing revs up again," Creel said. "It's sort of what sent her mama off with A. W. Richard. 'Here, you've got her,' she sez. 'I cain't take the slurs I git ever time I drive her to a checkup. Or seeing it happen to her, either.' So she ran."

"But it's okay for *Dez* to live out there nex to her and her doofusy new hubby," Allegra said.

"We tried having Dez visit for the holidays," Creel said. "It didn't work out."

"Why not?"

"I hate his rotten guts is why," Allegra said. "He's jes like Mama, a deserter."

"He'd changed," Creel said. "Talked tough n dirty. Liked to strut around in briefs. Bragged bout all the money he had n how 'def' his mama Mrs. Richard thought he was. Teased Allegra bout her hand, when wunst he was her self-appointed big-brother champion. I chucked him out."

I left my stool, to kneel in front of Allegra with my hands on her knees.

"I can see why you're so frustrated and angry. And I can see"— I nodded at her hand—"why you're scared. How must it feel to have your body turn into something not-you. Into cold and alien stone?"

Before she could answer, Creel said, "It's taken it nine years to git that far. So it's her. And it's not cold. Touch it n see."

Allegra nodded, giving permission. I touched the back of her hand, running my finger along her wrist and the top of her forearm. These smooth faceted surfaces had warmth, a glassy counterfeit of body warmth, and held within their murkier green depths a net of veins. The History, I mused heartbrokenly, of the Princess of Vista Grove. I left off stroking Allegra's arm and began to stroke her cheek.

"It's *her*," Creel said. "It grows with her. She can even move it. It makes her, you know, *unique*."

"Mr. Jamison, she'd be unique without it. And if only this made her unique, you and I would have to pray for blown-glass eyeballs or genuine tortoise-shell skulls to confirm for us our uniqueness."

Head cocked, Creel Jamison just stared at me.

"What do you plan to do when this emerald invasion reaches her shoulder? When it spreads up to her neck and down through her torso?"

Allegra began to cry.

"O child, I'm sorry." To Creel, I said, "I don't think you're a bad man, and certainly not a deliberate abuser, but I have to report this."

He spun about, propped his elbows on the counter, dropped his chin into his hands.

"Don't you dare," he whispered tightly.

"Why not? *How* can I not?"

I'd begun to regret allowing Epifanio to return to town. I half expected Creel to threaten me, with physical violence or a destructive lawsuit, but instead he said, "Because it won't do no good, ma'am."

"You don't know that."

"I do know." Still not looking at me, he slammed one fist down on the counter. "Not only am I not a 'bad man,' I'm not a neglectful one, Mrs. Hewitt. There's nuthin you can do for my baby by reporting this I haven't already given a shot, or mebbe two, mysef.

Bout all you can do is make sure the press comes baying in, sniffin n snappin n leg-hikin like a pack of mangy snoopsome hounds."

"There has to be some treatment." I patted Allegra's back; she sniffled into my sweater.

"Only one that Dr. Desautels n his high-powered researcher friends ever agreed on."

"Okay. What's that?"

Allegra pulled back and said: "Cut it off."

"Yeah," Creel said. "Amputation."

Creel and Allegra drove me home, Allegra huddled between us in the truck as if sending her mind—her entire self—into some other realm, where the curse of her hand became an asset, where the denizens had resilient bodies of shatterproof glass, bodies that winked in the sunlight like bright transducers.

Or maybe she just felt numb, sledgehammered by all that had happened that afternoon.

What had happened?

Most important, I'd caved. I'd let Creel convince me not to report to DFACS, Child Protective Services, or our regional medical center Allegra's extraordinary complaint. Creel had already done all he could. Her condition, although admittedly weird, didn't represent an immediate threat to her life. Nor was it painful. Her glove was the only prophylactic—against ridicule if not further spread of the crystals—that she needed now. If I disclosed a secret that they'd screened for years from our pillaging world, I'd kill their last hope of a joyful Christmas. For, as Creel saw it, the nastiness of Dez's early exile back to Amarillo had already smutched the season.

"Remember," I told him as they dropped me off. "You've got to stay in touch over the holidays."

"Course," he said.

"And I'm taking Allegra shopping on Friday."

"Thet's fine too."

They drove off, Allegra slumped against the passenger door, her arm tucked out of view, her abstraction from the moment so keen that she reminded me of a kid in a Walker Evans photograph from the Great Depression.

On Wednesday, I got a letter from Creel. He'd scrawled it in longhand, with a No. 2 pencil; it took me at least a minute to decipher any sentence of six words or more. I reproduce the letter (legibly) here:

Dear Mrs. Hewit,

Thanks for agreing to our agreement. Thanks for caring about Allegra. She loves you right back. I want you to believe I would never hurt or in any way shape or form put in jprdy her health/happiness. I am her father, she is my blood, I see her as a living breathing Gift of God. I also believe all things— *all things*—work together for good even if we can't always see His finger pointing like an arrow past all the evil crap at Glory.

Many people wld lable Allegra's condition *unnatural*. Even Dr. Desautels used that word once to me, in front of her—good Christan though he is—& I wanted to bust him for it. Well it may be strange or unpresidented or whatever but I don't think it's unnatural. A truely great book I found maybe 15 yrs ago—*The Seven Mysteries of Life*—helped me to see that what's hapening to Allegra doesn't make her a freak or a spawn of Satin. Look— "Putting it in terms of evolution"—*I* am not a Cretionist, I believe in God-sparked Evolution—"when a bunch of milling molecules makes its initial change toward what is generally considered life.... they begin to line up, to sort themselves, to form rows,

179

layers, lattices. In short, they crystallize .... &
this is why the crystal is the basic structure of
life, of order, & why ordered solids from rock to
wood to muscle to bone to gene are describable as
crystal." You can look this up if you get the book,
it's on pg 445.

Tests show the microscopic crystals in Allegra's
hand—wrist, forearm, & maybe even right on up if it
doesn't stop—are *triclinic*, layered in little boxes
w/ unequal axes & oblique cnnctng angles. That's
not *unnatural*, it's just the way some crystals grow,
& some of them—crystls, I mean—grow like rcngzd
life forms. Under a microscope, for exmpl, bauxite
looks like clumps of garden pees, asbestos like hair,
limonite like aspearagus sprouts. So why shd we get
all hot & bothrd if cells in a God-made human creture
start going to crystl in her & lining up in beutiful
tilted boxes. No reson but fear.

I don't fear, Mrs. Hewit. God's in charge, even
in this. Crystls conduct electrcty, & piezoelctrcty
shows up everywhere in living tissue. So the charge
that God has He puts in animal & vgtbl cells to make
it power their senses—hearing, feeling, taste, & so
on. It irks me people can't see that, knowing how
they see. Anyway, Allegra's special, a one of a kind
wonder, but she's *not* unnatural, & I love her like I
lov myself.

Yrs sncrly, Creel J.

An extraordinary letter: puzzling, troubling, full of cagy truck-
driver or garage-mechanic eloquence. Non-Southerners, I understood, would probably conclude from it that Creel was a religious
fanatic. Me, I regarded him only as a believer with a single self-

decided agenda, namely, Allegra. And maybe that agenda *did* qualify him as a fanatic.

For me, the troubling part of Creel's letter didn't lie in its references to God, but in its attempt to persuade me—and, more important, himself—that the crystal takeover Allegra was enduring, again, signaled a benign manifestation of His divine ordering.

A wistful hope. Pure self-delusion.

Allegra—if not tomorrow, next year, or even a decade down the line—would die of her affliction. It would . . . well, *petrify* her. From fingertips to foot soles. From nails to pate. Vista Grove's city councilors, if she petrified here in the county, might one day put her on the Post Office lawn, as an Oz-ish memorial to herself. And if, in her final vitreous state, she could still move a little, hooray. City employees wouldn't have to reposition her every week to keep our Bermuda from browning and blowing off.

That night I dreamt of Allegra; in fact, of all my charges at Vista Grove.

Class by class and grade by grade, our kids filed into the cafeteria buck-naked: lumpy gnomes and trolls in amongst the agile sylphs and leprechauns. Not only were they naked, they were transparent (but more like plastic anatomical figures than like ghosts). Their nakedness—this detail underscored the fact that I was dreaming—made no difference to any of them. They all behaved like veteran nudists, completely at ease with bare fannies and air-stroked genitalia. When they sat down to eat, the cameraman in my subconscious dollied in for a closeup on Allegra.

Her lunch tray held dozens of cubes of shimmering lime Jell-O; nothing else. She spooned them down. They filled her from her clear-plastic toes to her knees, from her knees to her hips, from her hips to her armpits, and from her armpits to the jut of her willful chin.

As her classmates ate—pizza, green beans, canned corn, bran muffins, rice pudding, the standard cafeteria fare—they acquired clothes.

Only Allegra turned emerald-green from toe to crown. On her last few bites she packed Jell-O into her sinuses, and up into her cranium, with a severe gusto.

Finally, all the other kids, fully dressed, turned toward her to gawk.

Allegra sat amidst them like a transmogrified princess, as petite as an elf, as green as bomb-hot chrysoberyl. The sight of her, once she'd finished popping Jell-O cubes, stirred long but self-conscious laughter.

On Friday, without coming in, Creel dropped Allegra off at my house. I took her shopping. As Christmas gifts, I bought her a long-sleeved blouse, some elbow-length blue-silk gloves, some mittens, and a pair of leather dress gloves.

"I only need one of each of em," she said.

"It's cold enough now to wear both gloves. Don't discard the extras. They're not really extras."

At Vaughn's Hardware, with money she'd put aside from her allowance, Allegra bought her dad a gabardine work shirt and a rubber-headed mallet. The mallet was to pound shelving into place without scarring the boards, a mistake to which Creel's impatience frequently recommitted him.

"Anyone else to buy for?" I asked.

"Who? Not Dez. Absodamnlutely not Mama. You mebbe, but if so, I wouldn't buy in front of you."

"Like I've done you?"

"Thet's different. We had . . . fun."

Vaughn's doesn't gift-wrap so we returned to my house to wrap Allegra's presents for Creel. Allegra insisted on doing the job herself. She slipped off her mended glove and set to work, her left hand moving as easily as her right. I watched it, alert and grateful, thinking that for these few moments she had entrusted to me her most cherished secret—with Creel unavailable to give his imprimatur to the disclosure.

"What do you want to happen?" I said.

She raised her hand. *The* hand. "Bout this?" I nodded. She resumed gift-wrapping, shook her head. "If I had three wishes, I'd wish for it to turn back norml. If thet didn't work, I'd wish for it to fall off hurtlessly while I sleep, like a lizard's tail. Then I'd git me a silver hook-hand n run Eddie Staley straight into Pinson Quarry Lake."

"What if *that* didn't work?"

"My third wish? Jes to gemmify all over, I guess."

" 'Gemmify'? Is that your word, Allegra?"

"I don't know. Mebbe it's Creel's. Mebbe I got it out of thet book he likes to crib from. Anyway, it's what I think is happenin, Mrs. Hewitt. Ever day."

She had a tiny purse, from which she removed a creased paper scrap. "Read this." Someone had typed its message— maybe even Allegra, whom I imagined tapping away earnestly at a battered Remington:

....crystallization is essentially a cooling,
settling-down and going-to-sleep process in which
structure is formed by atoms expending energy and
radiating heat as they compose themselves like a bear
getting ready to hibernate. The crystal's energy
leaks away most easily from its edges and easiest of
all from its outer corners and protruding points (pg.
451).

"While it grows, the green stays warm. But what I think's happenin is, I'm coolin down. Gemmifyin. I'll prolly end up like Sleeping Beauty fore her prince showed up to plant thet magic kiss on her."

I put my finger on a bow Allegra was tying.

She said, "They's one good thing to remember, though. Jes one, but a really priddy neat one."

"What's that?"

"When I gemmify all over—cool down to total deadness—well, my body—my *corpse?*—I don't think it'll rot, it'll jes lay out somewhere n . . . you know, *erode*."

I spent three days of my Christmas break in Savannah, at a Ramada Inn near the Civic Center, where I attended a road-show mounting of *The Phantom of the Opera*. I needed a respite from Vista Grove Elementary and my fatiguing caseload.

Over the first four days of the holidays, in addition to my attentions to Allegra, I'd helped Epifanio admit a fifth-grade boy to Manumission, a local clinic specializing in therapy for youthful sex offenders; accompanied a sobbing third-grader to the funeral of her mother, a victim of breast cancer; and tried to comfort a distraught second-grader who'd dialed 911 when his parents—a carousing mother and a perpetually soused step-dad— abandoned him for two days in a shotgun rental property with no food, hot water, or lights.

Allegra's case preoccupied me, though. After sitting high in the balcony at *Phantom*, and catching maybe half the words in its libretto, I returned to my motel room fuming and unable to sleep. So I rummaged up a sheet of stationery and wrote Creel Jamison a letter:

> I'm keeping my end of the bargain [*I believe I
> wrote*], but I worry about Allegra more and more. She
> told me after our mini-shopping spree that she thinks
> she'll eventually succumb to the vitality-freezing
> process advancing from her left hand. The Latin word
> applicable here is *sinister*, meaning "on the left" or
> "unlucky," and in today's English "threatening evil"
> or "presaging trouble." How can we ignore a sign so
> conspicuous, Mr. Jamison, and so dire?
>
> I suggest that you reconsider and possibly even

follow through with the amputation option. You must have thought long and hard about it already—I don't assume you've summarily dismissed it—but should it afford a surgical stop to the threat to Allegra's life, with no unforeseen physical side-effects or any chance that the crystallization process might begin again, then surely your daughter deserves to benefit from it.

Please let me hear from you. I will return to Vista Grove two or three days before New Year's. My warmest holiday greetings.

Once home, I swung by the Post Office to see what mail had come. Amid the mostly unwelcome deluge, I had a yellow card summoning me inside for a package pickup. This package was a 4" X 6" box wrapped in tan paper, with Allegra Jamison's return address. From its grease-pencil printing, I knew that she had mailed it herself.

Inside the tan wrapping, which I tore off while parked in front of the Post Office, I found gold-foil Christmas paper, a smushed yellow drugstore bow, and a note, whose printed message went: "SORRY THIS IS LATE. I TELL CREEL I DONT WANT TO HAVE MY HAND, ACTULLY MY ARM CUT OFF. NOT NOW. LIKE HE SAY, ITS ME AND I AM IT."

I flipped the note over: "IF I DO GET IT CUT, I LIKE YOU TO HAVE IT. ITS VALUBLE, CREEL SAS. I AM SICK OF IT BUT YOU CULD PUT IT SOMEWERE IN YOU HOUSE TO REMEBER ME AND I WOOD BE HAPY. MERRY CRISTMAS, ALLEGRA."

I laid her note on the dash, pulled the Christmas paper off my gift: her favorite old paperback of *The Arabian Nights*.

Early in January, the kids came back. Allegra smiled at me every time we passed in the halls. She had stopped wearing her mother's glove over her secret hand, choosing to flaunt instead either the blue silk glove or the fawn-colored leather one that I'd bought her before Christmas at Pinson's.

In a way, I suppose, I now considered her (with a scrum of midnight mental qualifications) a resolved case. Or, at least a semiresolved case. I turned the bulk of my time to classroom cutups, underachievers, and troublemakers; the chronic butts of others' lampoons, the self-esteem-shorn, and dumb-as-dirt space cadets; abuse victims, scowling quasi-psychos, and maladjusted newcomers. My list goes on.

Late in the month—freezing cold, no snow—Beth Peaden ran past my office. Ran back. Peeked in.

"Quick, Juanita! There's a commotion on the playground! A veritable riot, looks like!"

I ran coatless down the hall, out the side door, and along Vista Grove's cyclone fence to playground zero. An icy wind, or winds, stabbed through me like a convocation of darning needles. Boys from two of our fifth-grade classes had Allegra Jamison penned into a gravelly corner of the yard. Rob Pino clung like a spider to the fence, wedging himself a foot or so over her head with the fingers of one hand and the soft toes of his sneakers. From his free hand, a blue silk glove streamed, whipping frenziedly about as he led his buddies in a chorus of chimplike hoots. Eddie Staley hooted louder than Rob, feinted menacing runs at Allegra, and laughed when Rob lost his grip, nearly barrel-rolling down on her.

"*Geek, freak!*" the boys chanted: "*We grabbed a peek at her hand! / Geek, freak! / Lookit her wickity hand!*"

As Beth, Mr. Buchanan, and I converged on the spot, some of the boys parted truculently to let us through. Allegra became visible—clearly visible—for the first time. She stood facing her tormentors, her left arm raised. Every time one of them, including Eddie, feinted toward her, she pivoted to catch the anticipated blow on her coruscating green arm. The sight of Beth Peaden, Mr. Buchanan, Mr. Vicic, and me all bearing down on her seemed to enrage her further. She smacked Rob with the back of her hand, clubbed Eddie between the eyes, knocked a kid I couldn't identify out of her way, and broke across the yard on a desperate run toward the pecan grove bordering our school to the north.

Luckily (I guess), it was Friday, the one day Mr. Buchanan lets us dress casually. I had on jeans, an embroidered cambric shirt, and low-cut beige sneakers. I took out after Allegra. She could fly, though, and wriggled through a gap in the gate that I would not've fit through even if I'd drunk an Alice-in-Wonderland shrinking potion. *"Allegra!"* I cried as she pelted like sixty through the stately naked grey columns of the grove, the pecan trees' winter branches blooming atop them like huge, luminous ganglia. She ignored me. And kept running. And had almost disappeared by the time— fingers raw, teeth clacking—I pulled the collapsing gate far enough inward to let me squeeze through it after her.

"Catch her!" Mr. Buchanan yelled. "Bring her back!"

Permission to pursue. I trotted through the grove looking for footprints, knee-clipped shrubs, sneaker-trod brown grass. I found nothing but open chapels among the symmetrically spaced pecans and cold wind funneling through their connected halls. Allegra had gone to ground as surely as a fox.

I estimated the temperature at 35° F., with a wind-chill factor dropping it to 20° or less. Suddenly, though, the sun came out, a white fish-eye behind and above me. Swathes of skim-milk blue washed out around it, in bands that rippled into the skyey greyness ahead. The fish-eye didn't warm me any, but the wafting blue lifted my spirits. I crossed a narrow asphalt access road separating the pecan grove from what looked like an illegal dump site. By this time, though, I'd given up my trot for a winded stroll, one hand at my waist and the sweat on my shoulder blades cooling like . . . well, a crystal whose energy has started to leak away "from its outer corners and protruding points."

I found Allegra in the unlicensed dump.

On a refuse mound overlooking a plain of toppled freezers, discarded golf clubs, and gutted TV sets, she stood with her sinister arm raised in blessing or renunciation. A blessing for the scarred earth, I thought, or a hopeful renunciation of the stone cancer in her hand. The fish-eye sun rayed through it, revealing its changed bones and mutated veins. It threw wheeling green lattices down across the debris and blazed with the redemptive authority of a lightning rod.

"*Allegra!*"

Perhaps thirty yards separated us. In spite of the wind, Allegra heard me and turned. Tears dirtied her face. Her eyes showed no sign of recognition. However, her hand stayed up so that when she drew it once from right to left across her body, I realized that she meant this slow wave for both greeting and farewell. A salute and a valediction.

Come back with me! I started to cry. But didn't because she plunged sure-footedly down the mound, keeping her balance even as pop-top rings, rotten cardboard, pickle jars, quicksand coffee grounds, etc., etc., squirted out from under her. At the bottom, she ran on, weaving among appliance husks, bleached animal corpses, and other wreckage until out of sight. Hugging myself, I turned and walked back to school.

Allegra had seriously injured Rob Pino, Eddie Staley, and a boy named Chris Ritter in her single-handed efforts to hold her tormentors at bay. Good for her, I thought. But the wound to Rob's arm, the cut on Eddie's face, and the queer gouge in the Ritter boy's chest had nasty edges and a sickening depth. Lots of stitches. Lots of outrage. Both of Eddie's parents came to school to berate Mr. Buchanan. The threat of multiple lawsuits hung in the air like a blur of August no-see-ums. It wouldn't have surprised me if the families of our half-pint provocateurs had put together a lynch party and a torchlight parade to the Jamisons' trailer.

The upshot of the recess attack on Allegra was that Creel Jamison quit Nathan Crowder's truck brokerage and pulled her out of school. In fact, the two of them must have hightailed it out of

Vista Grove, and maybe the state, as soon as Allegra managed to pick her way home and explain to her daddy what had happened. I've never seen Creel or Allegra again, and I don't think that anyone else in town has either.

Over a long weekend in February, when Beth Peaden's husband Matt flew to Jacksonville on business, Beth stayed with me. We had a pajama party, behaved like over-the-hill teenagers, and talked a lot about the Jamison case. I felt released from the stricture of confidentiality because (1) dozens of us had seen Allegra's hand; (2) the Jamisons had fled like guilty assault suspects; and (3) Beth had followed Allegra's case all year, insofar as she could, as her teacher.

"I figured a disease," Beth said. "Never . . . *that*."

"How could anyone figure the displacement of human tissue by minute triclinic crystals? No way."

"The condition dooms her. So, so bleak." Beth shuddered. In fact, she began to lose her composure. "A *horror*."

"Maybe not."

"Oh, no? She's like the guy in the Poe story 'A Cask of Amontillado,' who gets bricked up behind a wall. That fella only had to wait days to die. Allegra has to live with her doom—a more horrible kind of bricking up—for . . . well, who knows for how long?"

"A more *beautiful* kind of bricking up."

"Don't romanticize it, or her family life, or her fate."

"Beth, I go bump against more hopeless, intractable cases than Allegra's almost every week. None more *unusual*, I grant you, but many sadder and a few even harder to envision turning out acceptably."

The second-grader whose mother's sleazoid lover burned him all over the torso with a cigar. Six- and seven-year-old rape victims of both sexes. A conscienceless sixth-grader, possibly a case of fetal-alcohol syndrome, who hanged a stray dog in our gymnasium. Foster children swapped from home to home for the entire duration of their schooling. Chronic liars. I couldn't think of any one of these kids who didn't seem as profoundly afflicted as Allegra, even if their cases would never provide fodder for a weekly "investigative" tabloid or a TV show about Astonishing Conundrums.

"Allegra's mama ran off when she was two," Beth said. "Her older brother probably molested her."

"But her daddy loves her, and she's lived continuously in his household since infancy."

"He's a God nut. He picks her up and moves her every time there's trouble."

"He picks her up and moves her," I echoed. "And he seeks meaning even in the bleakest anomalies."

Mexican standoff. We popped popcorn, watched *The Seventh Voyage of Sinbad* on TBS, and went to bed. Beth fell asleep. I writhed about in my blankets, thinking of Allegra, of how much and genuinely I missed her. She was dead to me—like a child felled by leukemia or a prodigal vanished into a plague-ridden land. Sleepless, I turned on a lamp and picked up my copy of *The Arabian Nights*. Going through "The Young King of the Black Isles," I came upon this passage:

> The enchantress went immediately out of the
> Palace of Tears to fulfill [the sultan's] commands,
> and by the exercise of her spells soon restored to
> the young king his natural shape, bidding him,
> however, on pain of death, to begone from her
> presence instantly. The young king, yielding to
> necessity, retired to a remote place . . . .

My hand, holding the book, fell asleep, but I could not and sat waiting for slumber in my overwarm room.

God's Hour

Tillery always dropped in at the Twelfth Street Tavern to watch *God's Hour*.

In the United States, the earthly emissaries of the Deity had chosen CBS to broadcast the program. Watching it at eight o'clock (EST) every Thursday evening on the network of the disembodied eye was mandatory, so it always had a one-hundred percent share of the ratings for its time slot. The other commercial and cable networks simply went off the air for that hour.

Tillery, a convicted child murderer, eased his way through the crowd in the Twelfth Street Tavern, keeping his elbows in and perfunctorily apologizing to anyone he bumped. A man already at the bar politely insisted he take his stool. Tillery murmured a listless thanks, climbed up on the stool, called for a beer, and turned his ashen eyes on the magnesium-bright screen mounted like an oversize mirror behind the bar.

"I can't stand television," said the burly man sitting next to him. "I'd rather dig ditches than watch most of the garbage they try to cram down our throats, but I *love* this program. I mean, I out-and-out *love* it. I wouldn't miss it for five nights in a Hollywood harem."

"You die if you miss it," Tillery said.

"Well, there's that," the burly man admitted, "but that's not the clincher. I mean, I always feel spiritually cleansed—inwardly refreshed, you know. As a kid, I wasn't a churchgoer, but in the three years the Deity's been on, well it's made me appreciate the rejuvenating aspects of worship."

Tillery, sipping his beer, gave the jerk a stare that shut him down as effectively as a slap.

After the first thirty-six episode season of *God's Hour* broadcasts (followed apparently by a summer of reruns), every detention center in the world had released its inmates. That was how Tillery escaped a life sentence for sexually brutalizing and killing, ten years before the first *God's Hour*, a snotty little Chicano twerp in El Paso. So, yes, the program had neutered even his old antisocial tendencies.

Tillery was glad to be out, he watched *God's Hour* faithfully, he was walking the straight and narrow—but unlike the meathead next to him, he *hated* the Thursday-evening broadcast. For one thing, after the program all that you could recall of it was its commercials. The regular sponsors were Coca-Cola, Chevrolet, Oscar Mayer Franks and Sara Lee Kitchens, whose colorful spots came on at roughly twelve-minute intervals, lucid little cheerleading sessions in the telecast's phosphor-dot ocean of hypnopedagogical vagueness. During the spaces between the commercials, you gazed blankly at the ineffably shining face of God, mindlessly imbibing Glory. No one knew *exactly* what these minutes consisted of, though, because memory failed, and it was technically impossible to videotape or by any other means reproduce a *God's Hour* segment.

Thursday was the evening of mandatory viewing—primarily,

said the Deity's earthly emissaries (most of them persons of great wealth and/or political influence called to service by apocalyptic dreams), because more folks were naturally home on Thursday than on the weekend and because God had no wish to alienate the rabbis, priests, ministers, and other responsible clergy who passed their collection plates on Friday, Saturday, or Sunday.

The CBS eye took shape on the screen, a Coca-Cola spot briefly effervesced, and a scary hieratic glow filled the tavern. Everyone fell silent. Eyeballs glazed, brains blanked out, and Tillery—resisting the irresistible—heaved a sigh that shuddered through his wiry chest. Caught in an even bigger than usual Thursday-night crowd, he was still somehow alone with his God, and an angry corner of his mind fought like crazy against this unasked-for pairing. Only wimps and madmen actively *sought* personal union with the Deity. Tillery remembered trying to miss *God's Hour* while still a prisoner. He had been shown a vision of hell—a hell uniquely suited to his own bellicose personality—that, regrettably, was altogether unforgettable. And he had never missed an episode since. You only got one chance. People who tried a second time suffered a fatal (but reportedly painless) rupturing of a cerebral brain vessel and passed in spirit to the hell revealed to them during their first misbehavior.

God is love, thought Tillery sardonically, not quite overcome by the mother-of-pearl images flooding him from the screen. Why did all the shits around him submit so docilely to this celestial brainwashing? You might have to park your heinie on a stool to watch it, but who but God said you had to surrender even your last down-deep scrap of personal identity to the autocratic First Farter's television show?

No one, that's who.

Absolutely no one who *counted*.

A Chevrolet commercial interrupted the hypnotizing blarney of the show's opening segment. Tillery drained his beer and asked for another as the turkeys around him shook themselves to life again, mumbled incoherently, turned to get their own refills. Whereupon the ad for the Nova was suddenly displaced by a nova of Godlight that plunged nearly everyone back into grinning stupefaction. Tillery's teeth were on edge, though, and an angel observing him would have seen a face locked in a resentful rictus.

Since the first telecast, wars had ceased, crime had vanished, terrorism had halted, and even petty disagreements had become a passion of the past. The supreme Being still permitted accidents, natural disasters, and the inexplicable terminal illness, but on the whole, His name had risen steadily in esteem over the past three years, and far fewer works on the problems of evil and pain were being published. The globe was a happier, much more serene place than it had been before the worldwide debut of *God's Hour*.

Ads for hot dogs and cheesecake punctuated the remaining parts of the broadcast, and Tillery used the Sara Lee spot to hurry to the rest room for a piss. Naturally, there was a line, but three or four guys made such a big deal of deferring to him that he was able to splash the urinal and get back to his stool before CBS signaled a resumption of the broadcast Godliness with the familiar earsplitting warning buzzer. Everyone else made it too, but some of the poor jokers had to finish with their legs crossed. And then it was over, and the second highest rated program in the land (probably because of its strong lead-in), a show about hard-boiled cops retraining as nursery school teachers, came on. Most of the tavern's clientele either turned away from the screen with their beers or filed out into the winter darkness, Tillery being one of those who opted to go. A cozy glow suffused him, but his apartment was empty, and in the morning he'd be back at his job as a foam-extrusion operator for an insulation firm on the outskirts of town. Happy, happy.

Someone at the Twelfth Street Tavern's door bumped him.

It was the lard-ass who'd been sitting beside him at the bar. He patted Tillery on the shoulder. "Say, fella, I'm sorry, really sorry. Will ya forgive me? Can ya, huh?"

"Yeah," Tillery mumbled. "Sure."

"Wasn't tonight's show great?" the jerk continued. "I mean, wasn't it just about the best and most upliftin episode in the whole ever-lovin' series so far?"

Tillery stepped back from the man. "Don't press your luck," he said. Then he eased himself sideways through the door—out into the God-pervaded night.

In the Memory Room

"This isn't my mother!" Kenny repeats, staring down at the dead woman in the Memory Room.

Kenny has a lumberjack's beard. His glasses magnify his eyes to the size of snowballs. His belly is so big that he cannot pull his maroon leather car coat tight enough to button it.

"I don't care what you guys say," Kenny tells the other eight members of Gina Callan's family arrayed behind him. "This . . . this *mannikin* isn't my mother!"

"Just who the hell you think it is, then?" white-haired Uncle Sarge Lobrano asks him. "Queen Elizabeth?"

Aunt Dot, Gina's sister, rebukes her husband: "Sergio!"

"This is the wrong woman they got in here! The wrong goddamn woman! My mother was beautiful, and this person—she looks like she's hurting. Still hurting."

"Kenny, it was a painful death," Aunt Dot tries to explain.

"Your mama's kidneys failed. She was retaining fluid. That's why her cheeks and jowls are so puffy."

The hostess who ushered Gina's family into the room says, "We did our best. I worked very hard to make her lifelike."

"My mother always wore glasses. We gave 'em to you. What the hell did you do with 'em?"

"Items to help make the likeness true are received at the desk, Mr. Petruzzi," the hostess tells Kenny. "Nobody passed her glasses on to me."

Kenny struggles to free his wallet from the hip pocket of his tent-sized trousers. From the wallet he extracts a photograph. "Didn't you get a picture, then? Here's the way my mother ought to look—beautiful."

He thrusts the photo at the hostess, a smart-looking, fortyish woman wearing slacks and a bulky fishnet sweater. Then, gesturing hugely, he declares again, "That's not my mother."

Vince—Uncle Sarge and Aunt Dot's son, a high-school football coach in Colorado Springs—takes his cousin's elbow. "Of course that isn't your mother, Kenny. It's only her body. Your mother's real self—her soul—is in heaven."

"I *know* where she is. But she doesn't look like *that*." Kenny flaunts the wallet photo. "This is how she looks, and this is the way I'll always remember her."

"That picture's five years old," Uncle Lyle says. "You can't expect your mother to look today the way she looked five years ago when she was in nearly perfect health."

"I can expect these bums to put the glasses we gave 'em on her, can't I?"

The hostess turns to Uncle Lyle, Gina's brother. "Mr. Sekas, I never received a photo of Mrs. Callan. Or her glasses. They never got to me."

"What you've done here," declares Kenny, "is a disgrace."

The hostess colors. But to preserve her professional dignity, she purses her lips and lowers her head.

Aunt Dot squeezes forward and puts her hand on the edge of the casket. "It's not just the glasses," she tells everyone. "Gina's not wearing earrings. Sis'd never dress up in such lovely clothes without putting on her earrings."

Claudia, Vince's nineteen-year-old sister, seconds her mother: "That's right. Gina isn't Gina without her earrings."

"Gina isn't Gina because these goofballs lost the picture we gave them. And her glasses, too."

"Mr. Petruzzi," the hostess says, the Memory Room seeming to contract about her, "if you gave us a photo and some glasses, we'll find them. But no one passed them on to me, and I had to make do as well as I could without them."

"It wasn't very good, was it?"

"Get this bugger out of here," Uncle Sarge directs Vince and Frank. Frank is Uncle Lyle and Aunt Martha's son, a pharmacist in Kenny's hometown, Gunnison.

Then Sarge turns to the hostess. "Kenny's upset—we're all upset—and you just gotta excuse him, ma'am. He depended like crazy on his mother. Even after he was this big grown man you see hulking here, he couldn't stop grabbing at her apron strings."

Like a couple of tugboats flanking the *Queen Mary*, Vince and Frank take Kenny's arms. Their huge, goggle-eyed cousin does not resist them. Instead he begins to blubber:

"She . . . she did everything for me. Loaned me money. Bought my clothes. Even if I came home at two in the morning, she'd crawl out of bed to fix me something to eat."

"She was that way to everybody," Claudia assures Kenny.

"And not just simple sandwich stuff, either. Gourmet doings. Omelets. Polenta and gravy. Steak and eggs."

Vince and Frank maneuver their cousin, the adopted son of Gina and the late Ernesto Petruzzi, toward the parlor beyond the Memory Room. Out of the pale of his dead mother's aura.

"She was my intercessor!" Kenny cries over his shoulder. "My champion when nobody else gave a damn!"

•

199

Alone with the dead woman, the hostess perches near the casket doing some careful repair work on the masklike face of Gina Sekas Petruzzi Callan. In the hermetic, off-white room, she feels again that she is inhabiting the remembered life of the deceased.

Frank Sekas's wife Melinda Jane has gone out into the February cold with Dorothy and Claudia Lobrano to buy some earrings.

All the other mourners—Uncle Sergio, Cousin Vincent, Uncle Lyle, Aunt Martha, Cousin Frank, and the distraught Kenny—have retired to the parlor, where they sit on lumpy divans or pace the worn carpet. A peculiar odor of lillies, nostalgia, and embalming fluid permeates the Memory Room.

It seems to the hostess that her subject is listening intently to her family's muted conversation.

Sergio Lobrano is saying, "It doesn't have to be open-casket, Kenny. You know that, don't you?"

"Aunt Dot wants it open."

"Now, look, let's get this straight. Your aunt's not bossing this business, and I don't want you saying afterwards that it was open-casket because that's how Aunt Dot wanted it, and your mother didn't look like herself, and blah blah blah."

"Uncle Sergio, I'm not—"

" 'Cause that'd be a cheap trick, Kenny. It wouldn't be fair to your Aunt Dot and it wouldn't be fair to yourself."

"Wait a minute," Uncle Lyle objects, and Aunt Martha chimes in, "Sarge, you haven't given Kenny a chance to—"

"I don't want him blaming his aunt for making a mockery of his mother at her own funeral, that's all."

Kenny's high-pitched, indignant voice startles the hostess: "I love my Aunt Dot, Uncle Sergio! I'd never do anything to hurt her—any more 'n I'd ever do anything to hurt my own mother. So what the hell're you talking here?"

"Well, I—" his uncle begins, audibly abashed.

"You didn't let me finish. I'm only saying that whatever Aunt

Dot wants, *I* want. And if we both want it, how could I ever trash her for something I've okayed myself?"

"Yeah," Sarge feebly confesses. "That's different."

"You didn't let me finish."

"Kenny, I'm sorry."

"It's okay," Kenny says. "Just don't try to tell me I'd ever do somethin' to hurt Aunt Dot."

"I won't. Believe me, I won't."

Conversation lapses, and the hostess, studying Kenny's photo of his mother, makes an unobtrusive adjustment to the lines bracketing Gina Callan's mouth. A familiar claustropbia menaces her.

Then she hears Vince say, "I wouldn't want some stranger trying to get my body presentable."

"Shhhh," Aunt Martha tells him. "Not so loud."

"I want to be cremated. I want my ashes scattered on the wind over the Great Sand Dunes National Monument. It's in my will."

Sarge makes a disgusted noise.

"Can you do that?" Kenny asks. "Can you have your ashes thrown out on federal land like that?"

"Who's going to stop you?" says Vince. "You just get somebody who's willing to go out there and do it."

"It won't be me or your mother," Sarge says. "What the hell's a punk like you doing with a will?"

"Be proud of him, Sarge," Martha says. "All most young people think about today is new cars or their next skiing trip."

"Not our Vince. He thinks about becoming a pollutant in some goddamn government showcase for sand."

"What's wrong with that?" Frank asks. "I'd like to be cremated myself. Dead's dead, and it's a helluva lot cheaper than a fancy-pants show like this."

In the ever-contracting Memory Room, the hostess imagines Frank rolling his eyes at the parlor's cut-glass chandelier.

"Gina wanted a Catholic funeral," Lyle intones. "Which is why

201

we're doing our best to give her one. Her marrying Wesley Callan, a joker with two divorces, didn't make it all that damn easy to set up, either. I had to talk to half a dozen different priests before Father McFahey agreed to do it."

"And that silly fart Callan isn't even coming," Sarge grouses.

"Are you sure?" Martha asks. "I told him over the phone he'd live to regret not coming up here."

Kenny says, "Yeah, well, he told me he wasn't going to listen to a bunch of R.C. mumbo-jumbo. He and his holier-than-everybody cronies in Gunnison're gonna put on some sort of memorial service of their own."

"Mumbo-jumbo?" Martha says.

"Yeah, 'mumbo-jumbo.' So I said, 'You've got your own sort of mumbo-jumbo to listen to, don't you, Wes?'"

Sarge laughs. "What'd he say to that, Kenny?"

"He didn't like it. But if you treat people lousy, it stands to reason you're gonna get treated lousy back."

"Those goddamn Jehovah's Witnesses drive me bats," Frank says. " 'Live Forever on Paradise Earth.' 'Blessed Are the One Hundred and Forty-Four Thousand.' 'Jesus Is Actually the Archangel Michael in Disguise.' Etcetera, etcetera. Aunt Gina was a saint to put up with three years of that malarky. A bona fide saint."

"And beautiful," Kenny murmurs. "Always beautiful."

"Wes may be a Witness," Martha declares, "but when he tucks it in, they'll cremate him—hear that, Vince?—and put his ashes in a jar and stick him on a shelf right across from Gina's vault in the Tower of Memories."

"But what about me?" Kenny asks. "Where am I gonna go? They saved no place for me, Aunt Martha."

Kenny's complaint reduces everyone else to silence.

In the Memory Room, the hostess makes a tiny incision in Gina's neck, swabs the vulcanized flesh around it, and seals the cut with a special mortician's adhesive. It seems to her that, now, she and her subject are straining hard enough to hear the snow whirl out of the overcast. It clings to their turn-of-the-century building like Colorado cotton, rectangles of frozen flannel.

The door opens, and a teenage girl comes into the room with a small manilla folder and a leather glasses case.

"I found these things upstairs," she says, giving them to the woman on the stool.

"Wonderful."

"What's wrong, Mrs. Dennis?"

"They'd've been a lot of help yesterday." Mrs. Dennis, the hostess, opens the envelope, removes the glossy photo, and tilts it to compare its likeness to the face undergoing renovation.

"But I wasn't here yesterday. I couldn't—"

"Never mind, Heather. Get on back upstairs."

The girl hesitates, collects herself, and leaves, going through the smoke-filled parlor past Kenny Petruzzi, the Sekases, and the Lobranos. Mrs. Dennis gets only a glimpse of the family before the door drifts shut again and she must return her attention to the dead woman in the casket.

—Forgive my Kenny, the corpse implores her. Ernesto and I spoiled him when he was little.

He isn't little now, Mrs. Dennis rejoins.

—His thoughtless behavior isn't really his fault. He never learned any responsibility.

Why the hell didn't he?

—I couldn't have children so we adopted. We were so glad to get Kenny, we went overboard to prove it. Ernesto gave him a diamond ring when he was six. He lost it the next day.

Mrs. Dennis merely stares at the dead woman.

—Kenny was the only thing Wes and I ever argued about, Gina Callan continues. Except for Wes's new religion.

Aloud, Mrs. Dennis says, "Same old story. Child won't accept original parent's choice of stand-in spouse."

—It wasn't that, the corpse informs her. Kenny was almost

203

thirty when Wes and I married. Ernesto'd been dead since Kenny was nine, and Kenny *liked* Wes. Or he did before the Witnesses got to him.

Then I had it backwards, thinks Mrs. Dennis, still working on her subject's throat: It was Wes who didn't like Kenny.

—Wes liked him as a person, only he couldn't put up with him being so flighty. When we got married, Kenny was just back from Vietnam. His wife had run out on him while he was over there and he didn't want to do nothing but play the dogs in Colorado Springs and Pueblo.

And Wes didn't approve of gambling?

—Oh, before he got converted, Wes'd play the dogs, too. It was Kenny's losing and borrowing money that drove him buggy.

But Wes loaned him money, anyway? Betting money?

—No, I loaned Kenny the money. Sometimes I just handed it to him. Sometimes he'd ask me for something to pawn. Jewelry, maybe, or silverware, and I'd give it to him so he could play his "system" and try to win back what he'd already lost.

Thinks Mrs. Dennis, No wonder Wes went buggy, Mrs. Callan. You were feeding Kenny's habit.

—It *was* a habit. A habit and an obsession. He had computer printouts and three-by-five cards about them damn dogs all over our house in Gunnison. His room downstairs . . . it looked the way an embassy looks when they have to shred their files. He was working out his "system." A system to make him rich.

And you fell for that?

—Well, sometimes, just occasionally, he'd win. When he did, he wouldn't think to pay us back for staking him. But he'd go out and buy me a color TV set or Wes some expensive hunting equipment. That'd stick him in a hole deeper than his evening's winnings, and Wes'd start ranting about Kenny being a numbskull and a moocher and a baby. A three-hundred-pound baby.

Painstakingly relining Gina Callan's eyes, Mrs. Dennis murmurs, "Seems like an accurate character assessment to me."

—No, wait. A month before I went into Fitzsimmons, he quit the dogs cold. Stopped going to the track. Wouldn't let his old betting buddies talk him into giving it another go. Even Wes was impressed. Even Wes.

Observes the hostess, But Wes isn't here.

—That's because my family's Catholic, and I wanted to be put to rest like a Catholic, and being a Witness has made it impossible for Wes to think about my religion without getting angry. It's got nothing to do with Kenny.

Except Kenny's Catholic, too. And hates your husband for his pious intolerance. And resents him for not being here.

—Kenny's *not* Catholic. After Wes and I married, he quit us. Now he's a Unitarian or something. Kenny hates the Catholics for refusing to let me take communion because I fell in love with and actually married a guy who'd been married twice already.

"Wheels within wheels," Mrs. Dennis tells the ceiling.

Reminisces Gina Callan:

—Our first years together, Wes had no faith but pro football. About four years ago, though, a doctor at Fitzsimmons botched the prostate surgery he needed. Wesley nearly died. These Witnesses got to him while he was suffering, talked to him, studied with him, poured their propaganda on him. He was down so far he bought it. Kenny says if only the Buddhists or the Hare Krishnas had reached him first, Wesley'd be that today instead. I wish they had.

I guess Wes was easier to take as a Denver Bronco fan than as a religious zealot?

—You bet. He wouldn't celebrate birthdays or Christmas. He wouldn't even buy me a stupid Valentine. He was afraid one of the brothers or sisters would call him "frivolous." That's when Kenny started to get fed up with *him*.

"I'm almost finished, Mrs. Callan." Mrs. Dennis leans back on her stool, studies her subject, and then removes the dead woman's glasses from their leather case and sets them on her nose, snugging the ear struts into her bouffant hairdo.

—I went into the hospital terrified, the bespectacled Gina Callan tells her hostess. I remembered how one of their lousy doctors nearly killed Wes, and *I* was afraid to die, afraid they'd push me to it the way they'd almost done him.

I suppose it's a cliché, Mrs. Dennis rejoins, but there are worse things than dying.

—Fear's one, admits the dead woman. And when I was really hurting, retaining water and so on, one of those army dorks . . . Wes called 'em *dorktors* right to their face, but they always seemed just to think he talked funny . . . came into my room and said, Mrs. Callan, you're dying. I think you should know. You've probably only got a few more hours. He didn't ask Wes, he didn't ask Kenny, he just took it upon himself to tell me.

My God, thinks Mrs. Dennis, genuinely appalled.

—That did it. That whomped the heart right out of me. Maybe some people'd be grateful to be told, but not me. I was thinking I'd make it, but what he said was absolutely chilling. I was . . . well, the only word that says it is *horror-struck.*

Mrs. Callan, I can imagine.

—They'd been taking me on and off various monitors and kidney machines, and sticking me with needles, and running plastic tubes in and out of me, and, well, I didn't last till morning. Kenny and Wesley sat there helpless beside me as I passed on. And being dead hasn't been half so bad as going terrified into that hospital and being told by some army quack . . . that *dorktor,* as Wes'd call him . . . that I was dying.

To herself, not to the woman's corpse, Mrs. Dennis thinks, How much more of this am I going to be able to stand?

—Know what terrifies me now? What ruins the death snooze I'm entitled to after sixty-seven years working and worrying?

No, ma'am. What?

—Wes'll be okay. He's got his religion to fall back on. But what's to become of Kenny?

Thinks Mrs. Dennis consolingly, He'll be okay, too.

—No. No, he won't. He never learned any responsibility. It was my fault, mine and Ernesto's, but poor Kenny's gonna be the one to pay for it. He's a baby. Still a baby . . .

Aunt Dot, Cousin Claudia, and Melinda Jane return from their shopping expedition. Mrs. Dennis and her subject can hear them coming down the carpeted stairs. The menfolk rise to greet them, while Aunt Martha blurts, "Those are wonderful, Dot. Those are Gina, all right. They're unquestionably Gina."

The women come crowding in, warning Kenny, Sarge, Lyle, Vince, and Frank to stay put. This is a female matter, cosmeticizing Gina, and Kenny and the guys will be allowed to look at her again only when Aunt Dot says she's presentable. Mrs. Dennis consents to their invasion—even though she cannot help feeling that they are barging into a torture chamber, not merely coming home with bangles with which to adorn their dead.

Melinda Jane shuts the door behind them.

"Ta da," says Claudia. She holds up a pair of beaten-brass earrings, with artificial pearls in the center of each clip.

"Thank God you got clip-ons," Mrs. Dennis tells her. "I know she had pierced ears, but the holes've closed up."

"Clip-ons, schlip-ons," Claudia replies. "All that matters is for 'em to look like her. These do."

"Big and jangly" says one of the aunts.

"Gina through and through," says the other.

Everyone in the Memory Room stares down at the dead woman. The hostess realizes that her subject, who stopped transmitting at the first sound of the women's return, is basking in their approval. For the first time since entering the mortuary, Gina Callan feels good about herself.

"Okay," says Aunt Dot, taking a deep breath and wiping her eyes with her sleeve. "Get Kenny in here."

Someone opens the door. The men bunch up, squeeze through, and approach the casket. Kenny shoulders his way to the front.

"Whaddaya think?" Martha asks. "Isn't that more like it?"

For a moment, Kenny merely stares. His bug eyes dart from his mother's hands to her rouged face and back again. Then he turns and, locating Mrs. Dennis, reaches out and grabs her hands.

"This is my mother," he tells her. "You goofballs finally got it right."

"Thank you. Your relatives helped."

"She's beautiful again—as beautiful as I remember."

"Thank you," repeats the hostess.

"You found her glasses. Her picture, too."

"One of our employees found them. Heather Thompson."

"Heather Thompson deserves a raise," Kenny cries. "I'm gonna buy her a box of candy. You, too. Both of you."

He releases Mrs. Dennis, turns again to the casket, and lifts his arms in a dramatic gesture of thanksgiving.

"This is my mother," he proclaims. "God bless everybody here for giving me back my mother."

Alone again with the bereaved dead woman, Mrs. Dennis sits down wearily on her stool.

—Wes never came, Gina Callan tells her. And Kenny's gonna be lost without me. Absolutely lost.

"Shut up!" the hostess shouts, trying to reclaim her room. "Do you think you're the only goddamn stiff whose troubles I've got to listen to? Is that what you think?"

Gina Sekas Petruzzi Callan ceases to transmit.

"That's better," Mrs. Dennis whispers, cupping her face in her hands. "Who the hell do you guys think you are, anyway?"

Life Regarded as a Jigsaw Puzzle
of Highly Lustrous Cats

Your father-in-law, who insists that you call him Howie, even though you prefer Mr. Bragg, likes jigsaw puzzles. If they prove harder than he has the skill or the patience for, he knows a sneaky way around the problem.

During the third Christmas season after your marriage to Marti, you find Howie at a card table wearing a parka, a blue watch cap with a crown of burgundy leather, and fur-lined shoes. (December through February, it is freezing in the Braggs' Tudor-style house outside Spartanburg). He is assembling a huge jigsaw puzzle. The Braggs give him one every Christmas. His challenge is to piece it together, unaided by drop-in company or anyone else, before the Sugar Bowl kick-off on New Year's Day.

This year, the puzzle is of cats.

The ESB procedure being administered to you by the Zoo Cop and his associates is keyed to cats. When they zap your implanted electrodes, cat-related memories parachute into your mind's eye, opening out like fireworks.

The lid from the puzzle's box is Mr. Bragg's—Howie's—blue-print, and it depicts a population explosion of stylized cats.

They are both mysterious beasts and whimsical cartoons. The puzzle lacks any background, it's so full of cats. They run, stalk, lap milk, tussel, tongue-file their fur, snooze, and so on. There are no puzzle areas where a single color dominates, a serious obstacle to quick assembly.

Howie has a solution. When only a handful of pieces remain in the box, he uses a razor blade to shave any piece that refuses to fit where he wants it to. This is cheating, as even Howie readily acknowledges, but on New Year's Eve, with Dick Clark standing in Times Square and the Sugar Bowl game only hours away, a man can't afford to screw around.

"Looking good," you say as the crowd on TV starts its rowdy countdown to midnight. "You're almost there."

Howie confesses—complains?—that this puzzle has been a "real mindbender." He appreciates the challenge of a thousand-plus pieces and a crazy-making dearth of internal clues, but why this particular puzzle? He usually receives a photographic landscape or a Western painting by Remington.

"I'm not a cat fancier," he tells you. "Most of 'em're sneaky little bastards, don't you think?"

Marti likes cats, but when you get canned at Piedmont Freight in Atlanta, she moves back to Spartanburg with your son, Jacob, who may be allergic to cats. Marti leaves in your keeping two calico mongrels that duck out of sight whenever you try to feed or catch them. You catch them eventually, of course, and drive them to the pound in a plastic animal carrier that Marti bought from Delta, or Eastern, or some other airline out at Hartsfield

•

210

Penfield, a.k.a. the Zoo Cop, wants to know how you lost your job. He gives you a multiple-choice quiz:

A. Companywide lay-off
B. Neglect of duty and/or unacceptable job performance
C. Personality conflict with a supervisor
D. Suspicion of disloyalty
E. All, or none, of the above   ·

You tell him that there was an incident of (alleged) sexual harassment involving a female secretary whose name, even under the impetus of electrical stimulation of the brain (ESB), you cannot now recall. All you can recall is every cat, real or imaginary, ever to etch its image into your consciousness.

After your firing, you take the cats, Springer and Ossie (short for Ocelot) to the pound. When you look back from the shelter's doorway, a teen-age attendant is giving you, no doubt about it, the evil eye. Springer and Ossie are doomed. No one in the big, busy city wants a mixed-breed female. The fate awaiting nine-year-old Jacob's cats—never mind their complicity in his frightening asthma—is the gas chamber; today, though, you are as indifferent to the cats' fate as a latter-day Eichmann. You are numb from the molecular level upward.

"We did have them spayed," you defend yourself. "Couldn't you use that to pitch them to some nice family?"

You begin to laugh.

Is this another instance of Inappropriate Affect? Except for the laughing gas given you to sink the electrodes, you've now been off all medication for . . . you don't know how long.

On the street only three years after your dismissal, you wept at hoboes' bawdy jokes, got up and danced if the obituaries you'd been sleeping under reported an old friend's death.

Once, you giggled when a black girl bummed a cigarette in the parking lot of Trinity United Methodist: "I got AIDS, man. Hain't no smoke gonna kill me. Hain't time enough for the ol' lung cee to kick in, too."

Now that Penfield's taken you off antipsychotics, is Ye Old Inappropriate Affect kicking in again? Or is this fallout from the ESB? After all, one gets entirely different responses (rage and affection; fear and bravado) from zapping hypothalamic points less than 0.02 inch from each other.

Spill it, Adolf, Penfield says. What's so funny?

Cat juggling, you tell him. (Your name has never been Adolf.)

What?

Steve Martin in *The Jerk*. An illegal Mexican sport. A joke, you know. Cat juggling.

You surrender to jerky laughter. It hurts, but your glee isn't inappropriate. The movie was a comedy. People were *supposed* to laugh. Forget that when you close your eyes, you see yourself as the outlaw juggler. Forget that the cats in their caterwauling orbits include Springer, Ossie, Thai Thai, Romeo, and an anonymous albino kitten from your dead grandparents' grain crib on their farm outside Montgomery. . . .

As a boy in Hapeville, the cat you like best is Thai Thai, a male Siamese that your mama and you inherit from the family moving out. His name isn't Thai Thai before your mama starts calling him that, though. It's something fake Chinese, like Lung Cee or Mouser Tung. The folks moving out don't want to take him with them, their daddy's got a job with Otero Steel in Pueblo, Colorado. Besides, Mouser Tung's not likely to dig the ice and snow out there. He's a Deep South cat, Dixie-born and -bred.

"You are who you are," Mama tells the Siamese while he rubs her laddered nylons, "but from here on out your name is Thai Thai."

"Why're you calling him that?" you ask her.

"Because it *fits* a cracker Siamese," she says.

It's several years later before you realize that Thailand is Siam's current name and that there's a gnat-plagued town southeast of Albany called, yeah, Ty Ty.

Your mama's a smart gal, with an agile mind and a quirky sense of humor. How Daddy ever got it into his head that she wasn't good enough for him is a mystery.

It's her agile mind and her quirky sense of humor that did her in, the Zoo Cop says, pinching back your eyelid.

Anyway, Daddy ran off to a Florida dog-track town with a chunky bottle-blonde ex-hair dresser who dropped a few pounds and started a mail-order weight-loss-tonic business. He's been gone nine weeks and four days.

Thai Thai, when you notice him, is pretty decent company. He sheathes his claws when he's in your lap. He purrs at a bearable register. He eats leftover vegetables—peas, lima beans, spinach— as readily as he does bacon rinds or chicken scraps. A doll, Mama calls him. A gentleman.

This ESB business distorts stuff. It flips events, attitudes, prefer- ences upside-down. The last shall be first, the first shall be last. This focus on cats, for example, is a *major* distortion, a misleading reenvisioning of the life that you lived before getting trapped by Rockdale Biological Supply Company.

Can't Penfield see this? Uh-uh, no way. He's too hot to screw Rockdale Biological's bigwigs. The guy may have right on his side, but to him—for the moment, anyway—you're just another hu- man oven-cake. If you crumble when the heat's turned up, great, zip-a-dee-zoo-cop, pop me a cold one, justice is served.

Thing is, you prefer dogs. Even as a kid, you like them more. You bring home flea-bitten strays and beg to keep them. When you live in Alabama, you covet the liony chow, Simba, that waits every afternoon in the Notasulga schoolyard for Wesley Duplantier.

Dogs, not cats. Until Mouser Tung—Thai Thai—all the cats you know prowl on the edges of your attention. Even Thai Thai comes to you and Mama, over here in Georgia, as a kind of offhand house-warming gift. Dogs, Mister Zoo Cop, not cats.

Actually, Penfield says, I'm getting the idea that what was in the *forefront* of your attention, Adolf, was women. . . .

After puberty, your attention never *has* a forefront. You are divebombed by stimuli. Girl's faces are billboards. Their bodies are bigger billboards. Jigsawed ad signs. A piece here. A piece there. It isn't just girls. It's everything. Cars, buildings, TV talking heads, mosquito swarms, jet contrails, interchangeable male callers at suppertime, battle scenes on the six o'clock news, rock idols infinitely glitterized, the whole schmear fragmenting as it feeds into you, Mr. Teen-age Black Hole of the Spirit. Except when romancing a sweet young gal, your head's a magnet for all the flak generated by your media-crazed century.

"You're tomcatting, aren't you?" Mama says. "You're tomcatting just like Webb did. God."

It's a way to stay focused. With their faces and bodies under you, they cease to be billboards. You're a human being again, not a radio receiver or a gravity funnel. The act imposes a fleeting order on the ricocheting chaos working every instant to turn you, the mind cementing it all together, into a flimsy cardboard box of mismatched pieces.

Is that tomcatting? Resisting, by a tender union of bodies, the consequences of dumping a jigsaw puzzle of cats into a box of pieces that, assembled, would depict, say, a unit of embattled flak gunners on Corregidor?

Christ, the Zoo Cop says, a more highfalutin excuse for chasing tail I've never heard.

•

Your high school is crawling with cats. Cool cats, punk cats, stray cats, dead cats. Some are human, some aren't.

You dissect a cat in biology lab. On a plaster-of-Paris base, guyed upright by wires, stands the bleached skeleton of a quadruped that Mr. Osteen—he's also the track and girl's softball coach—swears was a member of *Felis catus*, the common house cat.

With its underlying gauntness exposed and its skull gleaming brittle and grotesque, this skeleton resembles that of something prehistoric. Pamela van Rhyn and two or three other girls want to know where the cats in the lab came from.

"A scientific supply house," Coach Osteen says. "Same place we get our bullfrogs, our microscope slides, the insects in that there display case." He nods at it.

"Where does the supply house get them?" Pamela says.

"I don't know, Pammie. Maybe they raise 'em. Maybe they round up strays. You missing a kitty?"

In fact, rumor holds that Mr. Osteen found the living source of his skeleton behind the track field's south bleachers, chloroformed it, carried it home, and boiled the fur off it in a pot on an old stove in his basement. Because of the smell, his wife spent a week in Augusta with her mother. Rumor holds that cat lovers hereabouts would be wise to keep their pets indoors.

Slicing into the chest cavity of the specimen provided by the supply house, you find yourself losing it. You are the only boy in Coach Osteen's lab to contract nausea and an overwhelming uprush of self-disgust; the only boy, clammy-palmed and light-headed, to have to leave the room. The ostensible shame of your departure is lost on Pamela, who agrees, in Nurse Mayhew's office, to rendezvous with you later that afternoon at the Huddle House.

"This is the heart," you can still hear Osteen saying. "Looks like a wet rubber strawberry, don't it?"

As a seven-year-old, you wander into the grain crib of the barn on the Powell farm. A one-eyed mongrel queen named Sky has dropped a litter on the deer hides, today stiff and rat-eaten, that

Gramby Powel stowed there twenty or more years ago. Sky one-eyes you with real suspicion, all set to bolt or hiss, as you lean over a rail to study the blind quintet of her kittening.

They're not much, mere lumps. "Turds with fur," Gramby called them last night, to Meemaw Anita's scandalized dismay and the keen amusement of your daddy. They hardly move.

One kitten gleams white on the stiff hide, in a nervous curl of Sky's furry belly. You spit at Sky, as another cat would spit, but louder—*sssssphh! sssssphh!*—so that eventually, intimidated, she gets up, kittens falling from her like bombs from the open bay of a B-52, and slinks to the far wall of the crib.

You climb over the rail and pick up the white kitten, the Maybe Albino as Meemaw Anita dubbed it. "Won't know for sure," she said, "till its eyes're open."

You turn the kitten in your hands. Which end is which? It's sort of hard to say. Okay, here's the starchy white potato print of its smashed-in pug of a face: eyes shut, ears a pair of napkin folds, mouth a miniature crimson gap.

You rub the helpless critter on your cheek. Cat smells. Hay smells. Hide smells. It's hard not to sneeze.

It occurs to you that you could throw this Maybe Albino like a baseball. You could wind up like Denny McClain and fling it at the far wall of the grain crib. If you aim just right, you may be able to hit the wall so that the kitten rebounds and lands on Sky. You could sing a funny song, "Sky's being fallen on, / Oh, Sky's being fallen on, / Whatcha think 'bout that?" And nobody'll ever know if poor little Maybe Albino has pink eyes or not. . . .

This sudden impulse horrifies you, even as a kid, especially as a kid. You can see the white kitten dead. Trembling, you set the kitten back down on the cardboardy deer hide, climb back over the crib rail, and stand away from the naked litter while Sky tries to decide what to do next.

Unmanfully, you start to cry. "S-s-orry, k-kitty. S-s-sorry, Sk-sky. I'm r-r-really s-sorry." You almost want Gramby or Meemaw

216

Anita to stumble in on you, in the churchly gloom and itch of their grain crib, to see you doing this heartfelt penance for a foul deed imagined but never carried out. It's okay to cry a bit in front of your mama's folks.

I'm touched, Penfield says. But speak up. Stop mumbling.

For several months after your senior year, you reside in the Adolescent Wing of the Quiet Harbor Psychiatric Center in a suburb of Atlanta. You're there to neutralize the disorienting stimuli—flak, you call it—burning out your emotional wiring, flying at you from everywhere. You're there to relearn how to live with no despairing recourse to disguises, sex, drugs.

Bad drugs, the doctors mean.

At QHPC, they give you good drugs. This is actually the case, not sarcastic bullshit. Kim Yaughan, one of the psychotherapists in the so-called Wild Child Wing, assures you that this is so; that antipsychotics aren't addictive. You get 20 milligrams a day of haloperidol. You take it in liquid form in paper cups shaped like doll-house-sized coffee filters.

"You're not an addict," Kim says. (Everyone at QHPC calls her Kim.) "Think of yourself as a diabetic, of Haldol as insulin. You don't hold a diabetic off insulin, that'd be criminal."

Not only do you get Haldol, you get talk therapy, recreational therapy, family therapy, crafts therapy. Some of the residents of the Wild Child Wing are druggies and sexual-abuse victims as young as twelve. They get these same therapies, along with pet therapy. The pets brought in on Wednesdays often include cats.

At last, Penfield tells an associate. That last jolt wasn't a mis-hit, after all.

The idea is that hostile, fearful, or withdrawn kids who don't interact well with other people will do better with animals.

217

Usually, they do. Kittens under a year, tumbling with one another, batting at yarn balls, exploring the pet room with their tails up like the radio antennas on cars, seem to be effective four-legged therapists.

One teen-age girl, a manic-depressive who calls herself Eagle Rose, goes ga-ga over them. "Oh," she says, holding up a squirmy smoke-colored male and nodding at two kittens wrestling in an empty carton of Extra Large Tide, "they're so soft, so neat, so . . . so *highly lustrous.*"

Despite Kim Yaughan's many attempts to involve you, you stand aloof from everyone. It's Eagle Rose who focuses your attention, not the kittens, and E.R.'s an untouchable. Every patient here is an untouchable, that way. It would be a terrible betrayal to think anything else. So, mostly, you don't.

The year before you marry, Marti is renting a house on North Highland Avenue. A whole house. It's not a big house, but she has plenty of room. She uses one bedroom as a studio. In this room, on the floor, lies a large canvas on which she has been painting, exclusively in shades of blue, the magnified heart of a magnolia. She calls the painting—too explicitly, you think—*Magnolia Heart in Blue.* She's worked on it all quarter, often appraising it from a stepladder to determine how best to continue.

Every weekend, you sleep with Marti in the bedroom next to the studio. Her mattress rests on the floor, without box springs or bedstead. You sometimes feel that you're lying in the middle of a painting in progress, a strange but gratifying sensation that you may or may not carry into your next week of classes at GSU.

One balmy Sunday, you awake to find Marti's body stenciled with primitive blue flowers, a blossom on her neck, more on her breasts, an indigo bouquet on the milky plane of her abdomen. You gaze at her in groggy wonderment. The woman you plan to marry has become, overnight, an arabesque of disturbing floral bruises.

Then you see the cat, Romeo, a neighbor's gray Persian,

propped in the corner, belly exposed, so much like a hairy little man in a recliner that you laugh. Marti stirs. Romeo preens. Clearly, he entered through a studio window, walked all over *Magnolia Heart in Blue*, then came in here and violated Marti.

My wife-to-be as a strip of fin de siècle wallpaper, you muse, kissing her chastely on one of the paw-print flowers.

You sleep on the streets. You wear the same stinking clothes for days on end. You haven't been on haloperidol for months. The city could be Lima, or Istanbul, or Bombay, as easily as Atlanta. Hell, it could be a boulder-littered crater on the moon. You drag from one place to another like a zombie, and the people you hit up for hamburgers, change, MARTA tokens, old newspapers, have no more substance to you than you do to them, they could all be holograms or ghosts. They could be androids programmed to keep you dirty and hungry by dictating your behavior with remote-control devices that look like wrist watches and key rings.

Cats mean more to you than people do. (The people may not be people.) Cats are fellow survivors, able to sniff out nitrogenous substances from blocks away. Food.

You follow a trio of scrawny felines down Ponce de Leon to the rear door of a catfish restaurant where the Dumpster overflows with greasy paper and other high refuse. The cats strut around on the mounded topography of this debris while you balance on an upturned trash barrel, mindlessly picking and choosing.

Seven rooms away from Coach Osteen's lab, Mr. Petty is teaching advanced junior English. Poetry. He stalks around the room like an actor doing Hamlet, even when the poem's something dumb by Ogden Nash, or something beat and surface-sacrilegious by Ferlinghetti, or something short and puzzling by Carlos Williams.

The Williams piece is about a cat that climbs over a cabinet— a "jamcloset"—and steps into a flowerpot. Actually, Mr. Petty says, it's about the *image* created by Williams's purposely simple diction. Everyone argues that it isn't a poem at all. It's even less a poem, lacking metaphors, than that Carl Sandburg thing about the fog coming on little, for Christ's sake, cat's feet.

You like it, though. You can see the cat stepping cautiously into the flowerpot. The next time you're in Coach Osteen's class, trying to redeem yourself at the dissection table, you recite the poem for Pamela van Rhyn, Jessie Faye Culver, Kathy Margenau, and Cynthia Spivy.

Coach Osteen, shaking his head, makes you repeat the lines so that he can say them, too. Amazing.

"Cats are digitigrade critters," he tells the lab. "That means they walk on their toes. Digitigrade."

Cynthia Spivy catches your eye. *Well, I'll be a pussywillow*, she silently mouths. *Who'd've thunk it?*

"Unlike the dog or the horse," Coach Osteen goes on, "the cat walks by moving the front and back legs on one side of its body and then the front and back legs on the other. The only other animals to move that way are the camel and the giraffe."

And naked crazy folks rutting on all fours, you think, studying Cynthia's lips and wondering if there was ever a feral child raised by snow leopards or jaguars. . . .

Thai Thai develops a urinary tract infection. Whenever he has to pee, he looks for Mama pulling weeds or hanging out clothes in the back yard, and squats to show her that he's not getting the job done. It takes Mama two or three days to realize what's going on. Then you and she carry Thai to the vet.

Mama waits tables at a Denny's near the expressway. She hasn't really got the money for the operation that Thai needs to clear up the blockage, a common problem in male Siamese. She tells you that you can either forfeit movie money for the next few months or help her pay to make Thai well. You hug Mama, wordlessly agreeing that the only thing to do is to help your cat. The operation goes okay, but the vet telephones a day later to report that Thai took a bad turn overnight and died near morning.

Thai's chocolate and silver body has a bandage cinched around his middle, like a wraparound saddle.

You're the one who buries Thai because Mama can't bring herself to. You put him in a Siamese-sized cardboard box, dig a hole under the holly in the backyard, and lay him to rest with a spank of the shovel blade and a prayer consisting of grief-stricken repetitions of the word please.

Two or three months later, you come home from school to find a pack of dogs in the backyard. They've dug Thai Thai up. You chase the dogs away, screeching from an irate crouch. Thai's corpse is nothing but matted fur and protruding bones. Its most conspicuous feature is the bandage holding the maggoty skeleton together at its cinched-in waist.

This isn't Thai, you tell yourself. I buried Thai a long, long time ago, and this isn't him.

You carry the remains, jacketed in the editorial section of the *Atlanta Constitution*, to a trash can and dump them with an abrupt, indifferent thunk. Pick-up is tomorrow.

One Sunday afternoon in March, you're standing with two hundred other homeless people at the entrance to Trinity United Methodist's soup kitchen, near the state capitol. It's drizzling. A thin but gritty-looking young woman in jeans and sweat shirt, her hair lying in dark strands against her forehead, is passing out hand-numbered tickets to every person who wants to get into the basement. At the head of the outside basement steps is a man in pleated slacks and a plaid shirt. He won't let anyone down the steps until they have a number in the group of ten currently being admitted. He has to get an okay from the soup-kitchen staff downstairs before he'll allow a new group of ten to pass.

Your number, on a green slip of paper already drizzle-dampened, is 126. The last group down held numbers 96 to 105. You

221

think. Hard to tell with all the shoving, cursing, and bantering on the line. One angry black man up front doesn't belong there. He waves his ticket every time a new group of ten is called, hoping, even though his number is 182, to squeeze past the man set there to keep order.

"How many carahs yo ring?" he asks. "I sick. Lemme eah fo I faw ouw. Damn disere rain."

When the dude holding number 109 doesn't show, the stair guard lets number 182 pass, a good-riddance sort of charity.

You shuffle up with the next two groups. How many of these people are robots, human machines drawn to the soup kitchen, as you may have been, on invisible tractor beams? The stair guard isn't wearing a watch or shaking a key ring. It's probably his wedding band that's the remote-control device. . . .

"My God," he cries when he sees you. "Is that really you? It is, isn't it?"

The stair guy's name is Dirk Healy. He says he went to school with you in Hapeville. Remember Pamela van Rhyn? Remember Cynthia What's-her-name? When you go down into the basement, and get your two white-bread sandwiches and a Styrofoam cup of vegetable soup, Dirk convinces another volunteer to take over his job and sits down next to you at one of the rickety folding tables where your fellow street folk are singlemindedly eating. Dirk, who, as far as you're concerned, could be the Man in the Moon, doesn't ask how you got in this fix, doesn't accuse, doesn't exhort.

"You're off your medication, aren't you?" Your hackles lift. "Hey," he soothes, "I visited you at Quiet Harbor. The thing to do is, to get you back on it."

You eat, taking violent snatches of the sandwiches, quick sips of the soup. You one-eye Dirk over the steam the way that, years ago, Sky one-eyed you from her grain-crib nest.

"I may have a job for you," Dirk says confidentially. "Ever hear of Rockdale Biological?"

●

222

One summer, for reasons you don't understand, Mama sends you to visit your father and his ex-hair dresser floozie—whose name is Carol Grace—in the Florida town where they live off the proceeds of her mail-order business and sometimes bet the dogs at the local greyhound track.

Carol Grace may bet the greyhounds at the track, but, at home, she's a cat person. She owns seven: a marmalade-colored tom, a piebald tom, three tricolor females, an orange Angora of ambiguous gender, and a Manx mix with a tail four or five inches long, as if someone shortened it with a cleaver.

"If Stub was pure Manx," Carol Grace says, "he wouldn't have no tail. Musta been an alley tom in his mama's Kitty Litter."

Stroking Stub, she chortles happily. She and your mother look a little alike. They have a similar feistiness, too, although it seems coarser in Carol Grace, whom your balding father—she calls him Webby, for Pete's sake—unabashedly dotes on.

A few days into your visit, Carol Grace and you find one of her females, Hedy Lamarr, lying crumpled under a pecan tree shading the two-story house's south side. The cat is dead. You kneel to touch her. Carol Grace kneels beside you.

"Musta fell," she says. "Lotsa people think cats are too jack-be-nimble to fall, but they can slip up too. Guess my Hedy didn't remember that, pretty thing. Now look."

You are grateful that, today, Carol Grace does the burying and the prayer-saying. Her prayer includes the melancholy observation that anyone can fall. Anyone.

Enough of this crap, Penfield says. Tell me what you did, and for whom, and why, at Rockdale Biological.

Givin whah I can, you mumble, working to turn your head into the uncompromising rigidity of the clamps.

Adolf, Penfield says, what you're giving me is cat juggling.

Alone in the crafts room with Kim Yaughan while the other kids in

Blue Group (QHPC's Wild Child Wing has two sections, Blue and Gold) go on a field trip, you daub acrylics at a crude portrayal of a cat walking upside down on a ceiling. Under the cat, a woman and a teenage boy point and make hateful faces.

"Are they angry at the cat or at each other?" Kim asks.

You give her a look: What a stupid question.

Kim comes over, stands at your shoulder. If she were honest, she'd tell you that you're no artist at all. The painting may be psychologically revealing, but it refutes the notion that you have any talent as a draftsman or a colorist.

"Ever hear of British artist Louis Wain?" Kim says. "He lived with three unmarried sisters and a pack of cats. His schizophrenia didn't show up until he was almost sixty. That's late."

"Lucky," you say. "He didn't have so long to be crazy."

"Listen, now. Wain painted only cats. He must've really liked them. At first, he did smarmy, realistic kitties for calendars and postcards. Popular crap. Later, thinking jealous competitors were zapping him with X-rays or something, the cats in his paintings got weird, really hostile and menacing."

"Weirder than mine?" You jab your brush at it.

"Ah, that's a mere puddy-tat." Then: "In the fifteen years he was institutionalized, Wain painted scads of big-eyed, spiky-haired cats. He put bright neon auras and electrical fields around them. His backgrounds got geometrically rad. Today, you might think they were computer-generated. Anyhow, Wain's crazy stuff was better—fiercer, stronger—than the crap he'd done sane."

"Meaning I'm a total loss unless I get crazier?" you say.

"No. What I'm trying to tell you is that the triangles, stars, rainbows, and repeating arabesques that Wain put into his paintings grew from a desperate effort to . . . well, to impose order on the chaos *inside* him. It's touching, really touching. Wain was trying to confront and reverse, the only way he could, the disintegration of his adult personality. See?"

But you don't. Not exactly.

Kim taps your acrylic cat with a burgundy fingernail. "You're not going to be the new Picasso, but you aren't doomed to suffer as terrifying a schizophrenia as Wain suffered, either. The bizarre thing in your painting is the cat on the ceiling. The colors, and the composition itself, are reassuringly conventional. A good sign for your mental health. Another thing is, Wain's doctors couldn't give him antipsychotic drugs. You, though, have access."

"Cheers." You pantomime knocking back a little cup of Haldol.

Kim smiles. "So why'd you paint the cat upside-down?

"Because *I'm* upside-down," you say.

Kim gives you a peck on the cheek. "You're not responsible for a gone-awry brain chemistry or an unbalanced metabolism, hon. Go easy on yourself, okay?" Dropping your brush, you pull Kim to you and try to nuzzle her under the jaw. Effortlessly, she bends back your hand and pushes you away. "But that," she says, "you're going to have to control. Friends, not lovers. Sorry if I gave you the wrong idea. Really."

"If the pieces toward the end don't fit," Howie tells you, "you can always use a razor blade." He holds one up.

You try to take it. Double-edged, it slices your thumb. Some of your blood spatters the cat puzzle.

A guy in a truck drives up to the specimen-prep platform and loading dock behind Rockdale Biological Medical Supply. It's an unmarked panel truck with no windows behind the cab. The guys who drive the truck change, it seems, almost every week, but you're a two-month fixture on the concrete platform with the slide cages and the euthanasia cabinet. Back here, you're Dirk Healy's main man, especially now that he's off on a business trip somewhere.

Your job is both mindless and strength-sapping. The brick wall around the rear of the RBMS complex, and the maple trees shielding the loading dock, help you keep your head together. Healy has you

225

on a lower dosage of haloperidol than you took while you and Marti were still married. Says you were overmedicated before. Says you were, ha ha, "an apathetic drug slave." He should know. He's been a hotshot in national medical supply for years.

"We'll have you up in the front office in no time," he assured you a couple weeks ago. "The platform job's a kind of trial."

The guy in the truck backs up and starts unloading. Dozens of cats in slide cages. You wear elbow-length leather gloves, and a heavy apron, and feel a bit like an old-timey Western blacksmith. The cats are pieces of scrap iron to be worked in the forge. You slide the door end of each cage into the connector between the open platform and the euthanasia cabinet, then poke the cats in the butt or the flank with a long metal rod until they duck into the cabinet to escape your prodding. When the cabinet's full, you drop the safety door, check the gauges, turn on the gas. It hisses louder than the cats climbing over one another, louder than their yowling and tumbling, which noises gradually subside and finally stop.

By hand, you unload the dead cats from the chamber, slinging them out by their tails or their legs. You cease feeling like a blacksmith. You imagine yourself as a nineteenth-century trapper, stacking fox, beaver, rabbit, wolf, and muskrat pelts on a travois for a trip to the trading post. The pelts are pretty, though many are blemished by vivid skin diseases and a thick black dandruff of gassed fleas. How much could they be worth?

"Nine fifty a cat," Dirk Healy has said. That seems unlikely. They're no longer moving. They're no longer—if they ever were—highly lustrous. They're floppy, anonymous, and dead, their fur contaminated by a lethal gas.

A heavy-duty wheelbarrow rests beside the pile of cats on the platform. You unwind a hose and fill the barrow with water. Dirk has ordered you to submerge the gassed cats to make certain they're dead. Smart. Some of the cats are plucky boogers. They'll mew at you or swim feebly in the cat pile even before you pick them up and sling them into the wheelbarrow. The water in the wheelbarrow ends it. Indisputably. It also washes away fleas and the worst aspects of feline scabies. You pull a folding chair over and sort through the cats for the ones with flea collars, ID collars, rabies tags. You take these things off. You do it with your gloves on, a sodden cat corpse hammocked in your apron. It's not easy, given your wet glove fingers.

If it's sunny, you take the dead cats to the bright part of the platform and lay them out in neat rows to dry.

Can't you get him to stop mumbling? Penfield asks someone in the room. His testimony's almost unintelligible.

He's replaying the experience inwardly, an indistinct figure says. But he's starting to go autistic on us.

Look, Penfield says. We've got to get him to verbalize clearly— or we've wasted our time.

Two months after the divorce, you drive to Spartanburg, to the Braggs' house, to see Jacob. Mr. Bragg—Howie—intercepts you at the front gate, as if apprised of your arrival by surveillance equipment.

"I'm sorry," he says, "but Marti doesn't want to see you, and she doesn't want *you* to see Jake. If you don't leave, I'll have to call the police to, ah, you know, remove you."

You don't contest this. You walk across the road to your car. From there, you can see that atop the brick post on either side of Mr. Bragg's ornate gate reposes a roaring granite lion. You can't remember seeing these lions before, but the crazed and reticulated state of the granite suggests they've been there a while.

It's a puzzle. . . .

As you lay out the dead cats, you assign them names. The names you assign are always Mehitabel, Felix, Sylvester, Tom, Heathcliff, Garfield, and Bill. These seven names must serve for all the cats on the platform. Consequently, you add Roman numerals to the names when you run out of names before you do cats:

Mehitabel II, Felix II, Sylvester II, Tom II, and so on. It's a neat, workable system. Once, you cycled all the way to Sylvester VII before running out of specimens.

As a fifth grader in Notasulga, you sit and watch a film about the American space program.

An old film clip shows a cat—really more a kitten than a cat—suspended to a low ceiling by its feet. It's a metal ceiling, and the scientist who devised the experiment (which has something to do with studying the kitten's reactions to upside-downness, then applying these findings to astronauts aboard a space station) has fastened magnets to the cat's feet so that they will adhere to the metal surface.

The scientist has also rigged up a pair of mice in the same odd way, to see if they will distract, entice, or frighten the hanging kitten. They don't. The kitten is terrified not of the mice (who seem to be torpid and unimaginative representatives of their kind), but of the alien condition in which it finds itself. Insofar as it is able, the kitten lurches against the magnets, its ears back, its mouth wide open in a silent cry. On the sound track, a male voice explains the import and usefulness of this experiment.

No one can hear him, though, because most of the other kids in Miss Beischer's class are laughing uproariously at the kitten. You look around in a kind of sick stupefaction.

Milly Heckler, Agnes Lee Terrance, and a few other girls appear to be as appalled as you, but the scene doesn't last long—it's probably shorter than your slow-motion memory of it—and it seems for a moment that you are that kitten, that everything in the world has been wrenchingly upended.

"I know it seemed to you that evil people were trying to invade and control your thoughts," Dr. Hall, the director of Quiet Harbor, tells you. He pets a neutered male just back from a visit to the Gerontological Wing. "But that was just a symptom of the scrambled condition of your brain chemistry. The truth is. . . ."

•

Fatigued, you slouch out the rear gate of Rockdale Biological. Your apartment—the three-roomer that Healy provided—is only a short distance away. A late-model Lincoln Town Car pulls alongside you as you walk the weed-grown sidewalk. The tinted window on the front-seat passenger's side powers down, and you catch your first glimpse of the raw-complexioned man who introduces himself as David Penfield. An alias? Why do you think so?

"If you like," he says, "think of me as the Zoo Cop."

It's a permission you don't really want. Why would you choose to think of a well-dressed, ordinary-featured man with visible acne scarring as something as déclassé as, Jesus, the Zoo Cop. Is he a detective of some sort? What does he want?

The next thing you know you're in the car with Penfield and two other tight-lipped men.

The next thing you know you're on the expressway and one of the Zoo Cop's associates—goons?—has locked the suction-cup feet of one of those corny Garfield toys on his tinted window as a kind of—what?—mockery? rebuke? warning?

The next thing you know you're in a basement that clearly isn't the soup kitchen of Trinity United Methodist. The next thing you know you're flat on your back on a table. The next thing you know you don't know anything. . . .

. . . Marti's body is stenciled with primitive blue flowers, a blossom on her neck, more on her breasts, an indigo bouquet on the milky plane of her abdomen. You gaze at her in groggy wonderment. The woman you one day marry has become, overnight, an arabesque of disturbing floral bruises.

"Marti," you whisper. "Marti, don't leave me. Marti, don't take my son away."

Penfield, a.k.a. the Zoo Cop (you realize during your descent into the puzzle box), isn't a real cop. He hates you because what you've been doing for Healy is vile, contemptible, evil. So it is, so it is. He

229

wants to get Healy, who hasn't been around this last week at all, who's maybe skipped off to Barbados or the Yucatan or Saint-Tropez.

Penfield is an animal-rights eco-terrorist, well-financed and determined, and the ESB zappings to which he and his associates are subjecting you are designed to incriminate, pinpoint, and doom old Dirk and *his* associates, who obviously deserve it. You too. You deserve it too. No argument there. None.

Christ, Penfield says, unhook the son of a bitch and carry him upstairs. Dump him somewhere remote, somewhere rural.

You visit the pound for a replacement for Springer and Ossie, gassed three or four years ago. The attendant tells you there are plenty of potential adoptees at the shelter. You go down the rows of cages to select one. The kittens in the fouled sawdust tumble, paw, and miaow, putting on a dispirited show.

"This one," you finally say.

"Cute." The attendant approves. Well, they'd fire her if she didn't. The idea is to adopt these creatures out, not to let them lapse into expendability.

"It's for Jake, my son," you tell her. "His asthma isn't that bad. I think he may be growing out of it."

"Look at my puzzle," Howie says, yanking the razor blade away from you. "You've bled all over it. . . ."

Reading the Silks

ONCE BEYOND A TIME, Makoto Asaeda journeyed south to escape the Cataclysm. He hiked out of Kitakyushu, staying clear of the vacant houses, the wrecked machines, and the ruby-eyed beasts aprowl in the denuded forests. He also avoided the human savages hunched over the dead dray animals littering the island. Scooping meat from the carcasses, these devolved beings frightened Makoto— as did all the disconnected, ragtag people on blind horses and lame oxen, hundreds of refugees inching nowhere.

A week into his own retreat, Makoto coaxed an abandoned tank more than two hundred kilometers. At last it stalled on a spit of sand, and he emerged to see a half-naked fisherman seining the surf for fingerlings and crab. He traded this man a rosary of spent cartridge shells for a dinghy voyage into the East China Sea, an obstacle course of mines and listing vessels. Shipboard, Makoto slept for the first time in weeks—but his dreams fretted him, for he had no guarantee that any sort of improvement awaited him to the south.

As it happened, Makoto sailed for weeks, periodically switching vessels and bartering passage all the way to the Sakishima Islands, the Philippines, and the Celebes Sea. Finally, after disembarking among the rocks on a forbiddingly tropical shore, he killed a coney for dinner and continued hiking southward. On this new island—or was it a peninsula, the fat nose of a flooded continent?—Makoto encountered fewer refugees, so many fewer that he began to regard himself as one of the last human beings alive. Trudging through a stripped jungle of bloated orchids and shrapnel-blasted trees, he found that this idea, even if false, gave him a shiver of dreadful self-importance. It also profoundly frightened him.

THREE DAYS, OR THREE HUNDRED, PASSED. Makoto, balanced on the edge of a marshy tabletop, gazed down into an immense crater full of decapitated cypresses and ragged refugee tents. At the crater's heart, ringed about by the besodden tent city, sprawled a castle of glass, white-metal braces, and milky skylights. Once before a time, Civilization had boasted a million structures as complex and bright as this one, but Makoto, who hadn't seen one for a while, sucked in his breath through parched lips.

How could anyone repudiate hope when such a lovely monument to human creativity had outlasted the Cataclysm?

Ineluctably, the lattice-work palace drew the traveller down to it. Outside its gate, Makoto encountered a band of people knocking for entrance. Clad in frayed denims, rubber-thonged sandals, and tie-dyed headbands, some were locals. Others let Makoto know that they had journeyed farther than he had. This structure—the House of Abiding Calm—was their mecca, for in the wake of the unraveling of the TransMundi Computer Web, it promised serenity. Butterflies of every sort, they told Makoto, floated in the conservatory, and the Lady Yoko Kamiko was attempting to read their silks in order to reimpose order on the prevailing chaos.

Dreamers, Makoto mentally castigated them, certain that nothing could counteract the ruin inflicted by the skirmishes, looting, and penny-ante wars following the shoreline floods and the collapse of TransMundi.

Clearly, he reflected, "reading the silks"—studying and then interpreting the exquisitely patterned wings of butterflies and moths—was the least workable of all such flighty answers to the nightmare of the Cataclysm. These people at the gate, his rivals for sanctuary, were crazy. Or else the Lady Yoko and her hirelings had royally hoodwinked them.

"She's a living saint," a devout woman assured him. "She'd let everyone in if so many visitors in the flight chambers weren't a hindrance to her work."

"Piss on that!" cried a skinny white man from whose yin-yang headband hung twenty or so tin campaign buttons and the rusty caps of some American softdrink bottles. "She's a witch. We want out of that"—a nod at the sodden tent city—"and into her retreat"—a nod at the gate of the butterfly house—"but she lets only a few of us in at a time and, even then, just long enough to tantalize us."

Others chastised this gaijin for ingratitude, and Makoto noted that some of these people were holding boxes or kerchiefs that they proudly showed around.

In their boxes and kerchiefs lay the pupae or caterpillars of immature lepidoptera. Only petitioners who had brought such gifts were allowed to enter Lady Yoko's house; therefore, Makoto traded a coin that his father had once given him for a small box containing a tufted gypsy-moth larva. The negotiating was hard, but once he had persuaded the woman with the queer little caterpillar to yield it, he knew that he had decided correctly.

When the handicapped gatekeeper finally allowed six petitioners to enter, Makoto was among them.

"YOU HAVE A SINGLE HOUR," said the gatekeeper, a quadriplegic plugged bodily into a three-wheeled chair. He took their gifts and smugly passed them through. "After that," he cautioned, "you must return to this room and exit with your fellows."

Saint, thought Makoto, but another part of his mind rejoined, Witch! Nevertheless, he used the first portion of his hour to walk through a barnstorming royal air force of British orange tips, four of which landed—weightlessly—on his clothing.

Makoto also used this hour to dodge the languid acrobatics of a pair of giant atlas moths, creatures doomed to mate and die because they had neither guts nor tongues. He heard the eerie flutings of a tiger moth with timbal organs on either side of its metathorax. He watched a Palamedes swallowtail settle on a dwarf magnolia near a recycling waterfall; he marveled as an emerald-banded swallowtail loop-de-looped him like a delicate leaf striped with an emulsion of verdigris.

"Nearly all silk is obtained from the silkworm, *bombyx mori,*" spieled the quadriplegic to some of the other visitors, escorting them to the gate. "Silks such as shantung and tussah are the products of various Asiatic *saturniidae.*" He kept up this blather even as he gyroscoped this way and that, distrustfully searching for stragglers.

Makoto remembered seeing a linen-clad worker in the chamber in which the atlas moths had danced. Ducking out of the gatekeeper's sight, he hurried there to plead with this woman to trade clothes with him—her unisex jumpsuit for his torn shirt and grubby khaki trousers. To his surprise, she did so, for her duties in the House of Abiding Calm fatigued and bored her.

"The Lady Yoko," she said, "is so involved with her rejection of meaninglessness that she and Ranier"—the gatekeeper, apparently —"drive us like oxen."

And so this woman escaped with Makoto's group while he crouched beneath a wooden bridge in a chamber crowded with tuliptrees.

AFTER THE COASTAL FLOODS AND THE TRANSMUNDI COMPUTER

CRASH, the world's economy had also plummeted. Once before a time, Makoto knew, things had run—sloppily perhaps, and not always amicably—without benefit of a planetwide web, but not for decades. And so its collapse, along with the advent of the Greenhouse Effect, had spawned suspicion, panic, assault, and all the other vices spelling Cataclysm, the long-expected demise of Civilization.

Biological weapons had contributed, as had "weather control," crop-strangling chemicals, guerrilla-launched concussion bombs, and a battery of other nonnuclear options. It wasn't sad, Makoto thought. It was stupid. Maddening. He regretted his own bemused part in the early rioting and killing.

Someone had dropped a rotten mango from the bridge. Along with the putrifying pears and bananas in nearby chambers, the mango was meant as food for some of the lepidoptera. In fact, a flamboyant moth was tapping into the burst fruit.

But what seized Makoto's attention was the severed spiderweb in the lower branches of the tuliptree through which the mango had ripped. The spider from the web dangled free, struggling to rappel back up into its polygonal heart. One strand waved forlornly in an eddy from the ventilation units.

Thought Makoto, That poor spider is us.

Like radioactive fleas, stars leapt into the sleek black pelage of the night. Makoto emerged from beneath the bridge to marvel at them through the glass roof. Too bad he had no one to share their beauty. He would have welcomed even Ranier, the imperious cripple who had taken his larval offering and let him in. However, he had only the butterflies, none of which flew at night.

Head back, Makoto swallowed the sky, thankful that guerrillas had spared the House of Abiding Calm. Had a simple respect for the wonder it conserved dissuaded them? A mysterious regard for the Lady Yoko?

No matter. The house had its own power supply, water

sources, and temperature-regulating units. It was a self-contained cosmos, and Makoto was lucky to be there.

He fell asleep in a bank of purple thrift. When he awoke, Lady Yoko was kneeling beside him in an iridescent kimono. Ranier, in his motorized chair, gazed down from a face like a tin collander wrapped in flesh-toned rubber.

A hazy sun had replaced the stars, and the liquorish stench of decaying fruit permeated Makoto's new clothes. Startled, he sat up so quickly that the dour quadriplegic laughed.

"Jumpsuit aside," noted Lady Yoko, "you don't much resemble our disloyal Trinh."

THEY ALLOWED HIM TO STAY because Trinh had to be replaced—but Makoto's method of extending his sojourn did not endear him to Ranier. What persuaded Lady Yoko, however, was the obvious fact that Makoto had living grey matter between his ears.

Once before a time, he truthfully told her, he had troubleshot the cybernetic pincers on an undersea harvester engineered and built by a company in Kitakyushu. But that employment had washed away along with the TransMundi Computer Web and all the mutually dependent apparati of Civilization-at-Large.

Makoto had barely escaped the continuing Reaction Riots without making a few involuntary blood donations. For that reason, and that reason only, he had murdered two children—one of them armed with a battered Uzi—and then gone on to search and despoil the flood-damaged, paper-walled house of his victims.

"Please forget all that," Lady Yoko said. "I have need of you, Mr. Aseada."

Makoto passed his days running computer simulations of the life cycles of metalmarks, hairstreaks, checkerspots, noctuids. When he had finished the runs already plotted by Lady Yoko, he was asked to do food-supply predictions, habitat-improvement calculations, and a lovely evolutionary simulation that, when screened, burned dizzying haloes into his retinas.

Makoto learned that the Butterfly Effect had to do not with butterflies (or not only with them), but instead with the minute structure in a seemingly chaotic flow of data. And yet he wasn't doing the work that the people at the gates had told him about. He wasn't—as was the enigmatic Lady Yoko, his employer and patroness —"reading the silks."

Unlike most butterfly conservatories, the House of Abiding Calm had several different chambers, chambers designed for the needs of many different species. Makoto learned the dimensions, temperature settings, and humidity levels of each room. He grew accustomed to the cathedral whirr of stained-glass wings as monarchs wheeled in squadrons after warming their silks in the pale heat of a mackerel-eyed sun. He got used to the bourbonish rot of the fruits that the butterflies liked. He habituated himself to helping Ranier, whose surliness only increased. Never, though, did he accustom himself to the sudden appearances and the even swifter vanishings of Lady Yoko, the premier monarch of the house.

The conservatory crowned a polygonal underchamber in which were located its off-web computers and the guts of its control systems. Makoto didn't like to go down into this mazelike region because it reminded him of the bunkers he'd lived in during the first days of the Cataclysm—but his duties required it, making him glad for any chance to go upstairs, even if only to help Ranier.

One morning, when Lady Yoko's factotum seemed especially surly, Makoto said, "Suppose I turned your chair over, bastard."

Ranier wheeled back and regarded Makoto as if he had uttered a great inanity. "It can't be upset. Its autostabilizers wouldn't allow it. Besides, I'm a part of this chair. It and I are—" he searched for a word—"symbionts."

"Why do you treat me like an enemy, Ranier?"

"Because we're rivals. The Lady Yoko's love is *mine*—by right of precedence."

ABOVE THE CHAMBER OF MONARCH BUTTERFLIES reposed the office and bedroom of Ranier's cruel mistress. Makoto first saw this sanctum about three months after his arrival; it shocked him to find that its floor was transparent from the upper side, so that he and Lady Yoko seemed to be suspended in a polarized limbo thirty feet above a milkweed forest ornamented by orange and black silks.

Awe. Dizziness. An irresistible urge to grab for support.

But Lady Yoko turned him to the white walls of her work space, upon which were silk-screened in large decorative ovals the scaled fore and hind wings of countless kinds of lepidoptera. Here, then, she *read the silks*—after generating their images on her computers' screens and transferring them by a sophisticated electronic process to scrolls of expensive shantung.

What messages did she harvest from the metallic patterns of the wing scales? What meanings from the whorls, the peacock eyes, the opalescent streaks, the glinting herringbone wimples of her babies' magnified wings? Makoto, rapt, stared at the silks in mingled awe and consternation.

"I see in these scale patterns a link between the animate world of earthly insects—under the Eye of Heaven a tiny, but beautiful, life form—and the macrocosm of the universe," Lady Yoko said. "In the randomly generated beauty of my charges, Makoto, I also discern a telling minor of the planets, stars, and galaxies doing timeless minuets through the farthest reaches of outer space."

Hearing this odd speech, and agonizing to make it parse, Makoto realized that either Lady Yoko was mad or else she had uncovered an entomological urim and thummin previously unknown to humanity.

After equating the underwing venation of *Ornithoptera priamus* with the structure of a solar system thousands of light-years away, and the predawn skittishness of her fritillaries with some unusual meteorite activity near Jupiter, Lady Yoko took Makoto to her bed. Here she enjoyed him.

Makoto, meanwhile, sought not only to acquit himself well but to calm his pounding heart. He never quieted his heart, partly because he felt tested and partly because in Lady Yoko's darkened

bedchamber a butterfly the size of an owl and the color of greased
gunmetal hung above their exertions like a disapproving angel. The
kaleidoscopic shadows strobing from its wings presaged—in
Makoto's mind—the death of an inhabited world in another
galaxy.

REPEATEDLY, THEREAFTER, LADY YOKO HAD MAKOTO LIE WITH HER
in different spots throughout the house. Over time, his reluctance
to yield totally to her eroded.

The woman, if mad, was mad in a way defining connections,
not divisions, among animate and insensate phenomena. Also,
without becoming transparent to him, Lady Yoko had begun to
reveal aspects of her character worthy of sympathy, of admiration,
maybe even of love.

She told Makoto of the psychological frailties of her father, the
quirks of temperament that had kept her mother and her at
loggerheads, the somersault of fate that had transformed her from
a politics-weary diplomat in Kuala Lumpur into the Empress of the
House of Abiding Calm—even though, like Makoto himself, she
seemed ignorant of the island, peninsula, continent, or fallen lunar
sea on which its dead builders had erected it.

Grappling ceased; bona fide love-making began. They coupled
on terraces, feathered by squadrons of Day-Glo orange revelers.
They interfaced beneath a tuliptree near the Oriental bridge.
Brilliant scales on brilliant wings hymned their marriage. They
whispered—Lady Yoko to him, Makoto to her—as they glided,
buoyant scull on shantung water. Always, moths and butterlifes
surrounded them with murmuring hosannas of flash coloration.

Briefly, Ranier disengaged. The quadriplegic motored away
from Makoto every time he saw him coming. When work or
accident forced the two together, Ranier was slavishly pleasant, as
if fearful that Makoto's new role as lover gave him the authority to
send him into the fetid wastes created by the Cataclysm and the
Reaction Riots. Belatedly realizing the depth of Ranier's hurt,

Makoto started to worry about how flagrant his and Lady Yoko's bouts of love-making had been, and still were.

After telling his mistress that the gatekeeper felt for her an unrequited passion, Makoto was stunned, and then appalled, to learn that she hadn't known. Whereupon, guilt-ridden, Lady Yoko decreed that from now on they must conceal their trysts.

Phantom-of-the-opera melodrama, thought Makoto, making love to Lady Yoko in a chamber housing a population of death's-head moths—for the smell of rotting fruits had an aphrodisiac effect on them, and it was impossible, thus seized, to abstain from devouring each other.

Obsession, reflected Makoto. Soul's attraction to soul told through rampant physicality. Maybe they weren't good people, but they were exemplary, if driven, lovers.

ONLY DAYS LATER, THE QUADRIPLEGIC HIT BACK—by tricking Makoto into that same chamber with a tale about dying death's-heads: they needed tending. As soon as Makoto was in, though, Ranier triggered the bolts on the chamber's door panels. Makoto was stranded there, alone but for the weirdly agitated moths. What did Ranier plan to do now? Release a hissing drug into the hall?

Makoto *heard* something—a faint but stridulent chirping. It grew louder; louder and louder and louder. Listening to it, Makoto understood that Ranier had miked the room. Now, his adversary was incrementally powering up the volume, so that the papery rattle of the death's-head moths would first annoy, and then pain, and next deafen, and finally madden him.

In the early evening's white sky, a gibbous moon wobbled like a deflated soccer ball. Makoto, holding his hands to his ears and reflexively grinding his molars, was looking up through the roof of the conservatory.

Suddenly, the Moon exploded. It repeatedly exploded. Makoto could hear nothing but the emphatic rattling of the moths, a rising drone that made a continuous backdrop to the silent destruction of

Earth's natural satellite. Chunks of lunar maria rocketed outward, leaping into invisibility as the night sky engulfed them.

Proscribed laser weaponry, Makoto mused. A hangover hiccup of stolen "defense" technologies.

Although the death's-head moths around him stopped chirping, their wings went crazy; the air was a cataclysmic blur. Lady Yoko, summoned by the Moon's death, appeared outside the chamber, saw her lover among the frantic moths, bemusedly released him.

Makoto told Lady Yoko nothing of Ranier's attempt on his life—or, at least, on his sanity. He allowed her to suppose that his own carelessness had led to his imprisonment. The Moon, like much of the Earth, was ruined, so thoroughly blasted that it had jagged satellites of its own, orbiting fragments whose albedos ringed the mastectomized Moon like necklaces of chipped pearl.

Given that catastrophe, Ranier's attack hardly seemed worth fretting.

The weather changed.

Rains thrummed down like dissolving pebbles.

According to a visitor from Kampuchea, the seas were slouching inland "like hungry sharks on legs."

"RANIER WAS A SAILOR ON A PEACEKEEPING SHIP stung by a missile between Grand Cayman and Swan Island over thirty-five years ago," Lady Yoko told Makoto.

"That old? A man well into his fifties?"

Lady Yoko allowed this deduction to stand. "Ranier came apart in the attack like a modular doll. His rescuers flew him in gell-cushioned collops all the way to Melbourne—where, in those days, a team of laser surgeons had won acclaim putting rich Humpty Dumpties back together again."

Ranier's life, Makoto realized, was something of a miracle, for he had never been rich and his wounds had been severe. The U.N. organization charged with his peacekeeping mission had cleared the way for Ranier's surgery, then paid his bills. Today, however, the U.N. no longer existed, superseded years ago by TransMundi and more recently by chaos.

Apart from weather changes and the vivid nightime necklacing of the planet, the shattering of the Moon—where, Makoto recalled, at least three nations had run primitive bases—had no great impact on activities in the house. It had saved his life (or, at least, his sanity), but otherwise the daily business of caretaking the fragile lepidoptera went on as it always had.

What an irony.

People had died, and were still dying, because of the Moon's unexpected chain of eruptions, which, in turn, had led Lady Yoko to rescue Makoto from Ranier. Now, though, the Moon's death, and the deaths of all those affected by it, weighed less heavily on Makoto than would the demise of a single leafwing or swallowtail.

TEN DAYS, OR TWENTY-ONE, WENT BY. Makoto began to forget about how humanity had impoverished the night.

"They live ten to twenty-one days," said Lady Yoko. "Seldom longer."

In the chamber sheltering apollos, peacocks, painted ladies, brimstones, and mourning cloaks, Makoto had begun to recognize individuals. It hurt when they died.

In fact, during their love-making marathons, he and Lady Yoko had to squeeze from their minds the dismaying knowledge that the beautiful creatures were dying even as they protracted their own pleasure. Donning their clothes after one such tryst, the lovers looked up to see Ranier's chair launch itself from a catwalk high above the skylights.

It hurtled off the ramp, hung suspended for a moment, plunged through the glass (thunderheads billowing behind it like monstrous, dirty parachutes), and tumbled so dreamily that Makoto could make out every detail of Ranier's emotionless face.

Shards of glass fell with him, a glittering spray.

Makoto thought that a man plunging from the Moon could not have plummeted longer than did Ranier, who, after impact, repeatedly somersaulted, plowing through banks of verbena like a combine. He was so snugly jacked into his chair—his "symbiont"—that its plugs and connectors declined to release him. Meanwhile, a multitude of butterflies spiraled upward into the transfigured sky.

A day later, having struggled to free Ranier from the chair, they dressed him in a silken shirt patterned with tropical ferns, palm fronds, poinsettias, and orchids. Then they set him in his battered chair again and put his chair in a chamber with unbroken skylights. Soon, the Polynesian shirt began to draw butterflies, as did the suety-sweet beginnings of the decay process.

"This is exactly how I want my own funeral to be," Lady Yoko said. "Promise me, Makoto."

Although he considered it unlikely that he would outlive her, Makoto promised.

"ONE BRIGHT BUTTERFLY FLUTTERING IN AN AUTUMN WIND can perturb the motion of distant galaxies," Lady Yoko told him a few evenings later in her lofty office. She was reading silk screens, imputing to the designs in the wings of her charges pregnant correspondences to the appearances of gas clouds, black holes, quasar radiation, and newly forming galaxies. Makoto gave her a dull nod. The extra work he was doing had sapped his strength. Nor could he shake the belief that Ranier's mummifying body sat astride his shoulders.

"Look here!" Lady Yoko blurted. Pointing out the novalike eyespots on the silk-screened wings of a tropical birdwing, she declared that they had flared into existence only since Ranier's spectacular suicide.

"A cataclysm unlike anything we have ever experienced is taking place out there," she said, gesturing skyward, beyond the orbiting debris of the Moon.

"Explosions in great stellar chains. Many civilizations—not

just those centered on a single planet—are dying. The indifferent engines of star-formation and -destruction have doomed them, and there's nothing we can do."

Lady Yoko added that these events were occurring simultaneously with the mutations of the patterns on her silk-screened wings. As a result, the light from the exploding sister galaxies symbolized by the eyespots on this New Guinea birdwing would not reach Earth for thousands of millions of years.

That disaster was too far away to mourn, even if Makoto decided to believe in it. The loss of the bases on the Moon had precedence over Lady Yoko's conjectural eyespot tragedy—just as did Ranier's suicide and the lingering effects of the earthly Cataclysm that had driven Makoto from his home island of Kyushu.

I can only hold so much, Makoto thought. I can only embrace so many corpses at once. It was better to embrace the living, even if their warmth was fleeting and their defining spirit as hard to hold as the inchoate plasmas drifting between the suns.

Lady Yoko, turning from her silks, intuited his confusion. She led him, bewildered by such concern, into her bedchamber.

There, a moth the size of an owl fluttered above their embrace less in judgment than in blessing. Makoto and his lady made love, made love, made love, and the silks that came to cocoon them seemed proof against both decay and decipherment.

Icicle Music

Chimes on the roof, like icicles being struck in sequence by a small silver mallet.

Wind whistled away the icicle shards, hurled them back together somewhere above Danny's bedroom, turned their disconcerting chimes into a hair-raising electronic drone, then boomed so fiercely over cottonwood grove and nearby river that he had to suppose he'd only imagined the eerie icicle music.

Or had he? It was Christmas Eve, 1957 (to be exact, very early Christmas morning), and maybe those unearthly chimes were coming from another Soviet spaceshot, a beep-beep-beeping sputnik passing over Van Luna, polluting Kansas's atmosphere with commie radiation and a sanity-sabotaging barrage of high-frequency sound pulses. Who could say?

Danny got up. Careful not to rouse his mother (who ordinarily commuted thirty-plus miles, roundtrip, to her job in personnel at

McConnell Air Force Base in Wichita), he crept barefooted into the boxy little house's living room. He let the Christmas tree in the corner—light-strings unplugged, foil tinsel agleam, fragile glass ornaments minutely rotating—emerge from the gloom.

Had Santa come yet? Ha! Danny wasn't misled. He was twelve, had been for more than a month. And even if he hadn't just had his birthday, he hadn't believed in Santa for three or four years. And he hadn't really bought the scam of Jolly Saint Nick's year-end gift-giving since the year Esther Jane Onions let him take her bubblegum in a "kiss exchange"—a double-dare-you bet with Freddie DeVore—in the bushes behind the grain elevator off Depot Street.

Danny'd been, yeah, nine that year. The kiss exchange—Esther Jane's breath smelling just like her last name—had made him feel funny. He'd never do *that* again. It had destroyed his faith in Freddie DeVore's friendship, the inevitability of girls, the reliability of nearly everyone. (Even Ike with that famous grin, for which his folks had voted in '56, was probably a cheat, fudging golf scores and "forgetting" to report on his taxes all the money he'd won.) Anyway, E.J.'s breath, Freddie's refusal to ante up the agreed-upon Eddie Yost baseball card, Ike's secret sins, and three more disappointing years had forever numbed the kid in him.

Nine. Ten. Eleven.

And—*wham!*—he was illusion-free, a twelve-year-old dreaming of his driver's license, his first legal beer, and the full assumption of Daddy Pitts's role as head of household and chief provider. The rotten skipout. In fact, Danny hoped his dad was in jail somewhere this Christmas, or in a cardboard box over a steam grate in K.C. or Topeka, or even—sucks to him, anyhow—in a wooden one under a pile of gooey black Kansas dirt. It'd serve the bum right.

Actually, "Santa"—Milly, Danny's mom—had already come. His main present, unwrapped, lay on the green flannel tree skirt under the scrawny pine he'd chopped down on Mr. Arno's place. It glinted there like the sword of a medieval Turk.

It was the shotgun he'd begged for, a gas-operated "automatic" 12-gauge, the kind that absorbed some of its recoil instead of kicking back like a colicky mule. Even in the darkness, Danny could tell it was beautiful. His mom must have set aside ten—no, *fifteen*—bucks a month for most of this past year to buy it for him. He went to the tree, lifted the gun, let his fingers roam it from red-velvet-edged buttplate to the evil-looking shark-fin notch of its front bead, dumbstruck by the deadly power in his arms.

Two small packages, wrapped, lay beside the shotgun, and Danny guessed that they contained shells. Kneeling and hefting one of these boxes, he confirmed his guess. Now he could go dove hunting with Brad Selley. Not *now,* of course—but in the morning, after he and Mom had had their Christmas together.

His immediate problem was that morning, even if Mom got up at six or so, was still a good four hours away. The wall clock in the kitchen (designed to resemble the pilot's wheel on an old-fashioned clipper ship) said so. Figuring himself safe for a time, Danny sat down Buddha-style, the shotgun in his lap, and meticulously removed the slick red paper from one of the boxes of shells. Then, holding his breath, he slipped in one shell, aimed the gun at the cockeyed angel atop the tree, faked pulling the trigger, and faked, too, the 12-gauge's rumbling discharge: Ka-SHOOOOM! An imaginary explosion sloshed back and forth in his mouth and throat.

Then, upon lowering the shotgun, Danny heard the wind die. He heard a faint, panicky pawing overhead and the same dreamy icicle music that had called him from sleep. Dad had built their place near Van Luna's riverside dump, on a muddy patch of land inherited from Mom's grandparents. It was two miles from the city limits, a mile from their nearest neighbors, and the boy began to wonder if a crook—or a couple of crooks, a whole *army* of them—had cased their house, decided it was an easy hit, and showed up tonight (Christmas morning) to break in, bag up all their silverware and presents, and then skedaddle, booty-laden, into Arkansas or Oklahoma.

247

Danny, holding the 12-gauge, got up and backed away to the door of his own bedroom. The popping icicle music continued, as did the scrabbling on the rooftop shingles. Then both the chimes and the pawing ceased, and there was only a hushed curling of wind—and Danny's heartbeat, like acorns falling into a rusted gasoline drum—to suggest that God had ever created sound waves or that the universe had ever before experienced them.

The living room had a fireplace. Dad had built it (lopsidedly, Mom accused, and the cattywampus fireplace supported this gripe) of river stones and second-rate mortar. He'd put in no damper. When it rained, huge drops whistled down the flue, hit the inner hearth, and splattered the living-room rug with inky soot. Disgusted, Mom had stopped trying to use it. In fact, she'd stuffed the throat of the chimney with wadded-up sheets of the *Wichita Beacon* to keep the oily rain from further staining the hearth rug.

Now, to Danny's dismay, a crinkled ball of newspaper fell out of the chimney into the firebox. A second sheet cascaded down, and a third, and a fourth. Then, a pair of booted feet appeared in the firebox, dangling down uncertainly, both boots as worn as harness leather. *Whumpf!* The boots crashed through the crumpled newspaper to the hearth. Two skinny legs in mud-fouled khaki materialized in the shadows above them. With a grunt and a muttered curse, a man in a heavy red-plaid coat kicked away the papers, ducked out of the firebox, and hobbled over to the tree, carrying what looked like a grungy World War II duffel bag.

Santa Claus? thought Danny. Father Christmas? Kris Kringle? Saint Nick? Or just a chimney-shinnying thief?

The man's duffel *looked* empty. It hung down his back like a collapsed parachute. His greasy white hair squeezed out from under the roll of his red woolen sailor's cap to tickle the frayed collar of his jacket. In spite of the darkness, Danny could see the man clearly, as if his unexpected arrival had triggered an explosion of ghostly amber light.

Then, turning, the intruder looked straight at him.

Danny ducked out of sight. A moment later, though, he peered back around and saw that Klepto Kris Kringle had a pale, stubbly beard and a pair of bleak, ever-moving eyes.

What if he weren't just a thief? What if he were a rapist or a murderer? What if he had his sights on the shotgun now in Danny's arms? Assuming, as seemed likely, that he'd staked out their house and watched Mom bring it home . . .

Danny (Danny told himself), you've waited too long. You should do something. You've got the draw on him, don't you? Why are you being so wishy-washy?

"Hold it, mister!" Danny said, stepping out of the doorway and leveling the barrel of his Christmas gift on the intruder. Santa— no, the lousy burglar—twisted an ornament off the tree and hurled it all the way across the room. It struck the lintel over Danny's head, showering pieces of feathery, mirrored plastic. A flashing, quick-silver rain of tiny knives.

Ducking, Danny thumbed the safety off and shot. The blast spat flames, a burst of orange and blue that knocked Danny backward into a pile of clothes in his bedroom.

Klepto Kris howled.

The Christmas tree toppled, like a bombed pagoda bringing down all the bamboo chimes, hammered-tin animals, and folded-paper fish hanging from its dozens of eaves. The noise was loud. The entire house shook. Had there been an earthquake?

Golly, Danny thought, struggling to his feet. My shotgun's a gas-powered job. It's not supposed to kick.

"Danny!" his mother shouted from her own bedroom. *"Danny, hon, are you all right?"* She sounded panicked, downright rattled. For a moment Danny regretted squeezing off a pellet pattern in reply to a desperately flung Christmas-tree ornament. But all he'd done was issue a command—a reasonable command, given the circumstances—and Klepto had tried to take his head off. If the 12-gauge had been in the other guy's hands, Danny knew, *he'd* be dead now. Gut-shot by a stinking burglar on Jesus's birthday.

He met his mom outside their bedroom doors, which were across the hall from each other. At first, Klepto seemed not to be there any longer, as if he'd simply vanished, but then Mom saw a rotting boot dangling down from the throat of the chimney. *"What's that?"* She grabbed Danny's shotgun, rushed to the tree, kicked its fallen branches aside, found a box of shells, replaced the spent shell and added four more, then ran to the fireplace.

Danny was already there, reaching repeatedly for the toe of the visible boot, as if it were the persnickety beak of a cottonmouth. Each time he grabbed for it, it struck back. So Danny reached and pulled away, reached and pulled away.

Who wanted to get booted in the kisser? And why (now that he thought of it) had Mom taken his shotgun? He had more right to it than she did. After all, blood dripping into the wadded-up pages of the *Beacon* proved that he'd hit his target.

Then the boot withdrew, a storm of soot whirled from the smoke chamber above the missing damper, and both he and Mom were fitfully coughing, waving their hands and colliding with each other in their attempts to back away.

When the soot storm subsided, Mom knelt and pointed the barrel of Danny's shotgun up the angled flue.

"Come down here, you snake! Who do you think you are, stealing our Christmas?"

The burglar's soot-dislodging climb went on.

Mom, fiery-eyed, shouted, "Come down or I'll shoot!"

"Don't do it," Danny warned her. "You'll hit him in the butt, maybe, but most of the pellets'll come back on us."

That was good enough for Mom. Flicking on a light as she ran, she headed through the kitchen to the back door. Danny followed, still aching to get the shotgun back but no longer conscious of the biting cold. Mom hit the porch light, ran down the steps into the yard, gimped barefoot over the brown grass to a spot from which she and Danny could see the black jut of the chimney, and reached out a hand to halt Danny beside her.

Danny gaped.

No moon sailed the indigo velvet of the Sedgewick County sky, but every star visible from the northern hemisphere had winked into being up there. He was dazzled. It was hard to make out if the smear on the roof—the bundled silhouette of the man he'd shot—was a living thing or merely a phantom of starlight, wind, and jittery shadows. Danny saw this figure hoist itself out of their chimney, stumble over a lofty plain of shingles, and fall atop a four-legged shape with a white flag for a tail and two black branches of horn for headgear.

Unless he was imagining things, there was a deer on their roof, a buck with twelve to fifteen points. The guy who'd tried to steal their Christmas was mounting the jumpy creature. He encouraged it —*"Up, Blitzen, up!"*—to fly him to safety over both the riverside dump and the rooftops of their sleeping town.

"Stop!" Mom shouted. "Stop or I'll shoot!" She sounded just like a sheriff on a TV cowboy show.

"No, Milly!" the man on the roof pleaded. "Don't!"

"Clifton?" Mom murmured. Then, louder: *"Clifton?"*

The compact little buck (a courser, Danny thought, like in "The Night Before Christmas," which Mrs. French had read them on the day before their holidays) soared up from the house. It lifted like a dream creature, pawing the night air and defining both itself and its desperate, neck-clutching rider against a blowing purple scrim of stars. All Danny could do was marvel. There should have been seven other reindeer (if the words of that silly poem counted for anything), but one was about all Danny could handle.

The deer—the courser—drew an invisible circle over their back yard. Mom and he looked up to see its glinting hooves and white belly. Then the thief sprawled across the deer took a shiny ball from the pocket of his coat and nearly unseated himself sidearming it with all his wounded strength at Mom and him.

"Here's something for you, Milly!" And the stolen ornament—a second one, Danny realized—shattered on Mom's forehead.

"Ouch!"

"Merry Christmas to both you and the brat, bitch! And to all a good ni—"

Mom brushed fragments from her hair, raised the shotgun, took aim at the departing courser, and fired. Rider and mount received the ripping impact of the pellets. A cry from the man. A brief, anguished bleating from the reindeer.

The man fell headlong into the yard. The animal veered toward the dump, legs flailing, but crashed onto the barbed-wire fence Mom had put up to keep rabbits and stray dogs out of their vegetable garden. Its body crumpled the rusty strands of the fence, slicing itself open on the barbs.

Meanwhile, Mom thrust the weapon into Danny's hands and ran to the shotgunned intruder.

Danny ran to see whatever he could see.

The intruder—the would-be reindeer pilot—was dead, his neck broken, his head tilted away from his coat as if it wanted nothing to do with the hobo corpse to which it still so obviously belonged.

"Clifton," Mom said. "You stupid fool."

At his mother's direction, Danny hauled the deer off the fence, gutted it, and spent the remainder of that unending Christmas dawn butchering the deer on the back porch. They could use the venison, Mom said, and if 1958 wasn't any better than 1957 had been, they'd need a lot of it.

Meanwhile, Mom dragged the dead man into the dump; planted him in the cottony guts of a hide-a-bed sofa; wrestled the sofa into a mountain of ancient tires, mushy cardboard boxes, splintered orange crates, and broken tool handles; doused the heap with lighter fluid from her Ronco and a gallon of gasoline siphoned from her pink-and-charcoal Rambler stationwagon; and threw a burning Winston into all that jumbled trash to light it.

The pyre burned all night, a surrealistic flickering that Danny could see through the screened-in porch on which he was processing the carcass of the flying deer. Later, Mom helped him wrap all the different cuts of meat in smooth butcher paper—steaks, roasts, spare ribs, reindeer burgers. Then they washed their hands, limped into the living room, and sat down cross-legged next to the toppled tree to hunt for their presents.

"Was that Dad?" Danny said, avoiding Mom's eyes.

"Yeah."

"It didn't look like him."

"He'd changed a lot."

"Why?"

"I don't know. You'd have to ask him. Which, I guess, isn't possible anymore."

"He called that deer Blitzen. It flew."

"Yeah, well, Papa didn't always tell the truth." Mom dug the boy's only gift to her out from under a waterfall of tinsel. "Ah, this is great. How did you know I wanted a handmade ashtray? The way the colors swirl together—pretty."

"Thanks," said Danny, rubbing his shoulder.

"I'll exchange the gun for one with less kick. You've got my word on it. Please don't let it ruin your Christmas."

Mom leaned over and kissed Danny on the nose.

Then she handed him his other presents: a complete set of the plays of Shakespeare and a poetry book by a man Mom called William Butler Yeets. Danny didn't think he'd get to them very soon.

"I am—I mean, I *was*—the boy in that story," Daniel Pitts told Philip, the worried young man sitting next to his bed in a hospital room in Denver. The blinds on the only window had been hoisted; the icicles on the exterior cornice hung down like the barrels of a glassblower's panpipe.

"You don't mean me to take it as true, do you?" said Philip.

253

Once upon a time, Daniel had known Philip's surname. Tonight—Christmas Eve, 1987—he couldn't recall it. His memory did better with events of a decade, two decades, even thirty-plus years ago. Ancient history.

"Why not?" There were tubes in Daniel's nose. The plastic bag of an IV drip hung over him like a disembodied lung.

"Your mother killed an intruder, then burned his corpse in the Van Luna dump?"

"Yes."

"Okay, Daniel, if you say so. What about 'Blitzen'?"

"See Moore, Clement Clarke. *I* didn't name the creature."

"The creature's name's a red herring." Philip grimaced. "What about its reality?"

"Specious, I guess. At least as a courser. Mom probably shot my dad as he was fleeing into the cottonwoods. She bagged the poor deer purely by accident."

"There *was* a deer?"

"I butchered it. I used a hacksaw, a hammer, a dozen different knives. We had venison for months."

"Not a talent we'd've ever attributed to you, Daniel." Philip meant the actors and aspiring playwrights in the theater projects that Daniel raised money for and directed.

"Meat processing?" Daniel said.

Philip gave him a faint smile. "Your mother wasn't prosecuted for the slaying?"

"It was self-defense. Or property-defense, call it. Besides, no one ever found out."

"Your dad's bones are still out there in the dump?"

"I guess. But even if his bones are still there, his surviving aura isn't. Not always, anyway."

Philip wanted an explanation. Or *pretended* to want one. He was trying to be kind. Daniel was grateful. At this crucial pass, he thought it important to narrate the fallout of what had happened on that long-ago Christmas morning.

"My father—his ghost, anyway—appeared to me ten years later. To the day. Christmas, nineteen sixty-seven."

"In Van Luna?"

"No. I left there after graduating high school. I vowed never to go back, Philip. A vow I've kept."

"So where were you?"

"Cross-country skiing over a meadow of snow and ice-laden trees in the northwestern corner of Yellowstone Park. A scene out of *The Empire Strikes Back*, Philip. Unearthly. Alien. Some of the trees had gusted together, and then frozen, in architectures of special-effects weirdness. The sky looked nickle-plated, but with a light behind it like thousands of smeared-out coals."

"And your dad—the ghost?"

"Hold on, okay?" Daniel opened his eyes as fully as he could, given all the plastic tubing. "I had a hemispherical tent. On Christmas Eve, I pitched it near a fountain of spruces. I snuggled deep into my sleeping bag. I listened to the crazy-lady arias of the wind. A super feeling. Peaceful. Exhilarating."

"Yeah. Alone on Christmas. Thirty-five below."

"Toward morning, before dawn, icicle music woke me. (If you've never heard it, I can't explain it.) A guy in a red-plaid coat was quivering like geyser steam outside my tent."

"Klepto Kris?"

"A.k.a. Clifton Pitts. He—it—sort of modulated in and out of existence with the moaning of the wind. Then he retreated, backing away toward the mountains. I had to throw on my coat and boots and go after him."

"Just what I do when I see a ghost: I chase it."

Daniel, taking his time now, breathing as if invisible crystals of ice had interthreaded the air, told Philip (who, he remembered, almost always ran lights for him) that his pursuit of his father's aura had been successful: He had caught up with it.

The ghost had questioned him, wondering why Daniel was alone on Christmas day, what he'd done with his life, and how, at his young age, he'd escaped taking up an M-16 in the war against the Reds in Southeast Asia. A Pitts—a strapping kid like Danny—should have volunteered.

"Did you tell him how you'd 'escaped'?" Philip asked.

"I told him. And he—it—retreated, fading away into the wind so that I wasn't able to follow it any longer. A bit later, after eating, I began to think I'd hallucinated the haint's visit. The cold. The high, thin air. It wasn't unlikely, the possibility my mind had played tricks."

"Sounds good to me. Better than a visitation."

"Except—"

"Yeah?"

"Right after thinking I'd hallucinated my dad's visit, I looked around and saw my sleeping bag was gone. My father—his ghost—had taken it."

"An animal dragged it off, Daniel. Some other outdoorsy dude stole it while you were chasing your mirage."

"No. There'd've been signs. Tracks. Footprints. Something. And I hadn't been gone that long."

"What would a ghost want with your sleeping bag?"

"To kill me, Philip. As soon as I recollected that it had come on an anniversary—the tenth anniversary of Clifton Pitts's death—I knew why it had come. An eye for an eye, a tooth for a tooth. On Jesus's birthday."

"A sleeping bag?"

"Not just that. As soon as I'd realized what was happening, my tent blew away. It flipped back, beat against the trees, whirled off into the clouds. I was miles from the nearest town. Without my tent or sleeping bag, I was screwed."

"But you got out okay."

"I followed some elk tracks to a hay bale left out for them by a tenderhearted rancher. Pure luck."

"But you did get out."

"No thanks to Papa Pitts."

"Who's haunted you every Christmas?"

"No. Only on ten-year anniversaries of that reindeer shoot in Van Luna."

Philip cocked his head. "What happened last time?"

"In 'seventy-seven, he materialized in an intensive-care unit in Wichita. On which occasion he stole my mother."

"You saw it?"

"It began with icicle music—this time, though, from a hospital cart turning over in a hall. Test tubes shattering." Daniel shut his eyes. "Festively."

"You'd returned to Kansas to be at your mom's bedside?"

"Yes. Dad showed, too. It annoyed him, how well I was doing. Healthy-looking, hedonistic, contented. Mom's lung cancer was a nice counterbalance for him—proof that the woman who'd killed him wasn't immortal. And that her son—his son as well—might also be vulnerable. In fact, after taking Mom's soul, he assured me that my heyday was over. *Our* heyday."

Daniel remembered that he had received this news while staring perplexedly at his mother's waxen face. Then the ghost (an unseen mirage to all the medical folk traipsing in and out) had begun to fade, Milly's soul—the ghost had kissed her—fading with it. How did it feel to be swallowed by a mirage?

"He told you that?" Philip said. "Our heyday was over?"

Daniel blinked a yes.

"How do you suppose he knew?"

"Who can say? Maybe he guessed. Or maybe it was just redneck spleen. A cartoon of 'Rudolph the Red-Nosed Reindeer' on a TV in a seventh-floor waiting room rubbed him wrong; he wasn't happy about the way the war'd turned out; he didn't like the peanut farmer in Washington. Grievances, grievances."

Philip got up, walked around the sick man's bed to the window. He seemed agitated. "This is another ten-year anniversary. To the day, Daniel. He's due again."

"Right. Maybe you'd better split, Philip."

"I'll drop in again tomorrow. With Mario and Trent."

"Gary," Daniel said. "I want Gary to drop in."

"Gary was a sweet man, Daniel. But he's gone. We can't recall him to us. You know that."

"I know that."

"Hang on, okay? Just hang on." Philip leaned down, touched his lips to Daniel's brow, and murmured, "Goodbye." Then, finally, finally, he exited.

The radio at the nurses' station down the hall was broadcasting carols. An intern and a candy striper were dancing together just outside Daniel's room. Someone at the other end of the floor blew a raspberry on a noisemaker. The intern peeked in, sporting a cap with plastic reindeer antlers. Daniel waved feebly to let him know his getup was amusing. Satisfied, the intern backed out.

Fa-la-la-*la*-la, la-la-*la*-la.

Outside Daniel's window, faint icicle music. The glassblower's panpipe hanging from the cornice had begun to melt, releasing long-pent melodies.

"Come on," Daniel murmured. "Come on."

He couldn't wait. He wanted his father's bitter ghost to get a move on. If it materialized in the room and stole his soul, that would be a welcome violation: a theft and a benediction, the first Christmas present his daddy had given him in over thirty years.

Come quickly, Father. Come.

The Ommatidium Miniatures

A IS FOR APHID. Emmons could never recall his mother without thinking of the ABC books of microscopic phenomena that she had compiled to amuse him during long summer afternoons on Tybee Island. A microscopist of acknowledged creativity, Kathleen Emmons had published one of these books under the off-putting title *An Abecedary of the Near Invisible*. To almost everyone's surprise, it became a best-seller. For the next few years you couldn't find a home with elementary-school-age children anywhere in the country without a copy of her book lying on a coffee table or sticking out of a bookcase.

"A Is for Aphid," it asserted. And on the facing page, looking to young Emmons more like bug-eyed outer-space monsters than like microscopic insects, a herd of potato-shaped aphids elephant-walked the magnified branch of a muscadine vine. Deeper into the picture book, you learned that "D Is for Diatom," "M Is for

Microchip," "R Is for Rotifer," and you saw the stunning micrographs illustrating these statements. But the siphon-nosed aphids at the outset of his mother's book were the creatures that had fascinated Emmons as a boy, so he'd leapt at the invitation of International MicroDyne and begun preparing for his drop-down. He'd done so not only to test the minute engines of the company's new technologies but also to solder a spiritual link with his past—when *he'd* been little: an embryonic personality struggling to creep out from the shadows of his mother's success and his father's international reputation.

THE INCREDIBLE SHRINKING MAN. On the seventh floor of the IMD Sensor and Actuator Center in a northern suburb of Atlanta, Emmons sat in a conference room watching a video of a 1957 sci-fi film he had previously avoided having to see. Watching the movie was one of the weirder requirements of the field-test training that McKay had masterminded for the pilot of the company's first microremote; and as "Scott Carey," the movie's common-man protagonist, shrank to the size of a three-year-old boy, a mouse, and, finally, a bipedal cockroach, Emmons's attention wobbled.

"I can't believe you've never seen this," said McKay, leaning into him in the carpeted dark and flinching when Carey stabbed his straight pin up into the belly of an attacking spider. "It's a certifiable classic."

But Emmons thought it smart to refrain from confessing that he hated the movies, that he had always hated the movies, and that he was grateful to his parents for encouraging him to develop other interests. He kept his eyes—not his mind—on the oversized screen and said nothing. McKay, a personnel rather than a research-and-development specialist, sincerely believed that even MicroDyne's brightest technicians could benefit from the psychological training provided by a sci-fi "classic" like *The Incredible Shrinking Man*, and when an executive of his rank took that tack, what else could you do but comply?

"TO GOD THERE IS NO ZERO." For now, high on the screen, Scott Carey, who had squeezed into his garden from a window ledge in the basement, was gazing at the impossibly distant stars and all the muddled galaxies. "That existence begins and ends," said the actor Grant Williams in the film's final voice-over narration, "is Man's conception, not nature's. And I felt my body dwindling, melting, becoming nothing. My fears melted away, and in their place came acceptance. All this vast majesty of creation, it had to mean something. And then I meant something, too. Yes, smaller than the smallest, I meant something, too. To God there is no zero. I still exist!"

And B is for bullshit, thought Emmons, for it appeared to him that all he had seen in the film—denial, alienation, degradation, struggle—refuted Carey's concluding cry of existential yea-saying; indeed, Carey's fears about his own insignificance, and life's ultimate meaninglessness, had been *underscored* by the fact that he was going to go on shrinking forever.

BEING THERE. McKay had the lights brought up. He still got a boost from the film's upbeat gloss on the existential ramifications of littleness.

"Going down isn't easy," he told Emmons. "It's different from light microscopy, different from electron microscopy, and different from doing hands-on manipulations with a stereo-microscope assist. *Being there*—down among the dust mites, so to speak—is an *intenser* sort of microscopy, Emmons. Even if, on the literal level, you're operating a tiny waldo, doing watchmaker tasks with silicon pincers the size of an ameoba's paws.

"You have to overcome the possibility of 'dimensional shock' and take your bearings from the point of view of a nematode, say, or a spider colt. You have to learn to see again, at what I like to call 'ground zero.' Theoretically, it seems smart to work your way to the needed redimensionalization slowly. Which is why I've asked you to watch *The Incredible Shrinking Man* and then to discuss it with me."

Emmons discussed the film with McKay, certain that his boss was enjoying their talk—as he had the movie—immeasurably more than he was.

FROGS AND PHILISTINES. During their talk, McKay noted that Science—Emmons could hear the capital—had long ago declared that certain species of frog could not see anything in their environment inapplicable to their day-to-day existence. They were selectively blind to whatever failed to advance their survival or immediate well-being. The nonessential was invisible to them. A dragonfly at mealtime would loom like a helicopter, but an animal neither edible nor threatening—a wading heifer, for example—would splash by unregarded.

Scowling, McKay noted that some human philistines had a similar trait; namely, an inability to see anything that so much as hinted at parentheticality or irrelevance, *i.e.*, the microscopic.

Emmons's mind cast back to his mother's abecedaries: McKay was preaching to the converted. If A wasn't for aphid, then it was for amoeba; if F wasn't for follicle, then it was for flea. The naked human eye could not distinguish two dots less than 0.1 millimeter apart, but from an early age he had trained himself to see all that the human eye *could* see.

How, then, was he either a frog or a philistine?

His mother had helped make him sensitive to the invisible—the infusoria in a vial of creek water—and his father, whose namesake Emmons was, had made these lessons stick by seeing to it that he often felt like a mere protozoan. In fact, of late Emmons secretly saw himself as someone whom others did not fully register: a spear carrier in a play or some anonymous urban scarecrow sleeping in the gutter.

F IS FOR FATHER, F IS FOR FLEA. The Emmonses' beach house on

Tybee Island had always been full of dogs: Newfoundlands, poodles, Russian wolfhounds. It had also been full of fleas.

As McKay lectured, Emmons recalled his father striding shoeless in his tennis whites over the rattan mats on their concrete porch. Fleas jumped from the mats onto the damp cotton of his father's sweat socks, where their hard little bodies took on the instant visibility of commas or periods. His father picked off each flea with his thumb and forefinger and dropped it into the hot tapwater in an otherwise empty fish tank.

Lying on their pinched sides, the fleas kicked pathetically on the surface. Finger-jabbed, they spiraled, still kicking, to the bottom, where, eventually, the kicking ceased.

The elder Emmons, who seldom played very long with his namesake because his son usually netted more shots than he returned, would spend the rest of the morning decoying, seizing, and dunking fleas, moving from spot to spot on the mats to entice fresh generations of vermin to spring onto his socks. This intellectual celebrity, the computer scientist and backdoor cosmologist who had extended and redeemed his once discredited mentor Edward Fredkin's science of "digital physics," would scold young Emmons for failing to capture fleas, too.

To the world at large, he held up the dictum that the universe is a computer—that atoms, electrons, and other subatomic particles are built from infinitesimal bits of information; that reality is grainy; and that there exists a single underlying programming rule to account for the movement and purpose of each of its constituent grains—but to his twelve-year-old son on Tybee, in the microcosmos of his family's summer retreat, he preached filial devotion, a more disciplined forehand smash, and the philosophical-cum-recreational benefits of flea-tweezering.

MICROSCOPIC RAIN AND A MIDGET'S PARASOL. "In a sense," McKay was saying, "Carey was lucky. He shrank by degrees, with plenty of chances to make adjustments."

263

Emmons, returned from his flashback, became aware of the dense particulate rain in his boss's strangely appointed office. Decay products from the radioactive gases thrown off by the ceiling tiles and the Sheetrock walls rained down as an invisible but inescapable fallout. The air was afire. It fell in charged veils, sleeting, draping, folding back on itself to repeatedly stipple his boss with iotas of disintegrating matter. Also, the molecules on the surface of McKay's aircraft carrier of a desk were migrating aside to allow the falling particles to penetrate and rape it.

A guilty horror seized Emmons as he watched the rain, a shower clearly imperceptible to McKay, who was jawing about "acclimating declensions" and giving odd examples:

"The smallest adult human being recorded, Emmons, was a Mexican midget called Zuchia Zarate. At seventeen, Señorita Zarate stood two feet and two inches tall and weighed not quite five and a half pounds. This nineteenth-century freak could have stepped from one of the Montgolfiers' balloons, popped a parasol, and floated safely to earth. On her trip down, she could have leisurely scrutinized a torrent of high-altitude plankton: pollen grains, lichen fragments, the spores of fungi, bacteria, algae, and so forth. If MicroDyne could bring off that easy a drop-down, Emmons, you'd have no sweat accepting your littleness."

But Emmons kept thinking how handy the señorita's parasol would have been: a shield against the invisible deluge.

"LET'S GET SMALL." McKay's office was a museum of the minute. It contained an elegant miniature of the living room of the Tybee Island beach house—down to a baby baby grand piano, an itsy-bitsy computer station, a dinky fireplace with even dinkier andirons and grates, a collection of foraminifer shells, and a gallery of framed Kirkuchi patterns (diffraction images of various alloy particles as created and photographed inside a transmission electron microscope) no bigger than postage stamps.

A newt-sized plastic doll of Emmons's canonized father sat in a wicker rocker in this mock-down of their old beach house, gazing at the Kirkuchi patterns and thinking godly thoughts. McKay paid no attention to these items, he'd seen them so many times before, but Emmons knew that this miniature architectural tribute to his father had triggered his flashback as surely as had McKay's jabber about frogs and philistines. The urge seized him to grab the father doll and pop it between his fingernails as if clicking the carapace of a flea—but, even as a tiny doll, his father remained a Micromegas in Emmons's view and he couldn't do it.

Elsewhere in McKay's office there were Lilliputian cathedrals, miniature divans, Tinker Toy forts, and a display case containing gnat robots, beetle jeeps, electrostatic motors, and microdozers. The spiders that had draped some of these furnishings with gauze were living creatures, just like Emmons, but everything inanimate in the room mocked him by seeming more cunningly made.

"Ever see a tape of Steve Martin doing his classic 'Let's Get Small' routine?" McKay had just asked. "God, I love that routine. Think 'high' for 'small.' You'll get a grip on microminiaturization as a kind of occupational addiction. Look around. You can see why a shtick like that would appeal to me. . . ."

INADEQUACY, IMPOTENCE, INSIGNIFICANCE: A TRACT. That evening, in his apartment, Emmons worried that even his competence as a microremote engineer hadn't given him the sense of self possessed by a pompous company shill like McKay. Would going down— getting smaller—do the trick?

If H isn't for humility (an abstract noun), then it's for hydra (a tube-shaped freshwater polyp with a mouth at one end ringed by tentacles). And another definition of hydra is "a multifarious evil not overcome by a single effort." How to cope with the fact that the hydra he'd been struggling to defeat wasn't any sort of evil, but rather the achievements of a mother who'd classified over a thousand species of nematodes and a father who'd led the world's scientific community toward the one computational Rule governing every nanometer of space and perhaps explaining everything?

Forget that Fredkin's Rule—as his father had dubbed it—was still incompletely teased out. Forget that many scientists still blasted both the elder Emmons and the late Fredkin as, at best, "inspired crackpots." *Emmons* was now an Olympian name. Although the son bearing it was proud of his name, he was also cowed by it, mindful of the meagerness of his own efforts in comparison to his parents'. He seemed doomed by the scale of their reputations to fall on his face in any attempt to match them. He was too small to rival their successes, a bacterium in a life-extinguishing drop of acid: Scott Carey with a Ph.D. in microengineering.

"IT'S A DIDINIUM-EAT-PARAMECIUM WORLD." Germaine Bihaly, who lived across the complex's parking lot, showed up at his door with a tray of Cantonese carryout boxes, each one a small soggy chalet packed with steamed chestnuts, sweet-and-sour meats, plump shrimp, or vivid strings of slime defying identification.

"Share?" she said.

Emmons let her in. Bihaly was a travel agent, whom he had met over the telephone while booking a flight to a sensor-and-actuator conference in Berkeley. Later, he had coincidentally found her to be one of his neighbors.

They ate Chinese sitting on the ad sections from the *Atlanta Constitution*. Emmons explained why he felt like the incredible shrinking man and told her how, as part of his training, he'd had to watch an old sci-fi flick and then listen to McKay gab about its applicability to the piloting of microremotes.

Unsympathetic, Bihaly said, "Hey, Emmons, it's a *Didinium-eat-Paramecium* world," a joke between them ever since he had shown her his mother's sequential micrographs of a predatory ciliate seizing and absorbing another ciliate species nearly twice the *Didinium*'s size. Wasn't he a big boy? Couldn't he take care of himself in the sharkish corporate world?

Later, Emmons, frightened and tentative, hovered over Bihaly's body like a gar above the remains of a hammerhead's kill.

THE NIGHT TESTIMONY OF LEEUWENHOEK. Bihaly stayed anyway, and Emmons dreamed that he was an animalcule in a moist cavern among a population explosion of such creatures, all fidgeting, feeding, and reproducing in a balmy darkness not unlike that of MicroDyne's company pool.

What most upset Emmons about his presence among these nameless microorganisms was the heightening of his own namelessness by their large numbers. The indeterminacy of the Where in which he and all the other tiny beasties multiplied also bothered him. But, at last, a voice spoke over, around, and through him— like God making a proclamation—and he knew that he and the bacteria around him were cliff-dwelling on the speaker's gums.

"I dug some stuff out of the roots of one of my teeth," boomed the dead Dutch lens grinder and scope maker, Anton van Leeuwenhoek, Emmons's host. "And in it I found an unbelievably great company of living animalcules, amoving more nimbly than I had seen up to now. The biggest sort bent their bodies into curves in going forwards, and the number of animalcules was so extraordinarily great that 'twould take a thousand million of some of them to make up the bulk of a coarse sand grain."

In his sleep, Emmons shriveled.

"Indeed, all the people living in our United Netherlands are not as many as the living animals I carry in my own mouth." Emmons had once read that Leeuwenhoek attributed his lifelong ruddy health to a hot Ethiop beverage—coffee—that "scalded the animalcules" in his mouth. Emmons's arms reached out for Germaine Bihaly, but they could not find her.

ARTIFICIAL FAUNA IN A DAY-CARE ZOO. For the past seven months, Emmons had stopped nearly every morning on the edge of the day-care courtyard. He watched the kids swarm over the fiberglass backs of pink dinosaurs or the extruded-foam statues of giraffes.

Today, he saw a mechanical crane lowering into the courtyard an armored monster so much like a menacing alien crab that most of the kids dashed into the arms of day-care workers to escape it. Emmons knew it for the jungle-gym simulacrum of a dust mite, magnified thousands of times. Its body plates and serrated front claws were gigantic. Detracting from its realism, size aside, was the absence of magnified counterparts for the carpet fibers, hair strands, and skin flakes that cling to living dust mites.

"Educational, don't you think?" said McKay, appearing behind Emmons as if from nowhere.

Emmons stayed mute. He imagined the kids climbing on the dust mite like parasites on parasites, *ad infinitum*. A team of workmen positioned the yawing statue on its base, and Emmons wondered if possibly there weren't a few situations in which it might not be so bad to be parasitized.

THE RELATIVITY OF TIME CONSCIOUSNESS. "When you're down there, Emmons, you'll feel like the Methuselah of the microverse. That's because your eyes and hands will be electronically plugged into the ommatidia and manipulators of your remote. Generations will come and go, but you'll endure.

"Your consciousness—unlike poor Scott Carey's—will be up here in the Sensor and Actuator Center with me, President Sawyer, and the kids out there in the courtyard, but you'll be interacting with critters for whom a second may be an hour and a day a lifetime. That could rattle you."

McKay pointed to the hummingbird feeder on the far edge of the fiberglass zoo and to the ruby-throats hovering about it.

"Those guys have a metabolic rate higher than that of any other bird or mammal, Emmons. About twelve times that of a pigeon, about a hundred times that of an elephant. A second for a hummingbird is equivalent to two or three minutes for a whale. Just imagine what an hour down in the microdimensions could be and remember that as you observe and actuate, okay?

"You've got to have this conception of yourself as being in two places at once, but you've got to subordinate your real-world self to the one on microsafari. Otherwise, you'll screw up. We don't sweat the screw-ups for MicroDyne's sake, Emmons. One day, we'll mass-produce microbots in the same kind of volume that the folks in Silicon Valley do microchips. It's *your* well-being we're worried about. We don't want to take a raving loon or a mindless artichoke out of actuator harness."

McKay consulted his watch. Less than two hours to drop-down. It would roll around in either an eyeblink or an ice age, depending on which of his anxieties Emmons set his inner clock by.

TELEMETRY VS. MANNED REDIMENSIONALIZATION. Bihaly could not understand why International MicroDyne, or any other multinational mass-producing flea-sized actuators and invisible sensors, thought it necessary to plug the eyes and mind of a human being into the tiny contraptions that were already evaluating the safety of space-shuttle parts, encoding new functions on gallium-arsenide chips, and overseeing the manufacture of other microbots.

"Hell, Bihaly, to boldly go where no one's ever gone before," Emmons told her. "Why weren't we satisfied to fling only a lander at Mars? Why do our astronauts perform EVAs when a machine could do the job a helluva lot more safely?"

Bihaly continued to object. Emmons wasn't going to shrink, not like that guy in the sf film; in fact, he wasn't going to go bodily to the microdimensions at all. But, according to McKay, there was a psychological hazard as forbidding as the prospect of stranding an astronaut on Titan.

"So please tell me," Bihaly said, "why you've chosen to be the first MicroDyne employee to accept the risk?"

"It's pretty simple, really. I want to send back this message to McKay: 'That's one baby step for ameoba-kind, one gigantic step for Yours Truly.' Ain't it a shame the lousy drop-down's not going to be televised?"

THE MAP IS NOT THE TERRITORY, THE NAME IS NOT THE THING
NAMED. McKay took him into the hermetic, dust-free room in
which he was to execute the drop-down and perform his mission.
"Dust-free," McKay hurried to qualify, in the sense that only the
target area—a bell of clear glass eighteen inches in diameter and six
high—contained any dust, organic debris, or moisture. As for
Emmons himself, he would not really be in this room, but in a
nearby operator's booth, jacked into the microremote prototype
beneath the glass bell in the center of the otherwise vacant floor of
this otherwise featureless chamber. In sterile yellow boots and
coveralls, the two men stared down on the bell.

"My Mildendo," Emmons said.

McKay lifted his eyebrows.

"The capital city of Lilliput," Emmons said. He saw that the
dome's inner circle had been quartered into pie wedges of jungle,
desert, ocean, and a landscape of Mondrianesque microcircuitry.
It was a map, a relief map. As a very small boy, he had once taken
a Texaco road map from the glove box of his dad's Audi and studied
it as if it were a two-dimensional kingdom, convinced that the
names of towns were the town themselves and that dot-sized
people really lived there.

A fantasy that his mother's microscopy had given a credibility
that even beginning grade school hadn't undermined.

Today the fantasy had come true. The map was the territory
(even if the name was still not the thing named). As he and McKay
knelt to examine the bell more closely, Emmons had the unpleasant
sensation that he was both a demiurge to this little world and one
of its puny inhabitants.

O IS FOR OMMATIDIA. What must it be like to be a gnat gazing up
through the bell at McKay and him? Would the ommatidia of one
of those tiny insects even register them, or would their images be
fragmented into so many repeating split screens that the creature's
brain rebelled against the overload?

An ommatidium—as Emmons and half the population of the United States had learned thirty years ago from *An Abecedary of the Near Invisible*—is one of the light-sensitive facets of the compound eye of a fly, a honeybee, or a dragonfly. The dragonfly, his mother's book had said, has more of these honeycomblike optical drupes than does any other insect, nearly thirty thousand.

Emmons loved the word: *Ommatidium*.

Dragonflies saw the world fractured, divvied up, split-screened to infinity, which, of course, was also the way that Emmons lived his life and saw reality. It was the same discontinuous, grainy, particulate world amplified in his father's brilliant reworking of Fredkin's private science, digital physics. And just as thousands of ommatidia working together brought useful information out of the fundamental graininess of the world, so, too, might Fredkin's Rule precipitate from the countless information bits of the universe one crystalline truth that made perfect sense of the whole.

Emmons said it to himself as a mantra: Ommm-atiddy-*ummm*. Ommm- atiddy-*ummm*. Ommm-atiddy-*ummm*.

"You'll see more when you're down there," McKay said, puffing as he climbed off the floor. "From a human vantage, the bell's pretty damn empty-looking and ordinary-seeming. But there's stuff in there, all right, and you'd best get to it."

Emmons, standing, had a dizzying image of thousands of immense, cockamamie avatars of himself backing away from the dome and fading off into a vast blue muzziness.

INSIDE THE MICROTAUR. Emmons entered the operator's booth and, with McKay's and two businesslike technicians' help, placed himself in harness.

His invisible vehicle—the one at the very center of the sealed dome—was smaller than a weevil nymph, much too tiny for unassisted detection. Its dimensions qualified it as a micro-, rather than a nano-, technological wonder, but it had not been manufactured by the whittle-away process employed for most of

271

MicroDyne's current wares; instead, it had been drexlered—built up atom by atom—from virtual nothingness, so that it had not only a clear exterior shape under the scanning electron microscope, but also an intricately made interior, or cockpit, with fine one-to-one correspondences to all the controls in the human-scale operator's cab.

Outwardly, the remote resembled a cross between an armor-plated combat vehicle, moving on treads, and an eight-armed crab. Emmons regarded it as the spider-mite equivalent of a modern tank and the mythological centaur, a kind of high-tech microtaur.

Strapped into his seat and plugged into the vehicle's sensors and actuators, Emmons finally received the signal for drop-down. Obediently, he hit the switches in their proper sequences. *Wham!* Brobdingnagian landscapes bloomed, and he was there, an intruder in the pettiness and majesty of the microdimensions.

DOWN AMONG THE DUST MITES. "That's one baby step for amoeba-kind," Emmons said, but the realization that he was moving forward on tiny caterpillar treads made him cut short the guff. He could float, he could tractor, he could shinny, and, by the unfurling of veil-like wings, he could even fly a little, escaping by a hair the fate of insects so nearly weightless that the Brownian movement of random molecular action could buffet them to doom.

What he couldn't do was walk—not as a person walked, anyway—and his first true dimensional shock, all training aside, was the weirdness of this lack. Simulator trials had been helpful, but not wholly to the point. After all, the incredible shrinking man had not had to give up his body as he dropped toward the infinitesimal, only the dumb assumptions that size bestowed dignity, that whatever was small was willy-nilly of no import. The great whales of the seas and the bacterial populations in the human gut, Emmons knew, were . . . well, *equally meaningless lifeforms.*

But not being able to ambulate as human beings usually do— that was a bitch. Down among the dust mites, you had to motor like dust mites. If you didn't do in Rome as the Romans did, you could count on going nowhere but crazy. Frustrated, Emmons slapped at switches like a kid trying to undercut an upright Babel of ABC blocks.

REVERBERATIONS FROM THE VOICE OF GOD. "Emmons, you idiot, stop that!" McKay thundered from afar. "I can't believe you're behaving this way! You haven't done a blasted thing yet!"

But Emmons could believe it. He was a child again, overwhelmed by his father's disdain, lost in an utterly mystifying world.

"Easy," God advised. "Caterpillar into Quadrant Dust Jungle. We'll try the microchip wirings after you've had a chance to take your bearings there."

Emmons settled down; he headed the microtaur into Quadrant Dust Jungle, treading through a gray tangle of pet hairs, grease-coated cotton fibers, cat-flea eggs, pollen grains, skin scales, severed strands of spider webbing, and lopsided arches of unidentifiable gunk and fuzz.

Initially, this alien landscape fascinated Emmons, more by its grotesquerie than by its "beauty," but the longer he piloted the microtaur the more grim and monotonous it seemed. He was reminded of boyhood car trips across the panhandle of Oklahoma.

Boredom was settling on him when he saw a scale-freckled dust mite micrometering over the detritus-cobbled terrain, and he neared the retiring critter, a sort of cow-cum-crayfish, just to see what it would do.

It sensed the microtaur and switched directions. Thus baited, Emmons caterpillared after the mite, careful not to overtake it in his zeal to enliven things.

Relatively soon, he came among dozens—hundreds—of other such mites grazing through the spun-dust jungle of the quadrant. They were microdimensional cattle, heifers of the waste declensions of the very small.

"Reorient your vehicle and head for the EPROM chips in Quadrant Microprocessor!" demanded God.

Grudgingly, Emmons obeyed.

TAKING THE TOUR. Over a period of days, Emmons's microtaur did a grand promenade of the bell, creeping into the separately sealed Quadrant Microprocessor to perform Herculean cutting, pasting, and wire-connecting labors on the wafers arrayed there and incidentally clabbering them with debris from Dust Mite Territory.

Never mind, said McKay; it was the execution of the preassigned tasks that mattered, not their ultimate results, for under optimum conditions their results were entirely predictable. It was the doing of them by hands-on intervention at "ground zero" that was being tested.

"A is for A-OK," the godly McKay intoned. "Good job, Emmons."

In the control booth, Emmons took nutrients through IV stylets and fatigue-offsetting electrostimulus through the wires externally mapping his nervous system.

His microtaur entered Quadrant Living Desert, where its treads terraced a landscape of sand grains, humus particles, and buried seeds. Beneath this promise squirmed springtails and earthworms, creatures out of the Dune books, while beneath them unraveled miles of fungal mycelium and loop snares.

The microtaur's drexlered claws seized nematodes, tardigrades, and Pantagruelian lice. It brought minute soil samples into its collection baskets, then tractored out of Quadrant Living Desert into its final microenvironment, Quadrant Waterworld.

Here, it unshipped flagellate oars to power it through a realm of rotifers, ciliates, and diatoms.

Despite his various energizing hookups, Emmons was exhausted. He hadn't slept for days. If he failed to get some sleep soon, he would begin—even in this hallucinatory realm—to trip out. McKay and MicroDyne were hard taskmasters. He hated them for protracting his mission and for holding him so long in actuator harness. A pox on the bastards.

A RENDEZVOUS WITH MYTILINA. Emmons's microtaur sculled through Quadrant Waterworld and all its light-shot, alga-forested grottoes, bucking, releasing ballast, sounding, rising again.

Eventually, it neared a branching filamentous tree, jewel-green in the submarine stillness, on which a single crystal rotifer had gingerly perched. By its thornlike toes (resembling paired tails), its red eye-spot (like a speck of blood in a minute package of egg white), and its transparent shell (or lorica), Emmons knew it for a representative of the genus *Mytilina*.

It bobbed in the currents stirred by the MicroDyne vehicle, but otherwise appeared unalarmed even though Emmons understood that the rotifer was aware of his approach. In fact, it actually wished for him to close with it so that they could converse.

"McKay," he said, activating his throat mike, "this is weird. A goddamn rotifer wants to talk with me."

When no one in the Sensor and Actuator Center replied, Emmons knew that the *Mytilina* had willed his isolation from his coworkers and that a meeting with the creature was inevitable.

"Son," it said. "Son, what do you think you're doing?"

HOW CAN THE PERCEIVER KNOW THAT WHICH COMPOSES ITS APPARATUSES OF PERCEPTION? Each separate hairlike process ringing the mouth of the rotifer wiggled at its own ever-altering rate. The sound waves generated by these "smart" vibrations belled out through the water, colliding with, building upon, or subtly damping one another as the *Mytilina* itself required, so that by the time the shaped wave-front struck the sensors of his vehicle, it was— Emmons could think of no other appropriate term—"recognizable human speech." On the other hand, Emmons realized that the speaker was actually either God (not McKay & Friends, but the

275

Living God) or his own celebrity father in the guise of a microorganism.

"Maybe this is just my way of trying to help deduce the Rule," Emmons replied. "Didn't you always claim that the basic units of reality are very small, that the universe only seems continuous because we can't see the parts from which it's made? It's like a pointillistic painting by Seurat seen from a long way away. Walk closer and you see the dots. The same with Sunday's funnies. Take a magnifying glass and you'll see the specks of colored ink making up Linus's security blanket."

The crimson eye-spot of the bobbing rotifer pulsed, growing and shrinking at the whim of some inner cadence.

"Derek," it said, "can eyes composed of the smallest units in existence perceive those units? Do you really believe such a situation possible or likely?"

(Either the Deity or my dad is scolding me, Emmons thought. Give heed.)

"Remember," the *Mytilina* said, wobbling on its algal perch. "If the universe is a computer, everything happening as a result of its existence is innately incapable of understanding that it runs at the *direction* of that computer. The software, Derek, can't know the hardware—just as ommatidia the size of the smallest grains comprising reality can never see those grains. Put another way, they can never know—perceive—themselves."

KNOW THYSELF. The rotifer talked to Emmons for mind-made ages; the purpose of the mystic computer of the universe—to answer the question posed by its hidden creator—was obvious. But both the answer and the question itself remained obscure to the universe's sentient representatives because the algorithmic program running to provide the answer was still in process. Not even God—as the *Mytilina* itself could attest—had the answer yet, and no one could guess how much longer the program had to run before it burped out its solution.

Emmons's head began to ache. Other "wheel animalcules" drifted into view, curlecuing toward his father's emerald tree like pixels filling a computer screen.

"Join us, Derek," the rotifer said. "Escape that shell you're hiding in and join us here in Quadrant Waterworld."

It confessed that although he might never learn the question God had posed the universe, being too small to perceive anything that vast, and too integral a part of the program in process to have an objective vantage on it, he might yet learn a few things that would repay him for slipping out of harness into the amniotic warmth of the very small.

Emmons, in the submerged microtaur, saw this as the best offer he'd had in years. Doggedly, he started to prise up electrodes, unplug jacks, strip away wiring, and pull out IV stylets. Free at last, he would crawl into the ejection tube and shoot himself into the tiny water world now harboring both his father and God.

Z IS FOR ZERO, WHICH TO GOD DOES NOT EXIST. McKay ordered two burly technicians into the barricaded control booth. But before they could restrain him, Emmons—sweaty, pop-eyed, thick-tongued— fell back into his padded chair as if siphoned of all memory and will. The operator's cab was a shambles. (His microremote yawed in an emerald orchard of algae and glassy rotifers.) Feverishly, McKay and his cohorts worked to revive Emmons.

Bihaly's appearance wasn't providential—she had been wor-rying about the drop-down—but McKay's decision to let her in before the company doctor arrived may have been. "Rick," she said, using her private diminutive. "Rick, look at me."

Emmons's eyes opened. Above him, the faces of Bihaly, McKay, and the doctor orbited one another like kaleidoscope jewels. He felt nothing—not relief, gratitude, or panic—only a fine, pervasive nothingness drifting through him like pollen through the foliage of evergreens. So what? Nothingness was okay. It might even be survivable. To God, after all, there was no zero.

Emmons had been down for slightly more than four hours, a fact McKay's blurred watch face withheld from him. Again, no matter. Eventually, his eyes would adjust. Maybe, when they did, Bihaly, who had called him back from that which cannot see itself, would still be there and, with her, he would try to understand all that had ever happened to him.

I, Iscariot

*When evening comes, he arrives with the
twelve. And as they reclined at table and were
eating, Jesus said, "So help me, one of you eating
with me is going to turn me in."*

*They began to fret and to say to him one after
another, "I'm not the one, am I?"*

*But he said to them, "It's one of the twelve,
the one who is dipping into the bowl with me. The
son of Adam departs just as the scriptures predict,
but damn the one responsible for turning me in. It
would be better for that man had he never been
born!"*   —Mark 14:17-21

*And right away, while he was still speaking,
Judas, one of the twelve, shows up and with him a*

crowd, dispatched by the ranking priests and the
scholars and the elders, wielding swords and clubs.
Now the one who was to turn him in had arranged a
signal with them, saying, "The one I'm going to kiss
is the one you want. Arrest him and escort him
safely away!" And right away he arrives, comes up
to him, and says, "Rabbi," and kissed him.
And they seized him and held him fast. . . .
—*Mark* 14: 43-46[1]

Before sunset, in a field where potters dig clay for their vessels, the dead man twists beneath hundreds of rose-purple blossoms. Otherwise the tree's branches gleam naked, and the field stands empty of either weed or shrub.

Four men in dirty tunics and split sandals creep into view and spot the hanged man. Even if they had not seen him, their arrival downwind would have betrayed his presence, a strange mix of flower scent and meaty bloat. One of the men covers his mouth and nose with a sleeve.

The bladefaced man in the lead says, The women were right. He pauses a moment before adding, He's got to come down before sunset, or he'll pollute the field.

A stocky man with wiry knucklehair and eyebrows makes a show of gagging. Already has, he says. The bastard done it a night back, Cephas. Can't you smell him?

Still, says Cephas. We have to take him down.

Why? He's gone to Sheol, to everlasting shadow and dust, and the field's already defiled.

Because if it was you, Thaddaeus, you'd want the same.

---

[1] Robert J. Miller, ed. *The Complete Gospels: Annotated Scholars Version*. Revised & Expanded Ed. (San Francisco: Polebridge Press [HarperCollins], 1994), p. 47, p. 48.

It isn't me, even if we shared a name.

The four men argue. Then, silently, they cross the field single-file, like soldiers separated from their army in a hostile land. The sun, ever dropping, flattens and runs, reddening even further the potter's field that the tree already spectacularly brightens.

None of the men has a knife to cut the rope. Two nights ago Cephas had a sword, but lost it. He regrets its loss because none of the others wants to untie the noose that has strangled their former colleague. Thaddaeus, the stocky man, turns his face away, but leans into the bole of the redbud with all his might, pushing the tree into the bruised glow spreading outward from the west.

A taller man with callused hands and a beard like flaming straw helps him. Cephas leaps and grabs the bough supporting the hanged man. His weight draws the limb down. The stench of decay nearly overwhelms him, and he cries, John! Andrew!

Cephas' brother, Andrew, lifts the dead man's swollen feet and walks him out horizontal to the ground.

The rope, already rotten and fraying, snaps. The corpse pitches headfirst to the clay, twisting so that upon impact its abdomen bursts and an iridescent snake of bowel gushes out.

What a rank bugger! says Thaddaeus.

John, the tall man with the flaming beard, stands back from the corpse and recites,

> *When he is judged, let him be found guilty.*
> *And let his prayer become sin.*
> *Let his days be few,*
> *And let another take his office.*[2]

Selah, says Andrew. What now?

---

[2] *Psalm* 109:7-8 in *The Wesley Bible: New King James Version* (Nashville, TN: Thomas Nelson, Inc., 1990), p. 869. See also *Acts* 1:16-20.

Nothing, says Cephas, half-snarling. A day late, he's down from his tree. Let the dogs and vultures take him.

Thaddaeus begins to weep: a strange, indeed, a discomfiting sight in so powerful-looking a man. I wish we could trade this body for the other, he manages. I wish we

knew where the other body lay, says John. But we don't, and there's an end to it.

Cephas nudges the fallen corpse with a toe. Then the four men stalk single-file back across the field toward the city, warily inspecting the landscape's shadows for bountyhunters and informants. They skulk totally out of view. All that remains, framing their vanishment, is the crimson-tinted mother-of-pearl face of a computer monitor.

A day or two after the event inspiring this dramatization, some women start calling the field Akel Dama, or Blood Acre, and the name sticks, like wet clay to an amphora taking watery form on a potter's wheel.

Two thousand years later, the faux-event's resuscitants, including the hanged man himself, gather in a twilight space at once measurable with a carpenter's tape and so depthfully vast that it mirrors the world. The farther you go into this space the more detail and dimension it acquires.

In fact, its whiteness exfoliates into rainforests, cities, amphitheatres, palaces, and halls, almost as if you have run through a series of nested realities to this false courtroom at the shifting center.

The resuscitants—electronic simulacra, with reconstituted memories of their bodily lives—dispose themselves about the space, primarily on its edges. They will emerge into view at any legitimate call, then soliloquize, testify, and/or enact as the proceedings demand.

How do you plead?

Please. In what matter?

That of the Messiah's betrayal to the Judean authorities.

Yes. Of course. I handed him over.

Guilty, then.

But I didn't understand what I was doing. I never realized they'd haul him away for judgment and nailing.

Come, Mr. Iscariot. Do better.

Help us recognize him, they said. We know him by the commotion he's made, but his face remains unfamiliar to most Jerusalmites, even to some who've heard him preach, for they heard him from a distance. With these and similar arguments they cajoled me.

And so the kiss of betrayal?

The kiss of identification. No more. The others slander me because it turns the eye from how cravenly they fled, like chickens in a hawk's oversoaring shadow.

And now you rat them out in turn.

I say the truth, even if Pilate himself pretends not to recognize it.

So how do you plead?

Of leading the Judeans to him, guilty. Of betraying him, innocent. Altogether innocent.

Resuscitants appear in period dress. They look anomalously time-elided, extras in a pre-Lucan costume drama. But with them in modern attire appear the e-clones of some celebs as familiar to a latter-day netist as Brando or Heston to any longtime film buff.

The prosecution team, for example, includes e-clones for Avery Stills, Rebecca Mormile, and Henry Albornoz, while the even more famous defense team features dopplegängers for Wendy Grice, Hirofumi Satoh, and Dakota Browning. The Chief Justice of the United States Supreme Court—an e-clone of Paul Ogilvie—presides.

Either simultaneous or delayed cable feeds serve the computerphobic. In fact, television broadcasts garner such prodigious ratings that the major entertainment networks have preempted nearly all regular programming for gavel-to-gavel coverage of what aficionados early on christened the Trial of the Millennium. (CBS, predictably, calls its own focus on the virtually self-propagating proceedings Eye on Iscariot.)

Jury members, who never appear onscreen, vary widely in age, ethnicity, and socioeconomic status. They do have one odd quality in common: In offline negotiations preceding the trial, both defense and prosecution agreed that to qualify for duty these e-entities must manifest as religion-neutral or -indifferent. Both sides, it seems, feared any juror with a theological or a rationalist axe to grind and thus decided to exclude such specimens.

Do you swear to tell the truth, the whole truth, and nothing but the truth, so help you God?

My Yes is Yes, and my No, No.

You won't take the oath?

Yeshua taught that oaths echo like wind in the mouths of scoundrels. I'm not a scoundrel.

The Avery Stills e-clone rises. I object, he says. Your Honor, this is a blatant evasion.

The simulacrum of Chief Justice Ogilvie ignores him. By what would you agree to swear, Mr. Iscariot?

I won't swear, either as oath or profanation. None of us does. Probity cloaks any follower who takes to heart Yeshua's teachings.

Objection, says the Stills e-clone.

Why?

Your Honor, Mr. Iscariot stresses an apostolic association he stands accused of betraying. Letting him sidestep the oath is like granting him permission to lie.

Relax, Mr. Stills. What prevents any sworn testator from lying?

Your Honor, the issue isn't

Address the question, please.

One's personal integrity. Or one's fear of one's god. The figure shrugs and sits back down.

Take the stand, Judge Ogilvie tells Iscariot.[3]

The trial programmers and the electronic infrastructure supporting them begin to merchandise Iscariot. T-shirts; plastic cups; toy lambs; stenciled tunics; foam-soled sandals; Betrayal™ playing cards, board games, and computer games; two-faced silver coins (in laminated rolls of thirty); vials of a puttylike substance jocularly identified as spikenard; a set of porcelain plates depicting not only Iscariot, but Lucifer, Lancelot, Iago, Benedict Arnold, and Vidkun Quisling; flowering Judas seed catalogues; intricately carven tillboxes; flexible plastic figurines of Iscariot, Brutus, and Cassius writhing in the triple mouths of Satan. . . .

> *"The soul that suffers most," explained my Guide,*
> *"is Judas Iscariot, he who kicks his legs*
> *On the fiery chin and has his head inside. . . ."*[4]

Not to mention covers on *Newsweek, Time, U.S. News & World Report, New Yorker, GQ, Wired, Rolling Stone, Esquire, Mother Jones,*

---

[3] From here on, we drop the cumbersome neologism e-clone and its various situational corrolaries; however, every proper name in this transcript implies it.

[4] John Ciardi, trans., *The Inferno* by Dante Alighieri (New York: Mentor Books, 1954), Canto XXXIII, vv. 61-63.

TV Guide, The Atlantic Monthly, Redbook, Byte, Christianity Today, People, Omni, Sassy, Psychology Today, Science Fiction Age, St. Andrew's Messenger, TriQuarterly, Outland, Apostolically Yours, Playboy, Hebrew Studies, The Paris Review, Century, Science News, Trial Lawyer, Modern Horticulturist, and *CRANK!* (to list a provocative representative sample).

Favorite T-shirt designs include silkscreened portraits of Iscariot scolding Mary about the spikenard, filching from the disciples' moneybox, dipping bread in the Upper Room, kissing an already savvy Yeshua in the Garden of Gethsemane, scattering his bloodmoney in the Temple, standing selfconsciously naked in a YMCA lockerroom, driving an antique Edsel, propositioning the First Lady, chug-a-lugging a Coca-Cola, stealing home in a game between the Angels and the A's, eating a Pizza Hut calzone, and twisting slowly from a redbed tree in the potter's field known as Akel Dama.

The most popular T-shirt slogans include

I, ISCARIOT

EYE ON ISCARIOT

I^3 = ISCARIOT IS INNOCENT

I = ISCARIOT, I = IMPENITENT

I SCARE IN A RIOT . . . HOW ABOUT YOU?

ISCARIOT HAPPENS

DOESN'T ISCARIOT MEAN SNAIL?

A KISS IS STILL A KISS

HANG OUT WITH JUDAS, A REAL BREAKNECK GUY

JUDAS, JUDAS, JUDAS . . . THERE'S SOMETHING ABOUT THAT NAME

IF HE HADN'T SQUEALED, HOW WOULD WE HAVE HEALED?

12 - 11 = ISCARIOT

AN APOSTLE AMOK SET SALVATION'S CLOCK

WHAT, ME BETRAY?

GET A GOOD PRICE FOR YOUR SOUL

IF YOU LUV YEHUDDAH, YODEL!

BASE, VILE, LOW, MEAN, SICK & NASTY!!!

ISCARIOT, BOOTH, & OSWALD: HITMEN OF THE MILLENNIUM

and under the name ISCARIOT:

> Caiaphas
> Is an ass,
> Pilate
> Is all apeeve.
> Upon my word,
> I love the LORD . . .
> Till late
> Come Friday eve.

ONLINE LOGOMACHY (I)

Isn't it unusual for a defendant to testify on his own behalf at the opening of a trial?

This is an electronic simulation.

Maybe so. But ordinarily the prosecution would have to build its case, wouldn't it? That way the defense would have substantive arguments to rebut.

Other circumstances prevail here.

How so?

The prosecution, so to speak, has already had more than two thousand years to build its case.

In the court of public opinion?

Right. Exhibit A, for example, has been floating around almost since the beginning of the movement.

Exhibit A?

The Christian scriptures. The New Testament, specifically the 13th chapter of John.

Why John? Why that chapter?

John Boy's the only evangelist who has Jesus unequivocally finger Iscariot as the betrayer.

No way. All four gospels so identify him.

As the bringer of the kiss. Beyond that, though, it's all hearsay, innuendo, defamation, even false witness.

At which point a participant in the discussion types in the following passage:

> . . . *And as they were eating, he said, "So help*
> *me, one of you is going to turn me in."*
>
> *And they were very upset, and each one said*
> *to him in turn, "I'm not the one, am I, Master?"*
>
> *In response he said, "The one who dips his*
> *hand in the bowl with me—that's who's going to*
> *turn me in! . . . It would be better for that man*
> *had he never been born!"*
>
> *Judas, who was to turn him in, responded,*
> *"You can't mean me, can you Rabbi?"*
>
> *He says to him, "You said it."*
>
> —*Matthew* 26:21-25[5]

That pretty much brings it down to Judas, doesn't it? He dipped his hand in the bowl with Jesus.

Exactly. And Jesus turns his direct question right back on him.

Hey, they all dipped their hands in the bowl with him. It was a communal Passover meal. And Jesus may have turned every disciple's question back on him. The guy had a canny Socratic streak, Hebraic version thereof.

So why's Judas get whomped for special censure?

That damn kiss. In the fallout from the crucifixion, poor Iscariot catches a shitload of retroactive stigmatization. A classic case of scapegoating.

Yeah. Also note that the genuinely guilty disciple had a heavy stake in laying the blame on someone else, and Judas, whom Jesus sent out for some purpose, wasn't around to defend himself.

---

[5] *The Complete Gospels*, p. 107.

Neither that evening nor the next day—when his despair at the Rabbi's death and his eleven false friends' lies caused him to go out and hang himself.

You're saying that a disciple, or disciples, scapegoated Iscariot in the same way that Caiaphas and his pals scapegoated Christ?

Sure. Why not? If you're a believer, Judas may have died for your sins just as profoundly as Jesus did.

One big difference.

I'll byte. Go on.

Iscariot had the rope in his own hands.

Right. But if you want to get into the metaphysics of omnipotence, we could argue that point too.

Go back to that remark about a genuinely guilty disciple. If not Judas, who? Peter? Levi? John?

Maybe Iscariot was no more guilty than any of the rest of the disciples. On the other hand, maybe one of them wanted to protect his own ass.

Because John pulls the trigger on Judas, in that unlucky chapter 13, expect Dakota Browning to go after his e-clone in a withering cross.

Fireworx, spiderfolk. Fireworx!

Hey, anybody want to trade a Grand Unified Theory tee with a silkscreened lower intestinal tract on it for an I, ISCARIOT jobbie?

Get outta here. . . .

Hirofumi Satoh stands next to the witness box so that he can lend Iscariot emotional support and survey the courtroom (including its unseen spectators and the differently invisible netists peering in on the proceedings). Although of less than average height by his own era's standards, Satoh makes Judas, despite his beard, appear small and childlike. The elegant box in which Iscariot sits visibly downsizes him, too.

Describe your individual relationship with the Rabbi, Satoh says. He speaks with the accentless facility of a trained news anchor.

Good. Quite good.

Do you think he liked you?

Of course. He liked everyone. This open-souled regard for everyone was the main burden of his tidings.

Do you think he esteemed you over others?

He called me to discipleship. He allowed me into the inner circle of the twelve.

And how did he esteem you within that inner circle?

As highly, or nearly as highly, as any other. Once he said that we twelve would sit on twelve thrones in judgment on the twelve tribes of Israel.

Yes, Satoh says. Matthew recorded the saying.

He added that we would receive a hundredfold blessing and inherit eternal life. Why would Yeshua have said such a thing to a betrayer?

Objection, says Henry Albornoz from the prosecution's table. The witness wants us to engage in bootless speculation.

Judge Ogilvie looks at Albornoz. Ordinarily, counsel may object only to opposition counsel's inappropriate tactics, not the testimony of a witness.

But this is

Basic stuff, Mr. Albornoz.

Albornoz shakes his head.

Satoh turns to Judas as if no interruption has occurred: So you had a satisfactory, even an exemplary, relationship with the Rabbi?

I did.

What of your dealings with the other chosen eleven?

Iscariot hesitates. Then he says, Good. No trouble. Not really.

A little trouble, maybe? If so, Mr. Iscariot, you now have both occasion and cause to tell us.

Iscariot's posture—head down, shoulders slumped, hands on knees—suggests his ambivalence. An unseen spectator coughs. Satoh lays a hand on the edge of the witness box. Eventually, Iscariot looks up. He begins to talk, a quaver in his voice and a longdistance stare in his eyes. The stare, pursued into closeup, opens out into a rocky desert landscape. . . .

JUDAS

In my home village of Kerioth, just beyond the Jordan in Decapolis, I heard of Yeshua at the very beginning of his ministry. In only a few months' time, he had numerous followers, some of whom had come to him from as far away as Beersheba in Idumea. In comparison, my journey to him seemed easy.

At this time, he'd chosen only four or five of the twelve he later appointed fully. But in synagogue after synagogue around the Sea of Galilee, I heard him speak in parables; saw him heal the sick and cast blaspheming demons out of possessed unfortunates.

In Capernaum, I helped the friends of a paralytic remove some rooftiles and lower him on his mat into a crowded house where Yeshua had gone to preach. Looking down, I see that man struggle to his feet, seize his bed, and stride into the night to the chorusing alleluias of his friends and maybe half the thunderstruck throng.

A day later, following Yeshua about the lake, I separated myself from the crowd and happened upon him and his first five disciples encamped in brushwood lean-tos beside the sea: James and John, the sons of Zebedee, whom he called Boanerges, or Thunder Brothers; two more brothers, Simon Peter and Andrew; and Levi, the son of Alphaeus, a toll collector whom the others at first resented as a professional leech.

What about you? Yeshua asked me when I sat down unbidden at their cooking fire. What do you do?

I told him (and, of course, the others, who had begun to eyeball me through the flickering shadows) that I worked metal, making knives, pitchforks, and tilling instruments. I showed him the knife I carried as an example of my workmanship. He hefted it admiringly on one palm. He even set the edge of my knife to the heel of his hand, producing a thin beaded crimson line more black than red in the firelight. Then he smiled and asked me my name, and the blood on his hand—nor did I imagine this—vanished.

Too giddy to marvel, I said, Judas of Kerioth.

Ah, said Simon Peter, whom Yeshua already sometimes called Cephas, then we'll call you Iscariot.

But why? I asked him.

He presumptuously combines Kerioth and sicarius, Yeshua said.

Sicarius? I said.

It's Latin for dagger man or assassin. Maybe Cephas thinks you have Zealot written across your forehead.

I said, I make knives, but I avoid politics. The kingdoms of this world fall to ruin. I seek the everlasting, Rabbi.

Well said. You wish to follow me?

I want nothing else.

Then give me consent to disarm you.

I didn't understand, but Yeshua correctly read in me total surrender to whatever he purposed. Indeed, so reading me, he flung my knife, blade over haft, into the soft tarnished pewter of Yam Kinneret, the Galilean Sea. Yeshua's five not quite disciples laughed. Me? I felt no loss at the sinking of my knife, only joy, a heady exhilaration at my unexpected welcome among these men.

Looking back, I note a grisly joke: the one who named me dagger man carried a sword into the Garden of Gethsemane and struck off the ear of Malchus, the high priest's slave. He did so just as a platoon of Roman soldiers and some of the priestly constabulary laid hands on Yeshua.[6] Of course, he acted from both love of Yeshua and a gnawing fear that he had never truly merited the Rabbi's favor.

---

[6] A.N. Wilson, *Jesus: A Life* (London: W.W. Norton & Co, 1992), pp. 203-206. Wilson argues that Malchus, meaning king, may have been Saul, the Christian persecutor who later became the apostle Paul. Saul, after all, had been "the first of the Jewish kings" (206).

None of us merited it. I understand, though, that Malchus, the man whose ear Simon Peter severed, came to recognize that fact better than any of the chosen twelve, including the five on the shore with us on the night that Yeshua looked with favor on me, a Decapolean; in all respects but my allegiance to God and the son of Adam, a foreigner.

In subsequent days, Yeshua met headlong the devout, the forsaken, and the frenzied who searched for him along the lake shore. He preached, healed, and evicted demons. Often he did so from, or near, a fisherman's boat, to keep the crowds from overwhelming him. His labors wore him out. He withdrew to the hills. Through Simon Peter, he put out a call for the other seven—beyond the first five companions—whom he would appoint as dependent ministers.

Astonishingly, at least to me, Yeshua included me in that number. I was the only one of the twelve not also a Galilean, a fact that told against me on the night of the Passover and on the day of the crucifixion. A fact that tells against me now, I fear.

ONLINE LOGOMACHY (II)

Probably so.

You think?

Absolutely. He lacked the others' geographical roots and the loyalty that usually goes with compatriotism.

One way of looking at it.

You have another?

The other eleven, or a significant number of them, held his foreignness against Iscariot.

Oh, please.

To deflect attention from their own inglorious behavior on the night of their master's arrest, they conspired to frame him for betrayal.

A chestnut. A stale chestnut.

Yeah. Well. That old stranger-in-a-strange-land argument slices two ways.

293

A FAN LETTER

Dear Judas,

Hang in ther. Your cute yo now that. I evn
lik it wen yo suk in & chue on sum of yur beerd.
Fiona my sister sas its grosss but she has no tast
she is a filisten to be biblucl about it. Wich I
would lik to be with yo if I cud kno you to luv you
an luv you to kno you to be biblucl agan.

The Jap layer of yurs say he knos how you feel
me too. Fiona one nite mist kerfew & my dad sed
heed ring my neck if I didn rat her out where she
waz. So I tol. Fiona when she got hom & fond out
come don to my room to lay lik a reel hevy diss on
me. You Judas she yelld to me you stnking liddle
Judas. But I, I don think you stnk an if yo weren
jess a online emmige Id lik to mary you. So will
you I men lik mery me?

XXX 000. Luve,

Renata Smith-Koester

Wendy Grice resembles a bird, small and quick-moving. Her attire
suggests a goldfinch in the process of trading its grey winter
plumage for the yellows of spring. Iscariot regards her hopefully.

So the other eleven disciples sometimes made you feel your
foreignness, she says.

Sometimes.

Give the court a specific instance of their prejudice.

Iscariot considers, then says: Yeshua gave us instructions
before sending us out as his agents. He told us,

*"Heal the sick, raise the dead, cleanse the lepers,
drive out demons. You have received freely, so freely
give. Don't get gold or silver or copper coins for
spending money, don't take a knapsack for the road, or*

*two shirts, or sandals, or a staff, for 'the worker
deserves his food'. . . . "*

—*Matthew* 10:8-10[7]

Did you and the others obey these instructions? asks Grice.

Insofar as we could. But the business about not taking coins with us troubled a couple of the Galileans. What if there were an emergency? What if those we helped forced money on us, saying that we should take it as an offering to the poor?

What did these worriers decide?

That it would be wrong to make no provision for a crisis and equally wrong to refuse alms for the poor.

Did you agree with the Galileans on these points?

Yes, I fear I did.

So how did the eleven demonstrate their regionalist bias against you, Mr. Iscariot?

None of them wanted to stand as our group treasurer, for fear that taking the job would breach the Rabbi's instructions and prove a stumbling block to salvation.

Salvation?

Yes. Yeshua had also said that everyone would hate us twelve because of him, but that those of us who held out to the end would find our reward.

So no one volunteered for the job?

Not even Levi, the former toll collector. I won't do it, he said. I've set aside my old ways, and sorting through coins again would only pollute me beyond saving.

Grice gives the jury a moment for this news to register, then turns to Judas and says, So the eleven Galileans foisted the unwelcome job on you?

The job and the moneybox.

---

[7] *The Complete Gospels*, p. 75.

In Jesus' presence?

Oh, no. Out of it. Everyone understood that it would transgress his guidelines and reveal our lack of faith to keep a moneybox. But our fear of the unforeseen overcame our trust in Yeshua's farsightedness.

Why did you agree to act as treasurer?

I was backed into a corner. If I refused, how would I ever gain the others' acceptance?

Did acceptance come, once you'd taken this unpopular job?

No. Not at all.

What occurred instead?

The others accused me of filching from the kitty. They even said I'd taken the job to insure access to these middling sums.

Did you ever betray the others' trust?

What trust? But, no, I never pilfered. In fact, I gave more to our treasury than any of the others, who could pocket whatever they took in without making any sort of account to the entire group.

Mr. Stills would probably say that you could misrepresent or hide donations as easily as anyone else.

I guess I could have, but I never did.

Why didn't you?

I loved the Rabbi. I believed his words. And I wanted the respect of the eleven Galileans he had chosen along with me as his inner circle.

No further questions.

We will now take a ten-minute recess, says Judge Ogilvie.

A POEM ON THE NET

He has a finger in the till,
   Another in his eye.
He is a shameless, gutless shill
   For his abhorrent lie.

Once more to the tree, Sick Judas,
  Once more to the rope.
Hang yourself and thereby free us
  To rise from hate to hope.

Judas in the sky with diamonds?
  No, dirt-trapped, underground,
Mouthing cant and vulture-pie crumbs,
  Without a sound.

Dakota Browning, spiffy in designer buckskins, takes a turn for the defense questioning Iscariot:
    Which of the Galileans do you think most resented you?
    The three who believed themselves Yeshua's favorites.
    Namely?
    Cephas and the Thunder Brothers.
    Simon Peter and the sons of Zebedee, James and John, all of whom claimed to've seen Jesus transfigured on Mount Tabor?
    Yes.
    Which of the eleven went after your reputation the hardest, repeatedly and baselessly labeling you a thief?
    I don't know. Toward the end, they all seemed to regard me as an untrustworthy interloper. Thomas Didymus remained friendly, but of course he always demanded proof of any dubious assertion.
    Who would you name as the most persistent and implacable in his hostility?
    The one who called himself the beloved disciple.
    Dakota Browning turns to face the unseen jurybox. In other words, John the son of Zebedee?
    Without question, Iscariot says.

ONLINE LOGOMACHY (III)

In a rape trial, you can count on the defense attorneys going after the victim. She slept around, she dressed like a slut, she hung where a decent woman wouldn't hang, she was an infamous flirt, blah blah blah.

Your point, Clarence Darrow?

Dakota Browning & Friends intend to put the other eleven disciples on trial. Shoot, they've already started.

You think the eleven Galileans were victims of Iscariot's lies and chicanery?

Amen. We all were.

But if you buy the redemption myth, we were really all his beneficiaries.

I'm arguing legally here, not theologically. Cut me some slack. The biggest victim, of course, was Iscariot's master, but even Grice, Satoh, and Browning don't have the chutzpah to try to sabotage Jesus' reputation.

A minute ago you were griping about the ethical bankruptcy of defense attorneys. Now you call them spineless for behaving responsibly.

We'll see how they behave. Meanwhile, don't jump me for defending Peter and the boys from Iscariot's lawyers' calumny.

Aren't Peter and the boys, especially John Boy, guilty of that very sin? Likewise the evangelists who wrote down their self-serving stories?

Hey, they're evangelists, gospel-makers. They write under inspiration from the Holy Spirit.

Even those inspired of God can run with a beautiful or a holy lie, maybe especially those inspired of God. And if you don't believe in beauty, or holiness, or the lies occasionally undergirding them, then you have a duty to truth—should you believe in that—to dig for the ugly or corrupt foundations.

Pardon me, you blaspheming heathens, but I'm gone.

Farewell.

Au revoir. Auf Wiedersehen. Hasta la vista.

But another participant says, I'm still here. And I have no plans to tuck tail and run, even if Grice and Company drop a five-ton concrete block on the so-called beloved disciple.

THREE EXHIBITS FOR THE DEFENSE

A: *. . . Mary brought in a pound of expensive lotion and annointed Jesus' feet and wiped them with her hair. And the house was filled with the lotion's fragrance. Judas Iscariot . . . says, "Why wasn't this lotion sold? It would bring a year's wages, and the proceeds could have been given to the poor." (He didn't say this because he cared about the poor, but because he was a thief. He was in charge of the common purse and now and again would pilfer money put into it.)*

—*John 12:3-8*

B: *. . . Jesus. . . declared: "I swear to God, one of you will turn me in."*

The disciples stole glances at each other, at a loss to understand who it was he was talking about. One of them, the disciple Jesus loved most, was sitting at Jesus' right. So Simon Peter leans over to ask that disciple who it was <Jesus> was talking about. He in turn leans over to Jesus and asks him, "Master, who is it?"

Jesus answers: "I'm going to dunk this piece of bread, and the one I give it to is the one." So he dunks the piece of bread and gives it to Judas, Simon Iscariot's son. The moment <he had given Judas> the piece of bread, Satan took possession of him. Then Jesus says to him, "Go ahead and do what you're going to do."

Of course no one at dinner understood why Jesus had made this remark. Some had the idea that because Judas had charge of the funds, Jesus was telling him, "Buy whatever we need for the celebration," or to give something to the poor. In

299

any case, as soon as <Judas> had eaten the piece of
bread he went out. It was nighttime.

—John 13:21-30

C: *So <Mary> runs and comes to Simon Peter and*
the other disciple—the one that Jesus loved most—
and tells them, "They've taken the Master from the
tomb, and we don't know where they've put him."
       So Peter and the other disciple went out, and
they made their way to the tomb. The two of them
were running along together, but the other disciple
ran faster than Peter and was the first to reach
the tomb. . . .

—John 20:2-3[8]

Justice Ogilvie reads through the printouts given him by
Wendy Grice as Exhibits A, B, and C. He takes his time, using the
edge of an expensive letter opener to underscore each line of type.
Finally, he looks up.

Pardon me, Ms. Grice, but I'd think the prosecution eager to
enter these passages as exhibits for its side.

Yessir, says Grice. The folly of pride.

Really? They paint a rather unattractive picture of your client.

No more unattractive than the one they paint of John as a
braggart and a false testifier.

Objection! chorus Stills, Mormile, and Albornoz.

------

[8]Exhibit A appears on p. 227 of *The Complete Gospels,*
Exhibit B on p. 230, and Exhibit C on p. 242. The New King James
Version renders A's "expensive lotion" as "costly oil of spikenard"
(perfumed ointment), and B's "Simon Iscariot's son" as "the son of
Simon" and Jesus' direction to Judas ("Go ahead and do what you're
going to do") as the more specific, "What you do, do quickly." The
variant translations may impact the interpretation of evidence.

Sustained, says Ogilvie. Or would be if this weren't a friendly sidebar out of the jury's hearing. Please, everyone, relax.

Iscariot remains on the stand. Satoh paces the courtroom in front of the bench.

At length he says, You contend that John put in the frame and that his Galilean cohorts bought it.

No one but John could have heard what Yeshua said to him in the upper room, and I can't believe that the Rabbi named me to him.

Why did you go out?

Just as some of the others supposed, to make a contribution to the poor from our group treasury.

By this time Jesus knew that you kept a moneybox?

Sooner or later he discovered everything.

Didn't he rebuke you for your disobedience or demand that you disburse all your funds and chuck the moneybox?

Actually, he tweaked us for our lack of faith—a recurring theme with him because we recurrently gave him cause—and sent me out to do just what you've asked, discard the box. I gladly obeyed. It was a relief.

Why did he tell you, Do quickly what you have to do?

He was sharing new teachings and comfort with us, and he didn't want me to miss any more than I had to. Also, he feared that the Romans and the constabulary of the high priests might initiate a raid.

What happened to you on your errand?

I was named as an associate of Yeshua, placed under guard, and marched off to talk to Annas, Caiaphas' father-in-law, and then to Caiaphas himself.

About what?

They were always anxious to placate the Romans on festival days. Jerusalem's streets teemed with pilgrims, some reverent, some rowdy, and they wanted information.

So you told them Jesus' whereabouts for thirty pieces of silver. Right?

They said they'd nail me as a cutthroat rebel if I didn't help them. They also swore they only wanted to question Yeshua about any knowledge he might have of insurrectionist activity among the crowds. No one offered me even a tenth of a denarius for my help.

Didn't you think that these people might want to catch him in a punishable impiety? The priests and the Pharisees were no friends of yours.

With some heat, they mentioned Yeshua's cleansing of the temple during an earlier Passover, but . . . so what? Yeshua told us to expect the world's hatred. He also said we would overcome evil through faith.

When did you realize the authorities had lied to you?

Not until troops and temple police with torches and weapons jostled me along to the garden.

So you didn't betray the Rabbi.

Never. I loved him.

In your view, you did nothing wrong?

My crime was too much trust, or faith, in the intentions of the priests and the power of the Nazarene.

When did you come to doubt even the power?

When they tried him, scourged him, sent him stumbling along the Sorrowful Way, and hammered him to a cross. When even the eleven Galileans broke ranks and fled. Iscariot's voice cracks and he begins to weep.

Forgive me, Mr. Iscariot, but didn't you in fact receive thirty pieces of silver for your help?

At the moment of Yeshua's arrest, someone thrust a bag at me. I took it without knowing what it was. Later, I found it to hold a few crooked coins from the temple moneychangers.

Not thirty pieces of silver?

No.

What did you do with those crooked coins?

I returned to the temple in the morning and flung them at the feet of the scornful elders.

Then what? asks Satoh.

Judas rubs his temples, knuckles one eye, shakes his head. In his longdistance stare, online spectators can see reflected a canopy of rose-purple blossoms.

ONLINE LOGOMACHY (IV)

Matthew says that Iscariot went to the priests before the last supper and asked for a reward for handing Jesus over. The betrayer lies.

John was the only disciple who could've possibly known whom Jesus singled out as the culprit. Maybe he lied to the others, and Matthew, or Levi, tailored his gospel account to the cut of John's lie.

Whoa!

How so whoa?

You can't label John a liar on the matter of Judas' guilt and swallow whole his assertion that Jesus named the betrayer to him alone. Show some consistency here.

Okay, he lied throughout, during Jesus' earthly stay and after, in person to the other ten and on papyrus to posterity.

Christ, such cynicism!

Are you addressing the Lord or profaning his name?

Probably some of both. You Iscariot lovers seem to want to defame a hundred saints to redeem a single black-sheep creep.

A biblical desire. Jesus said, If someone has a hundred sheep and one of them wanders off, won't that person leave the ninety-nine in the hills and go and look for the one that wandered off?[9]

Gag me with an exegesis.

Whatever you want. Care to make a date?

---

[9] Matthew 18:12-13, *The Complete Gospels,* p. 90

DIVAGATION: AN ISLAMIC LEGEND

Pilate releases Barabbas to the rabble, who, by crying for the highwayman, have condemned the Nazarene to die. But at this very moment, God lifts Jesus bodily into heaven. Neither Pilate nor the crowd apprehend this miracle, owing to the fact that at this same instant God snatches up the traitor Iscariot, makes him over atom by atom to resemble the condemned Rabbi, and deposits him on the porch of the governor's house in Jesus' stead.

Iscariot cannot believe either his transformation or the severity of his plight. He cannot speak, either to protest or to explain. Who would believe him?

In a last effort to appease the crowd's bloodlust, Pilate has Iscariot scourged with a knotted cord weighted with slivers of oxbone. When this effort fails, Pilate allows his soldiers to drive the stumbling Judas into the courtyard. Here they strip him, cloak him in scarlet, and subject him to a variety of mocking torments. These culminate in his forced march along the Via Dolorosa.

Upon the cross, Iscariot tries to emulate the behavior that his master both preached and modeled. He repredicts the fall of Jerusalem. He forgives a repentent thief. He thinks, I die for the sinless Nazarene. And he says, Father, into your hands I commit my spirit. Whereupon, torn and breathless, he dies in the ascended Jesus' place.

From the Islamic perspective, the purpose of this story is to wreak justice and to discredit the resurrection. But to the e-clone of Judas Iscariot, the legend appears to require as profound a faith, or as foolish a credulity, as the orthodox passion narrative. If this electronic court convicts him of the betrayal of which greater Christendom already believes him guilty, will it sentence him to die on a rood of glowing pixels in the echoey virtuality of cyberspace?

THE PARABLES OF JUDAS

In an offline dream, Iscariot puts a series of parables before the court. He will say nothing to the judge, lawyers, jurors, spectators, and netists except by way of parable, so that what he dreams in his torment will evaporate totally upon awakening.

To no one's question but his own, he spins this parable:

The betrayal of God's empire of light is like a tiny bead of poison that a man drops into a well of sweet water from a hidden vial. Though the drop is even smaller than the pupil of a sparrow's eye, yet, when it spreads throughout the well and pollutes even the spring, all who come in faith to the water and drink, clutch their throats, fall to the ground, and die in an agony of perplexity and blindness.

He tells them another parable:

The betrayal of God's empire of light is like a cowbird that invades the territories of sweet-singing larks and lays a single egg in the nests of these songbirds so that when the larks' own eggs hatch, a black cowbird hatches with the larks' young, and takes their food, and crowds them from their nests, and displaces their parents' carols with croakings of raucous triumph.

Iscariot puts a third parable to the court:

The betrayal of God's empire of light is like a hacker who logs on with a stolen password, roams the system at will, and secretes within it a viral program that activates itself upon another user's inadvertent command. He then begins to convert coherent data into ceaselessly self-propagating hieroglyphs of nihilistic jabberwock. . . .

And so when Iscariot has finished dreaming these parables, he awakes in cyberspace, asweat and atremble, with each parable seared into his consciousness like a cigarette burn on a snowy linen tablecloth.

Dakota Browning says, Anything else you'd care to say in your own defense, Mr. Iscariot?

One thing. One thing only.

Go ahead.

Not long after time began, Lucifer betrayed God the Father out of ego and self-deception, supposing that he could somehow supplant the Creator.

Browning hopes to persuade the jury of his client's robust mental health. I assume you narrate metaphorically, he says.

I speak what I believe, Iscariot says.

Because your Yes is Yes, and your No, No?

Yes.

Although Browning appears dubious about issuing a second go-ahead, he says, All right. Proceed.

Not long after awakening as an e-clone, I learned that the evangelist John wrote in his gospel that Satan entered me. He reports that with Satan thus at work in me, I handed over our master.

You dispute both assertions?

I've never had an ego like Lucifer's and the most painful self-deception I've ever practiced was that built on my hope that the other eleven would one day warm to me. Iscariot halts and grimaces.

Do you need a recess?

No. Sometimes . . . well, sometimes I have bad, horridly oppressive dreams. In them—and often I think that this is one—food tastes salt and bitter, music turns to insupportable clamor, and the sun drops into eclipse, never to emerge again. I despair.[10]

---

[10] In *Lucifer: The Devil in the Middle Ages* (Ithaca and London: Cornell University Press, 1984), Jeffrey Burton Russell notes that people once cast Despair as Lucifer's daughter, who entices Judas to betray Jesus. "When Judas has done the deed, Despair prompts him to suicide, and the demons rejoice at his eternal damnation" (267).

Ogilvie leans toward Iscariot. Believe it or not, someone meant this trial as an antidote to despair.

Iscariot smiles wanly. A suicide has trouble believing that. But my resusication's taught me a lesson.

Tell us, says Ogilvie.

Despair is a harlot. Despite treason after treason, and sabotage after sabotage, God's empire of light never falls into total eclipse. Satan wages a futile war. Those who wage it with him wrap themselves in the pain and terror of their own self-betraying sins. Iscariot falls silent.

A fine lesson to learn, says Browning skeptically.

I had to die and come back to learn it.

Well. Yes. Anything else?

No.

No further questions, Your Honor.

Ogilvie looks to the prosecution. Cross-examination?

Rebecca Mormile half rises. To nearly everyone's surprise, she says, No questions, Your Honor.

ONLINE LOGOMACHY (V)

They had a chance to subject the jerk to a killer cross and they passed it up? What's wrong with these high-priced clowns?

Don't you mean clones? They're simulacra.

That's right. Nobody's paying them.

Maybe they think the defense did their job for them. I do.

The prosecution's blown it. Iscariot's got a fan club.

Yeah. Aficionados of Pol Pot, Hitler, and Attila the Hun love him.

No way.

There's always a way. Catch this bulletin-board doggerel from an admirer:

> Judas is my kind of strudel,
> A pastry both cheesey and fey.

Do you like him too? Then yodel:
Just open your gullet and bray.
If you love Yehuddah,
Who's really quite shrewd-a,
Don't bother to brood-a:
Just jap, double-cross, & betray.

I don't know, keyboards one discussant. There's a lot of ambivalence there.

Avery Stills rises. Your Honor, I'd like to call the evangelist John, a.k.a., the beloved disciple, to the stand.

John, a.k.a. Jonah Bar-Zebedee, emerges from the electronic courtroom's sea of unseen spectators, approaches the stand, and, despite Jesus' admonition to abstain from formal oaths, swears to tell the truth, the whole truth, etc., on a book containing a philosophical gospel that he himself allegedly wrote. The defense confers about this untoward swearing-in, but decides not to object to it.

You've heard Mr. Iscariot's testimony, indicting you as a liar and a slanderer, says Stills to John. Your response?

I stand by what I've written.

But the defendant claims

The light shines in the darkness, and the darkness did not comprehend it, interjects John. The same holds here, as it so often does.

Stills leads the witness through a point-by-point rebuttal of Iscariot's testimony. John denies any regional bias amongst the disciples against Iscariot, any collusion in burdening him with the moneybox, any conspiracy to scapegoat him, or any plan to drive him to suicide.

We never desired anything bad for our Decapolean brother, says John. Only fruitful growth in the spirit.

Why has he said what he's said?

Objection, says Wendy Grice. Counsel wants the witness to speculate on a matter in which he has a powerful bias.

With that understanding, we'll allow him to answer, says Justice Ogilvie.

Thus prompted, John says: The man hurts. His hurt speaks, and the speech shaped from it gives him ease.

You bear him no animosity for contradicting the testimony of your gospel?

None, John tells Stills. I bear something else altogether.

For instance?

Sorrow that he didn't live to see even one of the Rabbi's resurrection appearances. Sorrow that his own sorrow persists.

Stills turns to the defense. Your witness.

Grice moves to take Stills' place in the middle of the courtroom. She clasps her hands behind her back. She studies the floor.

ONLINE LOGOMACHY (VI)

She'll badger him twelve ways to Easter. Then Satoh'll go after him. Then Browning.

You sadistic goober, you relish the prospect. . . .

Grice turns to John. You saw yourself as Jesus' favorite, didn't you?

I did.

Giving you a self-proclaimed status rivaling that of Simon Peter, the rock on whom Jesus said he would build his church. Correct?

You say so.

Do you see yourself as a prideful man, Jonah Bar-Zebedee?

I hold myself in, well, a decorous esteem.

Really? A decorous esteem. Head down, Grice paces. Do you see yourself as a jealous or an envious man?

Only rarely.

Only rarely envious? Or only rarely aware of the tendency?

Objection! says Stills. Counselor descends to the catty.

True, says Ogilvie. But the ambiguity of the response does seem to warrant clarification.

I'm only rarely envious, John volunteers.

Why in your gospel do you refer to yourself in the third person as the beloved disciple or even the disciple Jesus loved most? asks Grice.

I didn't want to obtrude on the more important, indeed the most important, story.

Yet you give yourself a rather grandiose kenning and behave with self-described nobility under its label. Doesn't that strike you as immodest?

It would've impeached modesty to name myself outright and belied events to omit myself entirely.

So. Grice stops pacing. You really believed yourself beloved of Jesus beyond the other eleven disciples?

Each of us may've believed that.

Yet you recorded events supporting your self-perception as especially favored.

I saw what I saw, then told my story.

You recorded Peter's three denials of the Lord on the night of his arrest?

As did Matthew, John Mark, and Luke. The denials happened.

Okay, but you imply that you alone among the disciples saw the crucifixion.

One of us had to stand by him in his agony.

The others?

They fled, even Simon Peter. And Iscariot went out and hanged himself.

You write that from the cross Jesus gave his mother Mary into your charge?

I accepted it glady, and our Lord's mother remained in my household until her death.

You write that you outran Peter to the empty tomb?

Yes.

The relevance of your swiftness afoot to the meaning of the empty tomb escapes me. Do you think your foot speed certified your manliness? Your saintliness? Both?

It bore witness to my agitation upon learning that someone had taken our Lord from the tomb.

An agitation greater than Simon Peter's, right?

John shifts his weight. I'm a burlier man than Peter. I recorded my earlier arrival at the tomb not in relation to his later arrival but in relation to my turmoil over troubling news about the Rabbi's body.

Your getting there first didn't otherwise signify to you?

John shifts his weight again. No.

Wendy Grice goes to the bench for Defense Exhibit C. She reads, But the other disciple ran faster than Peter and was the first to reach the tomb. Grice looks up. You expect us to conclude from this that you didn't exult in your triumph? That you weren't in fact gloating over it?

Rebecca Mormile pops to her feet. Your Honor, counsel is browbeating the witness! And the relevance of all this to the guilt or innocence of Mr. Iscariot seem at best tenuous and at worst nonexistent!

I withdraw the question, says Wendy Grice. Rebecca Mormile sits down.

John leans forward in the witness box. I have a point to make. Ignoring the prosecutors' warning looks, he says, My account states forthrightly that Simon Peter entered the tomb first.

Grice snatches up the court's Bible and thumbs through it. Sir, your permission to place the witness's voluntary assertion in context.

Ogilvie nods his assent.

Grice says, After noting that Peter went into the tomb, the decorously self-esteeming John writes, Then the other disciple, who had come to the tomb first, went in also; and he saw and believed. Grice turns to the unseen jury. Does no one else detect a peculiar obsession here?

Mormile, pounding the table, pops up again. Your Honor!

Enough, Ms. Grice, says Ogilvie. Move on or wrap up your cross.

AN E-PISTOLARY PROPOSAL

Dear Producers, Trial of the Millennium:

This online courtcase of a despickable religious traitor from a couple thousand years ago has had its moments. It suggests some other possiblities to me as well. Use them as you see fit, altho of course I would like a mention in the front & back credits & a small cut of user fees, advertising loot, & future program sales.

Trying dead bastards who never went to trial is a winner all the way. As subjects for new proceedings, try: the Tamil suicide nerve-gas bombers who just hit the new soccer stadium in Jaffna; Lee Harvey Oswald; Adolf Hitler; John Wilkes Booth; Tomas de Torquemada. It'd probably be neat—i.e., entertaining, a jimmyjam ratings boost—to try a bitch or two, but I can't think of any. Marie Antoinette? Lucrezia Borgia? You guys can put researchers on this, right?

If you end up giving Iscariot the e-quivalent of the death penalty, I think you ought to hit him with something besides hanging. He's done that. Maybe you could introduce him virtually to complete vacuum, him being a moral vacuum & all. I have a program that I think would work for this. Give me a commission & I'll get busy on it.

pldflpp @ brwn.u.bkst.rtrd.

Grice lays the Bible aside and turns back to John. You heard Jesus whisper that the one to whom he gave the dipped bread would betray him?

Yes.

And you were the only disciple privy to this revelation?

Also true.

No one else could have known what Jesus told you unless you told the others in turn, right?

John says, Judas' presence in the garden with the troops would've also told against him. And did.

Even with Roman soldiers and Jewish police, our client's presence in the garden is subject to interpretation. And your interpretation condemns. Grice stares long and hard at John before saying, You write that when our client took the dipped bread, Satan entered him.

You say so, and you say correctly.

How did you know that Satan entered him?

I knew. It was apparent to me.

How, precisely? Did Satan pop into view and jump down Mr. Iscariot's throat? Did an evil fog that you detected by means of extrasensory perception or an acute sensitivity to invisible auras make Mr. Iscariot start glowing purple?

John raises his eyebrows and looks to Stills, Mormile, and Albornoz. He shifts his weight in the witness box.

Grice, virtually pouncing on him, says: *How did you know?*

John flinches. A moue of offended disappointment twists his bearded features. I heard you clearly. Did I understand you? Perhaps not, but loudness doesn't help.

Does taking questions from a woman trouble you?

John looks to Ogilvie, who shrugs.

Grice recites from Paul's First Epistle to Timothy from memory: Let a woman learn in silence with all submissiveness. I permit no woman to teach or to have authority over men; she is to keep silent. Do you find my sex a bar to candor and responsiveness?

Objection, says Avery Stills wearily.

Sustained.

Grice turns to Ogilvie. Still, sir, I believe you should direct him to answer my original question.

Ogilvie smiles. Straightaway, ma'am. The witness will answer the question: How did you know that Satan had entered Mr. Iscariot?

John looks back and forth from Ogilvie to Grice. How else could he have handed over the Rabbi?

In fact, says Grice, you deduced from your after-the-fact consideration of Jesus's arrest, and Mr. Iscariot's role in it, that Satan had entered our client.

Anyone could see it.

But, in fact, none of the other ten saw it all, did they?

None said they did.

Isn't it likely that you made this unverifiable assumption after misunderstanding Jesus' whispered words to you?

I heard what I heard.

Grice lowers her voice. Mr. Bar-Zebedee, a sagacious woman once said, Satan is a way of perceiving opponents.[11] Haven't you read Satan into our client because you read his presence in the garden as a betrayal?

John takes a deep, lung-filling breath. He looks away from Grice, shakes his head in annoyance.

Whether intentionally from malice or inadvertently from superstition, says Grice, gripping the witness box, you've demonized our client, sir, and created a monster that in fact exists nowhere but in your own religious imagination.

Objection! Mormile and Albornoz half-rise. Stills tilts his head back and smiles wide-eyed at the ceiling. Mormile says, Counsel

---

[11] Elaine Pagels, quoted on p. 63 of David Remick's "The Devil Problem," *The New Yorker* (April 3, 1995), 54-65. The remark synopsizes a major argument in Pagels' book *The Origin of Satan* (New York: Random House, 1995).

draws her own conclusions. Plus she's trotting out the stale relativistic notion that evil is a situational figment or illusion.

Grice says, I

Mormile gallops on: She should save it for late-night bull sessions with know-it-all adolescents.

ONLINE LOGOMACHY (VII)

Incoming! Incoming!

These two gals're cheetah mamas, ain't they?

Grice definitely gets my hydraulics working.

Please. Me, I endorse that stuff from 1st Tim. about all submissiveness. Unless they've dropped to their knees, females should keep their mouths shut.

Run for cover, guys!

What for? We know where you live, you pathetic synthetic-testosterone junkies.

Go easy. Can't we all agree that Grice and Mormile are both babes?

You've picked the wrong b-word, bonehead.

Help! I'm lost among these intellectual giants like a baby squirrel among ancient sequoias. . . .

Grice pivots toward the prosecution's table. I don't deny the existence of evil. I simply deny that it exists as some sort of preexistent counterprinciple in an ongoing combat with preexistent good. In that scheme, Rebecca, we all become pawns of the one or the other.

Interesting, says Mormile. But theologically suspect and irrelevant to this case.

Not at all, Your Honor. By reading Satan into our client, Jonah Bar-Zebedee denies to both Mr. Iscariot and himself, indeed to all of us, any capacity for self-generated evil. If Satan has entered our opponents, then Satan can't inhabit us. This attitudinal bias promotes the demonization of others and a smug sanctification of the self. It absolves us of the need to control our own native tropisms toward the dark.

Your Honor, says Mormile, this is heady claptrap.

Is it? says Grice. I propose a concept of good and evil that allows the prosecution to convict defendants on the basis of their own culpability, not on mere allegations of satanic possession. And what I propose doesn't automatically absolve our client, it simply requires a thoroughgoing demonstration of his guilt.

Demon? says John. Demon, stration?

Avery Stills motions Rebecca Mormile to sit and says, I think were arguing petty semantics here, Your Honor. Which, along with John's arrival from another cultural and religious dimension, has left him gasping to follow Ms. Grice's verbal loop-de-loops.

Grice looks to Ogilvie. The witness's milieu of origin laid the groundwork for ours. Nor do I think there's anything petty about alleging that Satan, Hebrew for God's most dogged adversary, has entered another human being.

Stills rises. John, didn't you make that allegation as a symbolic way of saying that Mr. Iscariot surrendered to his own evil impulses?

This way lies chaos, says Ogilvie, rapping his gavel. Mr. Stills, you're out of order. Ms. Grice, where do you suppose this digressive philosophical brouhaha is going?

I don't know, sir, but I'd love to hear the witness respond to Mr. Stills' out-of-order question. In fact, I'll repeat it: John, do you regard Satan as a symbol, a mere figure of speech?

Satan exists, John says. Satan entered Yehuddah Bar-Simon.

Did Satan leave Mr. Iscariot again?

I don't know.

What do you think? On the basis of your keen sensitivity to the Satan-inhabited, speculate for us. Did Satan ever leave Mr. Iscariot, once having entered him?

Perhaps when he hanged himself.

Why would Satan permit such a valuable instrument of his malevolence to hang himself?

He'd served his purpose.

So. You're saying Mr. Iscariot possessed free will only when Satan released him, at which time he expressed remorse for the latter's crime by hanging himself?

You say so, and I've also said so.

Then why're we trying Judas Icariot? Let's get Satan in here and grill him instead!

The electronic courtoom erupts in laughter and applause. With a look mixing amusement and disgust, Ogilvie pounds his gavel. Silence. Silence! The noise dissipates a little, and he says, We'll now take a thirty-minute potty-break! Another collapse of manners like this last one will result in my clearing the room and ordering these proceedings offline. A mild pox on all of you.

QUESTIONS FROM THE E-NUT GALLERY

Isn't grilling Satan a lot like tossing Br'er Rabbit into the briar patch?

Take the t off Br'er Rabbit and whattaya get?

Two thousands years older and one helluva culpability debt?

How does an e-clone take a potty break?

By shedding its impulses?

If this trial goes offline, where exactly does it go?

If a computer crashes & there's no one there to dash around in recursive panic, has it ever really been with the program?

Does anybody know Wendy Grice's private fax number?

ONE ONLINE SIDEBAR, WITH WITNESS AND JURISTS

Before Ogilvie can get to his chambers, Grice stops him and prevails upon him and her fellow attorneys to gather near the witness box for a demonstration of the potent consequences of demonization.

Demon? says John, standing down. Demon, stration?

Hold your right arm out in front of you at shoulder level and make a fist, Grice says. Bemusedly, John obeys.

This is highly irregular, Henry Albornoz says.

Hirofumi Satoh sighs and slaps a C-note into the palm of Dakota Browning's outstretched hand.

Stop that, Grice says. Take note. John here, a bona fide Thunder Brother, has several inches in height and who knows how many pounds on me?

Ogilvie compliantly ogles Grice. Stills checks his watch. The others glance back and forth between John and Grice, who is pressing down on his fist with her index finger.

Resist me, Grice says. Try to keep me from moving your arm downward. John resists effortlessly. Good. Very good. Grice withdraws her finger.

Your point? says Stills.

With your permission, I have a couple more simple requests to make of the witness. May I?

Exasperated, Stills gives her a curt nod and folds his arms across his chest.

Grice tells John, Relax. Lower your arm. Shake out the kinks. Good. Now extend it just as before and a make a fist. Excellent. Now lower your eyes and repeat the phrase I'm a bad boy clearly but not belligerently until I ask you to stop.

For heaven's sake, Wendy, says Mormile.

I mean it, Grice says. Come on, John. Say I'm a bad boy I'm a bad boy I'm a bad boy. . . .

This is demeaning, Albornoz says. We object.

It's all off the record, Browning says. Lighten up.

I'm a bad boy, John says over and over as Grice presses down on his fist with her finger. John grimaces and strains, but his arm drops steadily lower. His left eyelid succumbs to a noticeable tic. Grice removes her finger.

No one says a word.

Grice pats John's shoulder. Let's do it again. This time, though, look me in the eye and say with feeling I'm a good boy.

This time John successfully resists Grice. His tic goes away, and he smiles faintly through the tangled red shrubbery of his beard.

Do any of you legal geniuses require an explanation of this fascinating phenomenon? Ogilvie asks the prosecutors.

Bad boys' arms go down more often than good boys'? Rebecca Mormile says.

Neat trick, says Stills to Grice. You must really liven up a party with that one.

Trick? An enacted parable. It shows what a drumbeat of verbal abuse can do. I contend that repeated accusations of satanic influence drove Iscariot to surrender to the lie and hang himself.

It still doesn't prove him innocent of selling out Jesus, Albornoz says.

Then it's our boy's word against yours, says Browning.

And Matthew's, John Mark's, and Luke's, says Albornoz.

Later, says Ogilvie. Inflict your clouds of witnesses on the trial proper. Here they just befog my glasses.

A PROTEST FROM THE E-NUT GALLERY
If they bring on the rest of the apostles, this trial could still be in progress when Christ comes again.

Well, I'll be gone. Long gone.

The prosecution calls Jesus of Nazareth, says Albornoz.

A ripple of astonishment works through the courtroom, and every monitor screen worldwide gives back a panorama of the spectators, who, thanks to computer graphics, have flamelike tongues of fire on their shoulders and heads, as if each one were a votive candle. This surreal graphic is brief, however. The ripple among the spectators subsides, and the trial's programmers cut immediately to Justice Ogilvie, who appears in closeup like a great, ebony condor.

Impossible! he says, booming without raising his voice.

Why? says Albornoz, undaunted.

Because summoning him as a witness would be to induce the Parousia, and no mortal human being, whether of the flesh or the microchip, has that authority.

Albornoz says, But who better to clarify the issue of what he told John in the upper room?

Who indeed? says Ogilvie.

Without his testimony, sir, the question's likely to remain forever moot.

Them's the breaks, says Ogilvie.

ONLINE LOGOMACHY (VIII)

Puhwhozit?

Parousia. The Second Coming. You don't induce it.

ISCARIOT TO GRICE, A HYPERTEXT E-PISTLE

Dear Ms. Grice,

I've said I loved the Rabbi, and in truth I did. I first loved him from afar, I next loved him for the deeds of healing and exorcism I saw him do, and I finally loved the man for his charisma, holiness, and beauty. He had a comeliness of bearing, movement, voice, and repose that banished from the eye the middling imperfections of his face and body. For whatever reason—shame, perhaps—no evangelists wrote or spoke privately about these aspects of his attractiveness, but no one who met the Rabbi failed to see or admire them.

The prophet Isaiah may have foretold the coming of this man of sorrows, this mortal angel familiar with both grief and despisal, but Isaiah's prophecy miscarried in his vision of Yeshua's appearance. Do you recall how Isaiah, the son of Amoz, describes our deliverer?

He grew up before the LORD like a young plant
whose roots are in parched ground;
he had no beauty, no majesty to catch our eyes,
no grace to attract us to him.
He was despised, shunned by all,
pain-racked and afflicted by disease;
we despised him, we held him of no account,
an object from which people turn away their eyes.[12]

Yeshua drew people to him. No one but his enemies—
folks he'd outgrown, folks whose authority he challenged—
could fail to esteem him. Like me, he was a peasant, a man
who'd once made his living making practical goods with his
hands. In his case, benches, roof beams, and tables. In
mine, tools and weapons. Oddly, during my discipleship, the
only thing I ever saw him make was a corded whip with
with he careered through the temple, shaping panic among
the moneychangers and pigeonsellers. But that was after
I'd sought him out on the great lake and begged for a place
among his closest followers not with boasts or sighs but
with love and work. Despite my arrival from another land
and my awkwardness among the Galileans, these offerings
secured my place, and I found myself a movable home and
a sliver of reflected fame. In faith, apart from the Rabbi
and along with Judas Lebbaeus, I was an instrument of
healing, an expeller of demons, and a herald of God's
imperial reign.

I never wanted an infamy such as I have now, the
reproach of millions. Instead I wanted the regard of our
master and comfort in the night, things I tell you, along

---

[12] *Isaiah* 53:2-3 in *The Revised English Bible with the Apocry-*
pha (Oxford and Cambridge University Presses, 1989), p. 637.

with what follows, because Jonah Bar-Zebedee, my accuser, reports in his gospel that Yeshua said, And you shall know the truth, and the truth shall set you free[13], and because Didymos Judas Thomas reports in his less renowned gospel that Yeshua said, If you bring forth what is within you, what you bring forth will save you. If you do not bring forth what is within you, what you do not bring forth will destroy you.[14]

Spiritually speaking, honesty is the best policy. And so: One night we thirteen slept in scattered pockets along the shore between Capernaum and Bethsaida. We'd come together to talk about our work among the lake villages. In some we'd met success, in some consternation or rebuke. Weariness had fallen that night among the successful and unsuccessful alike. James and John, the Thunder Brothers, sleeping apart in two different spots, earned their nicknames.

I couldn't sleep, despite my fatigue. I left my place under a gnarled fig tree with Lebbaeus and Simon the Zealot; I wandered down the beach and found Yeshua lying alone in the chapel of an upturned, rock-braced fisherman's skiff. I knelt down and crawled in beside him. He opened his eyes and accepted me into the crook of his arm, and so we lay.

Later I put my lips to his ear, as if whispering, and one of my hands strayed to a place out of my view. Yeshua caught it by the wrist and with great gentleness touched

---

[13] *John* 8:32 in The New King James translation.

[14] *Thomas* 70:1-2 in Elaine Pagels' *The Gnostic Gospels* (New York: Random House, 1979), p. 126. Compare this version to those in *The Complete Gospels,* p. 316, and Marvin W. Meyer's *The Secret Teachings of Jesus: Four Gnostic Gospels* (New York: Random House, 1984), p. 32.

the back of it to his mouth. The water lapping at some nearby rocks and the uncanny sound of a hermit fisherman chanting a psalm from a boat far out emboldened me, and I twisted in Yeshua's arms as I was later to twist, they tell me, in Blood Acre. He smiled, a smile only faintly visible, and gripped me tighter.

Take rest, he said.

Yeshua, I said, I desire

But he put a finger to my lips and said, Whoever has come to know the world has discovered the body, and whoever has discovered the body, of that one the world is not worthy.[15]

I didn't fully understand, but it seemed that without encouraging me in my longing for him, he approved the sort of body talk that between male and female seeds the world and between loving others may at times stir both comfort and joy. His eyes said as much as his words, but I couldn't always see his eyes to read them. When I tried to move or speak, he said, Shhhh.

And then he said, How miserable is the body that depends on a body, and how miserable is the soul that depends on these two.[16]

Even this cryptic saying, despite his iteration of the word miserable, didn't feel like a scolding but like an openhearted attempt to pour light into me. Don't mire yourself in lust, Iscariot. Yet don't assume the soul so fragile or meatbound that it can't rise clean and smiling above the body's exultations.

This, I came to know, was not a teaching that Yeshua shared with everyone. That night, however, I lay back in the crook of his arm, well content, and slept. No other meeting like this occurred between us again, and yet I

---

[15] *Thomas* 80:1-2 in *The Complete Gospels,* p. 318.
[16] *Ibid.*, 87, p. 319.

never thought him avoiding me or disappointedly intent on picturing me to the Galileans as the serpent in their vineyard.

At dawn I awoke to find John casting a long shadow into the upturned skiff. He stared down at me with the disdain of a rich matron for a turd. I sat up, striking my head on the boat, and then rolled out from under it groggy and dazed. John made me feel like a harlot, an orgiastic devotee of Baal, and yet I'd done nothing, except in my mind, but lie beside the Rabbi and draw warmth from both his body and his presence. As for Yeshua, seeing the big fisherman, he propped himself up on his elbows and laughed heartily.

Look at you, he said. This morning you seem to wonder at my meaning when I said I'd make you fishers of men.

Maybe it was too early in the day. Maybe John didn't care to think the disciple from distant Kerioth even a twelfth so beloved as he. He bridled at the Rabbi's joke and lumbered back up the shore to his companions of the night.

From that day forward, he loved me less and less and I sweated like a slave to stay out of his way. I don't mean to brand John a vindictive lout, for my sins groan louder by far than his, but what Yeshua forgave me, I wish the world would forgive. My name has become anathema and filth. I'm not in the mouth of one of Satan's three heads, Ms. Grice, but I am indisputably in hell.

Your respectful client, Judas Iscariot

Your Honor, says Satoh, we'd like to enter this letter from our client as a deposition and as Defense Exhibit D.

Why don't you just put Mr. Iscariot in the box again? says Ogilvie. He isn't absent, after all.

No one in e-space is either altogether absent or altogether present, sir. We do this in the interest of saving time. Out of courtesy, we've already filed a copy with Mr. Stills and his associates.

Ogilvie looks to Stills. If you agree to the defense's request to enter the letter, I'd permit you to put Mr. Iscariot on the stand for a cross. But I have no bias in the matter either way.

Henry thinks it highly irregular, says Stills. But we have no objection.

Thank you, says Satoh. May we send e-copies to the jurors' fax screens, please?

Consider it done, says the stenographer, a robot retained in the courtroom out of atavistic sentiment.

Will you call Mr. Iscariot for a cross? says Ogilivie.

No, says Stills. He'd only lie again anyway.

Sustained! barks Ogilvie, looking toward Wendy Grice, who has half-risen from her place.

AN INFOHIGHWAYMAN HAS HIS SAY

My Ghod, the kisscheek from Kerioth's a real in-your-face faggot.

The proceedings proceed. Dakota Browning threatens to summon every Roman soldier who ever participated in or observed a crucifixion outside Jerusalem during the high-priesthood of Caiaphas.

We don't know much about most of those fellows, Ogilvie says. You'd get some pretty vague and inchoate resuscitants.

Browning yields on this point, but spends two days interrogating an expert on osculation, or kissing, with special attention to the socio-cultural import of nonromantic kisses in quasi-public places. A day later, he brings in aerial photos gridded to show the distances between Kerioth and the Galilean hometowns of the other eleven disciples, plus income charts, occupational statistics, and samples of each village's exports and home-grown foodstuffs. Over the new few days, Browning summons three vague and inchoate resuscitants who recall Jonah Bar-Zebedee lying to them about various matters; questions a lexicographer on the many connotations of the word

325

betrayal; and calls several heirs of the Fellows of the Jesus Seminar to testify that (a) the disciple John did not write the gospel so often attributed to him and that (b) even if Iscariot had in fact maliciously betrayed the Christ, he should receive along with his master shared credit for humanity's redemption. As Browning struts and preens, many people fight sleep and Ogilvie prompts giggles by making a show of holding his eyelids open with his thumbs. Browning yields to Satoh, and Satoh summons a night watchman from the Garden of Gethsemane.

Enough! says Ogilvie. Onliners've fled these proceedings in droves lately, and I'm sick of all the yammering.

Bless you, says Rebecca Mormile.

Ogilvie goes on to say, The jury will now decide, Is the defendant guilty or not guilty of betraying Jesus Christ?

The head juror, still out of view, asks Ogilivie if the jury may acquit Iscariot if it concludes there is a reasonable doubt of his culpability.

Yeah, yeah, says Ogilvie. You know the drill. Hop to it. And if you find him guilty, I'll have to think up a sentence commensurate with the crime, something worse than what he's already endured.

Maybe you could hang him and bring him back seven times seventy times, says the chief juror.

Stills says, If you favor the eye-for-an-eye approach, a crucifixion would probably

Enough! cries Ogilvie again. The jury will please retire and return us a verdict. Pronto!

THE VERDICT(S)

Your Honor, we the jury find Yehuddah Bar-Simon, a.k.a. Judas Iscariot, not guilty of betraying Jesus of Nazareth, his teacher, master, and Lord.

Grice, Browning, and Satoh trade highfives. The courtroom erupts in murmurs, cheers, hisses, applause, singing, and boos. A snake-dancing conga line of Iscariot supporters winds from the